Grown Folks Business

Also by Victoria Christopher Murray in Large Print:

Temptation
Joy

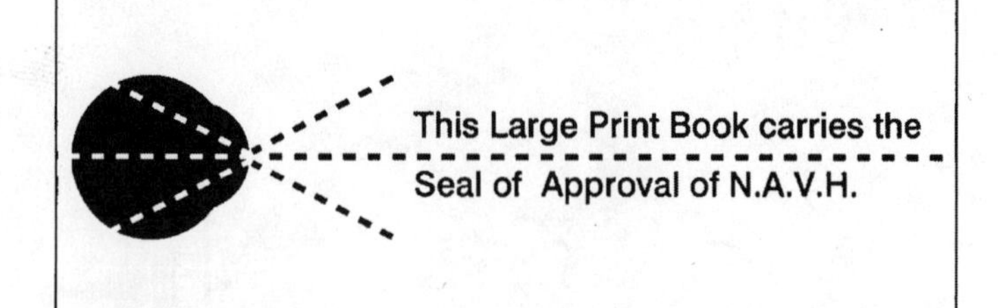

Grown Folks Business

A NOVEL

Victoria Christopher Murray

Thorndike Press • Waterville, Maine

This book is a work of fiction. Names, characters, places, and incidents either are products of the author's imagination or are used fictitiously. Any resemblance to actual events or locales or persons, living or dead, is entirely coincidental.

Published in 2006 by arrangement with Simon & Schuster, Inc.

Thorndike Press® Large Print African-American.

The text of this Large Print edition is unabridged.
Other aspects of the book may vary from the original edition.

Set in 16 pt. Plantin by Myrna S. Raven.

Printed in the United States on permanent paper.

Library of Congress Cataloging-in-Publication Data

Murray, Victoria Christopher.
Grown folks business / by Victoria Christopher Murray.
p. cm. — (Thorndike Press large print African-American.)
ISBN 0-7862-8713-6 (lg. print : hc : alk. paper)
1. African-American women — Fiction. 2. Triangles (Interpersonal relations) — Fiction. 3. Married women — Fiction. 4. Businesswomen — Fiction. 5. Gay men — Fiction. I. Title. II. Series: Thorndike Press large print African-American series.
PS3563.U795G76 2006
813′.54—dc22 2006009347

To: Bible Enrichment Fellowship International Church and my pastor, Dr. Beverly "BAM" Crawford

No matter how long I'm away, I always feel your welcoming arms when I return. The lessons I learn inside those doors motivate me to share the wonderful Word of God. Thank you, Pastor BAM, for teaching me, praying for me, and loving me.

To: Beulah Grove Baptist Church and Rev. Dr. Sam Davis

Thank you for being my church home away from home. I cannot tell you how much I appreciate your love and support with all of my novels. And a special thank-you for the idea for this book. The seed was planted on my first visit to Augusta, Georgia. (We had quite a discussion, didn't we?)

Acknowledgments

As always, I give glory and honor to God. I don't know any other way to live. I am thankful for all the blessings that He has given to me — including these novels to share with others.

Now, with that said, I'm not crazy about writing acknowledgments. In my last novel, I forgot two dear friends, Parry Brown and Marissa Monteilh. And then, others actually asked me why they weren't included in my acknowledgments. So I decided then that writing this part of the book is more stressful than the novel itself. When I thought about it though, I realized that I don't have to make a list thanking everyone I know. Everyone who is important to me knows it. So, no more acknowledgments for me!

Well, maybe just a few . . .

I do have to thank my parents Jacqueline and Edwin Christopher. The reasons for loving you are obvious, but who else has parents who go into bookstores, reface the books, and then tell the salespeople to order more? (Oops, was I supposed to keep that a secret?) I couldn't have bigger fans — with maybe the exception of my aunt, Joan Yearwood. I think you and my mom and dad are neck and neck when it comes to who will preside over the VECM fan club. Thank you for always believing in me from the time I was a little girl.

I have been blessed with a new team to support me on this writing journey. First, to my agent, Elaine Koster. There is no question. You are the best. By far. Period. Thank you for your never-ending belief in my writing. And to the team at Simon & Schuster. Wow! Cherise Davis, every single time your suggestions make the book better. I don't know how you do it; I'm just blessed to be one of your writers. Shida Carr, do you have any other authors? I don't think so. Thank you for making me feel like all the attention is on me. You are amazing. To the entire team at Simon & Schuster: Chris Lloreda, Marcia Burch, Debbie Model, and all the others who made me feel like part of the team from that very first meeting so long ago. Thank you!

To the African American bookstores who just never stop — every time I introduce a new book, you're there. I'm afraid if I start a list, I may leave someone out and I just wouldn't want to do that. So thank you, all of you. I hope to get a chance to visit every store with this novel.

And thank you, each and every reader who continue to support my novels and tell me that you want more. You keep reading and I'll keep writing.

Last, if I left out your name, please just fill it in here _______. And, I thank you for all that you've done for me too!

Now, as my daughter would say, "I'm out!"

Chapter One

"There's no other way to say this. Sheridan, I'm in love with someone else."

Quentin's words made Sheridan pause at the arch that separated the hallway from the kitchen. She glanced at the front door, where she had just kissed their children, Christopher and Tori, good-bye before they rushed to their school vans, eager to meet up with friends they hadn't seen during the Christmas holiday.

Sheridan stared at her husband before she twisted around to see if there was anyone behind her. Then her eyes rested on the television sitting on the kitchen counter, continuing the search for the source that delivered those words. Surely they hadn't come from her husband. She moved toward the dining table, where Quentin sat with his hands crossed in front of him, his head lowered, and his eyes away from her.

"What did you say?" she asked, feeling as if she'd walked into the middle of a conversation.

With effort Quentin raised his head. But

when he looked at her, his eyes spoke before he did. "I didn't mean to blurt it out that way," he continued, and then returned his stare to the table top. "I should have waited, for a better time, a better place. But . . . I needed to tell you."

"Quentin," she started, then paused, surprised by her outside steadiness, which didn't match her inside shaking. "What are you talking about?"

"I've been trying to find a way to tell you."

She shook her head, needing to clear all thoughts — anything that could be blocking her — interrupting her brain waves from making a direct connection with her mind. She couldn't be hearing this.

He stood, faced her, and now there was strength behind his eyes. "Sheridan, I don't want to hurt you. I really —"

"Did you just say you were in love with someone else?"

His Adam's apple leapt before he nodded. "I didn't want this." He paused, but his eyes continued talking, begging her for help. When she said nothing, his voice softened. "I never wanted to hurt you. I —"

Her mind's cobwebs cleared and his words made a clear path to her consciousness. She held up her hands, stopping him. "You never wanted to hurt me? Oh, yes, you did," she said, pushing away from him. "What you just said could only hurt." She took a deep breath. "So, you're in love . . . with someone else." She shoved the words through her throat. "When . . ." She paused, not sure she wanted to ask questions that would provide answers — the facts she wasn't ready to hear. But there was something she had to know.

"Who is she?" Sheridan whipped toward him, her hands contracting into fists. She imagined the fight. How she would beat the woman down. Then turn her rage on Quentin.

"We should sit down." Quentin held out his hand to escort her back to the table.

She ignored his gesture. "Who is she?"

He hesitated before he returned to where he'd been sitting and wiped his hands together. "First, Sheridan, please know this is not about you. I'm the one at fault."

Sheridan thought of a million retorts, but she held the curses inside.

Quentin said, "You have no idea how long I've wanted to tell you."

She held up her hand. "How long has this been going on? How long have you been seeing her?"

"It's not like that. It's not like I've been doing anything behind your back."

She almost laughed. "*Something's* been going on behind my back."

"I haven't had an affair, at least not the way you're thinking."

She looked at him as if he were speaking Portuguese. "How many ways are there to think about an affair, Quentin?"

"What I mean is that this is not about sex. That's why I know it's real."

It sounded like double-talk to her. "So let me get this straight." Sheridan paced across the tile floor. "You're in love, but you haven't been having sex. At least not the way I would define it. But you're in love and you needed to tell me because . . ." She stopped, wanting him to finish.

"I thought you'd want to know," he said. "I've wanted to be honest with you for so long."

"Well, now's your chance."

Quentin took a breath as if he thought it might be his last. "I wasn't looking for anyone. I wasn't sneaking around. This just happened. It was out of my control." He paused. "Sheridan, I've been fighting feelings for a long time, and I've finally faced the truth of what's been growing inside me. Something I thought was dead but is very much alive."

Her headache was instant, and the throbbing squeezed life from her. She wanted to listen, to understand, but only a few of his words pierced through her thoughts.

What just happened? An hour ago, they were having breakfast with their children, talking about Christmas and New Year's and the days in between. An hour ago, they were the Harts living the normalcy of family.

"I always wanted to be honest about this," he said.

What's going to happen to us now? her thoughts continued.

"It was not being honest that was destroying me and our life together."

What's our life going to be like now?

"I was miserable."

What am I going to do now?

"I tried to break it, deny it. But nothing worked."

"You know what?" Sheridan began. She hadn't heard too many of her husband's words. Her own questions overwhelmed her. "I don't want to hear any more."

Quentin stood as Sheridan rushed by him. "Honey, wait."

His words felt like a punch in her belly. She turned in slow motion. "What did you say?" Before he could answer, she continued. "You have the nerve to call me 'honey'? After just telling me you're in love with another woman. You just call me 'honey'?"

"It's not another woman."

"How could you call me 'honey'? What does . . ." She stopped, frozen. Even her heartbeat had ceased.

Finally she took short, slow steps toward the man she'd married seventeen years before. He stood stoically, as if he really meant what he'd said.

"What did you say?" The question squeaked from her.

It was the first time he looked straight into her eyes. "I am in love, but not with a woman. I'm in love with a man. I've fallen in love with Jett Jennings."

She wondered if he could hear the rumbling. The rumbling that began in her soles and rushed through her, filling her with the absurdity of it all. The cruelty of the news. The brutality of its suddenness. Sheridan raised her hand, and with the motion she'd practiced for a year in kickboxing, she served Quentin a right uppercut to his chin, then watched him wither to the floor.

She stared for only a moment before she stepped over him and stomped out of the room.

Sheridan was shaking.

"I'm in love with a man."

Those words played in her mind as she paced the long bedroom.

"I'm in love with a man."

She felt as if her heart had been pressed with a flaming-hot branding iron — the words permanently seared into her center.

"I'm in love with a man."

His words continued, taunting her as she marched past the dresser that held the picture of her and Quentin sharing wedding cake almost two decades before. She paused and stared at the pictures next to that one — the one with her, Quentin, and their son just moments after Christopher's birth. There was a similar picture with Tori. And six other framed photos that chronicled wonderful moments of their magnificent life.

Next to the pictures were the cards — the Christmas and New Year's cards they'd just exchanged, confessing their undying love and the promise of a bright new year.

"Sheridan."

His voice pulled her back. When she looked at him, she hoped to see something, some mark of the pain she'd caused when she dropped him to the floor. Something that could at least come close to the crushing blow her heart had taken.

"That's not the way we should handle this."

With those words, she wanted to hit him again, but she knew she'd used her free pass. He wouldn't let her get away with that twice. Even if he was a . . . She paused in her thoughts. What was he? Was her husband gay?

Her knees weakened, and she dropped to the edge of the bed.

He stepped into the bedroom and sat next to her. "You will never know how much I dreaded this," he said.

Their shoulders touched when he spoke, and she jumped away from him. She reached for an envelope she'd left on her nightstand.

"Sheridan, as much as I didn't want to do this, I couldn't live with this lie anymore."

She handed him the envelope. "Did you see this?"

He frowned as he took the letter. His glance was quick before he returned his eyes to his wife. His face was furrowed with confusion.

"It's from Tori's school," Sheridan explained. She wanted to start their day over — turn back the clock to before the sun even rose, before Quentin had even jumped from their bed and kissed her as he did every morning. "Tori's school fees are going up again next semester, and they want us to pick a payment plan."

"Sheridan . . ."

"We should pay in one lump sum like we always do."

"Sheridan . . ."

She stared in silence before she asked, "Are you gay?" Her voice trembled. She fought to keep her tears from falling.

Quentin's head barely moved in a nod. "I don't know what to call it. I know I've loved you, but at the same time I've been fighting other feelings for years."

Her eyes widened. "You haven't wanted me for years?"

"Oh, no. I've always . . . loved you. But . . ."

"I'm not really who you wanted. You'd prefer . . ." She stopped, unable to get the other man's name through her lips. The man she thought was her friend.

He lowered his eyes. "I didn't want to do anything about what I was feeling because

I didn't want to destroy us."

"But now you're fine with destroying me and Chris and Tori."

"I wish there was some kind of drug, some kind of medicine I could take to wash away these feelings. I've prayed —"

She held up her hands. "No you didn't. Because if you prayed, you would know what to do. If you prayed, we would never be talking about this."

"Sheridan, believe me. I have prayed, and that's why I had to tell you. I had to tell you the truth so that we can decide where to go from here."

She raised her eyebrows. "Decide where to go? Quentin Hart, you're a smart man. You know where to go."

He paused as if he'd heard more than just the words she uttered. Finally, he said, "I came to you as a first step. I want us to take our time before we make any decisions. So I was thinking I would sleep in the guest bedroom until . . ."

"Until what?"

He looked at her, but he couldn't hold her glance for even a second before he stared at the floor.

Sheridan said, "No."

"Okay." He nodded slowly as if he was surprised. "I was only thinking of you. But this is great, because I'd prefer to stay in here with you, keeping everything as normal as possible. It's better, especially for Chris and Tori."

"No."

Quentin frowned.

"I want you out of my house."

"What?"

"Quentin, are you out of your mind? Not only are you in love with someone else, but you just told your wife you want to be with a man. Do you think I'd want you anywhere near me? Do you think I'd want you near my children?"

"They're my children too."

She swallowed a mouthful of air to keep the scream inside. The scream that would inform him that Christopher and Tori wouldn't be his children much longer. From this point forward the children would belong only to her, not to some man who couldn't live life in the manner God planned. But she said nothing.

Quentin said, "This is not how we should handle this."

"You don't get a vote."

"I'm not leaving this house. Not until you understand that I love you and I love our children. But I can't fight what's inside of me anymore."

She pressed back her tears. He would not see her cry.

"Sheridan, we can't make quick decisions. That's why I have to stay here."

"Okay." She spoke as she moved toward her closet. "You stay." She dragged a suitcase from the chamber. "I'll pick up Chris and Tori from school, and we'll stay in a hotel."

Quentin closed her suitcase. "I think you're being overly dramatic."

God's grace covered her; stopped her from striking him again. "Let me break this down for you, Quentin. Nothing is more dramatic than having the man you've loved for seventeen years come to you one glorious morning and tell you your life has been a lie."

"It's not like that."

"Having him tell you that you don't have anything he wants." Her voice began to tremble.

"That's not true."

"Telling you you're . . . not good enough." She fought her tears.

Quentin reached for her, but she stepped beyond his grasp before he could touch her skin. "I'm not being dramatic, Quentin," she protested as the first tear rolled down her cheek. "I'm just trying to hold on to some form of sanity. I'm just trying to get from here to tomorrow."

In the silence that followed, Sheridan stared at the suitcase lying on their bed. Seventeen years of marital memories flooded her. "Please, Quentin," she whispered as she kept her eyes on their bed. "If you ever loved me, just leave."

A beat passed. "I'll go."

Only then did she look at Quentin. Those were not the words she wanted. She longed for her husband to take back all he'd said. To tell her he loved her, only her, and would forever. But she knew those words would never come.

She pushed through a dense fog as she stepped from their bedroom and walked down the stairs. Everything around her was familiar, but nothing was the same. The furniture, the wall hangings, the carpet felt out of order. Even the house knew the world had changed.

She opened the door to the home office for the business they shared: Hart to Heart.

This space was crammed with their love. A business built on the sweet words Quentin had written from the moment they met. The poetry he wrote for her, capturing her heart and her business acumen. It had been her idea to start a company — specialty gift cards. After Tori was born, they'd started small and had grown the venture to over one hundred thousand dollars annually: just a pittance compared to Quentin's income as an ob-gyn, but next to God and their children, Hart to Heart was a cherished venture. Their business was a manifestation of all that the Harts were about — their complete devotion to one another.

There was only one word to describe their business — successful. And now there was only one way to describe their marriage.

Sheridan stumbled to the walnut desk that sat in the middle of the room. She glanced around the walls, which held framed compositions of Quentin's most romantic expressions. As she thought about all the wonderful words he'd spoken and written through the years, she asked herself if any of those had been meant for her. And when she answered that question, she laid her head on the desk and cried.

It was an empty canvas of time.

Sheridan had no idea how long she'd sat at the desk, struggling to free herself from the overpowering emotions. But when she heard the front door open, then close, she raced to her bedroom. Behind the sheer curtains, she hid and watched Quentin roll two suitcases behind him. His shoulders were squared, he walked tall; he moved like a natural man.

He opened the back of the Mercedes SUV and slid the bags inside. When he closed the car's door, he stood still, staring at the front door to their home. Sheridan held her breath. Could this be it? Could this be the moment when he would come and tell her it was a mistake? That all he wanted was to spend eternity with her?

"Please, God. Make Quentin do the right thing," she whispered.

As if he heard her, Quentin looked up. She stepped from behind the curtains so he could see her. They stared at each other — until Quentin jumped into the Mercedes and rolled the SUV away. She watched until the car dipped around the curve of the cul-de-sac and out of her sight.

She stayed in place, staring at her empty driveway, and then she noticed Mrs. James, standing across the street, staring into her window. Sheridan turned away, before the neighborhood crier could see her tears.

She looked around her room, trying to

find a familiar space, but her bedroom was a foreign land.

She stumbled to the bed and rubbed her hand along the pillow that Quentin had laid his head upon just hours before. He had held her last night as they slept, the way he always did. The way he had promised he always would, from the day they married.

"The Bible tells us not to let the sun go down on our anger. And every night as we sleep, I will hold you, and you will know there is no anger inside of me. In my heart, there is only love."

She had melted at his words. Not only because she was sure he'd love her forever, but because she'd never dated anyone like him before — never knew a man who had such a strong relationship with God.

It wasn't like she'd had many relationships before Quentin. She'd met him when she was only nineteen, while visiting her doctor for a Pap smear. Quentin had been a third year medical student doing rotations at Harbor General. He'd taken her breath away the moment she saw him strut out of her doctor's office, grabbing her attention from the article she'd been reading in *People* celebrating Vanessa Williams — the first black Miss America. Sheridan had followed him with her eyes as he glided down the hallway going in the wrong direction — away from her. She wanted to yell for the six-foot, muscle-packed man to return. But all she did was marvel at how fine he was. She'd never seen a man with a bald head before — at least not one as young as this one seemed to be.

When the nurse took Sheridan into the examination room, she'd asked who that guy was in the white jacket.

The nurse had chuckled. "Every girl who has come in here for the last week has asked me that. He's a medical student working with Dr. Kennedy."

Sheridan had smiled, but her grin lasted for only a moment when she realized this student might be in the room when Dr. Kennedy examined her. How would she ever get a date with a man whose first vision of her was from down there?

It was almost funny, as Sheridan remembered that time now. She squeezed Quentin's pillow in her arms. She inhaled, grateful for the faint scent of Armani Man, which he loved. Grateful for the little bit of himself that he'd left behind. She wondered how long it would last.

She rolled to the center of the king-sized bed. She'd been so happy with Quentin that at times it had scared her. But she'd learned to live in the bliss. She'd thought her husband felt the same way.

"I've fallen in love with Jett Jennings."

Sheridan tried to remember the last time she and Quentin had made love, but even when she closed her eyes, she couldn't. It wasn't that there'd been a problem; it was just the holidays — the planning and gift buying and entertaining and celebrating. They'd been busy with life. And anyway, she'd learned a long time ago that they didn't always have to make love; they were in love.

She tossed Quentin's pillow onto the floor and jumped up from the bed. "You were the one in love, Sheridan. Not Quentin."

She caught her reflection in the mirror. Her shoulder-length, auburn-streaked hair was tied back; she was ready for her next beauty shop appointment. And the red crewneck sweatshirt and sweatpants hid the way she worked to keep herself in shape — for Quentin as much as herself. She had wanted him to be proud of her. And he had always told her that he was.

"Was it all a lie?" she asked her reflection.

Her reflection stared back as if she were a stranger.

"What is so wrong with me that my husband would want a man?"

Tears rolled down her cheeks as her answer.

She picked up the card Quentin had given her on New Year's, just four days ago.

What word can I use to describe
how I feel about you?
Happiness. Serenity. Joy.
None of those are enough.
You are my blessing,
my true gift from God.
Happy 2004.

When she read the card on New Year's morning, she'd held him until her arms got tired. He did it to her every time: every time he wrote, every time he spoke, he left no doubt in her heart that she was the forever love of his life.

"I'm in love, but not with a woman."

Sheridan shook those words from her head as she tried to remember again, when was the last time her husband had made love to her?

"I'm in love with a man."

She returned her gaze to the mirror and wondered what Quentin saw when he looked at her. The sweat suit hid her curves — made her look less feminine. Is that what it was? Did she make her husband long to be with a man?

The New Year's card slipped through her fingers and glided toward the carpet, landing face down.

"I've fallen in love with Jett Jennings."

Sheridan picked up the card and dashed into the bathroom. She tossed Quentin's words into the toilet. A second later she released the bile that rose within her. She freed herself of her pain until she was drained. Then she pushed herself up from the floor, stared at the emotional waste that filled her toilet, and with a breath, she flushed it all away.

Chapter Two

She really didn't want to do this.

Sheridan paused at the stove as the first school van stopped in front of the house. This was the late van; the one that brought home the children who stayed for extracurricular activities. Sheridan watched Tori jump out, wave to her friends, then run to the door.

For the fiftieth time, Sheridan wiped her face, hoping to erase all the emotional signs that had plagued her for more than nine hours. And she had counted every one of the five hundred forty minutes that tears had poured from her.

"Hi, Mom. I'm home," her nine-year-old screamed, the way she always did. But only today did Sheridan notice how *Father Knows Best*–ish her daughter sounded.

Sheridan sniffed back her emotions, plastered the best smile she could onto her face, and waited for Tori to bounce into the kitchen. "Mom, that smells good," she said as she raised herself on her toes and kissed her mother's cheek. "Yeah, chicken fajitas. My and Dad's favorite."

Sheridan had forgotten that part — how Quentin loved the whole-wheat fajitas as much as the kids.

"Are you hungry?"

"Yeah. Lunch was horrible today," Tori said, as if she knew how to whip up a meal. She dumped her backpack onto the floor. "I think the real cooks are still on Christmas holiday."

"How was dance practice?" Sheridan asked, pretending this day was normal.

"Okay. We got our assignments for the recital and I got the best part," she chatted. "But I'm not telling what it is. The show's in April. You and Dad are coming, right?"

Sheridan swallowed. It was a typical question about their typical life. "Now, sweetie, have we ever missed one of your special moments?"

Tori grinned. "Nope," she said, swinging her thick braids from side to side.

"Go change and get started on your homework. We'll eat in about an hour."

"Okay," she said. She grabbed her bag and said, "We're eating early. Will Dad be home by then?"

The question made Sheridan stop. She hadn't expected her lies to begin until dinner: casually, she would tell the children their father would be gone, but for only a few days. Simple lies for the most complicated event in her life.

"Mom?"

"Your dad had to go away on business."

"He didn't tell me that this morning."

Sheridan could hear the frown in Tori's voice. "No, he didn't, sweetheart, because this was an emergency." Sheridan turned and faced Tori as if that were the truth.

"Is everything all right?" Tori asked with her frown still in place.

Sheridan nodded. "It was just some medical stuff. But he said to tell you that he loved you and . . ." She couldn't think of anything else to say.

She had her first victory when her daughter's smile returned and Tori sang, "Okay. I can't wait for him to get home. I learned a new chess move and want to test it out."

Sheridan breathed, but she knew Christopher would never be that easy. Her son was curious, destined to be a journalist or a lawyer.

Fifteen minutes later, the inquisitive one barreled through the door. "Mom," he bellowed.

"Chris, why do you do that?" Sheridan asked the way she always did when he came shrieking into their house.

He grinned the way he always did. “What? Don’t you just love hearing your number one son’s voice? Maybe I should sing for you.”

Sheridan held up her hand. “Please don’t.”

“Why not?” Christopher pretended to be offended. “I was thinking about dropping out of school and hooking up with Alicia Keys. Can you imagine me and Alicia hitting that keyboard together?”

It was Sheridan’s first enjoyable moment of the day. Together she and Christopher laughed, and then together they said, “So, how was your day?”

Sheridan still marveled at how much her firstborn was like her. So often they said the same things, thought the same way. Their only difference was that while Sheridan preferred sweats, Christopher had developed a penchant for his father’s preppy look. Today he could have posed for an ad from *Junior Sportsman* magazine, with his khaki pants and white golf shirt underneath the brown bomber jacket he’d received for Christmas. He even wore the brown loafers, although they weren’t Gucci like the ones his father favored. But Sheridan knew even that was coming soon. Like Quentin, Christopher had acquired a taste for all things designer, while none of that appealed to her.

"You first," Sheridan said, knowing she'd never tell Christopher the truth about her day. "How was the first day back?"

"Cool. I'm lovin' that next year at this time I'll be a graduating senior on my way to Harvard or Hampton."

For the first time since Quentin had sucked the blood from her heart, Sheridan's smile was genuine. She was so proud of Christopher: his grades were almost perfect; he was the president of the junior class and captain of his golf team; his guidance counselor had already told him he'd probably be valedictorian. And he didn't give her or Quentin one ounce of trouble or worry — if she didn't count the distress she'd felt from the moment Christopher had passed his driving test. There was no doubt he was the second love of her life.

"Now your turn. How was your day, Mom?"

Her momentary joy dissipated. "Not much happened," she said before she could think about it. "Just the usual." She almost laughed at how crazy that sounded.

"What time is Dad going to be home? I need him to help me with my chip shots.

We have a father-son tournament coming up."

His simple words twisted her heart, threatening to wring the last of her tears from inside.

"Oh, I forgot to mention it, Chris. Your dad is out of town."

Sheridan returned to the chicken strips and green peppers and onions sautéing in the pan. She knew she wouldn't stand a chance if she looked at her son.

"Out of town? Where? Why? What happened?"

Sheridan knew for sure now — Christopher Hart was going to be an award-winning journalist. She shrugged, hoping the motion would diffuse his concern. "He's just covering for one of the doctors at some convention."

"Where did he go?"

She hadn't thought of that. "I don't know."

"Mom, you always know where Dad is. What's going on?" His tone let Sheridan know he wouldn't stop until he got an answer that satisfied him.

"Chris, why are you asking me so many questions?"

"Because something's not right."

It was going to take more than words to

convince him. “Chris, what’s the big deal? Your father rushed out of town. I know he’ll call me tonight. And if I need to reach him, I’ll call his cell.” She stopped, wishing she hadn’t mentioned that. She didn’t want Christopher or Tori suggesting they call their father. “Anyway, like you always say, ‘It’s no big deal.’ ” She turned to face him with as wide a grin as she could muster and playfully jabbed his arm.

He didn’t share her smile but retreated. When he picked up his bag and almost moonwalked out of the room, Sheridan exhaled. She couldn’t think of a time when she’d lied to her children, but she didn’t regret doing so now. She needed time; they needed time: she wasn’t about to blow up their world with this awful truth tonight.

The vision of Quentin in their bedroom, explaining why life had to be this way, returned to her mind, and she was surprised when fresh tears pushed from behind her eyes.

What was she supposed to say to her children? What would life be like for them once this news got out? Why did Quentin leave? What did she do? She sniffed back her tears. Crying wasn’t giving her the answers. She needed to go to the source.

Find out from Quentin what she'd done, how she could fix it now and bring him home. She looked at the clock. In a few hours, Quentin would call, she was sure of it. And they'd talk then. She took a deep breath. She could make things right. By this time tomorrow, her husband could be back where he belonged.

The black machine stayed quiet, as if it were punishing her with its stubborn silence. It was after ten and Sheridan couldn't believe Quentin hadn't called. He hadn't called to check on her or the children. He hadn't called to tell her he'd made a terrible mistake. He hadn't called to say he was coming home.

She grabbed the telephone and punched numbers into the handset. She tried to control her breathing as the telephone on the other end rang. After two rings, it was answered.

"Hey, girl, I was just going to call you," Kamora said. "I've gotta tell you about this bozo I had dinner with last night. The love handles on this guy were thicker than twenty-two-inch tires."

Sheridan couldn't find her laughter. "Do you have time for your best friend?" she asked with tears in her voice.

"What's wrong?" Kamora's cheer was gone.

That question released the floodgates. "Kamora, you're never going to believe . . ." Sheridan paused through her sobs. This would be the first time she'd say it aloud to someone other than her reflection. But if she didn't let it out, she'd burst.

"What's wrong?" Kamora repeated with urgency.

"Quentin . . ."

"You're scaring me," her childhood friend cried. "He wasn't in an accident, was he?"

Sheridan almost wished it was something like that. An accident. Something simple. Something she could fix. Something she could understand.

"No, Quentin's fine, but still, can you come over?"

"Is Quentin home?"

"No," she managed to say through the cries that rose from her center. Her husband would never be home again.

"Give me fifteen minutes."

Ten minutes later, Kamora stood at the front door, with a shopping bag in her hand.

"What's that?" Sheridan asked, still wiping water from her eyes.

Kamora held up the brown bag. "Some wine, girl. Three bottles. The way you sounded, I knew you needed something."

"I don't drink," Sheridan whispered as she closed the front door and led Kamora up the stairs to her bedroom.

"Don't you think I know that?" Kamora hissed. "But even Jesus understood the importance of wine in serious situations. Girl, why do you think his first miracle was changing some ghastly well water into one of life's finest liquids?" She held up one of the bottles, then used her foot to close the bedroom door behind her. "Anyway, this is plum wine. There's more plum than wine in this."

Sheridan wanted to laugh, but instead the tears came again, and she wondered if this emotional hydrant would ever drain completely.

"Sweetie," Kamora said, resting the bottles on the nightstand. She wrapped her arms around Sheridan. "What's wrong?"

Sheridan sniffed. "You're never going to believe this."

Painful seconds passed as this morning's episode played itself out for the thousandth time in her mind.

Sheridan sat on the edge of the bed and squeezed her hands together. She didn't want to say it, but at the same time she couldn't wait to put the words out there. "Quentin left me."

"What?" Kamora exclaimed as she knelt in front of her friend. "I don't believe you."

"It's true."

"Why would he leave you? This doesn't make sense."

Sheridan looked at Kamora, and her tears spoke for her.

"He left you for someone else?" Kamora whispered.

Sheridan nodded.

"Oh, my God. I cannot believe this." Kamora stood and paced. "Not Quentin Hart, Hope Chapel's Man of the Year. How could he do this?" She paused. "Sheridan, why didn't you tell me you guys were having problems?"

"I didn't know."

Kamora sat next to Sheridan and squeezed her friend's hands. She took a deep breath. "Are you sure, sweetie? I've heard every wife knows when her husband is seeing another woman."

"But what about when he's seeing another man?"

Kamora frowned, then paused, then smiled. "Oh, okay. I've gotta give you your props, girl. In the middle of all of this you still got jokes."

When Sheridan stayed silent and stared unsmilingly, her hands slipped from Kamora's grasp. Kamora's copper skin almost paled to pink, and she squinted as her eyes searched the room. "Where's the wine?"

"Let me get some glasses."

Sheridan stood, but Kamora pushed her back onto the bed. "No need for glasses, honey. This kind of news deserves wine straight from the bottle." She twisted the top off one of the bottles, turned it upside down, and swallowed a long gulp. She opened another one and handed it to Sheridan.

"Okay," Kamora began as she slipped to the floor and leaned against the wall, "I'm ready."

Sheridan was surprised at her calmness as she lay across the bed, sipped wine, and unfolded the story, talking without pause for almost thirty minutes. It was easier than she thought. After all, as she spoke, she realized this couldn't be her life. She was living these moments for someone else, and when she awakened, she and Quentin would have a good chuckle.

"And when he told me it was a man, I

hit him," Sheridan said.

Kamora laughed.

Sheridan said, "Knocked him to the floor with one of my best Billy Blanks moves."

"Aren't you glad I made you take that class?"

Sheridan nodded. "And I haven't even gotten to the worst part yet."

Kamora frowned. "There's more? Wait." She turned her bottle of wine upside down, emptied what was left into her system, and then wiped her mouth with the back of her hand. "Go," she said, signaling Sheridan to continue.

"It's Jett Jennings."

Kamora frowned. "What's Jett Jennings?"

Sheridan sat up on the bed and pulled her knees to her chest. She took another sip of wine, and waited for Kamora to understand.

A moment later, Kamora's eyes widened. She crawled toward the bed, with her empty bottle in her hand, and then climbed up to sit next to Sheridan. "Your superfine husband is kicking it with that giga-gorgeous man?"

Sheridan nodded. "But I think it's more than kicking it. Quentin said they're in love."

"I didn't know Jett was gay. Man." Kamora shook her head as if she was trying to get this news to go down as well as the wine. "But then again, I didn't know Quentin was gay either."

When Sheridan flinched, Kamora said, "Oh, honey, I'm sorry. This is just a little too much to take."

"Tell me about it."

Still shaking her head, Kamora said, "Remember when I told you all I wanted in life was to marry that man? When I met him at your Christmas party last year, I was willing to take my last breath if God would bless me and let me be with him just once." Kamora paused and fanned herself as if her body temperature had risen. "Whew! He was so fine I wanted to eat him with a spoon. I even started watching golf because of the brotha. I was going to do anything to make him my husband. But I couldn't get him to look twice at me."

"Now you know why." Sheridan took another sip. "But it's a good thing he wasn't searching for a wife so that he could hide in the closet, you know? I mean, can you imagine what would have happened if you had married him? Both of us would be sitting here tonight drinking wine." She paused. "Wait a minute. That's what we're doing anyway, huh?"

Kamora giggled and bounced back on the bed. But her laughter was soon gone. "Sheridan, this is some serious stuff."

"I know."

Kamora sat up. "What about the kids? What did Chris and Tori say?"

"Do you think I told them?" Sheridan shook her head. She had to take another sip at the thought of her children. "They think Quentin is away on a business trip. I couldn't handle telling them yet."

"I hear you. Girl, this is grown folks' business. I don't know how you're going to tell those babies." Kamora paused. "Chris is going to flip."

Sheridan took a sip of wine.

Kamora continued, "He's going to get the business once this news gets out."

This time it was two sips that Sheridan took from her bottle.

"And poor Tori," Kamora sniffed. "That little girl is going to be heartbroken." She was almost crying now. "How are your children going to handle this?" Kamora wailed.

Sheridan turned up the bottle and swallowed until the liquid burned her throat. "You know," she began, needing to talk about something other than her children, "I used to worry about Quentin leaving me for one of his patients."

"I remember," Kamora slurred.

"But when he didn't after the first few years, I got comfortable."

"As well you should." Kamora hiccuped. "He was faithful to you for all those years, girl."

Sheridan frowned when her friend lifted her empty bottle to her lips. She said, "Still, it was hard at first. I didn't exhale until Quentin walked through the door every night. But I never thought it would be as bad as this. I thought the worst thing would be if Quentin left me for a white woman."

"Girl, I hear you. That would've been awful." Kamora licked the lip of her empty wine bottle. "But look at it this way. This could have been way worse."

"I don't know how," Sheridan cried.

"Quentin could have left you for a white man."

Sheridan squinted, as she pondered Kamora's words. Then she chuckled. Then she giggled. Then she laughed. Kamora joined her, and their laughter turned hysterical. They laughed until tears came and their watery eyes reminded Sheridan of her pain. Kamora felt it too, and they cried.

"Kamora, what am I going to do? My husband is gay. A homosexual."

"I don't know . . ."

Sheridan frowned and lifted her finger to her mouth, signaling for Kamora to be quiet.

"What's the matter?" Kamora's whisper sounded like a roar.

"I heard something." Sheridan stood and wobbled a bit before she eased toward her door. She straightened her back and peeked into the hallway. Her master bedroom was at one end of the second floor, more than fifty feet away from the other bedrooms.

She stepped into the dark and glanced at Tori's, then Christopher's door. It looked as if the lights were out in both bedrooms.

When she returned inside, Kamora asked, "What was it?"

Sheridan shrugged. "I thought I heard something." She flopped onto her bed. "But it was wishful thinking. I wish I heard Quentin coming home." Her tears returned. "Kamora, how could I love a man for seventeen years and not know that everything he's said to me is a lie?"

Kamora cried with her. "Girl, Quentin lied to all of us."

Sheridan paused. Would her parents and the rest of her family and friends feel as cheated as she did? "What am I going to say? How am I going to explain this?"

"There are no words." Kamora sniffed as she opened the last bottle of wine.

"And what about church?"

Kamora frowned as she took a sip from the new bottle. "What about church?"

"How am I supposed to go back there? You know the news will leak out, and then . . ."

"Yeah, you know how church folk can be. Maybe . . ." Kamora stopped.

"Maybe what?"

Kamora shrugged. "Maybe you should find a new church home. You could always start going with me, but really I think you're going to be all right," she said. "You know why?"

Sheridan shook her head, wishing the pain — in her heart and in her head — would go away.

"Because God is going to help you through."

Sheridan looked at the wine bottle sitting on her nightstand. Her bottle looked empty. "I don't think God is too happy with me right now."

"Honey, what Quentin has done is not your fault."

Whose fault is it? Sheridan wondered. But she kept her questions to herself.

"You should go home so we don't wake the kids."

Kamora stared at her for a moment. "Are you mad at me?"

"Of course not. Thanks for coming over and supporting me."

"This is just what we do."

Sheridan wondered why her friend was screaming.

Kamora grabbed the edge of the bed and pulled herself up, still balancing the bottle of wine in her hand. But when she stood, she wobbled.

Sheridan frowned. "Maybe you should stay here."

"You don't think I'll make it home?" But before Sheridan could answer, Kamora glanced at herself in the mirror. "Oh, no," she said. *"Ssshhh."* She put her finger over her mouth. "Don't wake the kids."

Sheridan wanted to tell Kamora that she was the one being loud. But her aches — more mental than physical — kept her silent. Sheridan opened the door and peeped into the hallway. When she was sure it was clear, she said to Kamora, "You know where everything is."

"Some host you are," she said, handing Sheridan the last bottle of wine.

Sheridan waited until Kamora tiptoed down the long hallway and then closed the door to the guest bedroom. Alone, she looked down at the sweat suit she'd worn all day, then pushed away the comforter on the bed before she slipped between the sheets. She turned off the light but, a moment later, turned it back on — the way she did when Quentin was working late. She wanted her husband to know that even as she slept, she was always waiting for him.

Sheridan lay back and stared into the space. She tried to capture every relevant moment of her life with Quentin — the way they lived and loved, laughed and cried. It hadn't always been easy, but it had almost always been wonderful. No matter what was going on in life, she knew she always had God and Quentin. There was no place she had to go in this world without her husband. He was her protector, her security, her strength.

She held up her hand and watched her diamond wedding band sparkle in the bedroom light. She had just had the ring cleaned; it had been Quentin's idea when they'd been shopping two days before Christmas.

"I want your ring to shine as bright as the love I have for you that's inside of me."

Her husband had never left any doubt that his heart was filled with love. She just hadn't known — until today — that his devotion was not meant for her.

What did I do, Quentin?

She twisted the band, removing it from her finger, swallowing her emotions.

She fondled the ring between her thumb and forefinger and then tucked the wedding band under her pillow. When she closed her eyes, stubborn tears, refusing to obey her command to stay away, seeped through her lids. She sat up and took a long swallow of the still half-filled bottle of wine. Then she turned off the light. And when she closed her eyes, she slept.

Chapter Three

Someone was tap-dancing on top of her head.

"Mom."

Now the stilettos were stabbing holes through her skin.

"Mom."

The pain deepened as Sheridan struggled to open her eyes. When the morning light accosted her, Sheridan slammed her eyes shut.

"Mom, are you all right?"

She forced her eyelids apart. With the little strength she had in her arms, Sheridan pushed herself up. "Chris, is something wrong?"

He frowned as if those weren't the words he expected. "I was going to ask you that. Why are you still in bed? Are you sick?"

She glanced at the clock, frowned, and then asked herself the same questions. But as she slipped her legs from under the covers, yesterday's memory rushed to her consciousness. And then her head pounded. "I was up late last night, Chris," Sheridan explained as she tried to massage the pain from her head. “I was working.”

“I heard you and Aunt Kamora.” He paused and lowered his head. “Was she helping you with something?” he asked without looking at his mother.

Sheridan glanced at her son and frowned. Why wouldn’t he look at her?

“Was Aunt Kamora helping you with something?” he repeated, still keeping his eyes away from her.

“Yes.” She wanted to say more, tell more lies about something wonderful that she and Kamora had been doing.

“Okay. Go back to sleep; I’ll get Tori ready.”

“But I need to fix breakfast.” This time she moved her legs gingerly, but the pain stayed with her. Her temple throbbed, threatening to push her back onto the bed.

“I’ll fix Tori some cereal and you can go back to sleep. You look . . . tired.”

She wanted to protest. Assure her son that she could take care of him and Tori. But then she thought of Quentin.

“Okay,” Sheridan said, laying the comforter over her body with as much gentleness as she could. “I’ll be here when you get home.”

Her eyes were closed before Christopher stepped out of the room. She had to sleep to forget the wine. To forget Quentin.

But the dancing on her head began again, and moments passed before she realized that the assault was external. She grabbed the ringing telephone.

"Quentin?" she whispered as she squeezed her eyes shut.

"Sheridan."

The urgency in her mother's voice overrode the throbbing in her head. Her eyes opened. "Mom?"

"Honey, I need to speak to you."

Sheridan couldn't believe it. How did her mother find out about Quentin already? Impossible. But then she remembered how when she was a child her mother knew everything. Growing up, she was convinced that God tattled on her. But she thought God had long ago stopped that. He was supposed to be on her side — especially now.

"Mom, I . . . was going to call and tell you."

Her mother spoke over Sheridan's words. "Honey, when Quentin gets home from work tonight, can the two of you come over here? Without the children."

Sheridan blinked. Her mother didn't sound as if she knew.

"Sheridan."

And then she heard it — slight tears in her mother's voice. "Mom, what's wrong?" Sheridan gripped the receiver.

"Your dad and I need to talk to you and Quentin. It's important."

"Mom, uh, Quentin is out of town. On business. It was an emergency." She felt the need to make it a complete lie. "But I can come over."

"How long will Quentin be away?"

Forever. "I'm not sure."

Her mother sighed. "All right, but we really wanted to see both of you."

"Mom, please tell me what's wrong."

"It can wait, honey." The cheer Sheridan was used to returned a bit to her mother's voice. "We'll talk when you get here."

"Give me an hour," she said and then hung up.

When Sheridan swung her legs over the side of the bed, the hammering shifted from her head to her heart.

She pushed herself up and then looked back at the bed. It beckoned her to return. And she wanted to — she was exhausted from sorrow. But her mother needed her.

She took cautious steps from her bedroom to the guest room down the hall. She tapped on the door, but when there was no response, she knew Kamora had already made her way home. Kamora often used wine to wash away her concerns, so Sheridan was sure that Kamora had awakened alert this morning. Kamora's methods were something the two friends constantly debated. This morning Sheridan knew she'd been right all along. Drinking didn't solve a thing.

Sheridan moved in slow motion toward the master bathroom. The Jacuzzi tub summoned her, just as the bed had moments before. But she willed her eyes away and focused on the shower, twisting the faucet handles to full blast. Then she stripped and stared into the mirror.

Sadness had partnered with gravity and dragged her skin downward. Her eyes drooped, her cheeks sagged, the corners of her lips hung low. Every emotion she'd lived was engraved inside the creases on her face. She turned away before her eyes could begin to tear.

She placed her body under the showerhead. The pulsing liquid heat was soothing, freeing her from yesterday's memories and today's questions. But like a recurring nightmare, the pain-filled scenes returned and played in her mind. She remembered every horrible second — Quentin here, Quentin gone.

She twisted the showerhead to full blast and closed her eyes. She inhaled, then exhaled. Again. And again. The water was her conditioner, washing away the dirt with the pain. She stayed until calm pervaded her. She stayed until she knew she'd be able to walk without swaying and think without crying.

Stepping from the shower, she reached for her toothbrush. But a millisecond later, she snatched her hand back. Startled, she stared at the stand. There was only one toothbrush in place — the one with the pink handle. The blue-handled toothbrush was gone. She grabbed her toothbrush, and resisted the urge to open the medicine cabinet and take in other signs that her marriage was no more.

Inside their bedroom, she jumped into a gray sweat suit, keeping her eyes away from the dresser that now only held her bottles of perfume. She didn't dare look at the bed, still unmade, with only Quentin's pillows still in place. She grabbed her leather jacket from her closet and held her breath to keep his scent away. She hurried from the bedroom, dashed down the stairs and out of the house. She needed to get away from all that reminded her that her old life was now new.

Inside her Explorer, she sat for a moment, staring at the house, soaking in the same sight Quentin saw when he pulled away from his family.

How could he do this?

Sheridan eased her car from the driveway and eyed Mrs. James in her rearview mirror. Her neighbor didn't wave; she just glowered the way she had for the past ten years. Moments later, thoughts of Mrs. James were forgotten as Sheridan zigzagged through the subdivision, and tried not to notice the bare Christmas trees like the one she'd taken down with Quentin and the children just this weekend. At the stoplight, she tried not to see the man and woman who strolled in front of her SUV. But her eyes betrayed her and her glance followed the couple, huddled close, their love apparent.

The light turned green, and she sped away. But then at the corner, her eyes met with the Sizzler where, fewer than sixty hours before, Quentin, having decided she should have a cooking reprieve, had taken them all to dinner. And then a block and a half away, she passed Blockbuster, where on New Year's Day Quentin had surprised her with six DVDs and they'd laughed and cried their way through hours of comedy and drama. She swallowed the lump in her throat as she remembered that time they'd spent in bed, sharing emotions with the movies' characters. That was what she loved about Quentin; his sensitivity, never hiding his feelings behind some macho bravado.

Was that one of the signs she'd missed? As she turned onto the freeway, she asked herself for the millionth time what, when, where, how did this all happen? The questions were overwhelming.

She eased into the left lane.

My husband wants a man in his bed.

An eighteen-wheeler barreled down the 405 freeway behind her.

What did I do to drive him into a man's arms?

She sped up.

When was the last time we made love?

Sheridan slowed her car. It would be declared an accident; everyone would say how tragic it was. But before time could pass, Sheridan thought of Christopher. And then, Tori. And her mother. And father.

The boom of the truck's horn startled her. She floored the accelerator and screeched into the next lane. Car horns blasted, but she kept her eyes straight ahead, ignoring the obscenities hurled at her.

She breathed, as her heart rate slowed to normal. She couldn't believe she'd even considered that. Her children needed her. Her parents needed her. No, she'd have to find another way. Do something else to deal with the shame of it all.

Sheridan squeezed her mother tighter than she could ever remember holding her.

"It's all right, honey. Everything is going to be all right."

Sheridan nodded, grateful to hear those words. Her mother had no clue how she was soothing her daughter; she just always seemed to say the right thing.

"Where's Daddy?" Sheridan asked, closing the front door of the home where she grew up.

"In the bedroom." Beatrice Collins took her daughter's hand and led her into the living room. The space had barely changed in thirty years. The golden-colored couch with two matching chairs and the walnut coffee table all sat in the same place as when she had entertained her high school friends here almost every day more than twenty years before. "Cameron," Beatrice called, "Sheridan's here."

"So, honey, Quentin is away?" Beatrice asked as she sat on the couch and patted a space for Sheridan to sit next to her.

Sheridan sank into the ease of the old sofa and nodded, not wanting to lie to her mother again.

"You guys didn't mention that on Sunday."

"We didn't know," she said, glad she was able to speak some truth. "Daddy." She jumped up and hugged her father, needing his comforting embrace. As she looked over his shoulder, the pictures on the fireplace mantel smiled at her. Photos of her and Quentin and the children — all in yesterday's life.

"So, Daddy, Mom," she began, turning away from the memories, "what did you want to talk about?"

Cameron sat in the chair across from the couch and Beatrice joined him, resting on the full chair's arm. When she put her arm around her husband, Cameron said, "We wanted Quentin to be here. Your mother said he's away."

This time she lied with silence.

"I don't really want to tell you this alone."

Sheridan's heart took an extra beat. Her husband would never be by her side again, never be there to comfort her, or protect her, or love her.

Her eyes moved from her father to her mother and then back again. "Daddy, you're scaring me."

"Oh, no, baby. There's no need for that."

Beatrice stood and sat next to Sheridan again. She glanced at Cameron.

He said, "I have prostate cancer."

Sheridan gasped.

"Now, it's not that serious," Cameron continued.

"How can you say it's not serious?" Sheridan asked through the lump of fear in her throat.

Cameron leaned forward and squeezed his daughter's hand. "Because it's not. The doctor told me they found it early. With radiation —"

"Radiation?" Sheridan squealed.

"It can be treated," Cameron finished.

"But radiation?" Sheridan looked from her father to her mother. "That sounds serious."

"Well, my doctor is very optimistic," her father said.

"In fact, when the doctor told us your father had prostate cancer . . ." Beatrice paused and chuckled, and Cameron joined her. Sheridan looked at her parents with wide eyes. There was nothing funny about this. "Your father told the doctor he was fine with it," Beatrice continued. "He said he'd lived a blessed life and was ready to see Jesus."

Now Sheridan was sure that everyone in her world was spinning on a different axis. Her father was talking about meeting the Lord face-to-face and her mother didn't seem concerned.

Cameron said, "But the doctor told me at my age I would die of something else before the prostate cancer."

Sheridan looked from her father to her mother. Their chuckles continued, even through the words — *cancer, radiation, die* — that made her want to cry. It took minutes for Cameron and Beatrice to notice their daughter wasn't laughing.

"Honey," Beatrice said, "the key is they found this early."

"Really?" Her question was full of hope.

Cameron nodded. "For eight weeks, I'll have daily treatments, and in the end, I'll be fine. Anyway, you know what I believe," her father said. "Jesus is the name above all names — and that includes cancer. The devil has no power over me."

Sheridan took a deep breath. "So, you're going to be all right," she said, trying to keep her voice steady.

"Of course, sweetheart."

"Yes, your father will be healed, and he will shout God's glory from every rooftop." Beatrice chuckled again. "You know how your father is."

The smile that Beatrice and Cameron exchanged was one Sheridan had watched her parents share over the years. It was their secret code, a nonverbal language that only they spoke.

"Okay," Sheridan said as casually as she could. "When does this all begin?"

"My doctor's going to call me." Cameron patted her hand. "I wanted you to know, sweetheart, because I want you to be here for your mother. Now, we haven't said anything to your brother yet. We will, but not until we know more. I don't want him taking off from work and rushing down here. There's no need for that."

"He's going to be upset when he finds out." Sheridan squeezed her hands in her lap to stop their trembling.

Beatrice waved away Sheridan's concern. "Don't worry about your brother. I'll take care of him."

Sheridan knew her mother would do just that. She was a daddy's girl, but her brother could win a gold medal as a mama's boy.

"The main thing, Sheridan, is there's nothing to worry about. I'm going to be fine."

Sheridan put strength into her voice. "Well, that's good. I'm going to use the bathroom." She made sure she smiled before she rushed away.

Before Sheridan stepped into the lavatory, the fragrance of spring rain accosted her from the potpourri on the sink. Only the morning daylight filtered through the small window once she closed the door. But Sheridan didn't need light to move. Everything was still the same in the sea-blue room. The same rug covered the white tiled floor. The same plastic shelves sat above the commode, holding toiletries and old perfume bottles that gleamed as if they'd just been shined but were probably as old as she was. The small space hugged her with its familiarity. And she felt safe — to release the tears she'd been holding and hiding from the moment her father had uttered the words "prostate cancer."

Sheridan didn't care what her father said; he might be prepared to go, but she wasn't ready. Not now. Not ever.

She slid to the floor and let her tears flow.

Please, God. Don't take my father. Please, God.

And then she remembered her prayer from yesterday. How she had asked God to make Quentin do the right thing. And how Quentin had driven away from her as soon as she had said the prayer.

The memory made her sobs deeper, and she almost choked trying to keep her cries silent. She couldn't let her mother and father hear. If they did, they'd try to comfort her, and then they'd see the burden weighing on her and realize her tears were for something far beyond her father.

How can this be happening? To lose the two most important men in her life . . .

She prayed, "Dear God, please, God," until she couldn't say it anymore. After minutes she stood and turned on the water. She washed her face. And dried her tears. And prepared herself. Some way, somehow, she'd find a way to get through this. She had no other choice.

Chapter Four

It seemed impossible that life would continue.

Yesterday she'd lost her husband, and today she had to entertain the prospect of losing her father. Yet the fax machine was filled with customer orders requesting the best from Hart to Heart.

Sheridan's eyes scanned the final fax from one of their largest customers. Marcy, the owner of a Hallmark gift shop in New York, loved Hart to Heart. "Your husband is phenomenal," Marcy had quipped when she discovered it was Quentin Hart who wrote the emotionally stirring words for the sample cards they'd sent to her. "He makes love with his prose. You are a very lucky lady."

I'm not lucky, I'm blessed, Sheridan had thought as she beamed with pride then. She was sure she was going to throw up again now.

How was she supposed to care about Hart to Heart when the man who pulled her heartstrings had ripped the rope?

She closed her eyes, surrendering to her

emotional exhaustion. Even though she'd slept when she returned from her parents, she'd still been too tired to cook dinner and had ordered pizza. It had worked for the children — it had worked for her — until Tori began her assault.

"When is Daddy coming home?" Tori had asked as she slipped a piece of pepperoni into her mouth.

"I don't know."

It could have been her tone or her glare that silenced Tori and made Christopher stomp from the kitchen. Since that time, she'd heard little from either child.

The shrill of the telephone startled her. She grabbed the receiver.

"Sheridan."

She shot up straight in the chair. "Yes."

"How are you?" her husband asked.

Quentin sounded as if he were really away on business and calling to check on those he loved. "What do you want?" Her words sounded harsh — even to her ears. But what was she supposed to say? How was she supposed to act when all she wanted was for him to come home?

"I'm sorry I didn't call you last night. I wanted to, but I thought I should give you time."

In that instant, she felt it again. The longing. For her husband. For her life.

"Sheridan, are you there?"

"Yes."

"I want to come home."

She inhaled. That's what she'd been thinking.

"To talk."

She breathed. Almost smiled.

"To the children."

Her near-smile was gone.

"To let them know what's going on."

The hope chest that she had opened in her heart slammed shut.

"Sheridan, are you there?"

She wanted to be any place but here. "There's no need for you to talk to Chris and Tori. They're fine. They think you're away on business."

"Thank you for that, Sheridan. I think it's best if I tell the children myself."

"Tell them what?"

He paused. "I want to explain. That I'm not . . . coming home."

"You can't explain that to me, Quentin. How do you expect your children to understand it?"

"I want them to know that I'm still here."

No, you're not.

"And that I still love them and always will."

She wanted to ask him why the children should believe him when he'd said the same words to her for years. "Quentin, this isn't a good time."

"There's never going to be a perfect time."

"I just want to wait a few days. Wait until . . ." She paused. What did she want to wait for? For Quentin to change his mind and tell her the truth — that he wasn't in love with a man. That it was a lie he'd been told by the devil, and he'd come to his senses. "This isn't a good time," she repeated.

There was weariness in his sigh. "Don't do this, Sheridan."

"Don't do what?" She stood and paced across the length of the office. "Don't try to protect my children from this devastating news that will rip their hearts out the way you tore me apart?"

"Sheridan."

She was tired of hearing him say her name. "My father has prostate cancer," she blurted out.

"What? Oh, Sheridan, I'm so sorry."

"My mother called this morning," she explained, "wanting both of us to come over tonight. They wanted you to be there with me. They thought I would need you."

There was a moment of silence. "Do you want me to come over now?" he asked softly.

Please, yes. "No, not if you're going to leave again."

He hesitated. "If you need me, I'll be there."

She wanted to scream that he was a liar. A cheat. A low-down, dirty dog. But those were the words in her head, not her heart.

"I'm so sorry about Dad," he said through her silence. "And you know if there is anything I can do, I will. I love your parents, Sheridan."

But you don't love me, she wanted to cry. At least the words he'd spoken about her parents were the first words in the last twenty-four hours that she trusted. Quentin's mother had passed away and he had no relationship with his father. Beatrice and Cameron Collins had been his parents since he met them when he was only twenty-three years old.

"Now, I hope you understand why I can't deal with this. Why I can't handle making arrangements for you to talk to Chris and Tori."

"I understand how you feel, but this has

to be done. I'll come over tomorrow night."

She sighed.

"I can come over after dinner."

Will you stay?

"Please, Sheridan."

Exhaustion encouraged her to agree. "Whatever." She spoke as if the word took effort. Then she added in a much stronger tone, "But I don't want you saying anything to Chris and Tori about what's going on."

"They're going to ask questions. Especially Chris."

Another truth. "Tell them we're separating, but don't tell them you're a . . ." She stopped, daring him to finish her thought. When he said nothing, she said, "That's all we'll tell them, until I figure out what's best for them."

"I want what's best for them too."

Sheridan decided not to waste the words asking him how he could say that and then turn around and do what he'd done.

"Good night, Quentin." She hung up before she could hear his good-bye, before she would lose her pride and beg him to come home. She clicked the caller ID button to see where the call had come from. It was his cell phone.

Sheridan wondered where he was. Where he'd spent all of his hours away from his family. She hadn't allowed herself to speculate. But now the dam broke, and the questions flooded her. Was Quentin with Jett? Were they sharing a bed? Were they touching, caressing, kissing?

She tried again to remember the last time Quentin had made love to her. Still she couldn't.

The sting of the tears was immediate. *Quentin and Jett are together,* her mind whispered as if it were telling her a secret. She squeezed her eyes, wanting to release the images that came with her thoughts. Quentin and Jett. Having sex. Making love.

Her eyes snapped open and she grabbed her BlackBerry, scrolled through the address book, and clicked on Dr. Hong's number, then paused. Dr. Hong was her doctor — should she go to her with this news? But then she wondered what other doctor she could go to. A clinic was out of the question and she wasn't going to choose a physician from the Yellow Pages. Not even a recommendation from a friend was safe. Her own doctor was best.

She dialed the number.

"Dr. Hong's exchange."

"Yes," Sheridan said through deep

breaths designed to keep her tears at bay. "I'd like to leave a message for Dr. Hong."

"Go ahead, please."

"This is Sheridan Hart. I'd like to come in at her earliest appointment for a blood test." She paused, inhaled courage, and then said, "I need to have an AIDS test."

Chapter Five

Sheridan's fork slipped from her hand.

She glanced at Christopher and Tori, who continued to swirl the pasta onto their forks in silence, not seeming to notice what had just happened. Sheridan held her breath — *one, two, three, four, five.* And then the sound of the key jiggling in the front door lock.

"Daddy's home," Tori squealed. She jumped from the kitchen table and ran toward the door.

Sheridan squeezed her eyes shut. Even as she had tossed through the long hours of last night, then turned papers for a few hours in her office before she spent the rest of the day in bed, she hadn't been able to prepare her heart for seeing the man who was the source of her pain.

Tori's squeals of delight brought Sheridan back to the kitchen table. Although Tori ran to greet her father, Christopher stayed in place, and his stares made Sheridan twist in her seat.

"Chris, your father is . . . home."

He shrugged. His face remained stiff, without emotion.

"How's my best girl doing?" Quentin's voice floated into the kitchen from the foyer.

Although she couldn't see Quentin and Tori, Sheridan played the scene in her mind — Quentin lifting Tori waist high and swinging her around in a circle. A grin surely filled Tori's face; a smile certainly spread Quentin's lips.

Sheridan wanted to lay her head down and cry. In minutes, Tori's cheer would be gone. She looked at Christopher again. His face was taut, his cheeks were sucked in.

"Hey."

Sheridan looked toward the voice. Quentin stood in the archway to the kitchen, grasping Tori's hand.

"How are you?"

There was so much in his tone. It was their history she heard the most. Sheridan tried to smile, but her lips wouldn't move from the way they were pursed, protecting her — keeping all of her emotions of the past days inside. She pushed her chair back and cringed as the legs creaked against the tile. She lifted her plate from the table.

"Tori, finish your dinner," she said, keeping her eyes away from Quentin.

"I'm finished, Mom," Tori whined. "I just want to talk to Daddy."

The normal words she would have said, insisting her daughter return to her dinner, didn't come. There was nothing normal left within her.

As she piled Tori's plate on top of hers, Quentin said, "So, how are you, Chris?"

When there was no response, Sheridan looked at her son. His eyes were still on her, watching, waiting.

"Chris," Quentin called for his son's attention.

Finally he turned to his father. "Mom said you were away."

Even before she turned, Sheridan could feel Quentin's eyes on her.

"Yes," he said simply.

"Where're your bags?"

The dishes clanked against the porcelain sink as Sheridan almost dropped the plates.

"Sheridan, are you all right?" Quentin asked. She heard the concern in his voice.

She didn't want to respond. Didn't want to say a word to the man who was twisting her heart. The man she was still willing to beg to come home. She said, "I'm okay," because she knew her children were watching.

"Mom." In Christopher's tone, she heard his questions.

She faced her family.

"Chris, Tori. Your father wants to talk to you," she said, for the first time looking directly at Quentin.

Quentin's eyes locked with hers, and Sheridan could almost hear his silent plea. *Help,* she was sure he was screaming inside.

But she said nothing more and crossed her arms to keep her pounding heart inside her chest.

Quentin cleared his throat. "Ah, guys, let's go into the living room."

"Is something wrong, Daddy?" Tori asked. Her child's intuition didn't allow her to let go of her father's hand. She'd held him from the moment he'd walked through the door.

Quentin and Tori walked toward the other room, but Christopher stayed at the table.

Sheridan said, "Chris, didn't you hear your father?"

"What does he want to talk about?"

Sheridan stiffened. Something was in his eyes, in his voice. "Your dad's going to tell you."

He stood and moved closer to her. "I

want you to tell me."

Tears burned behind her eyes. She turned away and began rinsing the dishes. "Go into the living room, Chris. I'll be right there."

Seconds passed before she heard his steps. She placed the plates inside the dishwasher, wiped off the counter and the table, dusted invisible crumbs from the chairs, and then looked around for anything else to keep her away. But there was nothing left to do. She took a breath and joined her family, as it used to be.

Quentin sat on the couch, with Tori by his side. Sheridan walked to the fireplace and leaned against the mantel's edge. Christopher moved to stand next to her.

"Son, why don't you sit down?" Quentin motioned toward the love seat.

Christopher shoved his hand inside his jeans and shook his head. "I'm fine."

Quentin looked at Sheridan. But she stayed still.

"Tori, Chris, there is something I want to tell you." He cleared his throat. "First, I want you to know I love you."

"I know that, Daddy."

Quentin squeezed Tori's hand. "But your mother and I have decided . . . we need a little time apart. We need . . ." He glanced at Sheridan.

Sheridan pressed her lips together.

He lowered his head. "I'm going to be staying somewhere else . . . for a little while."

Tori's eyes widened, already filling with water. "Daddy, you're not going to be staying at home with us?"

"No, sweetheart."

"Where are you going to be?"

"I'm not sure . . . right now."

Sheridan swallowed the lump of fear those words put inside her.

"Are you and Mom getting a divorce?" Tori asked.

"Your mother and I haven't decided anything yet," Quentin said.

"Your mother and I"? Sheridan wanted to scream to her children that she had nothing to do with this. They should know she was the good parent, the one who had expected to keep their family together until the end of time.

"Sheridan," Quentin said. "Do you have anything to add?"

She shook her head.

Quentin sighed and turned toward his daughter. He lifted Tori's face with his fingers. "Nothing's going to change . . . not really." He wiped away Tori's tears with his thumb. "I'll see you all the time, and we'll still do things together and —"

"Why are you leaving us?" Christopher finally spoke.

Sheridan wanted to step to the center of the room, and shout, "Bravo." She held her smirk as she looked at her husband.

"I can't give you a simple answer, Chris."

Christopher shrugged. "It doesn't have to be simple."

Quentin said, "There are just some things your mom and I have to work out."

"Daddy, I don't want you to go," Tori cried as she wrapped her arms around her father's neck.

"Tori." Sheridan reached toward her daughter, and she ran from her father into her mother's arms. "Go upstairs, and I'll be up in a little while."

"Mommy, why is Daddy leaving?" Her grasp was tight around her mother's waist.

Sheridan kissed the top of Tori's head. She wanted to console her, assure her the world would be just as her father promised — nothing would change. But she knew words wouldn't soothe her daughter because she hadn't found any in the English language to bring comfort to herself. "Honey, go up to your room, and I'll be there in a while, okay?"

Sheridan could feel the nod of Tori's head before she ran upstairs, her sobs louder than her footsteps. Quentin stood, as if he wanted to follow his daughter, but he didn't move.

"I think Tori asked a good question," Christopher began as he closed the space between him and his father. They stood face-to-face, toe-to-toe, father and son. Sheridan watched and wondered when Christopher had grown taller. He was standing almost an inch above his six-foot father. "Why are you leaving us?"

"Chris," Quentin said and reached for his son.

"No love, Dad." He backed away, dodging his father's touch. "Just the truth. What's the real reason you're moving out?"

Quentin glanced at Sheridan, and she shook her head.

"Why are you trying to protect me?" Christopher said, raising his voice. "I want to know."

It's time to stop this, Sheridan thought. Before Quentin blurted out more than she wanted told. "Chris, your dad said all he's going to say."

"There has to be more to this than just you're leaving. Tori and I deserve to know." Christopher's voice quivered as he looked between his parents.

Sheridan said, "Like your father told you, we have to work some things out."

"That's not good enough."

"Christopher, we are still your parents," Quentin said. "You are not going to talk to us that way."

"Then I won't talk to you at all."

Sheridan watched her son march up the stairs. When she heard his bedroom door slam, she whispered, "That went well."

Quentin shook his head at her sarcasm. "We should have told them the truth. Lying never works," he said, as he turned back toward the couch.

She almost laughed. "You've been lying for seventeen years. Now you're a man with integrity? Please."

The soft lines of his jaw hardened, and he pressed his lips together as if he was trying to hold back words he might later regret. After a moment he said, "We're going to have to tell them. I want them to understand and know they will always be a part of my life."

It was Sheridan's turn to be silent.

"And you too, Sheridan." He paused. "I will always take care of you."

She looked at him as if she'd never seen

him before. "Quentin." She spoke softly, then stopped, letting his name rest between them for a moment. "How can you talk about love, and caring, and all of those things, and then just walk out of here? Like your family never mattered."

"You and the children have always mattered to me. That's why I waited so long and why it's so hard now."

"But none of this makes sense. I thought you loved me."

"I do." He shook his head. "I know it's difficult to understand."

She looked down at the floor. "Was it me?" she whispered.

"No," he said quickly and took steps toward her, but stopped when she stiffened. "Please believe me. This has nothing to do with you."

"How can you say that? Obviously, something was wrong. Something was missing for you." She squeezed her eyes shut, trying not to see Jett in her mind.

"This was happening long before I ever met you."

"That's the part I don't understand. You keep talking about all the years you've had these feelings. But then, what were the seventeen years with me about?"

"They were about loving you."

There it was again. Moving words, loving words, words that let her know she was cherished. Only now she knew the truth.

"Sheridan," he continued, "believe me when I say if there was any other way — if there was anything else I could have done, I would have done it. But I was miserable."

His words made her want to cry. She crossed her arms and pressed her lips together, trying to close off everything that had once been open to him.

Quentin stared at her for a moment. "You're not wearing your wedding ring."

It took a moment for Sheridan to understand. She turned her hand, staring at her bare left fingers. Then she frowned at him. "Why should I?"

He spoke no words, just lowered his eyes.

"I hope you didn't imagine you were going to have me and . . ." She stopped and held up her hands as if she were surrendering. "Anyway, I'm sure Tori will want to speak to you. And probably Chris, too. Where can they reach you?"

He walked to the mantel and stared at the photos of the four people who were the parts of the Hart family. It took a moment before Sheridan understood Quentin's silence. "Have you already moved in with Jett?"

His silence was louder this time.

"Quentin?" She called his name with dread and disbelief. And then the hours rushed through her. The hours she'd been living this nightmare, wondering what was wrong with her. Wishing she could have her husband back. Hours she'd spent blaming herself, feeling inadequate, insignificant. "How could you do this?"

"Sheridan, I'm sorry," he said, still turned away from her.

His words unwrapped the anger she'd been holding within. "I cannot believe you."

He faced her. "Sheridan, sweet—" He stopped before he finished. "I have to give this a chance. If I don't, I'll never know."

"So you really didn't want to stay here with me and the kids? All of that stuff you said on Monday was just show."

"No, I wanted to stay, but when you decided I should leave . . ."

"You were looking for permission to leave me and the kids to go live this lifestyle you know is wrong."

"Permission?"

"Well, if you're looking for permission,

Quentin, you're not going to get it. You're not going to get it from me or Tori or Chris or Pastor Ford or from anyone you know. If you're going to do this, you're on your own."

"I'm not looking for permission. I know what I have to do."

"And I know what I have to do. First, I'll be taking an AIDS test tomorrow."

Quentin took a quick step toward her. "I never exposed you to anything, Sheridan. I would never do that. The things that happened between me and Jett before . . ." He stopped when her face contorted with revulsion. "I was never intimate with a man," he whispered. "Not while we were together."

She almost screamed, then remembered their children. "I didn't know we weren't together, Quentin. You left home," she paused and looked at her watch, "barely sixty hours ago."

He looked away from her. "I promise you, I never exposed you to anything."

She chuckled, although there was no humor in her sound. "And tell me why I'm supposed to believe you."

"I never lied to you."

Sheridan shook her head. "What's so sad is that you don't get it. You're a liar,

Quentin. Your entire life is a lie, and you're acting like you don't realize that." She moved toward the stairs. But then she turned back to him. "I'll be speaking to an attorney. I want a divorce as quickly as possible."

His eyes widened as if he was surprised by her announcement. "Don't you think you're moving too fast? We need to wait —"

"Wait for what, Quentin?" Sheridan took slow steps toward him. When she stopped, she was standing so close, she could almost feel his heartbeat. Her breathing quickened as she felt the warmth of his breath through his full lips. She took in the dark speckles that sometimes blackened his brown eyes. She stared at the gleam of his freshly shaven head and inhaled his scent, knowing her nostrils would never forget him.

"Wait for what, Quentin?" she whispered again.

He didn't back away. "All I'm saying, Sheridan," he began, matching her tone, "is there are a lot of years and a lot of love between us. We need to wait until we're sure."

She stared at him for a moment before she backed away, putting as much distance as possible between the man she still loved and her heart. "I'm already sure because I'll never be what you want. I'll never be a man."

She rushed up the stairs but stopped when she heard one of the bedroom doors slam. She held her hand over her pounding chest and looked over the railing at Quentin. She could tell he had heard it too, and their fears were the same — had one of their children overheard them?

The Harts stared at each other for a moment longer before they both turned away. Sheridan was already in her bedroom when she heard the engine of Quentin's Mercedes. But this time she stayed away from the window. She didn't need to see him. She already knew where he was going.

The tears came again, but they were not the same as the ones she'd cried that morning, and yesterday, and the day before. Tonight, she cried because she couldn't contain her rage. This time she cried because all she wanted was for Quentin Hart to get out of her life for good.

Chapter Six

The kitchen screamed in silence.

The morning sounds were missing — no television blasting or siblings battling; Sheridan didn't even hear spoons scraping against the bowls as Christopher and Tori finished their cereal. She stood outside, away from their sight, preparing herself to greet her new family — as their single mother. She took a deep breath and spread her lips into a wide smile.

"Are you guys almost finished?"

Neither answered her.

"Tori, your van will be here in five minutes." She glanced at Tori's cereal bowl, still three-quarters filled with corn flakes, milk, and a sliced banana. "Tori, you have to get moving."

"I'm not hungry, Mommy."

Sheridan's heart fell to her knees — just like last night when she'd found Tori sobbing in her room. She'd held her daughter until she fell asleep, then went into her own bedroom to cry. But in front of the children, she would never show her anger. "You have to eat."

"I don't want to." This time tears accompanied her words. "Mommy, can I stay home? I don't feel well."

Sheridan sat next to Tori. "You're sad, huh?"

Tori nodded. Christopher pushed back, scraping the chair's legs against the floor. Before she could call him, he dashed from the room.

"I think school will make you feel better," she said, turning back to Tori. "You'll see your friends."

"But what if Joy or Lara ask me about you and Dad?"

"Why would they ask you anything?"

"But suppose they do? I don't want them to know."

Sheridan didn't have a response because she felt the same way. She didn't want anyone to know. Even though she'd told Kamora, she hadn't taken any of her best friend's calls since. She hadn't even spoken to her mother, even after Beatrice had left a message yesterday announcing that Cameron's radiation treatments would begin tomorrow. Like her daughter, Sheridan wasn't ready to share this shame.

Tori said, "Lara's and Joy's mother and father live with them. I don't want them to know that Daddy won't be living with us."

Sheridan wanted to just sit in the middle of the floor and cry. This was what Tori felt now, but what would happen when the world found out her father preferred a man to his wife? She wished she could keep Tori and Christopher home. Lock the doors. Bolt the windows. Unplug the telephone. Hide inside and just pray for Jesus to return.

"You know what, Tori? I can promise you two things. First, Lara and Joy will not ask you anything about your dad and me. And second, you'll have a wonderful day in school."

Tori pushed her bowl away, nodded, and stood. Sheridan waited until she heard Tori's steps on the stairs before she picked up the bowls Tori and Christopher had left on the table and dumped what remained into the garbage disposal.

"I'm leaving, Mom. I'm going to catch the van over at Darryl's house," Christopher said.

"Okay." She stared at her son dressed in jeans and a plain white T-shirt under his jacket. She frowned. Where were his khaki pants and golf shirt? He never dressed this way for school.

But she stayed silent and just wondered what he was thinking, what he was feeling.

"Have a good day, Chris."

He walked out the front door, and she tried not to question why Christopher hadn't hugged her the way he did every morning.

He just forgot.

"Mommy."

She tried to smile a little at Tori, who stood at the door with her backpack. "Yes, sweetheart."

"You promised I would have a good day at school, right?"

"Yes."

"Can you promise me something else?"

Sheridan nodded.

"Can you promise me Daddy will come home soon?"

Sheridan swallowed the lump in her throat before she said, "I can't do that, sweetheart, but not because I don't want to. I just don't know what the future will hold."

"But you told me I was going to have a good day."

Sheridan didn't have enough words to explain this life to her daughter. "I'm absolutely sure of that. But things with your dad and me . . . We have a lot to figure out."

"Okay," Tori said as if sadness had

wrapped itself around her.

"But there are some things I can promise you. I can promise that your dad loves you. And I love you. And in just a few days you won't be so sad. And in a few weeks life will . . . feel normal again."

Tori inhaled as if she was going to ask a question, but the blare of the school van's horn stopped her. Sheridan had never been so happy to hear that sound.

"We'll talk more after school, okay?"

She rushed Tori through the front door, kissed her, and then waved — like she did on normal mornings — as the van drove away. She closed the door and then leaned against it, praying that by the time her children returned, she'd be more prepared for their misery.

The moment she stepped away, she heard the front door's knob jiggle. She frowned when Christopher stepped inside.

"Chris."

"Mom."

They spoke at the same time.

"Did you miss the van?"

"No." He closed the door and dropped his bag onto the floor. "I told Darryl to have the van come here because I wanted to talk to you."

She glanced at the clock. "Chris, the van

will be here in a few minutes."

"Don't call me that."

Sheridan frowned. "Don't call you what, sweetheart?"

"Chris. I don't want to be called Chris anymore."

Her frown deepened, but then she laughed. "Okay, what's the joke? Is this something you and Darryl have cooked up?"

"It's not a joke, Mom. I don't want you to call me Chris anymore. Call me Christopher."

Her smile left when she saw his seriousness. "Chris . . . what are you talking about?"

"Mom, I'm serious." His voice quivered. "I want to be called Christopher."

"Okay," she said slowly.

His eyes left her and he stared at the floor. "I know about Dad."

She barely heard his words, but his expression was enough to tell her what he'd said. When Christopher looked up, there were tears in his eyes that matched hers.

"You know what?" she asked, although she knew what he was talking about. She remembered the sound she'd heard when she was speaking to Kamora. She remembered the slam of the door last night. She knew what he knew.

Christopher looked into her eyes. "I know why Dad's leaving us. I know there's something wrong with him. I know he's not a man."

She didn't have the words to agree or disagree. She simply wrapped her arms around his neck. "I didn't want you to find out this way," she whispered as she held him.

"But I did." His voice got louder with each word. "And I don't want to be anything like him."

"Chris," she began, but before she could continue, he interrupted her.

"Don't call me that, Mom. Chris could be a girl's name, and I'm nowhere near gay."

"Okay, calm down, Chris . . . topher." She motioned toward the living room. "Let's go talk."

"I don't want to." And then the sound that had saved her minutes before saved him now. Christopher wiped the single tear that had rolled down his cheek. "There's the van." He lifted his bag.

"It might be a good idea for you to stay home today," she said.

"No, I want to go to school. I just don't want to have anything to do with Dad ever again."

"Don't say that . . . Christopher. Your father loves you —" Before she could finish, her son rushed through the door. She hurried behind him, needing Christopher to understand that his father loved him and always would. But he jumped into the van before she could tell him that truth.

The van eased from the curb, taking her son and his pain away. She wanted to run after the vehicle and snatch Christopher back — hold him and make his hurt disappear. But just seconds later, the van vanished from her sight.

Minutes passed before she stepped back into the house and closed the door.

"Girl, I was about to hurl out an all points bulletin for you."

"I'm sorry," Sheridan said, pushing the cell phone earpiece more securely into her ear with one hand as she maneuvered the car with the other.

"I've been calling to make sure you were okay," Kamora continued her rampage. "You could have at least returned a sista's call."

"What can I say?"

"Just say you're okay."

Sheridan thought about Christopher and Tori and the pain of their morning. She wanted to tell her friend her life would never be fine again. "I'm okay."

"I'm glad. You'll let me know if you need to talk, right?"

Sheridan smiled. In her tone she heard Kamora's love. It was great to know that whatever she went through, her best friend would be there. Just the way Kamora had been since they'd met in the first grade. Just the way she thought Quentin would be for the rest of her life.

Kamora said, "I have a lot to tell you."

It wasn't often that Sheridan was eager to hear about Kamora's escapades as she searched for her perfect man. But this morning she couldn't wait to hear about her friend's latest exploits. She wanted to think about anything except where she was going and what she was about to do.

Kamora continued, "I've been doing a lot of research."

Sheridan frowned as she turned onto La Cienega. "Working on something for the office?"

"Girl, I ain't hardly thinking about my company. This is about you. You will not believe the things I found out about men like Quentin."

Sheridan's frown deepened. "What are you talking about?"

"You know," she said, as if Sheridan should be able to decipher her thoughts, "men who are married and sleeping with other men. There's a ton of research on this."

Sheridan sighed. "And why would I want to hear this?"

"Sweetie, I know this is hard, but you've got to know." Kamora spoke quickly, as if she felt a protest coming. "There is just so much of this going on. And the worst thing is women are the ones suffering."

I can attest to that, Sheridan thought.

"Let me read you something: 'Women are being victimized spiritually, emotionally, socially, but most importantly, physically by men who say they are straight but sleep with other men. Women are living with and dying for men who subsist inside a secret world, having sex with men and then running home to have sex with their girlfriends, fiancées, and wives. The tragedy lies not in the denial of these men to accept the fact that they are gay; the tragedy lies in the fact that the denial is so deep, very few insist on practicing safe sex, exposing themselves and their unsuspecting female partners to the deadliest of diseases.'"

Sheridan wanted to close her eyes but

instead swallowed hard as she eased from the freeway and turned onto Cloverdale Boulevard.

Kamora continued, quoting statistics on the number of men suspected of living on the down low. "And now black women are the fastest-growing group contracting AIDS." Kamora paused for just enough time to inhale. "Honey, I hate to say this, but" — she lowered her voice — "I think you should have an AIDS test."

Sheridan stayed silent as she pulled into the Saint John's Medical Center parking lot and turned off the ignition.

"Sheridan, did you hear what I said?"

"Yes."

"You may not want to, but an AIDS test is necessary because —"

"I agree with you," Sheridan interrupted.

"Really?" Kamora said, as if she hadn't expected her agreement so quickly.

"Yes." Sheridan's lips trembled as she stared at the two-story medical building. She could see the windows of Dr. Hong's second-floor examination rooms. "I need to protect myself and my children. I have to make sure I'm healthy."

"That's right, girl. I'm so glad you're looking at it this way." Kamora's voice softened. "Make the appointment and I'll go with you."

"That's not necessary."

"I'm not going to let you go through this alone. Just tell me when you're going and I'll be there."

"Now."

"What?"

"I'm going now."

"Don't you have to make an appointment?"

"My doctor will see me. I'm sure of it," Sheridan said, not bothering to explain that she'd made the appointment yesterday.

"O . . . kay. Well, I have some meetings this morning, but if you can go at about one . . ."

"No, I'm going right now. You've convinced me." She paused and blinked to keep back her tears of fear. "I'll just call you when it's over."

"I wish you'd wait for me."

"I have to do this now . . . before I change my mind."

Kamora paused. "Okay, but when you finish, we'll spend the afternoon hanging out. I have some plans for you."

Plans. Sheridan wondered what kind of plans she'd have to make after today.

Would her doctor tell her that her children were not only losing their father but that their mother was a victim of more than their father's verbal deception?

"Come by my office when you're done."

Sheridan was sure all she'd want to do was crawl into her bed. But she said, "Okay," and clicked off the phone. She took a deep breath before she stepped from her car.

Pushing back her shoulders, she strolled toward the medical building as if she weren't terrified. She marched to the receptionist's desk as if a cloak of confidence were wrapped around her.

The receptionist was on the telephone, and she smiled, her eyes asking Sheridan if she could please wait. Sheridan smiled back as if she had nothing but time.

But inside, Sheridan's heart wept. *Lord, please hear my cry. This is in your hands. You know what I need. You know what my children need. I worship you, I praise you, I thank you for your favor and I pray for your blessings . . .*

"Good morning, Mrs. Hart," the receptionist said, stopping her prayer. "You're a bit early, right?"

Sheridan nodded, because she couldn't speak.

"That's okay. You're blessed today."

"What?" She spoke louder than she expected. But she had just prayed for blessings.

"Dr. Hong's first appointment canceled, so I'll be able to get you in and out."

Sheridan nodded again. This was a blessing because that was exactly what she wanted. To get in. To get out. To get this over with.

Chapter Seven

Heaven wept.

The rain poured from the sky in thick sheets that blocked any view of Washington Boulevard from Kamora's Marina del Rey office suite. It had been pouring from the moment Sheridan left the doctor's office and slipped inside her car. The sudden storm caught everyone in the city by surprise — everyone except for Sheridan. She knew these were God's tears for her.

The downpour had made Sheridan call Kamora. "It's raining," she had moaned. "I want to go home." *And back to bed.*

But her friend would not be denied. "You owe me, Sheridan. I've been worried about you for days."

Sheridan begrudgingly gave in, knowing Kamora would not give up. Once she arrived, she'd been led into Kamora's office by her assistant with the explanation that Kamora was in a meeting.

Sheridan didn't think it was possible, but the rain poured from heaven harder. And the deluge of the sky's water took her back to another place, another time — the day seventeen years ago.

It was a day like today. A day when everyone who relished the L.A. life scratched their heads and said, "It never rains in Southern California." But on the day that she and Quentin had chosen to legally promise to love each other until the end of time, the sky had opened and released its water with such fury, Sheridan was sure God was telling her something.

She could imagine God's words, not unlike the ones her mother and father and brother had uttered. It had been a battle from the moment she and Quentin had announced their intention to marry.

"You're too young," her father had protested. "You should at least wait until you graduate from college."

"And why do you want to get married at the end of this month? Why are you rushing it?" was her mother's contribution to the heated argument. "This doesn't make sense."

Neither had voiced what she was sure they both wondered. But while her parents maintained their decorum, her brother had not.

"You're getting married?" her eighteen-year-old brother had asked incredulously.

"Why? Are you pregnant?"

The rolling of her eyes was her only answer, but she'd wanted to shout to everyone that she hadn't done a darn thing to get pregnant, although that had not been her will. It had been God's . . . and Quentin's.

"We should wait until we're married," Quentin had said the very first time their passion took them to the brink. "That's God's plan."

God and His plan occupied no part of Sheridan's mind when Quentin pressed his lips (and other parts of his body) against her. But no matter what she said, no matter what she did, Quentin never wavered.

"This is God's plan," he said, as if he'd been born with a triple dosage of willpower.

Sheridan had never understood Quentin. Most of her girlfriends had been having sex since high school. Although she hadn't been ready then, now, she was a nineteen-, almost twenty-year-old college student.

She was ready, but Quentin was not willing.

So when Quentin had taken her to breakfast for what she thought was a normal date and asked her to marry him, she'd wanted to grab his hand and sprint to City Hall. She loved him and couldn't wait to make love to him. She had no doubt they were made to be married to each other. No doubt at all — until everyone else voiced theirs.

But no one's spoken fears had stopped them, and on that day seventeen years ago, Sheridan and Quentin had taken the step to prove the world wrong.

By the end of their first year of marriage, it was clear that they'd known best. Although the two struggled to juggle school schedules and part-time jobs, and to pay bills that at times were overwhelming, still, they were delirious with happiness and much better together than apart. Five years into their marriage, Quentin was a licensed doctor and Sheridan was thrilled to be his wife and the stay-at-home mother of four-year-old Christopher.

"We were meant to be, Quentin," Sheridan whispered, as she watched the rain. "What happened?"

"Hey, girl," Kamora said, bolting into the office.

Sheridan wiped away the tears she hadn't, until that moment, realized were there. By the time she turned to Kamora, a plastic smile spread across her face.

Kamora hugged her friend. “I’m so glad to see you.”

“I’m glad to see you too.”

Kamora stepped back, stared at Sheridan, then waved her hand in the air. “Stop lying.”

Sheridan chuckled. “No, really. I’m glad you talked me into having lunch with you.” She lifted her purse as Kamora slipped into her orange leather jacket.

“Who said we were having lunch?” Kamora gathered her hair into a ponytail and wrapped a band around it. “I never mentioned food.” She hooked her arm through Sheridan’s and led her across the floor of her spacious office. “We’re going to have a lot more fun than just throwing down some catfish and greens. We’re going shopping.”

Sheridan groaned. “Kamora, I’m not in the mood. It’s raining.”

“So? We’re going to take one of my cars.”

“I don’t like to shop,” Sheridan whined, thinking of all the times her friend had dragged her through stores looking for that perfect outfit for that perfect date with that perfect man.

“And you think I care about what you like?” Kamora joked.

"I think you're being a bit insensitive considering what I'm going through."

"That's exactly why we're going. Think about it. There are a lot of ways to get back at Quentin —"

Sheridan's mind rushed back to last night. *"I have to give this a chance,"* was what Quentin had said.

Kamora continued, "— and we'll think about all the ways to really give it to him later. But for now, we're going to spend your husband's money."

"I never exposed you to anything, Sheridan."

Kamora said, "Think about it. Those designer clothes waiting with your name on them. And then imagine the look on Quentin's face when he gets the bill." Kamora giggled.

"The things that happened between me and Jett . . ."

"Where are we going?"

"That's my girl." They stepped into the elevator. "I was thinking about Rodeo Drive. Only the best for Dr. Hart's wife. After all, that's where *he* shops."

When they exited the elevator, one of the sleek black town cars from Kamora's limousine company, Ride and Shine, was waiting for them. Before they took two steps toward the car, the driver's door opened and a Shemar Moore look-alike jumped out. Sheridan's eyebrows rose at the way the young man grinned at his boss and the way her friend beamed back.

"Good morning, Ms. Johnson." Then the driver glanced at Sheridan. "Ma'am." He tipped the hat Kamora had all of her drivers wear and then pulled the door open.

"When did you get the new guy?" Sheridan whispered, glad to have something to take her mind away from Quentin.

Kamora's smile was still wide. "Jackson?" She said his name as if it were a synonym for *heaven.* "I hired him a week ago." She sighed. "But there's been a small problem." Kamora pressed the button to close the privacy window. Still she whispered, "No matter what I do, I haven't been able to get him to dip his pen in my inkwell."

Sheridan slapped Kamora's leg, but she couldn't hold back her giggles. At least for a few moments, she could live in Kamora's world.

Sheridan said, "I thought you had stopped dating your employees. You said it was trouble."

Kamora nodded. "But then along came

Jackson." She peered through the glass. "Look at him; even you have to admit that Jackson could make your temperature rise a degree or two."

Sheridan pursed her lips. "Excuse me if I don't share your enthusiasm for men right now."

Kamora took Sheridan's hand, her playful tone gone. "Girl, I really want you to be okay."

Memories returned. Of the good and the bad.

Sheridan nodded because she knew she couldn't utter a word without crying. She had never been filled with such anger, but still, sadness lingered.

Kamora asked, "How did it go this morning?"

Sheridan pulled back the image and shivered as she remembered the way Dr. Hong had smiled and politely not asked why she wanted an AIDS test. As the technician drew blood from her left arm, Dr. Hong had stood on the right and chatted about the weather. Three tubes of her life's liquid were drained, then a cotton swab was placed in the crook of her elbow before she was told the results would be available on Monday. And then she was dismissed. She was in and out, just like the receptionist had promised.

She shrugged, bringing herself back to the present. “It was just a blood test.” She paused. “But I don’t want to talk about this. Let’s go shopping.” It was happiness that she drew on her face, but only sorrow was sketched on her heart.

Sheridan leaned back into the soft leather seat of Kamora’s limousine. She stayed that way, even when Kamora took her hand and squeezed it, wordlessly telling her that she loved her and that life would be all right.

Sheridan wanted to believe that, but first, she had to live through the AIDS test results. And she wouldn’t know that outcome until Monday.

Sheridan stared at the clothes laid out on her bed: the white satin blouses, the pearl silk pants, the ecru linen suit, the eggshell knit dress, the cream suede ankle-length coat. She sank into the chair, and her glance moved to the bags torn open and tossed across the floor: Versace, Prada, Chanel. It looked like the back room of a Paris show during Fashion Week. *What have I done?* she wondered as she kept her eyes away from the receipts stacked on the nightstand. She couldn’t bring herself to add up all she'd spent.

I'm going to take this stuff back, she thought. She'd had her fun, running rampant through the stores with the platinum card she hardly ever used.

The slam of the front door interrupted her guilty thoughts, and she jumped up. She looked at the clock — only a bit after five. Neither of the children were supposed to be home yet. And she had not heard the normal shouts that announced her children's arrival.

She rushed into the hallway and called out. When no one answered, she frowned. She tiptoed down the stairs, her heart pounding with each step. She moved slowly until she stood at the bottom. "Hello." No answer. But then she thought, *How stupid is this? Greeting an intruder.*

She continued toward the front door.

"Mom."

She whipped around, her hand over her chest. "Chris, didn't you hear me call you?"

His eyes bored into her. "I told everyone in school today to call me Christopher. The teachers said that was okay."

His words reminded her of his demand this morning, and his sorrow made her forget the terror she'd felt. But even though hours had passed, she still didn't have words to comfort him.

Sheridan hugged her son, the way she always did when he came home. But she kept silent, not posing the question she asked every day. She already knew how his day was. She could tell by the way he stood in place, stiff, with his leather backpack still hanging from his shoulder and his hands stuffed inside his pockets.

"Christopher," she said his name slowly. "We need to talk."

"There's nothing to talk about. Dad decided it for us."

"But I want you to understand this has nothing to do with you."

"How you can say that, Mom? He's leaving me and Tori and you." When Christopher saw the look on his mother's face, his tone softened. "It doesn't matter. I've had a lot of time to think, and I've accepted the fact that I don't have a father anymore."

So much of her wanted to agree with her son. But it was only what she wanted for Christopher that made her say, "Your father loves you."

"How can he love me and a man at the same time?"

Sheridan pressed her lips together and

wondered how many times she'd asked the same question.

"Anyway, Mom, I'm real sure about the way I feel. But you don't have to worry." He put his hand on her shoulder. "If Dad doesn't want to be the man of the house, then I'll take over."

She wanted to tell him he was a man, but a young man. There was no need for him to take on responsibility he wasn't ready to carry. She would handle their home. She would handle him. But all that came from her lips was "Christopher . . . ," before he turned and barged up the stairs.

"Mom, I really don't feel like talking about this anymore."

"Christopher."

"I have a lot of homework," he yelled from the top landing.

Then he was out of her sight. And she was left standing in the middle of the hallway with more to say but without a son to listen. She had learned long ago that there was nothing inside of her that could force a teenage boy to communicate when he didn't want to.

She sighed. *Lord, you said you would never leave me,* she began the prayer in her mind. *And if there was ever a time that I needed to believe this, it's now.*

Please help me. Give me the words to say to these children. To comfort them and to help them find peace.

She stepped into the kitchen. Within an hour Tori would be home from dance practice.

As Sheridan pulled pans from the cabinet and then chicken from the refrigerator, she knew one thing she had to do. She had to call Quentin and tell him his son knew. Knew that his father was leaving for a man.

She didn't understand the way she smiled — just a little — inside. The small bit of joy came from her mind — from the way she imagined Quentin would feel once he heard this news. And then maybe tonight, when he laid his head on his pillow, he'd have an inkling of some of the pain she'd been carrying for more hours than she cared to count.

He answered his cell phone on the first ring. As if he'd been waiting for her call.

"Sheridan."

She paused and wondered how she should tell Quentin this news. She could drag this out. Or plunge the knife into his chest quickly. She couldn't decide as she paced inside the room she still thought of as their bedroom. Then she looked at the clothes piled on her bed. She had to finish packing all of the bags to make her round of returns tomorrow. She didn't have time to drag this out.

"Quentin, are you alone?"

There was a moment of silence. "Yes, why?"

"I have to tell you something about our family and I don't want anyone else involved."

"Is something wrong?"

How can you ask me that? I spent my morning handling your children and taking an AIDS test. "Chris found out. He knows why you left us."

He paused, then said, "You told him everything?" In his whisper, she could feel his panic.

Fury still raged inside her, but her shoulders sagged from the burden she carried for her children. No matter what she felt about Quentin, she wanted the absolute best for Christopher and Tori. No matter how much anger she harbored in her heart, she'd have to find a common ground where she and Quentin could come together for the sake of their children. "I didn't tell Chris anything, Quentin," she said, sucking the anger from her voice. "He must have overheard us last night." *Or he overheard me and Kamora,* Sheridan thought, her guilt building.

"I can't believe you, Sheridan. I thought you said you wanted to wait to tell the children."

She reared back at his tone. "Wait a minute —"

"I should have been the one to tell my son. I'm the only one who could make him understand."

"Don't fool yourself, Quentin," she said, squaring her shoulders and ridding herself of just a bit of the guilt. "You'd never be able to make any sixteen-year-old boy understand this."

Quentin sighed. "Well, what did he say?"

"I believe his exact words were" — she paused — " 'Call me Christopher because Chris could be a girl's name and I am nowhere near gay.' "

"You told him I was gay?"

Sheridan didn't know what upset her more — his rage or his surprise.

"No, he overheard us," she repeated slowly.

"Well, what did you say? Did you tell him that's not true?"

"How was I supposed to tell him that? You want me to lie to him the way you've lied to me?"

Several silent moments passed before he said, "How did Christopher take it? Was he angry?"

Sheridan sighed and wondered if this was the same man she loved last week. "How do you think he took it?"

"So he was angry."

Duh. "Yes." *Just like I am.*

"Oh, God. This is not what I wanted. I've got to talk to Chris and make him understand. Maybe I should come over."

I don't want you anywhere near me and my children.

Sheridan glanced at the clock. "It's too late now."

"Then tomorrow. I want to talk to my son."

No. "Fine. You can call him after dinner."

"Okay." He paused. "I bet you're happy, Sheridan. Christopher probably hates me."

Sheridan pounded her fist into her leg, imagining how it would feel to punch him again. She had defended him, told Christopher that his father loved him.

Quentin sighed. "I can't believe you did this."

She punched her leg harder. "Don't put this on me, Quentin," she said, her rage rising. "You left us. This is your problem, now you figure out how to fix it." She clicked the phone off.

I cannot believe that man, she thought as she stomped through the room and wondered who was this new man Quentin had become. He was not the man who she craved would come home. This man — she wondered how she had ever loved him.

She tossed the phone onto the bed, and when the handset bounced on top of the clothes, she paused. She stared at the items for a moment before she lifted the Chanel garment bag.

"I can't believe you, Sheridan."

She remembered Quentin's words as she removed the knit dress. She held it in front of her as she glanced at her reflection. She had to agree with Kamora; this dress was a knockout. *It'll look great on me this Sunday.* She glanced at the price tag. When she'd done that earlier, it had made her cringe. Now it didn't faze her.

In her closet, she hung up the dress, then picked up the pants suit.

"I can't believe you did this, Sheridan."

She held the pants suit in front of her. This raw silk two-piece would be perfect for her sorority's prayer breakfast. Again, she peeked at the price before she hung the suit in the closet. Almost an hour passed before her bed was clear, and her closet was full of designer labels.

She lifted the receipts from the nightstand and tossed them into the trash can along with any lingering remnants of the guilt she'd felt earlier. What she'd spent this afternoon was not her concern. It was Quentin's problem. And the way she calculated, his concerns were just beginning to add up.

Chapter Eight

The starkness of the white felt harsh.

Everything in the waiting area was white: the walls, the chairs, the floor. Sheridan wondered if the room felt sorrowful on purpose, to prepare family members. She wondered if one day soon, her parents and children would find themselves sitting in this room, waiting to see her one last time.

She jumped up from her seat.

"Mom, let's go out. There's a Starbucks across the street."

Beatrice shook her head and motioned for Sheridan to sit next to her. "No. I want to be here in case Cameron needs me."

Sheridan knew Beatrice would be inside the radiation room if it had been allowed. This was as far away from Cameron as Beatrice was going to be.

Beatrice sighed, and Sheridan took her hand. From the moment she'd arrived at her parents' home this morning, Sheridan had waited to see any signs of concern. But her parents were normal — lighthearted, full of jokes, as if they'd forgotten they were on their way to the hospital for

Cameron's first treatment to battle his body's invader.

But now as they sat, her mother's slight sigh was the first sign of a chip in the sturdy armor of strength and faith that Beatrice wore.

"You doing okay?" Sheridan whispered.

"I'm fine. I know God's got this."

Sheridan chuckled. "You've been hanging around Chris." The sudden burst of joy went away when Sheridan said her son's name. Would he demand that even his grandparents call him Christopher?

Beatrice said, "I do know that this is in God's hands. Your father and I have lifted this up to the Lord, so now He has to take care of it." She paused. "Did you tell Quentin?"

Why did you have to go there? "Yes," she said as if the word took effort. All morning she had prayed Quentin's name wouldn't even come up, although she knew she was praying for a miracle.

"When will Quentin be home?"

Never. "I'm not sure, exactly."

Beatrice waited and then when nothing more came, she said, "Not sure? What kind of business trip is this?"

Sheridan inhaled, hoping to breathe in courage, but none came. There was no way she could tell her mother the truth.

"What's wrong, Sheridan?"

How could she answer that with all that her parents were facing?

"Sheridan?"

Her mother's voice made her heart ache again, and she knew for sure this pain would never go away.

"Sheridan."

I'll just turn to her, smile, and make up some kind of story about how wonderful life is.

Sheridan twisted in her chair, but the moment she looked into her mother's eyes, the lies went away. The dam burst, and she cried as if she'd just heard Quentin's news.

Without a word or the passing of a second, Beatrice guided Sheridan through the hospital's halls. Finding what she was looking for, Beatrice pushed the bathroom door open and led her daughter inside.

Sheridan's sobs continued as Beatrice searched the space, making sure they were alone. Then she turned to her daughter.

"Now tell me," Beatrice said in her gentle yet stern way. With her fingertips, she wiped the water dripping from Sheridan's eyes, but she couldn't brush the tears fast enough. Fresh ones appeared before the old ones were gone.

"Mom, it's terrible."

"It can't be that bad. No matter what kind of disagreement you've had, you and Quentin have loved each other for a long time."

That declaration made her sobs quicken.

"Sheridan," Beatrice began, as if she were about to school her daughter on the intricacies of marriage, "there have been times when I've been so annoyed with your father that —"

"Quentin's left."

Beatrice's fingers stopped stroking Sheridan's face.

"Quentin's left me. He left me and the children and our home. He's gone."

Beatrice took a few steps back until she was leaning against the bathroom's long counter, shocked into silence.

"He left Monday morning," Sheridan began, and then the story surged forth like a roaring river. When she explained that Quentin had taken most of his clothes and moved out, Beatrice held her hands. When she told her that her husband was living with Jett Jennings, Beatrice hugged her daughter. Beatrice held her in the embrace, as if her arms would give all the protection she needed. When they finally separated, neither woman's eyes were dry.

"I . . . don't . . . know . . . I . . . don't . . . understand," Beatrice stuttered.

Sheridan shrugged, calm now, as if the release had been therapeutic. "Mom, I never saw it coming, or else I would have done something."

Beatrice hugged her again. "Oh, sweetheart. There is nothing you could have done. This is not your fault."

She heard but didn't believe her mother's words. "Mom, I don't want Daddy to know."

Beatrice frowned.

"He has so much to deal with right now. I don't want to burden him with this."

"Sheridan, there is nothing about you that would be a burden to your father."

"Still . . ." How could she tell her mother that she didn't have the strength to face her father? She'd always been his girl, the perfect one pleasing him every step of her life.

But now he would discover she was not perfectly wonderful. She had failed — as a wife. "Daddy has too much on his mind right now, Mom," Sheridan argued.

"*Hmph.* You know your father better than that. He can handle this, the cancer, and a whole lot more."

"Mom, please."

Beatrice took her daughter's hand. "Honey, your father and I haven't survived all these years of marriage by keeping secrets."

For Sheridan, that truism was full of pain. It was the reason why her marriage had died. Her life with Quentin was one big secret.

"You have to tell your father, Sheridan. I won't say a word, but only because it should come from you."

I don't want to, she thought. But she nodded as if she agreed.

"What about Chris and Tori?" Beatrice whispered even though they were still alone. "Do they know?"

Sheridan sighed, nodded, but could say no more.

Beatrice read her daughter's heart. "Are you ready to go back out there? I don't want your father to worry if he comes out and doesn't see us."

Sheridan glanced at her reflection in the mirror. She could pass for a woman who had her life together. If her father didn't look too closely, he'd never know.

Beatrice stepped into the hallway. Sheridan followed, and noticed the way Beatrice's shoulders slumped with more than the weight of her husband's disease. Sheridan was sorry for what she told her mother today. And for a whole lot more. She was sorry for all the agony she was sure was waiting in the days in front of them.

Chapter Nine

It was love sprinkled with concern that filled her heart when Sheridan helped her father into the Explorer.

"I don't know why you're treating me like some invalid," Cameron complained. "I can climb into this car just fine."

"I know, but can't a daughter help her father out every once in a while?" Sheridan tried to put cheer into her voice.

"Help your mother. She's the one who's old," Cameron kidded.

"Who you calling old?" Beatrice shot back from the seat. "If I'm so old, why didn't you realize I'm already in the car? It must be more than your prostate that needs help. While we're here, we need to check out your eyes."

Her parents laughed as Sheridan slammed the passenger door and then climbed into her own seat. She couldn't join in their laughter. Her thoughts were with her mother's admonition to tell her father the news.

After a few quiet moments, Beatrice asked, "So, how was it, Cameron?"

"Just fine," Cameron said in a tone that contradicted the fact that they were leaving his first radiation treatment. He twisted in his seat and reached for his wife's hand. "Just like Dr. Lees promised, the whole thing took about five minutes. It was the getting undressed and waiting and then getting dressed again that took all the time. This is going to be a piece of cake."

With that, Sheridan knew no more would be said about her father's cancer-killing visit. Her parents would not spend hours pining about what had happened or why. They would simply pray.

As Sheridan maneuvered through the streets, her parents chatted, but her thoughts wouldn't allow her to be with them.

How am I supposed to do this? she wondered as she stopped at a red light. She glanced at the car in the next lane. Inside, a man leaned across the space and kissed his female passenger. Sheridan's eyes were stuck; even when the light turned green and the car sped away, she stayed in place.

"Honey, the light is green."

She pushed down on the accelerator, and the Explorer jerked forward with a screech.

"Whoa, do you want me to drive?"

Cameron laughed.

She felt the tears coming. Yes, she needed her father to drive. To take over the car and everything in her life. To make it all better.

It wasn't until Cameron said, "Honey, what's wrong?" that Sheridan realized a tear had rolled down her cheek.

"I have to tell you something."

"Sweetheart, let's wait until we get home," Beatrice said.

Sheridan shook her head. She had to tell now, before she was overcome with the sadness that had started to grow at the sight of the loving couple and the realization that she'd never again share a moment like that with Quentin. "Daddy, Quentin left me. We're getting a divorce."

"What? When did this happen?"

For the second time too soon, she repeated the story of what was now her life. But this time she removed herself as the main character and became only the narrator. She was just getting to Jett Jennings when she eased her car next to the curb in front of her parents' home.

And again she had shocked one of her parents into silence.

Sheridan turned off the car's ignition and then waited for someone to speak.

"Daddy, I'm sorry."

"Sweetheart, what are you apologizing for? You didn't do anything."

"That's what I told her," Beatrice said.

"But I must have done something — even if it was not noticing the signs."

"Honey, none of us saw the signs," Beatrice said. "Cameron and I saw you and Quentin almost every week, and we didn't suspect a thing."

She spoke before she thought, "But you weren't sleeping with him."

Their opened mouths and wide eyes almost made her laugh. *I'm getting good at shutting them up,* she thought.

"Well," Cameron started and took her hand, "how are you doing?"

She shrugged. "I'm fine, I guess."

"Well, I want to talk to Quentin," Cameron said.

Sheridan smiled. "What are you going to do? Beat him up?"

Neither one of her parents laughed the way she'd expected, and she wanted to tell them that wasn't fair. They'd laughed about Cameron's cancer; didn't her tragedy deserve a chuckle or two?

"No, I'm not going to beat him up," Cameron said, as if he had considered it. "But over the years, Quentin and I have become close. He's always talked to me, and I can't think of a time when he needed to talk to me more."

"If I thought it would help, I would drive you to him right now. But nothing's going to change. It's not like he's with a woman." She paused, and the images rushed back to her. Quentin and Jett. "There's no chance of us reconciling." Those words put such a thick lump in her throat that for a moment she again wanted to die with her marriage.

"Do you want to come inside with us?" Beatrice asked.

"No. I want to be home when the kids get there."

Beatrice tsked, as if the thought of her grandchildren mixed with this news was too much. Cameron stepped from the car and then helped Beatrice from the back seat. For the second time that day, she saw the weight of her burden on one of her parents' shoulders. And it pained her once again that she'd caused them this grief.

"This is not your fault, sweetheart," her father said into the window as if he'd read her mind.

She nodded because she knew he expected her to.

"Call us?"

She pressed her lips into a smile. "I will.

Tonight." And then she drove away. In the rearview mirror, she looked at her parents standing shoulder to shoulder, watching and waving as their daughter and her tragedy drove away. Sheridan knew if they had their way, they'd go home with her and care for her until this pain passed.

But she was a long way from the days when hugs, chicken soup, and vanilla ice cream solved all that ailed her. With what she faced now, the only way her parents could help was if they had a direct line to the Lord. And with the way she'd been raised, she was pretty sure they did.

It was his hands that Sheridan remembered the most.

With tenderness, he caressed her. With compassion, he punctuated his speech with gestures. With grace, his fingers molded around the pen as he wrote those extraordinary words for Hart to Heart.

Sheridan glanced at the clock. She needed to take her thoughts away — away from the agony of the past five days. But how was she supposed to move on when her life had been about her husband and children?

Thank God for the children, she thought. Sheridan picked up her pad. The 2006 catalogue for Hart to Heart was already due. To keep her business going, she had to come up with new cards. New words that would help some man somewhere profess his undying love for some woman in his life.

She stared at the blank page in front of her and wondered if men who loved men gave their lovers cards. Would Quentin ever give a card to Jett? Would Jett ever bring flowers home to Quentin?

She grabbed the telephone and quickly dialed.

"Sis!" her brother exclaimed the moment he answered the phone. "What's up in your world?"

The familiarity of his voice draped itself around her, and she wished she'd made this call before.

"How are you, my dear brother?" Sheridan asked, not wanting to answer his question.

"It's all good. I'm wrapping things up here in the office so that I can get home."

"Big plans for the weekend?" She amazed herself. With all of this, she was able to breathe, walk, speak as if life was the same as before.

He said, "Naw. We were out all last weekend, so Rosemary and I are just going to kick it. The most I'll do is maybe take a bike ride along these mean streets of San Francisco. And then, of course, on Sunday there's football. Go, Raiders!"

Sheridan chuckled. "Tell Rosemary I said hello."

"Will do, but I know you didn't call me to ask what Rosemary and I are up to. So, to what do I owe the pleasure of this chat with my big sis?"

She took a deep breath. It was time to tell. She opened her mouth, but a lump lifted from her stomach, into her throat, stopping the words she planned to say. "Can't a girl just call her little brother?"

"First of all, little is hardly the adjective you can use to describe me," her six-foot-five, ex-college-linebacker brother chuckled. "And secondly, when was the last time Sheridan Hart called me to say hello?"

"I'm hurt."

"Ah, I'm just kidding," he said, although they both knew he wasn't. He was right. She didn't speak to her twenty-months-younger brother as often as she wanted. Life just got in the way. After all, she didn't have a lot of free time. She had children. And a husband.

Sheridan took another breath, sucked in some spunk, and said, "I do have something to tell you." She paused. "Quentin's gone."

"Where'd he go?"

"Away from me." Then the story poured from her. It was a practiced speech now. As Sheridan gave the details of the events of the past week, her brother stayed silent except for the occasional "I don't believe this" exclamations that punctuated her soliloquy. But as was their way, Sheridan included the parts she'd left out with her parents — the conversation with the children, the AIDS test, how Christopher knew the truth.

"And so where is he now?" he almost screamed when she finished.

Sheridan flinched at his question, and everything that she found painful to imagine rushed to her mind. She inhaled. "He's" — she paused and breathed — "with Jett." This was the part where she was sure the tears would come. And surprise filled her when she didn't cry. For days she'd been fighting to take her heart to a place where tears didn't live anymore. Maybe she was winning the battle.

"Ain't this some s—" He paused. "Well, praise the Lord anyway."

Sheridan couldn't help it; she laughed. Her brother always caught himself before he actually cursed. It amazed her: in all the years they'd shared on this earth, she'd never heard him say a bad word. She wondered how he stopped himself though, since he always came so close.

He continued, "I can't believe Q is going out like this." He whistled. "Do you need me to come down there?"

"For what?"

"Well, first, to help you get your divorce started."

"You're not a divorce attorney. What are you going to do, litigate him to death?"

"I'm glad you got jokes, but someone needs to look after you."

She couldn't count the number of times he'd said that. He couldn't have been more than five the first time he'd declared himself her protector, and he'd always lived up to that promise.

"I'm going to get the divorce papers started," he said, taking control. "And I know some people who know some people. You won't even have to wait the six-month period."

"Okay," she said because that was the easiest way to work with her brother.

"I still can't get over this. You know, I want to come to L.A. There are a few things I'd like to say to Mr. Q."

"I've already said everything that Quentin needs to hear."

"Maybe you left some things out."

"I don't think so. We were married for seventeen years. I know what to say to my . . . to Quentin."

His voice softened. "Sis, just be grateful he didn't waste any more of your life."

Sheridan shook her head. What was he talking about? Quentin hadn't wasted her life. Every week of those years, every minute of those days, she'd live again. She'd even breathe every second of this last week if it would bring back her life the way it used to be.

"Anyway, this is for the best."

Sheridan turned her attention back to her brother and frowned.

"You're still young," her brother continued. "You'll find someone deserving of you."

It was time to hang up. Her brother spoke as if he were swinging from a crazy tree. Talking about her finding someone else. Like she'd ever trust a man — besides her father, brother, and son — again.

Sheridan said, "I've got to go."

"When are you getting the AIDS test results?"

She could tell he was disgusted. "I'll

speak to my doctor on Monday and call you."

"Are you sure you're all right?"

"I'm a survivor. Destiny's Child has nothing on me."

"I just want to see that m— well, praise the Lord anyway."

"I'll call you in a couple of days."

"I'll call you tomorrow," he said. "Hang in there. I'll be praying."

She hung up and massaged her eyes. The call didn't bring her the comfort she had expected, but in a small way she'd found some consolation. The thought of her brother getting on a plane, flying for ninety minutes to Southern California to confront the man who had once been his friend, made her smile just a bit.

Her BlackBerry vibrated atop her desk. "Oh, no," she groaned when she noticed the message: "7 p.m. marriage retreat meeting." She'd forgotten; she and Quentin had done all the research for the couples' getaway and were supposed to review it with the board tonight.

Sheridan searched through her desk for the folder with Quentin's scribble on the outside. She stood and hurriedly grabbed her jacket and bag. In the foyer she yelled, "Chris . . ." Seconds passed before she said, "Christopher."

His bedroom door opened, and then her son appeared at the top of the landing.

"Christopher," she began, "I'm going to church. I'll be back in a couple of hours. I have my cell, okay?"

He nodded, leaned over the railing, and smiled. Sheridan took two steps back. How many times had Quentin watched her like that? "Okay, Mom. I'll take care of Tori. I'll take care of everything."

It was the second time he'd made that pronouncement — that he was now the man of the house. Sheridan shuddered. She still had to speak to him about that.

She rushed to the car. But when she put her key into the ignition, her hand stayed still.

She was supposed to be doing this with Quentin.

Preparing for Hope Chapel's tenth marriage retreat, the annual vacation for married couples.

She flicked her wrist and the engine revved up. And her stomach fluttered.

She was supposed to be doing this with Quentin.

Attending the retreat as husband and wife. As examples for the soon-to-be and newly married couples. But what kind of example would she be now?

She could imagine the comments: "Did you hear about the Harts?" and "I thought they had the perfect marriage," and "Just goes to show you the world is not what it seems."

In one movement Sheridan turned off the ignition and jumped from the car. "I can't do this."

She stepped into her home, and Christopher was standing there as if he'd been waiting.

"Did you forget something?"

She looked at him and wondered why she never noticed it before. Everyone said he looked like her, but tonight he sounded like his father.

"No, I just decided not to go." Sheridan rushed up the stairs. At the top she glanced down at her son. He was watching her, and his eyes told her he understood.

Inside her bedroom Sheridan made the call.

"Hi, Nicole, it's Ms. Hart," she said, trying to put a smile into her voice. "Is your mom or dad home?"

"Hi, Ms. Hart. Mom and Dad are on their way to church. You just missed them. Sorry."

I'm not sorry. "That's okay. I'll just leave

a message. Tell them, we . . . I . . . Mr. Hart and I are sorry we missed the meeting tonight."

"Okay." Nicole paused. "Is Chris, I mean, Christopher there?"

Nicole reminded Sheridan that Christopher's demand for a new identity went beyond their home. Still, it pleased Sheridan that Nicole asked for Christopher.

A year ago it had almost broken her heart when Christopher asked if he could go on a group date. She'd known it was coming, but she wasn't ready. His choice of Nicole eased her pain a bit. The two seemed perfect.

Christopher and Nicole attended the same school, were in Jack and Jill, were both active in church, and often found themselves at social events together with their parents, since their fathers were both doctors and their mothers officers in their chapter of Delta Sigma Theta. Nicole was the girl whom every mother requested for her son in her prayers to God.

So when Christopher announced last November on his sixteenth birthday that he and Nicole were now boyfriend and girlfriend, Sheridan and Quentin had given their approval — and the talk about the responsibility of dating as young Christians.

Sheridan was also pleased that they'd joined the Dating Forum at church, a program their pastor had developed a year before.

"Hold on, Nicole," Sheridan said. "I'll get Christopher for you." As she walked to her bedroom door, she allowed herself a small grin. She couldn't do anything about their father, but at least she could help Christopher and Tori maintain some semblance of their lives.

"Christopher," she yelled from her bedroom door. "Phone." He bounced up the stairs. "Nicole's on the phone for you."

Christopher stopped moving. "Tell her I'm not here."

Her grin turned upside down. "What's wrong? Are you mad at Nicole?"

"No. I can't do this right now."

His words were the same as hers just minutes before. She nodded, and like he'd done for her, she told him silently that she understood.

They stood for a few seconds longer. Eye to eye. Emotion to emotion. The security and comfort of life as they'd known it to be, gone.

"I'll take care of it," she said. And Sheridan turned away, ready to tell another lie . . . this time for her son.

* * *

The day had been as hazy as her memory was now.

Sheridan sat on the lawn, holding Christopher in her arms.

"Do you want me to hold him?" her father asked from one side of her.

"Let me." As her mother gingerly took the baby, Sheridan kept her eyes on the stage. The long speeches were continuing under the blazing June sun, and Sheridan didn't want to miss any part. In less than an hour, her husband would march across the stage, accepting his medical degree and taking them both to the land they'd dreamed of.

"I'm so proud of you, Dr. Hart," she'd told him that morning as she tightened the knot on his brand-new silk tie, which she'd spent almost forty dollars on. It had been beyond a splurge, but she'd remembered the way Quentin had eyed the tie when they saw it in *GQ* magazine. And although they couldn't afford it, by the time the credit card bill came, Quentin would officially be a doctor, albeit an intern.

Quentin had hugged her tightly, and inside his arms, she felt all of his gratitude. For the way she worked for the city of Inglewood while he studied for long hours and worked even longer hours.

But this was the beginning of the life they'd strived for together. In eight days Dr. Quentin Hart would begin his internship at UCLA.

"I want to give you the world," he'd said as he'd clasped the faux pearls around her neck. "In a few years you'll have a real string of these."

She faced him. "That doesn't matter to me. All I want is to be with you."

"And I with you . . . until the end of time."

She closed her eyes and held her husband tighter than she ever had, promising herself they would be this way forever. And as she stayed in his arms, she wondered where the ringing was coming from. She didn't want to break away, knowing in her heart that she had to hold on to him. But the ringing continued, growing louder, until she had to let go.

Her eyes opened; it took her a moment to focus and realize where she was. In her bedroom. In the present. Not with Quentin. Not in 1991.

She begrudgingly released her dream.

"Hello."

"Sheridan, were you asleep?"

She glanced at the clock. It was only a

bit after ten. When had she fallen asleep? "No."

Kyla said, "Nicole said you'd called, and I was concerned when you and Quentin didn't make it to the meeting tonight."

Sheridan cleared her throat, hoping to remove the grogginess and her memories. "Oh, there's nothing to worry about."

"You're not feeling well?"

The thoughts of yesteryear stayed with her. "I'm fine. I'm sorry I missed the meeting, but I wanted to get the hotel agreement to you."

"I'll pick it up tomorrow, or you can give it to me in church on Sunday. Everyone is excited about Hawaii. I'm so glad Quentin suggested it." She paused. "So, with the proposal completed, there's not much left for you and Quentin, right?"

There's nothing left for us. "Kyla, I'm really sorry to do this, but Quentin and I won't be on the planning committee anymore."

"Why? What's wrong?"

My husband prefers a man to his wife. "I can't talk about it now, but Quentin and I completed everything you needed. You don't need us anymore."

"That's not true. You're part of the marriage fellowship team. We will always need you guys."

Sheridan felt them building — the tears. Sadness once again, overriding the anger. But there was no way she was going to cry. "I'm sorry, Kyla," she quivered.

"It's fine," Kyla said. She paused and then spoke with a softer voice, "Sheridan, remember that I'm your friend if you need anything. At any time."

The battle to keep the tears away would be lost if she didn't end the conversation. "Thanks, Kyla." She hung up without saying good-bye. And then she had her victory. She didn't cry. But although she was triumphant over her tears, she couldn't defeat the ache. The ache that came as much from remembering their past as from trying to imagine her future.

Chapter Ten

Maybe this was getting easier. Maybe she could find normal in this abnormality.

Those were Sheridan's thoughts as she stepped from the shower. Even when she glanced at her toothbrush, standing alone, even when she opened the medicine cabinet, filled with only her toiletries, there were no tears.

Inside her bedroom, Sheridan jumped into a pumpkin-colored sweat suit and rushed downstairs into the kitchen.

"You get on my nerves," Tori shouted at her brother.

Sheridan almost wanted to applaud. Even the children understood that life had to move on. "Tori, don't talk to your brother that way." She spoke the same words in the same tone that she'd used a million times.

"He started it," Tori protested, giving her standard answer. "He told me that I was out of my mind because I didn't call him Christopher. And he's the one who's out of his mind because everyone knows his name is Chris."

Sheridan's thoughts of normalcy dissipated. "Tori, what's wrong with calling your brother Christopher, if that's what he wants?"

"I like Chris better than Christopher."

He said, "I don't care what you like. My name is Christopher, stupid."

"Mom!"

The chirping of her BlackBerry caught Sheridan's attention. As she searched in her purse, she said, "Christopher, don't call your sister stupid, and Tori, call your brother . . ." She stopped when she saw Quentin's number across the screen next to "missed call."

She stepped from the kitchen, away from her children, and wandered into the living room to listen to the message.

"Sheridan, hi, this is Quentin." *Does he think I've forgotten the sound of his voice?* "I, uh . . . well, I hope you're well." *Then why did you leave me?* "And, well, anyway, I wanted to make plans to get the kids." His sigh that followed let Sheridan know that his words were as absurd to him as they were to her. "Maybe tomorrow. After church, if you'll be going." *Why would he wonder if we'll be going to church? We always go . . .* "I, uh, won't be there." *Oh.* "I'll meet the kids outside. Or at your . . . our house. Whichever you prefer. Whatever is best for you." *Come home. Make this all go away. That would be best for me.* "So give me a call when you get this message. Uh, thanks . . . and Sheridan . . ." He stopped, ending his message.

Sheridan replayed the message. But no matter how many times she listened, it didn't help her understand how she'd gotten to this space as a single mom making visitation plans with her children's father.

Sheridan sighed. Even though she wanted to strap Quentin to a tree and play darts with his manhood, on the other side, she wanted to preserve the children's relationship with their father. They deserved that — even if he didn't.

She had no idea how Christopher and Tori would react to this news. Neither had mentioned Quentin, walking around as if only the three of them had ever lived in the house. She was sure Tori would want to see Quentin. And she was just as sure Christopher would not.

In the kitchen Sheridan stuffed her cell phone inside her purse and then turned to her children. In just minutes they'd fallen in love again, chatting as if moments before they hadn't been preparing for war.

"Hey, you two." She spread her lips into a smile she didn't feel. "Your dad . . . tomorrow." She paused as Tori's eyes widened and Christopher's eyes narrowed. "He wants to see you after church," she said as if she agreed with their new life.

"Yeah," Tori cheered.

Christopher glared at his mother for a moment and then turned and walked from the room.

"Christopher, wait." She rushed up the stairs behind him and caught his door just before he tried to slam it. "Christopher."

"No."

"No what?"

"I'm not going to see him, Mom. I don't ever want to see him again."

"He's your father, Christopher."

"Not anymore."

My thoughts exactly. "He will always be your father, and he wants to see you."

Christopher folded his arms and leaned back on his bed. Sheridan sat next to him. "I know you're mad right now, but you've got to know that your father loves you."

"How am I supposed to know that?"

Sheridan reached inside for words that would answer that question for both of them. "Because this has nothing to do with you. I know for sure that he loves you."

Christopher jumped from his bed. "I don't care if he loves me," he screamed.

"Christopher, watch your tone. There's no need to yell."

He continued as if he hadn't heard her. "I don't love him, and you can't make me love him. Just like you couldn't make him love you."

His words froze her heart.

"Mom?"

Both Sheridan and Christopher turned to Tori standing in the doorway.

"I love Daddy." Tori stood at attention, as if she were determined to make her position known. "I want to see him."

Christopher looked at his sister as if she had really lost her mind. He glowered at his mother and then stomped from the room.

Sheridan tapped on the door. "Christopher." She paused and waited. He'd been inside the bathroom for almost an hour — since he'd left her sitting in his bedroom wishing she'd slapped him for speaking the truth. *"Just like you couldn't make him love you."*

She couldn't remember what Christopher had said before or after, but she knew it would take a long time for those words to leave her.

"Christopher, this is enough. It's time to come out. Right now." Her tone carried her warning.

She stepped back and tapped her foot. Counted silently. She'd give him to ten. When she got to nine, the door opened.

He looked at the wall, the stairs, the floor. He looked at everything — except her.

The anger she felt floated away. She wanted to hold her son, tell him to cry, so she could cry with him. Just like she did with Tori almost every night.

But Christopher had told her he needed no comfort. "I'm fine, Mom" was all he said when she asked how he felt.

Now Sheridan knew he wasn't fine.

"Christopher, I'm sorry you're angry, but this is not how we're going to handle this, okay?"

He mumbled words she couldn't decipher.

"We need to talk," she said.

His tear-filled eyes finally met hers. "Mom, please don't make me go."

It was the way he trembled that made her blink back her own tears and reach for him. "Okay," she whispered as she held him. "We'll talk about it later. I have to take Tori to dance practice."

"Okay," he said before he hurried into his bedroom.

"Mom."

Sheridan turned, and there was Tori, with her own tears. Sheridan prayed for the day when her home wouldn't be filled with all this sadness.

"I'm ready," Tori said.

Sheridan nodded. "Wait for me downstairs." In her bedroom she dabbed at the water that seeped from her eyes and then inhaled, ready to be the strength for her children.

She yelled good-bye to Christopher, heard no response, and then rushed Tori into the Explorer. Silence stayed with them through the five-minute ride, and Sheridan was grateful when she pulled in front of the dance studio.

"I'll be here to pick you up at two."

Tori nodded but didn't move, her eyes straight ahead.

"Are you okay, sweetheart?"

Again she nodded. "Mom, are you going to be mad at me if I go see Dad?" Still she didn't look at Sheridan.

"Of course not, Tori. I want you to see your father if that's what you want."

She nodded again. "I do." Finally she

faced her mother. "I'm sorry, Mom, but I still love Daddy."

"I know," Sheridan said as she pulled Tori into her arms. *I still love him too.* She held her daughter for a moment longer before she said, "I'll call him, and by the time I pick you up, the plans will be all set, okay?"

It was a weak smile Tori gave her, but Sheridan was grateful for it. At least one-third of their household had something to look forward to.

Tori jumped from the car and trotted toward the building as if she'd suddenly found joy.

You're supposed to be on my side, Tori, Sheridan thought as she eased the car away. *You're not supposed to want to see your father.*

The guilt bombarded her right away. Those were not the thoughts of a loving mother. Still, a part of her was glad that Christopher shared her feelings.

Sheridan maneuvered the car into the driveway, glanced at her home, and then clicked on her cell phone. She dialed Quentin's cell, and the call went straight to voice mail. She dialed again. Same thing.

Where is he? she wondered, knowing this was his weekend off. She wanted the plans finalized before she picked up Tori — before she changed her mind about letting her go.

"Where are you, Quentin?" she asked aloud. And she prayed her mind wouldn't take her there again. To Quentin and Jett. Jett and Quentin.

"Golf!" She remembered his Saturday morning tee time. He'd canceled during the holidays, but since it was almost seventy degrees, she was sure where he was now. She glanced at her watch. She had more than thirty minutes to intercept him before he took to the course.

Sheridan backed the car from the driveway and then onto the 405 toward the private club in Bel Air. As traffic whizzed by, she glanced in the mirror, wishing she'd done her hair. Wishing she had on something other than her standard sweat suit uniform.

Why am I trippin'? It didn't matter what she wore or whether her hair was done; life was different now. *But he wanted me for all those years.* The other side of her told her that he hadn't.

Still, after she parked, she checked herself in the mirror.

She slammed her car door, and then she heard his laugh. It surprised her, the way it made her feel. The way it made her smile. The way it robbed her of her anger. She turned toward the laughter, and her heart didn't take another beat.

There was her husband. Walking from his Mercedes. In khaki pants and a navy golf shirt. With his Louis Vuitton golf bag draped across his shoulder. With a grin on his face. With Jett Jennings at his side.

She didn't want him to see her, but she couldn't move. She watched them walk, just feet away from her. Old friends. New lovers.

They chatted and laughed. A second before they stepped into the clubhouse, Jett turned. Eyes met. She stood, bolted in place. He stood, as Quentin disappeared behind the doors.

Jett's face filled with surprise. Hers stretched with sorrow. They stayed, staring, waiting for the other to move. He shifted first. Turned the ends of his lips upward into a slight smile. The ends of hers drooped down. She pressed her emotions through her eyes and prayed that he would know what she was thinking. Then, she prayed that God didn't punish her for those thoughts.

Jett understood. Took away his smile. Nodded slightly. Then, in the next moment, he was gone.

And still, she stood, shackled to the spot.

"Sheridan. Sheridan."

She didn't have the power to turn toward the voice.

"Sheridan." Francesca Mills scooted over, rolling her golf bag behind her. "Darling, what are you doing here?" Francesca stood on her toes to lift her five-foot frame tall enough to air-kiss Sheridan's cheek. "Don't tell me your husband finally got you to take up golf. That's wonderful. Perhaps we can play together some time. Are you playing today?" Francesca chatted as if Sheridan were talking back.

Francesca stepped back and eyed Sheridan's sweat suit. "You don't look like you're playing golf."

"I'm not," were the first words Sheridan was able to push through her throat.

"So what are you doing here? Are you meeting Quentin?"

"No." That was all Sheridan was going to say. Francesca Mills had made millions as an upscale interior designer, but she could have doubled her fortune as a gossip columnist. There was no way Sheridan was going to say anything more.

"Oh. Well . . ."

Sheridan hopped into her truck before Francesca's inquisition continued. "I've gotta run, Francesca."

"Oh. Well . . . I'll see you in church tomorrow. I wanted to ask —"

Sheridan slammed the door on the rest of Francesca's words and then sped off as if she had somewhere to go. She needed to get away fast, but no matter what the speedometer said, she couldn't get away from the image in her mind. The two men — one clean shaven, one with a short haircut. Both impeccably dressed. Either able to turn the head of any woman passing by.

But only one of them aware that he had just squeezed every bit of her life's blood out of her heart.

The image stalked her.

The picture in her mind of two men. With their heads tossed back, their laughter filling the air. No cares in their world.

The ringing cell phone forced her to leave her misery. She didn't want to answer, but when she saw the caller ID, she pressed the earpiece into her ear. "Hi, Mom," she said, trying to hide sadness behind cheer.

"Sweetheart, what's wrong?"

"Nothing," she sniffed. "How's Dad?"

"He's fine, but I want to know what's

going on with you."

Sheridan shook her head, knowing she wouldn't be able to drive if she said aloud what she'd seen five minutes before. "Nothing, Mom."

"Have you heard from Quentin?" Beatrice asked, her voice steady.

"Yes, but I can't talk about it right now."

"I understand." Beatrice let a beat pass. "You know we're praying for you."

"I know." Sheridan could imagine her parents in their bedroom, both on their knees until their joints ached.

"And the greatest battles are won during the midst of a storm."

"I know."

"I wish you'd talk to your father and me. We want to help."

"I know." She knew now how Christopher felt. She loved her mother but just wanted her to leave her alone — for now. "Mom, I'm fine. It's just hard."

It was her mother's turn to say, "I know." Beatrice continued, "But we're here. And the Lord's always there."

"Mom, can I call you back?" Those were all the words she had left.

"Sure, sweetheart. Call us later."

She clicked off her phone just as she drove up to her house.

* * *

The moment she saw his cell phone number, she picked up. She couldn't take the chance of Christopher or Tori answering the telephone.

"Sheridan, it's me."

She didn't say anything. It had been that way since she'd picked up Tori. Even though Tori was burning to ask, her daughter didn't inquire at all about the promise her mother had given her to have the plans finalized for her visit with her father. Tori asked nothing — as if she knew better.

And then the three Harts spent the quietest Saturday evening Sheridan could remember. Each in their own bedroom, after Christopher ordered pizza when it was clear Sheridan had no plans to cook.

She couldn't cook. She couldn't talk. She could barely walk. All she could do when she slept was dream. All she could do when she was awake was remember. Quentin and Jett.

"Did you get my message?" he asked through her silence. "I left one on your cell this morning."

Did Jett tell you he saw me? "I got it," she breathed.

"I was waiting; I was hoping . . ."

Jett didn't even mention me. "You can pick up Tori tomorrow," she said, trying not to imagine Jett sitting by his side as he spoke to her. "Come here. After church."

"Great." She could see his smile. "I'm really looking forward to seeing them."

"I said you can pick up Tori," she spoke slowly. "Not Christopher." Now she could see his frown. "He doesn't want to see you," she explained before he asked.

"What?"

She repeated what she'd said and then waited for his fury.

But his response was soft. "Maybe we should . . . insist that Chris come with me."

"Can't do that." Her answer was quick. "He's sixteen."

"Still . . . I'm his father."

You should have thought of that before.

"And I want to see him."

"He doesn't want to see you."

The silence that followed felt like a moratorium, and Sheridan was sure that at this time, in this place, even Quentin was grieving for the way they'd been.

"All right," he acquiesced.

His words shocked her. Where was his fight?

"I'll take Tori to lunch and maybe a

movie. And I'll talk to Chris when I pick her up."

Sheridan nodded but made no sound.

"Sheridan . . . are you okay?"

A beat passed before she said, "How can you ask me that? Are you looking for an answer to make you feel better?"

"No, I really want to know that you're okay. That's important to me."

She spoke quicker than she could think. "Then come home."

The moments of silence were even longer this time. Finally she said, in a tone that let him know she was setting the rules, "Just make sure it's only you and Tori at lunch. I don't want her around . . . anyone else."

She hung up before he could respond and sat absorbing the conversation. She had been convinced that Quentin would rage about Christopher. How he wasn't about to take no from a sixteen-year-old. How he was the father and Christopher was the son.

But Quentin hadn't battled at all. Not for his son. Not for his wife.

"Who are you, Quentin?"

She glanced at the clock. It wasn't even eight, but she wanted to crawl back into bed. Fall into unconsciousness so she wouldn't have to deal with any of her feelings — not the loss, not the anger, not the confusion, not the waiting for the AIDS test results.

She tossed the extra pillows onto the floor, but as soon as she placed her knee on the mattress, her wedding ring glimmered at her.

Sheridan frowned. It was supposed to be under her pillow, where she tucked it every morning. But somehow it had slipped to the center of the bed — almost to Quentin's side.

She picked up the wedding band and the telephone rang. She grabbed it without looking at the caller ID, sure that it was Quentin — ready to go to war to save his family.

"Hey, girl, do you have some time for your best friend?"

Sheridan looked at the ring between her fingers, then tucked the symbol of everlasting love back under her pillow. "What's up?"

"I'm on my way home from a date," Kamora said.

Sheridan looked at the clock, wondering if she'd misread the time minutes before. "This is a bit early, isn't it?"

"I'm just getting home from last night,"

she said as if she should win a medal. "I'm a few blocks away. Can I come by? I need to talk."

"Okay, but not here." The memory of Christopher maybe hearing her and Kamora that night had stayed with her. "Let's go to Starbucks. Come get me."

After telling Christopher, Sheridan waited at the front door until Kamora pulled up.

"So it's true," Sheridan said as she squeezed into the Lexus coupe. She eyed Kamora's low-cut leopard-print spandex dress. "You haven't been home."

"Girl, I've been on the world's longest date, and you'll never guess with who."

Sheridan shrugged. There was no chance of her guessing. Kamora was her best friend, but it was mostly because of the length of time they'd known each other. Since Kamora opened her business four years before, they hadn't shared the same circle of friends. Kamora was a creature of Hollywood. Her world overflowed with celebrities she'd met when they hired her limousine company, while Sheridan lived for her husband and children. Everyone she knew was connected to the four Harts.

Kamora said, "I finally got Jackson to

dip into the inkwell."

Jackson? Sheridan frowned. "Your driver?"

"He's not my driver anymore. After last night I decided to promote him to supervisor. But then this morning he performed tasks that earned him the position of vice president. And then this afternoon," Kamora sighed as she steered into the Starbucks parking lot, "I decided to sign my entire company over to him. Cars and all."

Kamora laughed, and Sheridan shook her head.

"So this is what you want to talk to me about?" Sheridan asked.

Kamora looked at her as if she were stupid. "Yeah." She smoothed the front of her dress as she slipped out of her sports car and strutted in her three-inch Jimmy Choos like she was a runway model.

Every man seated under the Starbucks' heat lamps twisted his neck to gape at Kamora as she pranced toward the door. She swayed her hips, tossed her golden-hair weave over her shoulders and pretended she didn't notice the tongues hanging out of opened mouths. Even women stopped speaking, stopped laughing, stopped drinking, and stared at

Kamora as if royalty were passing.

It was always that way when they were together. Most times Sheridan felt invisible, but it never bothered her. She was secure in who she was — before. And she wasn't looking for a man. She already had one — before.

Inside they ordered their drinks, and the gawking continued. Kamora chatted as if they were the only two in the place, but Sheridan knew her friend was very much aware. This attention was more precious to Kamora than the air she breathed.

"Let's sit over there." Kamora wiggled toward a table right in the center of the café.

"So . . ." Kamora crossed her legs and the hem of her dress rose up her thighs. She licked the slight bit of foam from the plastic cover of her Caffè Verona. "What do you think?"

"About what?" Sheridan slouched in her chair. Tonight, the stares bothered her. She felt like a cardboard cutout sitting next to Kamora. For the second time in one day, Sheridan wished she'd worn something else. Wished she'd done something with her hair.

Kamora said, "Girl, I am in love with Jackson."

"You said that last week, Kamora, when you were seeing what's-his-name."

Kamora dismissed Sheridan's words with a wave. "This time it's for real."

"You said that the week before when you were seeing what's-his-face."

Kamora pouted. "I really mean it this time, Sheridan. You know that I don't sleep with a man on the first date."

And that's supposed to mean . . . Sheridan took a sip of tea.

"But Jackson, he's different," Kamora continued. "He treats me like he really loves me."

Sheridan wanted to remind Kamora that she'd said that about all the men she'd been with. But she stayed quiet and stared at the steam rising from her cup.

"He told me he loved me from the moment he laid eyes on me."

Were you on top of him when he said that?

"He told me I had the most beautiful eyes he'd ever seen."

Maybe that's when you were on top.

"And he said that he could imagine me being the mother of his children."

I don't even want to know what you were doing when he said that.

Kamora said, "So, what do you think?"

"I don't think anything." *Except for the*

fact that I can't believe you slept with that boy. "I don't know Jackson."

"You met him. You spent the entire day with him."

"I spent the day with you, running into stores buying every variation of white clothing."

Kamora laughed. "Has Quentin said anything about the bill?"

"He hasn't gotten it yet. The Amex bill won't be here for another two weeks."

"I can't wait." Kamora leaned forward. "Anyway, how are you doing?"

Sheridan tried to keep her thoughts away from Quentin and Jett. Quentin and Jett this morning. Quentin and Jett tonight. "I'm okay."

"Have you talked to Quentin?"

"Right before you called." She paused. "He wants to see the children."

"Well, you knew that. No matter what I think of him, I know he's a good father. I knew he'd be hanging around your house. Shoot, that might make him come to his senses and keep his behind home."

"He wants to see them away from the house. He wants to take Tori out."

"Take her where?" Kamora sounded as if the thought offended her.

Sheridan shrugged. "To lunch, somewhere. He wants to take Chris too, but he won't go."

Kamora smiled as if that was good news, but then her smile was gone. "You're not going to let Tori go with Quentin, are you?"

Sheridan frowned. "Why wouldn't I?"

Kamora twisted her lips like she had a bad taste in her mouth. "Because you need to be careful."

"Of what?"

"Well, I would never let my children go into any homosexual environment —"

"You don't have any children."

"Because homosexuality is a spirit," Kamora continued, as if Sheridan hadn't spoken. "You have to be careful about having your children around people like that."

" 'People like that'? Quentin is Tori's father."

Kamora leaned forward and whispered, "But he's gay."

"You think you have to remind me?"

"I'm just sayin' you don't want Tori catching that."

Sheridan laughed. When her friend didn't smile, she said, "You're serious? What are you talking about? You think Tori can catch that like a cold or something?"

"I'm just sayin' you don't know where those spirits come from or what they do. You need to have complete control over your children. Quentin shouldn't have unsupervised visits." Kamora paused as one of the many Denzel look-alikes who frequented the coffee shop walked by. But the moment he stepped to the bar and kissed a woman on the cheek, Kamora continued as if she'd never stopped. "Not to also mention that what Quentin's doing goes against everything God says in the Bible."

Sheridan shook her head, full of disbelief. This was the same woman who had spent an entire night and then the next day in bed with a man she barely knew. Yet Kamora sounded as if only Quentin was bound for hell.

"I'm just sayin'," Kamora continued, "you gotta watch out. Girl, all sin comes from spirits."

"Who told you that?"

"Girl, it's in the Bible . . . somewhere. Just be careful. You gotta think about who your children are around."

What's the difference between you and Quentin?

"Anyway" — Kamora sat back and let one of her Jimmy Choos dangle from her foot — "you haven't seen a man until you see Jackson naked. And the way he . . ."

Sheridan's eyes wandered around the coffee bar as Kamora continued her litany of the virtues of her new man. She focused on the couple sitting at the next table. Then she watched the baristas as they whipped up exotic drinks that were once just called "coffee." She stared at the photo of Magic Johnson holding a Starbucks mug. Anything to keep her from asking Kamora why she was above God's word but Quentin wasn't. Kamora slept with every man who smiled at her, yet she sat in judgment.

Sheridan wanted to scream her thoughts at Kamora. But she just kept her cup to her lips and her eyes away from her friend. She said nothing because Quentin didn't deserve her defense.

Chapter Eleven

Who is banging on my door?

"Mom!"

It took every effort to open her eyes. Sheridan hadn't fallen asleep until the first morning light nudged its way through her window. All night her eyes had been open, seeing her husband with Jett. And even when she'd been gifted with minutes of rest, the stalker followed her into unconsciousness, pulling her awake to face the pain of her man with a man.

"Mom!"

"Come on in, Tori."

Her daughter bounced into the room wearing mauve Capri pants with a matching shawl. She pirouetted like the ballet dancer she was. "What do you think?"

"Looks good, but when did you start asking me what to wear?"

"I just want to know if you think I look good. I want to look nice for Dad."

Sheridan almost groaned. "You look great."

Tori paused. "Mom, you don't look good."

"I'm tired."

"You didn't sleep?"

"I worked late," she lied.

"Oh. Well, I'll be ready for church in a little while. Christopher's already downstairs."

Sheridan glanced at the clock. Even though she could be ready in thirty minutes, church was not where she wanted to be. People would be there. People who would ask, "Where's Quentin?" People who would stare and perhaps see her shame.

She said, "I'm not going to church today. You and Christopher can walk. Or call your Aunt Kamora and go to church with her."

"Okay, we'll call Aunt Kamora because Chris will never walk." She kissed Sheridan on the cheek and then almost skipped out of the bedroom.

Sheridan closed her eyes and prayed that God would keep away the stalker. Keep away the worry of the AIDS test. And she rested. But soon, the banging began again.

"Mom!"

It took enormous effort for her to rise. "Yes!"

Tori bounced in with a smile that wasn't contagious.

Sheridan said, "I thought you were going to church."

"We went." Tori frowned. "We're back."

Sheridan twisted her head toward the clock. It was almost two. She certainly didn't feel as if her eyes had been closed for over three hours.

Tori continued, "Dad's downstairs. He wants to see you before we leave."

Her first thought was, why didn't her husband just come upstairs to his bedroom? And then it made sense. This wasn't his bedroom.

Sheridan jumped up. "I'll be down in a minute." She wrapped herself inside her robe and rushed to the mirror. She undid the twist that held her ponytail and combed her hair. Then she rushed to the bathroom. Within minutes she'd brushed her teeth, washed her face, and prayed that Quentin would remember how he once loved the way she looked in the morning.

She scrambled out of her flannel robe and then searched her closet for the floor-length silk wrap that she'd ordered from Victoria's Secret years before. But she shook her head when she looked in the mirror.

Ridiculous.

She was back in her flannel robe and walking down the stairs a minute later. She almost smiled when Quentin looked up at her.

"Hey, you," he said.

Everything about the moment made her want to hold him. The way he spoke, the way he sounded. The way he looked, the way he smiled.

"Hi." Sheridan crossed her arms when she got to the bottom of the stairs. She glanced at Tori and wondered what her grin was about.

"Are you feeling okay?" he asked.

"Yeah, I was just up late last night." When he frowned, she was glad that she'd chosen those words. *I'll just let him wonder,* she thought.

"Mom worked late last night," Tori said.

Sheridan rolled her eyes.

"Oh." His smile returned. "I was hoping to see Chris too."

"We have to call him Christopher now, Daddy."

Sheridan noticed the muscle in Quentin's jaw tighten as he remembered Christopher's hurtful words.

Sheridan asked, "Where's Christopher, Tori?"

"He stayed at church for the afternoon service."

Sheridan and Quentin exchanged glances, knowing their thoughts were the same. Their son staying for an extra church service? They both knew the reason.

"Well, I'll see him when we get back." Quentin turned to Tori. "You ready?"

"Yup." Tori waved. "See you later, Mom."

Sheridan tightened the belt on her robe when Quentin turned to her. This was the point where he always kissed her. She waited, but then he stepped outside and closed the door without another word. She stood in place until she was sure he wasn't coming back to do what he'd forgotten.

At least this time she was dressed.

But Quentin didn't come into the house. He simply waved from the car when Sheridan opened the front door for Tori.

As she watched Quentin drive away, Sheridan was saddened. Her husband was way ahead of her, already settled in his new world, at ease with his role as a separated parent.

"Dad said he's late for a meeting," Tori explained when she followed her mother into the living room. "That's why we didn't go to the movies. But he said we'll go next weekend and that he'll call Chris . . . I mean Christopher, later."

Was he rushing to meet up with Jett? "Who's he meeting?" she asked, picking up the newspaper and trying not to sound interested.

Tori shrugged. "I dunno. But Mom, I had a great time. It was absolutely fantastic."

It was only lunch, Tori. "Really? What did you have?"

"Just a hamburger," she said, scrunching her nose as if the food wasn't part of it. Tori plopped onto the couch. "I'm excited because Dad's living in Encino and I've never been there."

Sheridan's heart beat faster. "He told you he was living there?"

"Yup." And then her smile faded a bit. "Mom, all week I prayed Dad would come home, but then today he explained why he can't."

Her heart stopped pumping blood through her veins. They had agreed not to say anything to Tori. Not yet. She put down the newspaper. "What did he say?" she squeaked.

"He said everyone gets to a point in their

lives when they have to figure out who they are. He said he waited until he was older to do that, and he was sorry because it hurt you and me and Christopher. But he thinks we're going to all be better because he is better. He said it's all about God's perfect timing."

How could he bring God into this? "Is that all he said?" Sheridan asked.

"He said that I might not understand it all now, but that I would soon. But I understand most of what he was saying."

Sheridan breathed. At least Quentin hadn't lost his complete mind. But still, how could he tell Tori he was living in Encino? Suppose she figured out that's where Jett lived?

"I still wish Daddy were home. I asked him if there was a chance of him ever coming back."

Sheridan's heart pounded.

"He said no," Tori said, her sadness apparent. "He said for a long time he's known he had to leave, but he didn't because he just wanted to leave his life, not us." Tori paused and frowned. "I didn't really understand that part," she said. "But he says he's happy, and I want him to be happy."

You're way ahead of me.

The joy that walked in with Tori returned to her. "And Dad said he can't wait for me to visit him in Encino and that we're going to always do a lot of fun things."

They were just words, but they pounded her head like a hammer. Sheridan massaged the top of her forehead.

"Mom, are you all right?"

"I have a little headache." She stood. "I'm going to take a nap and then I'll fix dinner."

"Don't worry about me." Tori leaned back onto the couch and rested her feet on the ottoman. "I'm not hungry."

Sheridan had barely closed her bedroom door when she grabbed the telephone. She punched the numbers on the handset so hard, her finger pulsed. Sheridan spoke the moment he answered, "Quentin, what do you think you're doing?"

"What did I do?"

"You told Tori you're living in Encino," she said in a tone that put an exclamation point after each word.

"So?"

"You didn't ask me if you could tell her that," she snarled. "Suppose she figures out that you're living with Jett."

"First of all, I didn't know I had to get

approval. And second, how will Tori figure out that I'm living with Jett? I didn't tell her that."

"At least you had the good sense not to."

"Well maybe I should have. We're going to have to address this with Tori . . . and Chris."

"Not until I say so."

"When did you become the rule maker?"

She wanted to curse him out. "When you walked out of our lives."

"I didn't walk out of your life, Sheridan. I think you're just upset . . ."

You think? "I don't care what you think. I want to know everything you're going to say to my children."

"If you weren't so angry, you'd realize how ridiculous that is and you'd realize what I did was good. It's the first step to telling Tori the whole truth."

"We're not telling her anything."

She heard his sigh. "Why are you so upset?"

She didn't know if it was his words or his calm that made her anger rise. "Because you're not here. You're not here to help me handle the children through this mess."

"Well, how are you going to handle it when someone tells Tori about me?" He paused. “Sheridan, please calm down and listen to me.”

She sat on the bed.

He said, “Even Chris could slip and say something.”

I didn’t think of that.

“I want to make sure Tori learns about this in the right way,” Quentin finished his argument.

“I know,” she said, reeling in her rage. “Look, Quentin. This is a bad situation —”

“It doesn’t have to be,” he interrupted her.

“But it is. You’re not here when Tori is crying herself to sleep or when I’m trying to explain this new life to Christopher.”

He hesitated. “Is it that bad?” he asked softly.

What are you, stupid? “Yes, but what did you expect? You’ve turned our lives upside down and you’re surprised that we’re having challenges?”

“I’m sorry, but believe me, the conversation with Tori was innocent.” He paused. “You know, maybe you and I need some time together. Maybe we need to sit down and talk . . . about this and other things. What about . . .” He stopped as if he had changed his mind, but then he continued. “What about meeting me tomorrow?” He hesitated again. "For dinner."

She paused with surprise. There was a lot for the two of them to talk about. But dinner . . . dinner with him might take her anger away, and she wanted to hold on to it and nurture it so it would grow and cause him the pain he'd caused her. Still she said, "Okay, let's meet at Carousels."

Now her words surprised him.

Sheridan said, "Before you ask, I'm sure. Let's meet at Carousels," she repeated. "I'll see you tomorrow night." She hung up before she could change her mind.

Yes, Carousels would be the perfect place. No chance of things getting out of hand in public; they were both much too civilized to allow that to happen. And maybe after a few hours with her at Carousels, Quentin would be reminded of the many things he seemed to have forgotten.

Chapter Twelve

The FedEx truck rolled away from her home and Sheridan tore at the envelope the delivery man had just left. It was what she thought it was. A thick packet. Legal papers. The top page said it all: "Dissolution of Marriage."

She flipped through the pages, glancing at the yellow sticky notes her brother had attached for her. After a few minutes, she tossed the packet aside. She couldn't believe the papers had come right now. Right when she had something so important to do.

She climbed the stairs, and tried to calm her trembling as she reached for the telephone.

"This is Sheridan Hart," she said when the phone was answered. "May I speak with Dr. Hong?"

The seconds moved like minutes as she waited. Her eyes wandered around her bedroom, and she paused at the pictures on the dresser. Her family. Her children. Her past.

"Hello, Sheridan, how are you?"

"Not good, Dr. Hong. I've just been waiting." She took a deep breath. "I'm calling for the results . . . of my AIDS test."

"I have them right here."

Sheridan closed her eyes, sat on the bed, and wondered why the room had turned so hot. And then she shook as the doctor told her the news.

"Thank you." She hung up without saying good-bye.

She was a block of concrete, unable to move from the bed. On memories, she drifted back, traveling to the beginning of their days. Her wedding day. Her children's births. Christopher's first day of school. Tori's first dance recital.

Now, because of God's grace, she'd have a lifetime of more memories. Christopher's graduation. Tori's wedding. The birth of her grandchildren. Her future.

Her blood did not carry a certain death sentence. She'd been spared.

Sheridan reached for her Bible on the nightstand. She knew the scripture by heart, but she wanted to read the words. *"The thief cometh not, but for to steal, and to kill, and to destroy: I am come that they might have life, and that they might have it more abundantly."*

This was her favorite scripture. God's

promise to give back better than the devil could take away.

Sheridan walked to the window. There was only a hint of the sun, but Sheridan felt as if a light beamed inside her.

"This is a sign." She'd been sure her life was over. The devil had stolen her husband, destroyed her marriage. She was convinced this was all designed to kill her.

But on the opposite side of misery, there was God. There was no need for her to pine for her past life when God promised her a future.

Sheridan turned away from the window, then did what she hadn't done in a week; she dropped to her knees. Thoughts of the past days flooded her, taking her through all of the emotions. There was so much she wanted to say to God. So much that she wanted Him to know.

Finally she prayed. "Forgive me. And thank you."

She stood, knowing that God understood. He would fill in all the words in the middle.

From there, Sheridan moved at space shuttle speed. She made the calls, jumped into the shower, and then slipped into a teal sweat suit. Inside her closet, she grabbed the cream pants suit she'd bought with Kamora and packed it inside a garment bag. Less than thirty minutes later, she hurried through the front door. In her car she snapped her fingers, rushed back into the house, grabbed the credit card from her office drawer. She stopped, the divorce papers catching her attention. But the moment of silence didn't last long. God's grace showed her that she had to release the grief. She smiled, then rushed through the door.

There was still enough time to have a drink at the bar.

Sheridan entered Carousels and glanced around the dimly lit space.

"Mrs. Hart?"

"Joseph, how're you?"

"I'm fine," the maître d' smiled. "Wow, you look wonderful. Things must be going great for you and Dr. Hart."

She only smiled. "I'm meeting Dr. Hart, but not for a half hour."

"That's fine. I can seat you now."

"No." She motioned toward the left side of the room. "I'll wait at the bar."

She could feel Joseph's eyes following her as she sauntered away. The bar was full, but there was one empty stool in between two men dressed in almost identical tailored suits. She eased onto the cushioned seat and almost fell off when she glimpsed herself in the bar's mirror. Her fingers fluttered through the edges of her new haircut. She'd never worn a style this short, and she'd held her breath as her hairstylist chopped off almost six inches of her tresses.

"Are you ready?" Crystal had asked as she held the oversized scissors in her hand.

Sheridan nodded, squeezed her eyes shut, and didn't face the mirror again until Crystal had finished. She couldn't believe how pleased she'd been when she saw the sleek bob ending inches above her shoulder. The angles framed her face, highlighting the sharp slope of her nose and the fullness of her lips.

"You look fab-u-lous," Crystal had said as she snapped her fingers three times in the air. In the salon's restroom, Sheridan had changed into the pants suit she'd carried with her and strutted out to whistles and cheers from the stylists and other patrons. Sheridan twirled as if she were the dancer in the family and embraced the compliments.

"I can't believe you finally stepped out of those tired old sweat suits," Luis, one of the stylists, sang in his singsong voice.

"You know what I always say: if you've kept it, flaunt it. And you are showing out, girl." He high-fived the stylist next to him.

Crystal said, "So, Sheridan, what brought about this change?"

Her smile dimmed, and then she waved her hand as if this transformation was about nothing.

"Hello." A voice from behind stole her from her thoughts. "What are you drinking?"

She had to turn a bit to see the intruder. And she couldn't help it. She smiled. From the gleam of his head to the tailored seams of his Italian suit, he was straight off the pages of *GQ* magazine. "I haven't ordered anything yet," she said.

"That's why I'm asking," he said in a tone that made Sheridan wonder if flirting was his job. "Whatever the lady wants, I'm willing to give her."

Oh, brother. "Thanks, but I'll order my own." She turned to the bartender. "I'll have a . . ." She paused. It had been years since she'd ordered a drink. It was just something that she didn't do as a wife and mother. "I'll have a chocolate martini, please."

When the bartender walked away, the man said, "All I asked was if I could buy you a drink. I didn't ask you to marry me."

"Really?" Sheridan pouted as if she was offended. She held up her left hand. "That's too bad, because I really need a ring for this finger." The voice was hers, but the words weren't. That was something Kamora would say.

The man leaned back and laughed so loud that others looked at them. Sheridan laughed with him.

"Excuse me."

In the mirror she saw Quentin behind her, his face stretched with surprise. She didn't know what shocked him more, her hair or her company. She didn't care.

"Hi, Quentin," she said, spinning around on her stool. "You're early."

He stared at her for a moment, but then his glance turned to the man. He held out his hand. "I'm Quentin Hart, Sheridan's husband."

She raised her eyebrows but said nothing as she lifted her drink. She motioned to the bartender to bring her check to their table.

"Nice to meet you" was all the man would give Quentin. And then he smiled at Sheridan and said, "It was really nice to meet you. And don't worry about that drink. I'll take care of it."

She smiled her thank-you and then followed the waiter to the table. Quentin held out the chair for her before he sat. She took the napkin from her glass and shook it onto her lap. When she looked up, Quentin was staring at her.

"What's wrong?"

"You look different."

You think? She tilted her head. "Do you like it?"

He nodded. "I do. I just didn't expect . . . What made you cut your hair?"

You. "I needed a change."

He nodded again. "Well . . . you look wonderful." He looked over his shoulder. "Who's your friend?" he asked, pointing his chin toward the bar.

Sheridan opened her menu and didn't even bother to look in the bar's direction. "Someone I just met."

"Today?"

Sheridan looked up with a frown.

"I was just wondering because" — he glanced at the crystal glass in front of her — "you don't usually drink."

A shrug was her response.

Quentin cleared his throat. "What are you having? The usual?"

She shook her head. "No, I want something different."

"Obviously."

"Do you know what you're having?" Sheridan asked.

He nodded. "The usual. So" — he placed his arms on the table — "you just woke up this morning and decided you wanted to do something different?"

She allowed herself to think back to the hour when Dr. Hong had given her the report — that she would not face death, but had received life. "I got some good news and decided it was time for me to push aside the anger and get on with my life."

"It's only been a week, Sheridan. Don't be so hard on yourself."

She jerked a bit at his words. "I thought you'd be happy that I wanted to put my anger — at you — behind me."

"I am," he said, and Sheridan wondered why he glanced at the bar again. "It's just that we both need some time. This is difficult."

She wondered what the difficult part was for him. He'd left, moved in with Jett, and never looked back. "I want to be like you. You're moving on."

Quentin's eyes darkened. "I didn't do this to hurt you."

She leaned forward and whispered, "Why did you do this?"

The waiter interrupted them. Sheridan

felt like she was on a ledge, waiting to be pushed.

They gave their orders, and she held her breath until Quentin continued, "I didn't leave because I didn't love you. I left because I finally loved myself." He sighed. "My intentions were to never give in to what I truly wanted."

"How long have you . . . wanted this?"

"All my life."

Three words that made her heart sink.

He continued, "When I was a little boy, I knew I was different. I didn't want to do the things or play the games that my friends enjoyed. And when I got older, I didn't have the same interest in girls or sports other boys had."

"So you were never interested in me?"

"Oh, no, Sheridan. I loved you. I still do. But I forced myself —"

"To love me?"

"No, I didn't have to force that. But I forced myself to live the American dream. I wanted to be part of this country's tradition. So I hid what was in my heart and molded my mind into what everyone expected. It was difficult, until I met you. I fell in love."

"So you didn't have those thoughts when we met, when we got married?"

"Not right after we got married, but soon they came back."

The image of Quentin with Jett at the golf course returned. And the stalker brought his other possessions: the images of them holding hands, caressing, kissing. She took another sip of her martini, hoping to drown the mental pictures.

He said, "In the last few years, I've been overwhelmed with these feelings and thoughts and desires. Every time I looked in the mirror, I came face-to-face with the truth. And then I met Jett."

She hated the way he said his name. Hated the affection in his tone. And she wondered, had it all been there before?

For two years they'd known Jett Jennings, a top-one-hundred player on the PGA tour. He had been a phenomenon years before Tiger. Retired, Jett moved to Los Angeles from Orlando to run the Jennings Foundation — a sports program for underprivileged children.

Knowing no one in L.A., he'd joined Hope Chapel and, as part of the church's Brother-to-Brother program, was paired with Quentin, who helped him get acclimated to the city.

Sheridan had been convinced it was a perfect match. Quentin was a wannabe golf pro, and Jett had just been inducted as an honorary member into Quentin's fraternity. A great friendship was born. Sheridan had called Jett her friend too. He'd attended family dinners, children's parties, and holiday gatherings. But Sheridan had been unaware that as she opened her home, Jett was stealing her most valuable possession.

Two waiters returned and placed the salmon lasagna in front of Sheridan and the filet mignon with cheese potatoes in front of Quentin.

Sheridan bowed her head, prepared to say a silent grace, when Quentin began, "Dear Heavenly Father, we come to you with praise in our mouths and thanksgiving in our hearts." His words surprised her. Quentin always blessed their food, but she hadn't expected him to do that now.

He continued, "We give you thanksgiving for the food we are about to receive. We pray that all impurities will be removed for the nourishment of our bodies."

Sheridan was about to say, "Amen," when Quentin added, "And Lord, we thank you for this time of healing, this time of understanding as two of your children come to you for guidance. We thank you and we bless you, Lord. We honor you and we love you. We give all praise in Jesus' name. Amen."

It wasn't until Quentin had almost stuffed his first forkful of steak into his mouth that he noticed her stare.

"What?"

"I was a little surprised." He frowned and she said, "When you prayed."

The creases in his forehead deepened. "I always pray."

But you weren't always gay. Sheridan picked up her fork and took a small bite of the lasagna.

"Do you think I love God less than I did last week?"

She stuffed her mouth with another forkful, giving her time. Then she said, "I don't —"

"I prayed to God for years," he said before she could finish, "asking Him to take this desire away from me. I prayed for Him to make me just like every other man. But although He blessed me with everything, He never answered that prayer. And I finally realized maybe no answer was the answer. Maybe He wasn't going to change me because this was how I was born. I would have never chosen this life. I never wanted to leave you or my children. But this is not about a choice."

"I . . . wasn't . . ." she stuttered.

He spoke over her words. "You know what gets me? People think if you're gay, it's about sex and you couldn't love God. Well, I knew I was different before I knew anything about sex. By the time I understood sex, the desire to be with men was already inside of me and it wasn't about sex alone. It was a complete attraction: emotional, physical, and, I believe, even spiritual."

Sheridan put down her fork and swallowed air. "You've had experiences . . . with men?" It was the question that had been incubating inside. One she was afraid to ask, but even more terrified to have answered.

His eyes filled with her pain. "Sheridan, I don't want to hurt you."

She swallowed more air and nodded. "I want to know," she said although her pounding heart told her she already knew.

He waited for a moment, then said, "It started so long ago. Learning how to hide the desires. Being careful not to stare at the guys in the locker room, or making sure I said something when the guys talked about girls. But then in college . . . my roommate." He paused and looked down into his plate. "It was the first time." His eyes met hers and he asked if he should continue.

She nodded.

"I can't explain how I felt. Except that I felt like I was home. But when it was over, I hated myself.

"I made a promise to God never to do it again. But it happened, over and over. It was a cycle of loving it and hating me. Every time became the last time."

Around them, customers ordered, waiters served. Talk and laughter filled the air. Life moved as if their conversation were normal.

Quentin shook his head as if the memories still hurt. "Whenever I was with someone, I felt free . . . until it was over. It was driving me crazy. I had to go to someone, but I didn't trust my friends. So, I told my father."

Sheridan sat back, surprised. In the years she'd known him, she could count on one hand the times he'd mentioned his father or anyone in his family. She knew he was an only child who lost his mother before she had time to leave him memories. But all she knew about his father was that Quentin hadn't spoken to him in all the years they'd been married. Although she probed, she'd never been able to get anything more from Quentin. She stopped when one day he'd told her in tears, "My father is dead to me, Sheridan. Leave it alone." She'd held him then, giving comfort, grateful that he had her parents. Now, she wished she'd asked more questions.

Quentin took a breath. "It was just me and my father for all those years. A hardworking man, a deacon in our church, who held three jobs to keep me in private school and when I told him I wanted to be a doctor . . ." He paused. "I will never forget the look on his face. He was so proud." Quentin's Adam's apple crawled up, then down his throat. "He told me then, that whatever I needed, he would give me. He said he would make sure I made it through medical school. In all the years with my father, he never said he loved me. But I always knew he did. And those words that day assured me that he did.

"So, although I was scared, I was sure I could talk to him. Thought I could tell him the truth."

She wanted to reach across the table and take his hand. But she was frozen in place.

"I told him. Asked him for help. Wanted

to know what I should do." His lips quivered. "The man I talked to that day wasn't the man who raised me. The man I talked to that day, who had never used a bad word in his life, cursed me until he couldn't speak anymore. Looked at me as if I belonged on the sole of his shoe. Told me that I was the son of a man, but that I was no man and that I had better pray that devil out of me before I burned in hell. Then, he screamed at me to get out of his house, and not to come back until I could prove that I was a real man." Quentin was silent, and then his words became softer. "All the love I thought he had for me left that day. And I promised myself two things. One, that I would be successful without him, and two, that I never wanted to see anyone look at me the way he did." He looked at her now. "But he scared me enough to drive me to my knees."

Tears stung behind her eyes. She didn't know why she wanted to cry. Didn't know if it was because his pain was now hers or because his history was news to her. "Why did your father react that way?"

He shrugged.

"You never asked him?"

He shook his head. "I called him. Told him I was sorry. That I would do whatever he wanted." He paused. "He told me I could come home if I would confess my sin in front of the congregation at church and allow the people to pray for me. Told me I had to stand up in front of five hundred people and tell them I had sinned; that I was a homosexual."

"Did you do it?" Sheridan whispered.

"No. I hung up and never called my father again. But I did pray. Prayed for hours at a time, for days, and within a few weeks, I met you. I knew God sent you. You were the answer to every prayer. And for a long time, I was right."

Her mouth felt as if it were filled with hundreds of cotton balls. "But soon, I wasn't enough."

"You were always more than enough of a woman. You were just never a man."

She'd said those words to him, but it hurt when he said them to her.

"I'm sorry." He pushed back his chair. "I'll be right back."

She didn't follow him with her eyes. Didn't do anything except stare at the knife that sat atop his steak, ready to cut away another piece of meat. She stared at the knife and then lifted her martini glass, swallowing all that remained of the drink.

When Quentin returned, Sheridan

pushed her plate away, motioned to the waiter. Ordered another chocolate martini.

"I'm sorry, Sheridan."

"I'm glad I know."

He took a long breath. "I never wanted you to know. Never wanted to see that look — the one my father gave me — again. But today, I felt I owed you."

She nodded and sat in silence until the waiter returned with her drink.

"I hope you understand," he said.

She took a sip of the martini. "I don't, not really." She took another sip, waited a second, and drank again. "But I have to accept that this is you. And I have to learn to live with this and without you."

He shook his head. "You don't have to live without me. I will always be there for you."

"But you will never again be there as my husband."

He opened his mouth, but said nothing; he cut a piece of steak and then looked at her with sad eyes. "I hope you believe I'm sorry."

"I do . . . now."

He nodded, and silence stayed with them for the rest of the meal. Sheridan kept her eyes on her plate, but she stole glances at the man across from her. It had only been a week since he'd told her who he was, but this revelation today put years between them. Quentin looked the same; his speckled brown eyes still devoured her. But his words and his thoughts were alien to her. Secrets that he'd kept made her realize she'd been sleeping with a stranger.

The silence stayed until the table was cleared.

Quentin said, "I want you to know I'll take care of everything — the mortgage, the car, all the bills. You won't have to worry about any of that."

She nodded, deciding it wouldn't help if she told him she hadn't expected it to be any other way.

"I'll put money into the account like I always did." He lowered his voice. "You will never want for anything, I promise. And the business — I hope you're going to keep it. We worked hard on Hart to Heart."

Again she nodded. This wasn't the time to tell him she got sick every time she went into the office and saw his words of love.

He said, "I'd like to be able to continue the business with you."

Not a chance.

"Maybe we can set up a schedule. I can come over once a week or so and we can work together. You think that might work?"

No. "I'll think about it."

He continued, talking about the children and how he wanted what was best for all of them. Sheridan nodded, as if she were listening, but her mind had left long ago. As she looked at him, Sheridan tried to erase him — from her mind and her life. But no matter what, he was still there. It was then that she realized she'd have to erase him from her heart first.

"So, does this sound okay to you?"

She shrugged because she hadn't been listening.

He said, "And I agree with you. We can take our time talking to Tori."

"Okay."

The silence that returned was heavier this time. Sheridan couldn't remember a day when they two didn't have words to share. But tonight proved their life as husband and wife, partners and lovers, was over.

"I need to get home to the children," Sheridan said as she slipped her purse onto her shoulder.

"I'd love to see them."

In his words, Sheridan saw some of his pain — the sting of not seeing his children every day.

"If you want to come by to see the children . . ."

His face brightened, but only for a moment. "No. But I would like to start calling them every day. This last week . . . it's been so hard."

She nodded. "Call them tonight." She bit her lip. "But I don't know about Christopher."

He nodded. "I have to talk to him."

"Let me talk to him first, and then I'll call you."

"Thank you." He pulled back her chair as she stood. More silence accompanied them as they stepped outside and handed their tickets to the valet. It was a relief to Sheridan when the Explorer came first.

When she turned to Quentin, all the days of their lives stood between them until Quentin leaned forward, closing that space. He kissed her cheek. "It was good to see you like this."

She didn't say the same but tried to smile as she stepped into her car. Quentin closed the door and wiggled his fingers in a wave good-bye.

As she pulled slowly from the lot, she watched in her rearview mirror the vision of the man she had once loved completely and still loved deeply. He stood in a navy blazer and tan pants; she wanted to keep that image in her mind forever. She kept her eye on him until her car rolled from the lot and she turned to the right.

Then he was gone.

But the joy she'd carried when she entered the restaurant was gone as well. The dinner was sad. The dinner was over. And they'd never return to Carousels as husband and wife.

Carousels had been their favorite restaurant for most of their married life. She remembered their first time there; it was the day they'd signed the papers making them homeowners.

"Oh, Quentin, this is too much," she'd exclaimed when she saw the model for their View Park home. "What are we going to do with five bedrooms?"

"Fill them with beautiful children who look like you." He had laughed at the look of horror on her face. "Okay, so we'll be satisfied with the two wonderful children we have. But don't worry about the bedrooms. After Christopher and Tori have their own, that only leaves two. And I figure we're going to need a guest bedroom, and a library, and a gym, and an office." He held his hand up to his forehead. "I think we need a bigger house."

She'd laughed. "Okay, I'm convinced," she said, even though the burden of being homeowners overwhelmed her.

When they signed the mortgage papers, she'd almost cried. "Do you know what our payments are going to be?"

"Sheridan," he began as he wrapped his arms around her, "you're a doctor's wife. We can afford this."

Sheridan knew Quentin's words were right. Still she wondered why they couldn't wait until there was more money in their savings. But money in the bank didn't matter as much to Quentin as it did to her. He had to be a doctor. It was one of the few professions that would support the life he was determined to live.

"Let's celebrate," he'd said that day as he helped her into their new Range Rover.

She shook her head. "I need to get home. Mom's watching Tori, and Chris will be home from school soon."

"Don't worry about the children."

She cocked her head and said, "I thought buying the house was crazy, but I know you've lost your mind now. There are two children at our home waiting for their mother."

"Not tonight. Your parents agreed to take them. We're not even going home."

It took her a moment to settle into the idea of an evening alone with her husband.

"Where are we going?"

"I found a new restaurant, Carousels. I've been dying to go there. And then, I got us a room at the Hilton at Universal Studios."

"Oh."

"Okay, it's not Maui, but we'll get there." He grinned. "In the meantime, we're going to have a blast at the Hilton."

"I didn't pack a bag. I don't have any clothes."

"The plans I have for you don't call for any clothes." He kissed her gently.

She'd moaned with love, and then spent two of the most glorious days with her husband, starting at Carousels and finishing on the balcony of their twenty-fourth-floor hotel room overlooking the Hollywood Hills.

It had been a wonderful time, but just another entry into the catalogue of all the blissful moments they had shared.

A car honked, and Sheridan jumped before she looked in her rearview mirror. She wondered how long she'd been sitting at the light, remembering what life had been.

"That's the end of it for me," she said as she sped onto the freeway. "I'm tired of remembering. Now it's time for me to forget."

Chapter Thirteen

Sheridan took a breath before she slammed the car door. A week had passed since she'd promised Quentin that she'd speak to Christopher. But as the days went by, she'd said nothing to her son. It was difficult enough, just trying to find comfort in their new life. And she'd hoped that time would bring forgiveness to Christopher's heart. But the passing of time did little to soften him. Each night when Quentin called, Tori ran to the telephone; Christopher stomped away.

Last night, when she insisted he talk to his father, Christopher had yelled, "I'm never talking to him again." He'd slammed his bedroom door. "I don't care if you put me on punishment for the rest of my life."

Quentin had heard his son's words and told Sheridan, "This can't go on."

"I'll talk to him tomorrow," Sheridan had said.

In his sigh, she heard Quentin's doubt, but in this case, she was on his side. As angry, as saddened, as frustrated as she was with the situation, she still wanted her children to have a relationship with their father.

Sheridan walked across the grass toward the clubhouse where Christopher's golf team held practices twice a month. This morning, she'd decided this would be the perfect day to have this talk. Tori was spending the afternoon with her friend Joy after dance practice. So Sheridan was free to take Christopher to lunch, pack his favorite foods into his belly, and then convince him that he should give up the fight of hating his father.

Sheridan opened the clubhouse door and Darryl walked out before she stepped inside.

"Hi," she greeted Christopher's best friend.

He grinned. "Hey, Ms. Hart."

"Where's Christopher?"

Darryl's smile left and he glanced at the boy next to him. "Christopher?" He said his name as if he had no idea who she was asking about.

Sheridan laughed. *Teenagers.* "Yes, remember my son? I came to pick him up."

This time, Darryl's glance went to the ground. "Uh, he's not here, Ms. Hart."

"Did he leave already?"

"Ms. Hart."

Sheridan turned toward the voice and smiled as Coach Matthews moved toward her. When she glanced over her shoulder, Darryl and the other young man were gone.

"Ms. Hart, how are you?" Coach Matthews said.

"Just fine. I came to pick up Chris."

The coach frowned. "Chris isn't here."

"I know, Darryl just told me. Can't believe I missed him. Anyway, how's he doing? He hasn't mentioned the father-son tournament recently. Is it still going on?"

The coach's frown deepened. "Ms. Hart, Chris quit the team last week."

"What?"

"Told me he didn't want to play anymore."

"No way."

The coach nodded. "I was shocked. You know, he was our best and was getting better each year." He paused. "I'm sorry. Maybe I should have called you and Dr. Hart. I was just sure he'd discussed this with you."

"He didn't say a word."

"I'm sorry, Ms. Hart."

She waved her hand as she turned to the door. "No problem. I'll talk to Chris when I get home."

"We'd love to have him back," the coach said before Sheridan stepped outside and rushed to her car.

Coach Matthews's words swirled inside her. Christopher had quit. Left his favorite sport. Stopped playing the game he loved — the hobby he shared with his father.

Sheridan turned her car into her subdivision and wondered where her son was. He'd walked out the door this morning. With his golf clubs. Said he'd be home before three.

As she eased her car past the tennis courts, the sound of cheers made her turn. To the left were the basketball courts. She slowed the car and squinted. Stopped and stared for long minutes. She got out of the car as Christopher dribbled the basketball down the court, pulled back at the free throw line, then shot the ball. It swished right through, barely touching the net. Young men swarmed around him, giving high fives, and a group of young girls cheered from the benches.

"Christopher," she yelled. Several heads turned, but not her son's. She called his name again. Even from sixty feet away, she could see his surprise. She waited as he gathered his clubs, said good-bye to the other players, stopped to hug one of the girls, then strolled toward her.

Her forehead creased into a deep frown. What was he wearing? It looked like a stocking cap, but she couldn't be sure.

"Hey, Mom. What are you doing here?"

She couldn't believe his question, but it was what he wore that had her attention.

"Christopher, what is that on your head?"

He grinned and patted the silk material. "It's a do-rag."

"A do-what?"

He repeated the word as if she should know. "It keeps my hair in place. Makes it look good."

She wanted to tell him he didn't have any hair — they kept his hair cut so short he was almost bald. But even if he had a six-inch Afro, she wasn't about to allow one of her children to prance around in public wearing a stocking cap. "Take that thing off," she demanded.

"But, Mom," he whispered and then looked over his shoulder as if he was afraid someone was watching.

"Take it off," she said again. "Or I'll take it off for you." He did as she ordered. "Now, what are you doing here?"

A moment of silence and then, "I decided to play ball today instead of going to golf."

She almost waited to see what other lies he would tell, but instead she said, "I just saw Coach Matthews."

The grin left his face.

"Get in the car," she said, turning back to the SUV.

"I'll walk home."

"Get in the car."

He dumped his clubs in the back seat and then jumped inside. "Mom, before you go off, I don't know what the big deal is. It's not like I need golf to graduate or anything."

"It's not about that, Christopher. It's about the fact that you lied."

"I didn't lie."

"You told me you were going to golf practice this morning."

"No, I just said I was leaving. And I did leave. So, I didn't lie."

She wanted to slap him. Slap him for being so smart, and for trying to get technical with her. Slap him for being so stupid, hanging out just blocks from his home.

He continued, "I said I was leaving and would be back by three. Remember?"

"You had your golf clubs with you, Christopher. You go to practice every other

Saturday with the team."

"But I didn't tell you I was going to practice."

She took a breath. "Why didn't you tell me you'd quit the team?"

He shrugged. "You didn't ask."

She gripped the steering wheel. "Christopher," she said, her voice rising with anger. "I'm tired of this game. You know that when you left this morning I thought you were going to practice. Just like you knew I wouldn't ask if you quit the team. Why would I ask that?"

When he stayed silent, she said, "You've been lying, Christopher." She held up her hand when he began his protest. "You've been lying with your actions and you know it."

She stopped the car in front of their house, but neither got out. "Why did you quit the team?"

He shrugged. "Didn't want to play anymore."

"You're going to have to give me more than that."

He started out the window. "I don't feel like playing anymore."

"Because of your father?"

He finally turned to her. "I don't have a father."

She sighed. "I'm so tired of you saying that."

"I don't know why. Last week, you told me you understood what I was feeling. But this week, every time he calls, you act as if it's okay and I don't get it."

"I do understand how you're feeling, but what I understand more is that it wasn't doing any good holding on to my anger. I was miserable."

"Dad made you that way."

"Initially, yes. But it was my choice to hang on to it or let it go. And I feel better letting the anger go."

He was silent for a moment. "Well, I'm not angry anymore either."

She exhaled, relieved.

Christopher said, "I just don't want to have anything to do with him."

Her relief was gone. "We really need to talk about this. I had planned on us having lunch —"

"I'm not hungry and there's nothing to talk about." He looked straight ahead, staring through the windshield, punishing her for deserting him and his anger.

She thought about dragging him to a restaurant anyway. Food could certainly change his mood. But then on the other side, there was nothing more wretched than spending time with a miserable teenager.

"Okay, go inside, but don't leave this house before I get back."

He looked at her. "Where are you going?"

"I'm going to get something to eat."

"You're going without me?"

"You can still go with me."

He shook his head, jumped from the car, grabbed his clubs, and then glared at her.

She pulled the car from the driveway and didn't look back. Didn't want to see the pain on her son's face. The pain she understood. The pain she agreed with.

But she couldn't tell him that. She had to do everything she could to get Christopher to lose his anger. Rage made you do ridiculous things — like quit a sport you loved. And Sheridan didn't even want to imagine what other kinds of behavior could come from an angry sixteen-year-old. She had to do something. Had to do something to save her son. The challenge was, she had no idea what to do.

Chapter Fourteen

"Mom, I'm really worried about Christopher," Sheridan said as she leaned back on her bed. As she spoke, her hands stroked the pillow where Quentin had laid his head just three weeks before.

"Honey, you have to give him some time. This is hard on Chris. He'll come around."

There had never been an issue in life where her mother couldn't reassure her, but Sheridan doubted her mother's assurances this time. For days she'd felt as if she were sitting on a ticking time bomb.

The feelings had started the previous Saturday when she found Christopher on the basketball court. For the next few days he'd hardly spoken, and he kept his promise never to speak to his father, even though Quentin called every night.

"I know this will pass," Beatrice continued, breaking through Sheridan's recollections.

"Do you want me to talk to him?" Her father's voice boomed through the line.

"Daddy, I didn't know you were on the phone."

"I know you didn't. I couldn't get a word in between you and your mother."

"Sheridan, don't listen to him. If your father had anything to say, we would have heard his one cent by now."

"See how she is, Sheridan? Your mother didn't even give me credit for two cents."

Sheridan chuckled. No matter what was going on, her parents never lost their joy. "Daddy, how're you feeling?"

"Great. I had another blood test today and the radiation is working — at least that's what my PSA results say. I could have told the doctors I was getting better. I didn't need a test. But I let the doctors do what they have to do. Anyway, let's get back to Chris. Do you want me to talk to him?"

"No, I'm trying to give him the space and time he needs. Maybe in a few days."

"I agree with Beatrice. Chris'll be fine. He's sixteen. His job is to make us all miserable. Don't you remember your brother?"

Sheridan laughed. "That's true, but I'm worried because I don't think this is just Chris acting out. He's really hurt."

"Maybe Pastor Ford can talk to him," Beatrice said. "Have you talked to her yet?"

"No," Sheridan said, although she had no intentions of that happening. Although she loved her pastor, she couldn't face her with this news. At least not yet. "I'll wait a few more days. Quentin will probably come by to see him."

"Speaking of Quentin, sweetheart, he called us this morning." Beatrice almost sounded apologetic.

Sheridan jumped from the bed. "He did?" She didn't know why she was so surprised. He'd always been close to her parents. Maybe the real surprise was that he hadn't called before. "What did he say?"

Cameron said, "Wanted me to know that he was thinking about and praying for me. Said he wanted to come by in a few days."

Beatrice added, "He told us that he loved us, just like he loved you and the children. He didn't want us to doubt that."

Cameron's turn: "And he apologized. Said he never wanted to hurt you."

"What did you guys say?"

Cameron chuckled. "Not much. Your mother answered the phone, and she was so shocked her tongue didn't move. It was a first."

"Well, I didn't hear you saying too much." Beatrice tried to be serious, but in seconds she was chuckling with her husband. "Sheridan, when we got off the phone, Cameron and I agreed we need to get one of those new telephones with that caller ID. I don't want to be caught off guard like that again."

Beatrice and Cameron laughed, but Sheridan didn't. It seemed to take a moment for her mother to notice.

"Sheridan, are you all right?" Beatrice asked, turning serious.

At the window Sheridan watched as a black Lincoln Navigator with tinted windows pulled up in front of her home. Even through the closed windows, she could hear the beat of the blasting music's bass.

The SUV's back door opened and Christopher jumped out. A young girl followed with a skirt so short Sheridan knew it couldn't have cost more than two dollars. There was hardly any fabric at all.

Who are those kids? "Mom, Dad, I have to go. Chris just got home."

"Okay, dear, call us tomorrow."

Sheridan hung up and ran down the stairs. She peered through the living room window.

The girl leaned against the back of the SUV and her skirt rose high; now Sheridan was sure she could see the child's underwear. As he moved to the back of the truck to talk to her, Christopher's grin was wide. The girl seemed to be doing all the talking, and Sheridan resisted the urge to rush outside and cover her son's ears.

But she stayed in place, too shocked to move. When the girl stood on her toes and kissed Christopher's cheek, Sheridan's daze dissipated and she rushed to the front door. No one seemed to notice her standing there as the girl climbed into the back of the Navigator, waved, and then the truck took off like it was on a speedway.

Christopher stood at the curb until the SUV was no longer in sight. He turned toward his home, paused when he saw his mother, and then moved toward her as if he always came home in a truck with teenagers she didn't know.

"Hi, Mom."

"Christopher, who were those kids?"

He shrugged. "Just some guys from around the way."

Her eyebrows lifted. "Some guys, huh?" She closed the door behind them. "Well, who are they? Do they go to your school?"

He laughed. "No, they graduated already. But Mom, they live around here, so you know they're all right."

"I don't know anything like that, Christopher. I don't know these kids, and you made a deal with your father and me that we would know all your friends."

"It's not like I'm hiding them, Mom. They dropped me off right in front of the house. If I was hiding something, I would have gotten out around the corner."

This was one of those deciding moments, when as a parent she had to say, had to do, the right thing. *I need a handbook.* "Christopher, what about your friends? I haven't seen Nicole or Darryl in weeks."

Christopher scrunched up his face as if a stench had suddenly filled the air. "I'm over them."

"What does that mean?"

Christopher sighed as if it took too much effort to explain this to an adult. "It means, Mom, that I'm growing up. I've outgrown the kids I grew up with."

Sheridan crossed her arms. "Oh, really?"

"Yeah. It was time for me to make some changes, and I met these guys." He smiled as if the thought of them brought him bliss. "They're cool. They're not kids, they're men."

His words scared her.

He turned toward the stairs, and Sheridan said, "Well, do these . . ." She paused, wanting to say "boys," but instead said, “Do these kids have names?”

“Uh-huh. Brendan and Gary,” he said.

“I think you left someone out,” Sheridan said, her glance following Christopher as he ran up the stairs.

At the top of the landing he looked down at her and grinned. “Oh, yeah. Brendan, Gary, and Déjà.” She was still standing in the same spot when she heard his bedroom door slam. She was still standing and wondering why just the sound of that girl’s name made her tremble.

Chapter Fifteen

"Ooohhh, I'm telling," Tori sang, as if those were the words to a song.

Sheridan allowed herself a quiet smile as she descended the stairs and paused outside the kitchen, stopping to check the mail. The days were moving ahead, pulling the three Harts into the future, and Sheridan was pleased. It had been almost a month, and she and the children were finding a way to be normal. It was amazing to her that as different as the world was, so much was the same. The children still got up and went to school, did their activities, came home, did homework, ate, and went to bed. In between they had their sibling wars and then made up, finding a way to become allies.

Life felt the same. Except for when the telephone rang every evening after dinner and Tori ran to answer it. And then there was the fact that every night she went into her bedroom alone.

"Ooohhh, I'm telling Mom," Tori sang again.

Sheridan opened her mouth, but before

she could speak, Christopher growled, "You'd better not."

Sheridan frowned but remained silent.

Christopher continued, "If you say anything, I'm gonna kick your butt."

Sheridan marched into the kitchen. They both looked at Sheridan as if she'd materialized from the middle of the floor.

"Mom, Christopher got a tattoo!"

It took a moment for the words to reach her brain, and then she laughed.

"Look at his arm," Tori continued her case.

Sheridan's laughter stopped, and she grabbed her son's arm, twisting him around. She gasped. "Christopher."

"What?" he asked, trying to lower the short sleeve of his T-shirt, even though his arm was still in Sheridan's grasp.

"What . . . is . . . this?" She couldn't take her eyes off the black dots that connected to form a cross with the letters *JIMH* down the center.

"It's a tattoo, Mom."

"You're not old enough to get one."

Christopher pulled away from his mother's hold. "The man said I was."

"I don't care who said that. What were you thinking?"

He shrugged. "I went with Brendan and

Gary. They got tattoos too. We all thought it would be cool."

"It's not cool, Christopher. It's not legal."

His eyes widened. "Why is it illegal to get a tattoo?"

"Because you're sixteen. You need permission. Who did this?" she demanded.

Christopher swallowed. "Mom, it's no big deal. I just wanted to be like the rest of the guys. They all got one."

"And you think that impresses me?"

"Why are you upset? I should be able to get a tattoo; it's my body."

"No, it's not, Christopher. Because, you see," she began, her voice rising and her finger pointing, "as long as I put food in it and clothes on it, it's my body. And you do what I say, when I say it, until you're able to take care of that body yourself. Do you hear me?"

He nodded.

"Where did you get that?" she asked again.

"Mom, I don't want to get anyone in trouble. The guy thought I was eighteen."

"Why did he think that?"

Christopher lowered his eyes.

Sheridan shook her head. "I don't even want to know. Just go to your room."

Christopher moved as if he were being set free. But before he got to the doorway, Sheridan said, "What is that on your arm anyway?"

He frowned, looked down at the black marking, and then looked back at her.

"I know it's a tattoo," she said. "What is it supposed to be?" Sheridan held her breath. She hoped those letters weren't the initials of that little girl in this new group of friends he'd found.

"It's a cross," he whispered. "That's why I didn't think you'd be mad, Mom."

She folded her arms. "And," she began, almost afraid to continue, "whose initials are those?"

"They don't belong to a person, Mom. The initials stand for . . . 'Jesus is my homeboy.' "

Sheridan's eyes opened almost as wide as her mouth. It took her a moment to sputter: "You can go now." As he bolted up the stairs, she added, "And you're on punishment until you're thirty-five."

She turned around and looked at Tori.

Tori said, "I think I'll go to my room too."

Sheridan nodded. "Good idea." It wasn't until she heard Tori's room door close that she sat at the table and held her head.

"Jesus is my homeboy"?

She grabbed the telephone and dialed. The moment he answered, she said, "Quentin, we have a problem."

There had been no signs that three people were in the quiet house when Quentin stepped through the front door. And Sheridan couldn't remember a time when she'd been happier to see him.

Quentin slipped his jacket from his shoulders and tossed it over the settee in the entryway like he always did when he came home. "A tattoo?"

Sheridan nodded. "A cross with the letters *JIMH* in the center." She shook her head as she remembered Christopher's explanation. "First, we have to get rid of the tattoo. Then I'm going to kill him."

Quentin sat on the couch. "I can help you with the first part. It can be removed by laser, I think."

Her sign was one of relief. "So now what?"

"I have to talk to him. We should have insisted that he speak to me before this."

"That wouldn't have changed anything. The only thing that would have made a difference . . ." She paused. "Never mind. Let me get him."

She called twice before Christopher came out of his room and stood at the top of the stairs. "Could you come down here, please?"

His hands were stuffed in his pockets. His eyes widened when he saw his father.

"Chris," Quentin said simply.

Christopher looked at Sheridan, as if for help. But she kept her arms crossed. Then he looked at his father. "I don't want to talk to you."

"I want to talk to you."

He chose the chair in the corner by the window, as far away from Quentin as he could get.

"Your mother told me about the tattoo."

Christopher kept his eyes away from his father.

"I don't care how mad you are at me. Or how mad you are at what's happened. I don't like what's happening to you."

Christopher looked up, and the glower in his eyes made Sheridan doubt her call to Quentin.

"Chris, what I want you to know is —"

"My name is Christopher now."

"Okay." Quentin's eyes moved between Sheridan and Christopher. "It doesn't matter to me what you want to be called. What matters is what you do. I know,

Chris . . . topher, that you knew better than to get that tattoo."

Christopher's piercing stare was louder than any spoken words.

"Why did you do this?" Quentin asked.

Christopher shrugged.

"You don't have anything to say?"

A beat passed. "Not to you."

Quentin pressed his lips together and stared back at his son.

This was a bad idea, Sheridan thought as she watched the war of wills. "You know what," she said, going to Christopher's side. "I think he understands now."

Christopher looked at Sheridan. "I'm sorry. Mom."

There was no way she could look at Quentin. She knew he wasn't finished, but she also knew that this was enough. If this continued, words would come out of Christopher that all three of them would regret. "Okay. You can go upstairs."

For the second time that night, Christopher raced away with the speed of an Olympic sprinter. She didn't look at Quentin until she was sure Christopher was away from the sound of their voices.

"I wasn't finished," he said.

"I'm sorry, but it was enough."

"He wouldn't even talk to me."

She wanted to ask, What did you expect? Did he really think he could move away from his family into this new life and not have it affect his teenage son?

"I didn't want it to be this way," he said, as if he heard her thoughts. "I left this house, but I didn't leave my family."

"There's not a difference to Chris. Really," she said, looking away, "I don't understand the difference either."

"You know, when I first told you about what I was feeling, I wasn't planning to move out."

She raised her eyebrows. "So you're saying that if I didn't insist you go, none of this would've happened?" She held up her hand before he could say anything. "It doesn't matter." She paused and looked at him. "And there's no turning back." She said it as if it were a warning. "What's important now are the children."

He nodded. "I agree. That's why . . ." He stopped. "I got the divorce papers. I was surprised."

"I told you I was going to file them."

He nodded. "I just don't understand the rush."

"And I don't understand why we'd wait."

He took a breath. "I want you to know

I'm not going to fight you. My attorney has looked over the papers, and I'm fine with everything. I just want to do this right."

You can't make a wrong right.

"Anyway," Quentin said, "We still need to talk to Tori."

"What do you plan to say to her?"

He shrugged. "The truth; that's what I want to live by."

Before she could stop herself, she said, "I guess that's a new thing for you."

Almost a minute passed. "I'm not your enemy, Sheridan. And I think if you want things to get better, you'd better stop treating me like I am."

He stood, grabbed his jacket, and slammed the door on his way out.

Chapter Sixteen

This was the reason she'd kept the message.

Sheridan pressed the number one on the dialing pad and listened to the message again. "Sheridan, this is Pastor Ford. I've missed you and Quentin in church the past few weeks, and Kyla Blake just told me you guys were no longer leading the planning committee for the retreat. I hope to see you in church tomorrow, but if not, please give me a call. I want to talk to you and Quentin."

Sheridan sighed, hung up the phone, and knew she had to go to church this morning. She hadn't been to church this year and now Pastor Ford was calling. If she showed her face, that would allay the pastor's concerns.

Sheridan stood and posed in front of the mirror. The St. John knit fit her even better now than it did when she'd bought it with Kamora.

Have I lost weight?

She made a mental note to check, but no matter what the scale said, the mirror said she looked good.

But the mirror can't see my heart.

That part of her was a long way from feeling fine.

And now, today. How was she supposed to handle church? How would she answer the question sure to come — where's Quentin?

She grabbed her Bible and purse, draped her jacket across her shoulders, finger-combed her hair, and then stepped into the hallway. She almost bumped into Christopher as he rushed through the hall.

"You guys ready?" she asked.

He looked surprised. "I . . . didn't know you were going to church, Mom."

"Why not?"

"Well, you haven't been going."

She lowered her eyes. "I'd been working late the past Saturdays."

His glance said, *Yeah, right.*

"Where are you off to in such a hurry?" she asked.

"Nowhere." His cell phone rang. Christopher pulled it from his pocket, then lingered in front of his bedroom as he whispered.

Sheridan moved slowly toward the stairs, trying to stay close enough to hear her son's conversation. But by the time she got to the bottom of the stairs, she knew nothing more. His monosyllabic responses were so soft she couldn't tell if he was still on the phone.

When he came down the stairs, Sheridan said, "Who was that?" She kept her eyes away from his, shifting items from one purse to another, all the time trying not to be too interested.

"Nobody."

She sighed inside. "Tori, are you ready?" she yelled.

Tori's bedroom door opened and she skipped down the stairs. "Hi, Mom."

At least one person in their home was happy.

"Mom, I'm going to walk."

Christopher's lips moved, but his words didn't make sense. "Who are you? And what have you done with my son?" Sheridan kidded.

He looked down at the carpet as if his answer was there. "I just want to walk." He glanced up, but his eyes wouldn't stay with hers. "I'll meet you at church. I'm going to the teens' service."

She eyed him a little longer. "Okay." She looked at her watch. "You only have twenty-five minutes."

Christopher nodded.

She turned to Tori. "Are you walking?"

"No," Christopher said quickly.

Both Tori and Sheridan turned toward him in surprise.

He added, "I don't feel like babysitting."

"First of all, no one has to babysit me," Tori said, resting one hand on her side as if she had hips. "And second of all, I wouldn't want to walk with your stupid behind anyway."

Sheridan smirked. "I guess she told you. Anyway . . ." Sheridan paused. *What are you up to?* "Just make sure you have your . . . behind in church on time."

In the car, as Tori chatted, Sheridan couldn't get her mind off her son. *What is Chris up to?*

Sheridan tossed her feelings aside. Christopher was a good young man. He'd never been in trouble. This tattoo had to be just a case of a teenager acting like the visitor to this planet that all teenagers were.

She twisted the car into the curve of the church's parking lot, and thoughts of her son dissipated as she eyed Francesca Mills edging her fire red Ferrari into a spot. Sheridan chose a space as far away from Francesca as she could find. But the moment Sheridan stepped away from her car, she heard the familiar screech. "Sheridan."

Sheridan shuddered, stopped, and then faced Francesca with as fake a smile as she could muster.

"Hi, Ms. Francesca," Tori said.

"Hi, darling." Francesca kissed Tori. "Whew," she said, turning to Sheridan. "It's been so hard catching up with you." She stood on her toes and blew her signature air kiss in Sheridan's direction. "I've left you a million messages. I had some questions about the marriage retreat. I have an idea for a workshop and . . ."

"I'm not on that committee anymore. You should talk to Kyla," Sheridan said, walking toward the church. She stretched her long legs, hoping to leave Francesca behind.

"What happened?" Francesca asked, somehow matching Sheridan's long-legged strides.

"Just talk to Kyla."

"Should I talk to Quentin?"

Sheridan stopped moving. "I said . . . talk to Kyla," she said in the tone she reserved for her children.

Tori leaned closer to her mother, while Francesca took a step back.

"I'm sorry."

Without acknowledging Francesca's apology, Sheridan took Tori's hand and walked into the sanctuary. She took a breath, glanced around, and then eased down the aisle, smiling at the familiar faces, waving at friends, not giving a hint of any of the turmoil she felt.

"Mom, today's the Sunday that the kids can go in with the teens. I'm going in there, okay?"

"Sure," Sheridan said, although it wasn't all right with her. She wanted Tori by her side, a shield to protect her from questions she was sure would come. But she couldn't put that on Tori. And her almost-ten-year-old loved the classes with the teenagers. She couldn't deny her that.

Sheridan sat on the left side of the altar, totally opposite where she and Quentin used to sit every Sunday. She glanced at her watch and wished she'd timed this better. Five minutes still remained before praise and worship. She should have walked with Christopher.

"Hey, Sheridan."

The greetings started.

"Love your hair, girl."

She held her breath.

"Where have you been?"

No one asked about Quentin.

When the praise team began the morning service, Sheridan released a lungful of air. But as she stood to join the worship and raised her hands in the air, she wondered why no one had asked about Quentin. Did everyone already know?

You're being paranoid, she thought, as she tried to focus on Jackie at the keyboard. But although she sang the words, her heart took her mind to other places: The day she and Quentin first came to Hope Chapel. The weekend when they attended their first marriage retreat. The Mother's Day when Quentin, in front of the congregation, proclaimed, "A million lifetimes would not be enough to hold all the love I have for you."

Her thoughts kept her so far away, she didn't notice when Pastor Ford stood at the pulpit. It wasn't until she realized that she was the only one standing that she eased into her seat.

But through the pastor's prayer, through the offering, through the sermon, Sheridan's mind kept her away from the present. She tried to remember the last time she'd come to church without Quentin, but she couldn't think of it. If Quentin didn't go to church, she didn't. Now there was a lifetime of Sundays — without Quentin — in front of her.

"We serve a God who is kind, and patient, and merciful, and faithful." Pastor Ford's voice made its way through her tangled thoughts. "But what happens when trials come? Does that mean that God is not kind and patient and merciful and faithful?

"Joseph had his trial when he was sold by his brothers; Shadrach, Meshach, and Abednego had their trials when they were tossed into the fiery furnace. Paul and Silas had their trials when they were thrown into jail. Each of them served the Lord."

Pastor Ford continued, "So, where was God's kindness and patience and mercy and faithfulness when they were going through?"

That's a good question, Sheridan thought.

The pastor's manicured fingers swept her shoulder-length bob from her face. She placed one hand on her hip, and with the other, she raised her Bible high in the air. "God was right there. He was there with Joseph and the Hebrew children and Paul and Silas. How do I know?" She paused, looked around the congregation, and said, "How do you think they made it through?"

The congregation applauded.

"Amen."

Some stood on their feet and waved their hands at the pastor.

"You better preach that word, Pastor."

"The Lord never promised you a trial-free life," Pastor Ford continued. "He never promised existence without tribulation. But He did promise to always be there. To help you make it through!

"God promises spiritual security in the midst of troubles."

Pastor Ford continued, but Sheridan never heard another word. She gazed at the pastor and wondered how she knew. Surely she'd planned this Word for her.

Was this what it was all about? Was this just a trial in the bumpy road of life that she had to endure? Was God still really with her?

"Sheridan, your AIDS results . . . are negative." She heard Dr. Hong and then asked herself how she could wonder if God was with her. His mercy had made sure she had her health.

As Pastor Ford strutted up one aisle and then down the other, teaching, Sheridan pondered Pastor Ford's questions.

If all of this was just a test, why did God have to choose this one for her? She would have much rather had something she could handle — Quentin losing his job, or one of the children having difficulty in school. Or even Quentin with another woman. She could pray for God's help with that.

You don't get to choose your trials, the spiritually mature side of her mind told her.

Sheridan sat through the rest of the service, and before the last note was played on the keyboard, she stood, ready to rush from the church. And then she remembered her children.

Sheridan tried to make herself invisible in the midst of the crowd, surrounding herself with people she knew only well enough to smile at.

At the door she glanced at her watch.

In another minute they'll both be walking home.

"Oh, Sheridan." Dana King walked up to her.

Sheridan smiled. If she had to talk to someone, she didn't mind Dana. She was one of her favorite sorors. But the look of tragedy covering Dana's face made Sheridan's heart beat faster. "Hi, Dana," she said, as if she were afraid to speak.

Dana pulled her away from passing ears. "I just heard. Tori told me that you and Quentin are getting a divorce," she whispered, just as Christopher and Tori walked up to them.

Christopher's eyes widened as he heard the woman's words.

"I am so sorry. I didn't know," Dana said. She glanced at the children, her face covered with pity. "If there is anything I can do, let me know."

In better days Sheridan would have asked what Dana thought she could do for a woman losing her husband. But now she couldn't move away fast enough. "Thank you, Dana," was all Sheridan managed. She looked at her children and her eyes told them to follow.

They hurried past the crowd that hovered at the church's entry — the eight o'clock service mixing with the eleven o'clock arrivers.

As they rushed to the car, Christopher asked, "Tori, did you tell Ms. Dana that Mom and Dad were getting a divorce?"

Sheridan clicked the remote to the car and jumped inside.

"I didn't tell Ms. Dana that," Tori said, and eyed her mother in the front seat.

"Well, why did she say you did?" Christopher almost screamed, although his lips barely moved.

Tori shrugged, and Sheridan didn't have to turn around to know that tears were building in her daughter. "I didn't tell Ms. Dana. But after the service Ms. Francesca asked me what was going on and I didn't know what to say."

"I can't believe you did that," Christopher roared.

Sheridan glanced at her son. "Don't yell at your sister. I never told either of you not to say anything."

But she wished she had. It never occurred to her that the rumors would begin through her children. But she should have known. Francesca Mills was a proficient gossip. She'd go to any level if she smelled scandal.

"I don't care what you say, Mom. What Tori did was stupid. It's nobody's business what's going on with us."

"But this isn't Tori's fault."

"I'm not stupid," Tori cried. "And if you had been in class, you could have helped me."

Before Sheridan could ask Christopher where he'd been, he said, "Because of you, everyone's going to know Dad's a faggot."

Sheridan was sure her world would end now. She peeked in the rearview mirror. A mixture of confusion and fear creased Tori's face.

Tori asked, "What are you talking about?"

"Dad's a —"

"Christopher!" Sheridan stopped him, glad that she was behind the wheel of a car. Otherwise, she was sure, she would have beaten him down.

No more words were spoken. When Sheridan pulled in front of the house, she shot Christopher a warning glance, and she was more than glad when he rushed into the house, leaving her and Tori alone.

Tori got out of the car, closed the door, and then waited for her mother.

What am I supposed to say?

Sheridan took her time, stuffing the church bulletin inside her Bible, pushing her cell phone inside her purse, and finally tucking her heart back inside her chest.

She turned to the door and pretended she was surprised. "You didn't have to wait for me, Tori."

"Mom, are you mad at me?"

"Of course not, sweetheart."

"Well, Christopher is and I don't know why. You and Dad are getting a divorce, right?"

"You didn't do anything wrong," she repeated, not answering the question.

Tori sighed when they stepped into the house. "Ms. Francesca just kept asking me, and I didn't know what to tell her."

"That's okay, sweetheart."

"Mom?"

Sheridan kept her back to Tori, knowing this was the moment.

"Christopher said Daddy is a faggot."

What am I supposed to say?

"What did he mean?"

If she had no sense, she would have sent Tori to Christopher. Let him explain it; let him tell his sister how Quentin had betrayed them all. But she loved her daughter too much to send her into Christopher's den.

She turned and made her mind strong. "There are some things your Dad and I want to talk to you about. I'm going to call him and see if he can come over, okay?"

It worked better than she thought. The idea of seeing Quentin seemed to take Tori's mind away from her question. "Okay." She turned to the steps and ran upstairs. "Let me know when he gets here."

Sheridan almost collapsed from relief when she heard Tori's door close.

This was the beginning. The world was colliding with their lives. Soon everyone would know what Tori had been told.

Sheridan picked up the phone and uttered the words that almost felt like a habit. "Quentin, we have a problem," she said when he answered.

For the second day in a row, Quentin entered the house that had once been his home. His eyes drooped, his cheeks sagged; he looked as weary as she felt.

In the living room she said, "Maybe you should move back home."

He looked at her with surprise.

"Just kidding," she whispered. "Just trying to lighten this mood." She sighed. "This whole separation thing is not going well, Quentin." She slumped onto the couch.

"I knew we should have said something to Tori."

"I never thought Christopher would say anything. Especially not the way he did." She shook her head, still unable to believe her son's words.

"Where's Tori now?"

"In her bedroom."

"And Chris?"

"He asked if he could meet some friends back at church." Sheridan didn't mention she'd had a small battle with Christopher when she asked why he missed church. He'd told her that he hadn't. That he'd been sitting in the back and Tori didn't see him. Sheridan wanted to quiz him more, find out what he was up to. But right now, her attention had to be on Tori. "I thought it would be best if he weren't here."

She was disappointed when Quentin seemed relieved. He used to be the strong one, the disciplinarian when the children needed it. He never backed away from anything. He faced everything. The Quentin of old.

"Are you ready to talk to her?" she asked.

Quentin nodded. "But let me speak to her by myself."

She was already shaking her head. "Why?" Sheridan frowned.

"Because this is something I need to do — father to daughter."

But you're not a real father anymore. "Fine, but I need to be there. Tori's going to need me when she hears this, Quentin."

"That's the problem. If you're in the room, she'll turn to you. I want her to turn to me. I want her to know that no matter what is going on, no matter what names someone calls me, I still love her, will protect her, and will be there for her."

"And how will my being in the room stop that?"

Quentin shrugged. "I'm playing a hunch. Don't worry. I'm going to tell her that I'm with Jett, but on a level that a nine-year-old can understand."

Her head was still shaking her objection.

"Please, Sheridan. All I'm going to say is that although I still love you, God put love in my heart for someone else too. And that just happened to be a man."

She wanted to tell him not to blame God, but she left it alone. She looked at her watch. "I'll give you five minutes."

It was his turn to frown. "What's with the time limit? I'm going to give Tori all the time she needs."

Sheridan knew he was right, but how could she let her daughter hear this news without her?

"Don't worry, Sheridan," he tried to assure her. "Remember I love our children as much as you do."

If that were true, we wouldn't be in this situation.

He put his hand on her shoulder. "I promise you this will be fine."

Why should I believe a promise from you? You said we'd be together until death.

Sheridan nodded, giving in. But the moment Quentin trotted up the steps and entered Tori's room, she ran behind him. She pressed one ear to Tori's door and then cursed the builder of their home. Solid walls, solid doors. She could barely hear their murmurs. Just proved they'd received their four hundred thousand dollars' worth.

Sheridan paced in front of Tori's room and tried to ignore the voices in her head. The ones that screamed she was deserting her daughter.

He left his family. He can't be trusted.

But then the other side of her spoke.

He's her father. He'll never say anything that will hurt her.

It was the part of her that wanted to preserve the relationship between Quentin and Tori that won, but Sheridan stayed close. When she tired of pacing, she sat, leaned against the wall, and kept her eyes on the door. The minutes were too long for her.

When almost thirty minutes had passed, she knocked on the door and stepped inside.

"Hi, Mom," Tori said, but she didn't look up. "I think I'm gonna win. This will be the first time I ever beat Dad."

Quentin and Tori sat on her bed, with a chessboard between them.

"Don't distract me, Tori. You haven't

won yet," Quentin said.

The two laughed and Sheridan frowned. She looked for signs of trauma — redness around her daughter's eyes, grief sketched on her husband's face. But there was nothing.

"Quentin?"

He glanced up, then straightened his back. "Oh, it's okay, Sheridan. Tori and I talked. We're good." He turned his attention back to his daughter. "Right?"

Tori nodded as she finally looked at Sheridan. "Dad told me about Mr. Jett. It's okay."

Then the two of them turned back to the chessboard, as if she weren't there. As if they hadn't just had a conversation about one of them being gay.

Sheridan left the two of them alone. She stood still in the hallway, washed in shock. But then relief took its place, and she began to understand. Tori possessed something that she didn't have. Nor did Christopher. Tori possessed the ability to love unconditionally.

Sheridan shook her head as she stepped down the stairs. She needed to have a talk with her daughter. Her nine-year-old could teach her something.

Chapter Seventeen

"Sheridan, it's Pastor Ford."

"Hello, Pastor," she said. *Dang,* she thought. Once again she vowed to purchase a phone with caller ID for the kitchen. "How are you?"

"I'm just fine. I was wondering if you had a moment to drop by the church this morning."

Sheridan frowned. She was mad at herself. If she'd gone to church last week, she was sure she wouldn't have received this call. But after the encounter with Dana, Sheridan couldn't bring herself to go back. Still, she should have known this day was coming. "I thought today was your day off," Sheridan finally said.

"It is, but that doesn't have anything to do with my wanting to see you."

Sheridan paused. There was no way she could walk into the pastor's office. She'd seen it too many times: Pastor Ford would take one look at a person and know everything going on in her life — including what she'd had for breakfast.

But on the other side, Pastor Ford had

always been there — during the best and worst of her life — as the Harts' spiritual leader, to guide, console, correct, and love. There was nothing she needed more right now than some of Pastor Ford's love.

"Can I come in at ten?"

"I'll see you at nine thirty," Pastor Ford said.

"Yes, Pastor." There was no doubt in Sheridan's mind; somehow Pastor Ford knew. Through one of the loudmouths in the church or through a whisper from God. Either way, she knew.

While she dressed, Sheridan volleyed thoughts in her mind: should she tell her pastor the whole story?

As she drove to the church, she still hadn't decided. As she walked to the doors, she still wrestled with her thoughts. As she stepped up to Etta-Marie, Pastor Ford's assistant, and hugged her, Sheridan gave up the struggle. She wasn't going to confess a thing.

Within seconds of Etta-Marie's announcing Sheridan's arrival, Pastor Ford swept into her outer office. It was clear that she was there just for this meeting. Wearing a gold velour pants suit, with her hair brushed away from her face, the pastor looked like she was about to work out — except for her face, perfectly made-up as if she were prepared for an *Essence* photo shoot.

Pastor Ford motioned toward the wingback chairs, and Sheridan sank into the soft leather.

"So, Pastor," she said with false cheer, "what did you want to see me about?" She smiled as if there was nothing new in her life.

"How are you, Sheridan?"

"Fine."

Without taking a breath, Pastor Ford said, "How are you and Quentin?"

"Fine," she lied again, and said a short prayer that God's wrath wouldn't crack through the ceiling, punishing her for her dishonesty.

Pastor Ford leaned forward. "Sheridan, if there is one thing I don't believe in it's —"

A liar.

"— gossip," Pastor Ford continued. "But I've heard rumors that concern me, and couple that with not seeing you and Quentin for weeks . . . that's why I asked you to come in."

"I was in church last week." Even to Sheridan it was a pitiful statement, stonewalling nothing.

"Sheridan, not only am I your pastor, but I'm your friend. I want to help."

Those words were the key, and Sheridan unlocked the door. With tears, she escorted Pastor Ford into the emotional dungeon where she'd resided for the past weeks.

"I cannot imagine a rejection worse than this, Pastor," Sheridan sobbed as she finished telling the pastor everything.

Pastor Ford reached for her tissue box and dabbed Sheridan's tears.

"I'm a woman being tossed aside for a man," Sheridan cried. "And the worst part is I can't imagine what I did to make Quentin do this."

"Sheridan, this has nothing to do with you. This is about Quentin and his decisions."

"I keep telling myself that, but . . ."

Pastor Ford exhaled what seemed to be a chest full of air. "Well, this wasn't what I expected."

"You said you heard rumors."

"Yes, but the talk was Quentin left. That's all." The pastor paused and shook her head as if she couldn't believe the news. She stood at the window. "Sheridan," she started, keeping her gaze on the scene outside, "this other . . . man.

Is it someone from the church?"

Sheridan stared at the pastor. *Where did that come from?* "Yes." Sheridan paused. About three months earlier Jett had stopped attending Hope Chapel. Sheridan hadn't asked why; she'd just assumed that the church was too far from the new home he'd purchased in Encino. Sheridan added, "It's someone who used to go to church here."

Pastor Ford's face washed with sadness.

The pastor didn't ask, but Sheridan said, "Jett Jennings."

A mournful groan filled the room as the pastor sank into her chair. "Sheridan, I'm so sorry."

Sheridan frowned. The pastor spoke as if somehow this was her fault. And then the memory rushed back — of the day Pastor Ford introduced Jett Jennings to the congregation and then made a personal introduction to the Harts.

"Sheridan, I want to see you and Quentin, together."

Sheridan shook her head. "There's nothing you can do, Pastor. Quentin has already moved in with Jett. And I've done everything I can to get over the loss and the anger. I'm trying my best to move on." She paused. "Besides that, it's too late anyway."

"It is never too late. Quentin loves you. And more importantly, I know he loves the Lord. If Quentin will just pause and listen, he'll hear God's voice. He can turn back. Give me his number."

Pastor Ford jotted Quentin's number on a pad. "When's a good time for you?"

"I'm available anytime." Sheridan was surprised by the hope in her own voice. What was she wishing for? She had slammed shut that hope chest in her heart and wanted it to stay that way. It was over. Quentin had told her so. She stood. "Pastor, thank you for always caring about me."

Pastor Ford hugged her. "Sheridan, I love you. And Quentin. And Christopher and Tori. There is no way I can not become involved in this. Quentin was this church's Man of the Year and I know who he is in the Lord. I don't know what this is about, but I know it's not of God. And I'm going to remind Quentin of that."

Sheridan nodded. She turned to leave, but then the pastor reached for her hand. "Before you leave, I want to pray for you."

She bowed her head and tried to listen to Pastor Ford's appeal to God for Sheridan to be blanketed with peace and for the scales to fall from Quentin's eyes.

But Sheridan couldn't get her pastor's other words from her mind.

"He'll hear God's voice. He can turn back."

Could there be a chance that Quentin would admit his mistake? Was there a chance that he would come home?

For the first time since he'd walked out the door, the prospect of his returning seemed real. But now a larger issue loomed before her. Her husband left her. For a man. After all the tears, all the heartache, did she really want him back?

The stalker waltzed through her mind with his images. Quentin with Jett. Holding hands. Caressing. Kissing.

"Amen," Pastor Ford said. When Sheridan opened her eyes, they were filled with tears.

Pastor Ford hugged her again. "My prayer is Quentin will be home very soon."

Sheridan nodded because she didn't have it in her to tell Pastor Ford the truth. The truth that no matter what epiphany Quentin experienced, she could never see herself in bed with him again.

Chapter Eighteen

"He'll hear God's voice. He can turn back."

Sheridan's mind hit the replay button, and the pastor's words played again. And again. And the hope chest that she thought she'd locked, opened.

Could I do it? she asked over and over. *Could I really take him back? Back in my bed?*

Throughout the afternoon and evening, as she chatted with Tori and Christopher during dinner and helped them prepare for school, Sheridan surprised herself as she began to embrace the hope that she might get her life back.

When the telephone rang, at nine sharp, she didn't have to answer it. Tori would get it before the third ring. When the ringing stopped, Sheridan tiptoed into the hallway. Downstairs only the kitchen light glowed, and Sheridan could hear Tori's chatter. The moment Sheridan turned toward her bedroom, Tori yelled, "Mom, Dad wants to talk to you."

"Okay," Sheridan said. Quentin never asked for her, and Sheridan knew he'd spoken to Pastor Ford.

There was hope.

"Hi, Quentin."

"Sheridan, Pastor Ford left a message on my cell."

She smiled.

"She asked for a meeting with the three of us," he said.

Anticipation made her heart pound.

"I have no intention of seeing her."

Her smile left with her hope.

"I don't know why you gave her my number."

Sheridan swallowed. "She asked for it."

"I don't need to talk to her."

It was only then that she noticed his tone, on the low end of anger. "You've always had a great relationship with Pastor Ford," Sheridan said. "Maybe she can help us now."

"I don't need any help, Sheridan. I know what I'm doing."

"If you're so sure, why won't you even talk to her? What are you afraid of?"

He hesitated and then said, "I'm not afraid. It's just that I know what she's going to say."

"How do you know that?"

Frustration was in his sigh. "How many sermons has she preached on homosexuality being a sin?"

"Probably the same number of sermons she's preached on fornication being a sin. Or lying being a sin. Or anything else. Quentin, Pastor Ford's not judgmental in that way. It's not like she wants to talk to you to prove you wrong . . . just . . ."

"Just what, Sheridan? She's going to tell me I'm wrong for what I'm doing. She's going to say I'm wrong for leaving my family. She's going to say I'm wrong for having this desire, for being in love with a man."

"And if she says that, Quentin, it's all true. This isn't right. You weren't supposed to leave me and Christopher and Tori."

"So what was I supposed to do? Suppress everything I've been feeling?"

"You were supposed to stay with your family, Quentin, and get the help you needed."

"I thought I was doing the right thing when I came to you, Sheridan. I'd heard those stories of married men on the down low, exposing their wives to all kinds of diseases. I swore I would never do that to you."

I don't know if this is much better.

"Look," he continued softly through her silence. "I thought you and I had found that space where you accepted me. I don't want to fight with you. It's not good for the kids and it's not good for us."

She wanted to tell him about the hope she'd had. The hope that was supposed to take him to the pastor's office and turn him back into the man he once was.

He said, "I'm sorry."

"You say that a lot."

"Because I mean it. I wish things were different."

His words left tears in her eyes and certainty in her heart. In her mind she tossed away the key to that hope chest, knowing she'd never look for it again. The storage space in her heart with her dreams and desires for life as Dr. Quentin Hart's wife was cleared forever.

"Good night," she said, ready to bring this all to an end.

"Wait, Sheridan. One more thing. I want Christopher and Tori to stay over here with me next weekend."

Those words dried her tears.

"I don't know if Christopher will come," he continued, "but I already talked to Tori, and she's excited."

Those words made her tremble.

"Next Friday, I'll pick Tori up from school."

Those words made her say, "I've got to go." She didn't wait to hear his good-bye. Sheridan tossed the phone onto the bed. Her hands were still shaking.

"He wants the children to come over to stay?" She spoke aloud, hoping the words would make more sense that way. They didn't.

How could he ask her that? To share their children with his lover.

She had never thought about this. Never thought about sending her children to spend the night with Quentin and . . . another man.

"Why can't he just see them here? Or take them out?"

She picked up the telephone and dialed quickly.

"Hey, girl," Kamora said the moment she answered. "What's up?"

"Do you have any more plum wine?"

"Oh, no, what's wrong?"

"Nothing, that was a joke," Sheridan said, only half kidding. "I've had a hard day and just need something to take my mind off . . ." She stopped.

"I want Christopher and Tori to stay over here with me next weekend."

She flopped onto the bed. "Just tell me something good. Something that will get my mind away from . . ."

"Oh, sweetie. It's still hard with Quentin, huh?"

"You don't even know."

"Tell me. I'm a good listener."

"You're the best, but that's all you've been doing. And I don't want to talk about me."

"Well I do have something I've been dying to tell you." Kamora chuckled. "Last night Jackson and I . . ."

Sheridan wasn't sure she wanted to hear anything about Kamora and Jackson. But it was something. Something that would drown out the words. Something that would drown out her thoughts. Something that would keep her mind away from a decision that she knew would change every single one of the Harts' lives.

Chapter Nineteen

Sheridan couldn't believe this was her first time seeing the doctor.

"Well," Dr. Lees began. "I like your progress, Cameron."

"So, my PSA is still declining?"

The doctor nodded. "It's not yet where we want it to be, but we still have three weeks of treatment. We'll get there. How're you feeling?"

Cameron beamed. "As if I've been lying on a beach in Tahiti."

"And I've been right next to him," Beatrice said.

Dr. Lees laughed and looked at Sheridan. "I need to hire your parents to teach patients that attitude is half the battle."

"Not attitude," Beatrice corrected him. "Faith."

Sheridan smiled at the doctor. "There you have it."

The doctor stood. "Okay, Cameron. Let's get you into the room."

Cameron kissed Beatrice's cheek and then followed the doctor to a room on the other side of his office. Beatrice and Sheridan left through the front door.

"We called your brother last night," Beatrice said, as they walked into the waiting area.

"Really? Did he fuss at you for not telling him about Dad?"

"He didn't go off like we thought he would, but he still wanted to come down here. Said with all this craziness happening, either he had to come down here or move us all up there."

"That's my brother." Sheridan laughed.

"He's concerned about you."

"I know. I haven't spoken to him this much since we were kids. He calls almost every day."

"He knows the meaning of family. It's killing him that he's so far away."

"I know. I'm so grateful for him. And for you and Daddy too."

"We haven't done anything."

"I can feel your prayers."

"We've been doing that."

"Thank you, Mom," Sheridan said, although her eyes were not on Beatrice. She was staring at a portrait of a man reading a book to a child. The picture tossed her thoughts back to Quentin and the images that had invaded her sleep and kept her turning throughout the night.

"How're the children?" Beatrice asked, rescuing her.

"Fine."

"That's all you're going to give me about my grandchildren?"

"They both seem to have found their place in this new life."

"But you haven't."

Sheridan shrugged. "Children are more resilient. Tori's decided nothing matters except that she loves her father. And Christopher . . ." She paused. "He doesn't want to have anything to do with Quentin. But even he's comfortable in his choice."

"But you haven't found your place."

Sheridan's stare returned to the portrait. "I go back and forth. At first all I wanted was to be back with Quentin. Then I was so angry that I couldn't stand the sight of him. But then I decided the best way was to make peace — not only for the children, but for my own sanity."

"That's a good thing. All the feelings you're experiencing are normal," Beatrice said.

"I'm just tired of feeling like a human tennis ball going back and forth."

"Be patient. You were married for so

long, every emotion you have is tied to Quentin."

"I want to feel normal again."

"You *are* normal. Even in the best of circumstances, we go back and forth. Life is a trail filled with curves and bumps. Sometimes it's smooth. Sometimes it's straight. All the time it's everchanging, just like you are."

Sheridan smiled at her mother's wisdom. "You sound like a philosopher."

Beatrice chuckled. "I'm no philosopher, but I am a woman of faith who understands this life. And I've been through my own trials. Right now, your dad's in some room having a life-threatening illness zapped out of him. But all I can see is the goodness of God. That we found the cancer early. That your father is responding to the treatments. That God is holding us up. I know He'll carry me through. And if He'll do it for me, He'll do it for you."

"I believe that. I just want to get to the other side." She paused. "But the other side looks a long way away. There's more confusion now."

Beatrice's eyes asked, *How could that be?*

"Quentin wants Tori to spend the weekend with him."

"She must be excited about that."

"He wants her to spend the weekend . . . with him and Jett. At their house."

It took Beatrice a moment to ask, "How do you feel about that?"

"It scares me. It never occurred to me that Quentin would ask this. He's seen Tori and Christopher at our house, and he's taken Tori out. I expected it to stay that way."

"He's used to spending more time with his children."

"I guess." She twisted to face her mother. "What would you do?"

"Oh, no. I don't tell grown folk what to do."

"I knew you were going to say that."

"But I will say this. No matter what you decide, remember that Quentin is still Tori and Chris's father. Knowing Quentin, the only thing he's done is left 1333 Belle Street. He left the house, not his children. God made him their father, even though the Lord knew a long time ago Quentin was going to do this."

"Quentin says that God made him this way."

"That's a hot potato — especially with this gay marriage debate going on. Your father doesn't agree with me, but I tend to side with Quentin."

"Really?" Sheridan leaned in closer to her mother.

"I said I *tend* to side with Quentin. I don't know for sure, but I don't know why anyone would choose this lifestyle. Too much heartache associated with being gay in this country. Especially being black and gay. Who would want that? But there is something I do know. And that is Quentin would never hurt his children."

"Mom, he's already hurt them. He's hurt all of us."

Beatrice was silent for a moment. "I understand what you're saying. Just take the time to pray about this. Go to the One who has all the answers."

Sheridan leaned across the chair and hugged her mother, feeling as if somehow, maybe the right answer could be within her reach.

Chapter Twenty

There was only one way to handle the bumper-to-bumper freeway traffic.

Sheridan punched the speed dial number on her cell phone.

"Chandler and Lewis."

"This is Sheridan Hart." She chatted with the receptionist for a moment and then asked for her brother.

"Hey, sis," he said, answering his phone. "What's up?"

"I just dropped Mom and Dad off. Dad's treatments are going well."

"Yeah, Mom just called. You know I'm mad at you for not telling me about Dad."

"They made me promise."

"Well, now make a promise to me. If anything else happens, promise you'll tell me no matter what those old people say. You know you can't trust anyone over sixty. They make dumb decisions."

Sheridan laughed. "Okay." And as quickly as it came, her glee was gone. "There is something I want to run by you." She filled him in on Quentin's request.

"I can't believe that nonsense." Sheridan

had to hold the phone away from her ear. "As much as I love Rosemary, if she ever pulled some crap like this, she'd never see our children."

"You don't have children."

"Good thing, because Rosemary would never see them. You're not going to let Tori go, are you?"

"I don't know what I'm going to do."

"Sis, it's a no-brainer. You don't need to spend a minute figuring this out. Homosexuality is a spirit."

"That's what Kamora said."

"I always liked that girl."

"No, you didn't. You said she was the fastest ten-year-old you'd ever met. And you were only eight."

"Well, we're not talking about Kamora. We're talking about what both she and I know. And that's that you can't expose your child to a spirit. And why would you want to? Quentin doesn't deserve to see Tori or Chris."

"How can you say that when he's their father?"

"Oh, please. He's more of a coward than a father. Leaving you and the children to live with some man. He's going straight to hell."

Sheridan sighed. "Quentin said he was born this way."

"I am so tired of that gay propaganda. That's just an excuse not to call a sin a sin. That's the biggest problem with all of this, Sheridan. Listen to me. Quentin is living in sin, but he doesn't call it a sin because he was *born* that way. I'm telling you, it's just sick justification." He made a sound that Sheridan knew was pure disgust. "These people have managed to turn a sin into an entire political agenda."

"I don't know what to believe."

"Believe the Word of God. The Bible tells you where God stands." He released a loud stream of air. "Every time I think of this, I want to come down to Los Angeles and kick Quentin's a— Well, praise the Lord anyway."

Her brother's rampage didn't amuse her. Sheridan said, "I've got to go. I'll call you later."

"You always do that when you don't want to hear what I've got to say, but I'm telling you, Sheridan, this is going to be one of the biggest decisions of your life. Your children are your responsibility."

"But he's —"

"And don't repeat that nonsense about him being their father. A real father would have kept his butt with his wife and his children. He ain't no kind of father. I'm telling you, Sheridan . . ."

Sheridan was sure he was still talking when she clicked the end button. She sighed. In one corner sat Kamora and her brother, steadfast in their belief that what Quentin was doing was wrong.

And then there was her mother. Much less stringent. Much more forgiving.

What am I supposed to do?

She wished she had someone to turn to — someone who would know exactly what to do. She was still shaking her head when she turned off the 405 and headed toward home.

Sheridan held her breath as if not breathing would stop the question from being asked again.

"Mom, did you hear me?" Tori asked, as she dipped her finger in the spaghetti sauce and scooped. "Did you talk to Dad about this weekend?"

Sheridan slapped Tori's hand away from the pan. "Stop that, honey. That's unsanitary."

"Okay," she said as she eyed the sauce. "But did you talk to Dad?"

It was the third time she had asked the question, and the way Tori stood, Sheridan knew her daughter wasn't going to go away. "I haven't had a chance to finalize anything."

"Okay." Tori grabbed her backpack and bolted up the stairs. "You can talk to him tonight. I'm so excited; Dad said he was going to make pancakes on Saturday" were the last words Sheridan heard before Tori scurried into her bedroom.

Those few words satisfied Tori, but Sheridan knew that wouldn't last. Tonight, tomorrow, or the next day it would come up . . . again and again. Until Tori and Quentin had the answer they wanted.

Why does he want her over there?

When she thought about *over there,* an avalanche of images flooded her again — of two men, touching, caressing, kissing, loving. She squeezed her eyes, pleased that the pressure helped to erase her mind's stalker's pictures.

She opened her eyes to clarity. No way. Tori could not go into Jett's home.

She'd expected relief. But none came. Tori would be disappointed, but what she feared was Quentin's reaction. She tried to imagine what he would say, what he would do, and it all scared her.

Hours later, after she'd fed her children, checked their homework, and then climbed into her own bed, she still hadn't found any words that would placate Quentin. And as she fell asleep, she realized there were no words in the English language that would make him understand. She knew for sure that a battle was about to begin and she prayed that at the end they would all be standing.

Chapter Twenty-one

The week passed as if life were normal.

Every morning, Christopher and Tori departed for school. Every afternoon, they returned to homework and dinner. Every night, Quentin called. Every time, Sheridan discovered new ways to avoid him.

On Tuesday night she'd run the water from her shower at full blast, and sat on the edge of the tub, pretending not to hear Tori shout, "Mom, Dad's on the phone. He wants to speak to you about this weekend."

On Wednesday she'd held a turned-off cell phone to her ear, pretending to be in the middle of a call. "I can't talk to him," she whispered to Tori, covering the mouthpiece as if someone were really on the line. "I'm talking to an important client for Hart to Heart."

And then last night, when she'd run out of indoor antics, she'd driven two blocks from her home, parked in front of the community center, and sat until she was sure Quentin and Tori's nightly ritual was over.

But today was the day she'd have to come out of hiding. According to Tori's breakfast chatter, the plans were set: Quentin would be picking her up this evening for a fabulous weekend in Encino.

"Do you know what this ten-inch stretch chili dog reminds me of?" Kamora asked, as she stuffed one end of the hot dog into her mouth.

Sheridan shook her head as she swallowed a bite of her Guadalajara hot dog. Kamora's call this morning, after Tori had skipped to the school van, had been the perfect antidote to the anxiety that was building inside her.

"Did you hear me?" Kamora asked, rescuing Sheridan from the thoughts of the argument that was sure to follow her declaration to Quentin.

"I heard you, but I don't know what it reminds you of," Sheridan said, her mouth full.

"It reminds me of Clark."

Sheridan frowned. "Who's Clark?"

Kamora licked her lips and smiled. "He's the new guy I'm seeing."

"What happened to . . ." Sheridan pressed her finger to her forehead as if that would help her remember. "What happened to Jackson?"

Kamora waved her hand as if she were swatting a fly. "History. That man got on my nerves. Too young. He was only thirty, you know."

"But you were ready to turn over your company to him."

"Well, thank God I didn't. And anyway," Kamora said, lifting the hot dog to her lips again, "changing her mind is a woman's prerogative. And so my prerogative is Clark."

Sheridan tightened her cape against the breeze that swept across the patio. This morning the weather had been walking-on-the-beach beautiful. But in just hours the spring-heat days of January had metamorphosed into storm watch 2004.

"Sometimes I worry about you, Kamora," Sheridan said finally.

Kamora frowned. "Why?"

"Because I wonder what you're looking for. It seems like you're trying to find something in all of these guys."

"Don't overanalyze it, Sheridan. I've told you before. I'm just a black woman trying to make it in a white man's world. I work hard. That means everything I do, I'm going to do it . . . hard."

When Sheridan's cell phone rang, Kamora motioned for her to pick it up, but she shook her head. "No, whoever it is will leave a message."

Kamora frowned. "Suppose it's Christopher or Tori?"

Sheridan didn't have to look at the screen to know who was calling. She breathed, relieved when her phone stopped buzzing. But when it rang again, Sheridan knew what she had to do.

"Sheridan, I've been trying to reach you," Quentin said when she answered.

"I'm sorry. I've had quite a busy week."

"Well, now that I have you, I'll be picking Tori up about seven tonight."

"Ah, I don't think that's a good idea, Quentin." She glanced at Kamora, who had pushed her half-filled plate aside. Her eyes were pasted to Sheridan's lips. "Tori won't be going with you . . . this weekend."

"What happened? Is she sick?"

"No. I just don't think it's a good idea."

She imagined his expression — the way his forehead creased and his eyebrows rose when he was confused. "What's not a good idea?"

She took a deep breath and then spoke the words as if they were all connected. "I don't think Tori should spend the weekend with you. I have to give it some more thought."

"What's there to think about? I'm coming to pick up Tori tonight."

"Quentin, please don't make this more difficult. I have custody. You left the children with me."

"Is that what this is about? You're punishing me, using Tori?"

"No."

"I never thought you'd go this low, Sheridan. You can't keep my children away from me."

"I'm not saying that. You can see Tori. You can take her to lunch or to the movies like you've been doing. But I want to think some more about her spending the weekend with you."

"That's right," Kamora whispered as she moved to the edge of her seat and popped a french fry into her mouth.

"Sheridan," Quentin said, while Kamora was still urging her on, "I will take any action I have to, to make sure I see Tori and Christopher any time I want."

His words surprised her. "Are you threatening me?"

"Call it whatever you want. But I'm not going to let you do this. I plan on being as much of a father to Chris and Tori now as I was before." He hung up before she could say another word.

In their years of marriage, there had never been a moment when Sheridan believed Quentin was capable of rage — until now. His tone made her quake with fear. *All I want to do is think about this some more.*

"That was great, girl." Kamora spoke with such cheer Sheridan thought she was going to stand and applaud. "You told him. He should have known better than to fight with you."

Sheridan looked at the phone. Remembered Quentin's words. Recalled his tone. "I'm not trying to fight. I just want to give this some more thought. I'm not sure Tori should spend the night over there."

Kamora tossed her napkin onto her plate as if the thought ruined her appetite. "Is that what he's asking? I cannot believe that man." She paused. "He's lucky you let him see Tori anywhere. If he was my husband, he wouldn't get the chance to even see our dogs."

"You're not married and you don't have any dogs."

Kamora continued as if she hadn't heard Sheridan. "You can't let Tori go over there and get all mixed up in that stuff."

"You're not going to start that again. Like he has some disease that Tori can catch."

"I'm just sayin', you don't want your child around that gay spirit. It's very serious because it's more than a sin. Homosexuality is the only sin God calls an abomination."

Sheridan shook her head. "That's not true."

"It is true; just look in the Bible."

"No, *you* look in the Bible. Look in Proverbs and see how many sins God calls an abomination, including lying."

Kamora twisted her lips, as if she doubted Sheridan's words.

"But you're not the first person I've heard say that. It amazes me the way people use the Bible against other people, but they never look at what they're doing themselves."

Kamora stared as if she were trying to figure out if Sheridan was talking about her. "I'm just sayin' that I know God hates the homosexual."

"And I don't believe that's true either. I know he hates homosexuality, but he hates fornication too." She paused and returned Kamora's stare. "Does that mean God hates the fornicator?"

Kamora leaned away from Sheridan. "If you're talking about me, what I do is not the same as what Quentin's doing.

It's not even close."

"Why not? Isn't a sin a sin?"

"Yeah, but fornication is not the same thing. Times have changed, Sheridan, and I think God understands that."

"Quentin could say the same thing, that times have changed. But don't you think God knew 2004 was going to come? And that men were going to want to be with men? And women were going to want to be with women? And everyone was going to want to have sex outside of marriage? And I'm not leaving myself out of it. I've been lying all week to Tori and Quentin. All of it, every bit of what each one of us is doing is a sin."

Kamora was quiet for a moment. "I'm just sayin' I don't know of any other sin in the Bible where God made His position so clear."

"What do you mean?"

"God destroyed an entire city because of homosexuals and their arrogance." When Sheridan said nothing, Kamora continued, "How could you even consider sending your child into Sodom or Gomorrah? No responsible mother would do anything like that." With her words Kamora tossed a twenty onto the table and stood. "Don't worry about your part. This one's on me.

The food and the advice." She stood and turned away, but then a moment later she swiveled back to face Sheridan. "And for the record, I know God is probably not happy with the way I lead every part of my life. But this is a hard walk, and God knows my heart. He knows I want to do right. He also knows I'm only human, but I guess that's hard for you to understand since you're so perfect."

This time when she turned, Kamora marched away from the table and never looked back to see Sheridan sitting there with shock on her face and sadness in her eyes.

The sun that greeted Sheridan this morning was now covered by gauzelike clouds that blocked the warm rays from reaching the city. But even though the day's light kept fading, Sheridan wasn't ready to go home. She needed to clear her head of the words from her brother and best friend.

"He may be their father, but he's a coward. He's going straight to hell." And Kamora's words of warning were not much different. *"How could you even consider sending your child into Sodom or Gomorrah?"*

Sheridan turned onto the Pacific Coast Highway and whizzed the SUV past the oceanside communities. She'd been sure she shouldn't let Tori stay with Quentin. But when she listened to her brother and Kamora, she almost found herself on Quentin's side.

What is the right thing?

She asked the question over and over until the first signs of drizzle splattered against her windshield. She turned around and sped back toward home. It was a torrential rain that greeted her as she drove further inland, and by the time she turned into her community, streets were already showing signs of flooding.

She eased around the curve of her cul-de-sac, and slowed as she noticed a Jaguar sports coupe in her driveway. She frowned, not recognizing the green vehicle. She edged her SUV next to the car and stared as she finally recognized the man in the driver's seat — Jett Jennings smiled slightly and waved.

I cannot believe he has the audacity . . .

Her heart pounded as she grabbed her purse and jumped from the Explorer. She stomped past the car, not caring about the way the rain pelted her slacks and matching cape. She was at her front door when she heard his footsteps behind her.

"Sheridan."

She swung toward him. Even with the rain hammering him, Jett still looked like a model in all black — jeans and a long-sleeved shirt. His short, curly hair was plastered to his head by the rain.

"What are you doing here?" she asked.

"I want to talk to you."

She said nothing.

"We're getting drenched. Can we go inside?"

Her clothes were already soaked, and she was sure her leather backpack would never look the same. But she would rather die in the rain. "Like I would ever let you step foot inside my home again."

He looked surprised and tried to stuff his hands deep into his pockets. He had difficulty keeping his eyes open as the raindrops struck his lids, making it difficult for him to see.

The rain pelted Sheridan like rapid fire, but she stood with her arms crossed, waiting.

"Sheridan, I'm not here to make trouble. I just want to talk to you."

It was only curiosity that made her say, "Speak your piece and be on your way."

He turned, glancing at the homes

around him, and he shivered. It was the cold that made him do that. The cold in the air. The cold in her eyes.

"I don't want to have this conversation out here. Your neighbors," he whispered.

He was right. She was sure Mrs. James was behind her heavy drapes, peeking, wondering what kind of craziness was going on in the Harts' household now. But not even Mrs. James mattered. "What about my neighbors, Jett? Should I be concerned because they may see us and wonder what we're talking about? Or maybe they already know; should I be concerned about my pride?"

He said nothing.

"I don't have any pride left, Jett. It left with my husband. I think you can find my pride and my husband at your house."

"This is not what I want. I don't want to be your enemy."

"Too late."

He blinked at her words. "I always thought you were my friend. I'd hoped we could stay that way."

"You're kidding, right? You want to talk about friendship with me?"

"I understand you're upset right now."

As she wiped water from her face, she wanted to tell him he didn't understand anything. He couldn't if he'd actually appeared on her doorstep unarmed. "What do you want, Jett?"

"I want you to let Tori spend the weekend with Quentin and me."

She laughed and looked at her watch; raindrops blurred the crystal. "I just told Quentin an hour ago, and he already has you here fighting his battle?"

"He doesn't know I'm here."

"Then you really need to take your . . . behind off my property." She turned and twisted the key in the lock.

"Sheridan, Quentin feels bad enough that he's lost Chris. Don't make him feel like he's lost his daughter too."

She whipped around, facing him again. "This is all Quentin's doing. He left, and now he doesn't want to deal with the consequences."

"This is not about consequences. This is about you being bitter and angry."

Her fingernails cut into the palm of her hand as she squeezed her hand into a fist. "Bitter and angry? You bet I am. Why shouldn't I be? After seventeen years of marriage I find out that my husband is a liar —"

"He never lied to you."

"— and a faggot."

Her words shocked them both, and a slight grin came to Jett's face. "I can't believe you went there."

She glared at him. "You need to leave before I call the police."

"I would welcome that. What do you think the police would say about your keeping a father away from his children?"

"Whatever they think, just remember, Jett, this has nothing to do with you. These are my children. This is my family."

"Chris and Tori are part of my family now too. No matter what you say."

She stepped toward him, ready to go toe-to-toe, although she had to look up to meet his eyes. "You know what I say? Come back to me when you can give Quentin a baby. Come back when you can give him everything I gave him."

"Obviously I'm giving him something." The sting of his words brought tears to her eyes. She stomped into the house, slammed the door, and wiped the dripping water from her face. The chime of the doorbell shocked her.

She checked the locks and then walked into the living room. Still she shivered. The bell chimed again, and she shivered some more.

Sheridan picked up the kitchen phone

and dialed. When Quentin answered, she yelled, "Your lover is in front of my house. You better come over here and get him before I call the police."

She clicked off the phone, just before the bell chimed again. Sheridan rushed to the door and pulled it open with such force, it banged against the wall.

"Get the h—" She stopped before she said the word and stared into Tori's face.

"Mom, I forgot my key."

She grabbed Tori's backpack. "Get in here." Sheridan's glance moved from her driveway to the surrounding houses. There was no sign of Jett. She closed her eyes, took a deep breath, and thanked God that Tori hadn't arrived minutes before.

"I'm all wet," Tori shrieked. "And I have to get ready for Daddy." Before Sheridan could respond, Tori ran up the stairs.

It took minutes before Sheridan followed her. With each step, her dread increased. She didn't know what she was going to say, but she knew, no matter what, at the end she'd have one unhappy child.

Chapter Twenty-two

"Christopher, Tori. I'm ready."

Sheridan stood at the bottom of the stairs. Christopher trotted down to meet her, but she still hadn't heard Tori's bedroom door.

It had been a long weekend. The daughter who Sheridan believed could teach a lesson on unconditional love proved there was no such thing. Tori moped her way through Friday night and Saturday, delivering the message that Sheridan didn't deserve her love.

"Tori, I'm not going to call you again."

Finally her door squeaked open, and Tori appeared, moving with all the speed of a sickly snail.

"It's time for us to go."

Tori said, "I want to walk to church."

"No," Sheridan said, and looked at Christopher. "We're all going in the car today. No one's going to be late."

Christopher shrugged. Sheridan and Tori may have been miserable, but the weekend had been good for him. Friday night he'd gone to the movies, and yesterday he'd spent the afternoon playing basketball with his newfound friends. When she'd asked to meet them, Christopher said he'd invite them to church.

In the car Christopher sat silent with a smile. Tori sat silent with a scowl. When Sheridan pulled up to the front of the church, Tori said, "Can I get out here, Mother?"

Sheridan rolled to the curb, and Tori jumped out a millisecond after the car stopped.

"I'm going to get out here too, Mom," Christopher said.

She parked the car and sat for a moment. For the first time since Quentin left, she was glad to be coming to church. She needed a word from God. Something that could help her with Tori . . . and Quentin. He hadn't spoken to her since Friday. No word from him . . . or from Jett.

Inside the sanctuary Sheridan smiled and waved, and as she sat, she pondered the fact that without Quentin at her side, women weren't greeting her the way they used to.

She glanced at her watch. There were still ten minutes before the service began. She flipped through her Bible, but then she stood and walked toward the bathroom.

She pushed open the door, and as she approached the restroom area, she heard, "I wasn't surprised at all. I always knew there was something up in the Hart household, okay?"

She stopped. And she was sure her heart stopped too.

"They were just too perfect." That was the shriek of Francesca Mills.

"Well, you know what I say — if your man is getting what he needs at home, he won't be looking outside, okay?"

Sheridan frowned. Those were the words of Jane Jones, who was as plain as her name, and had never been married.

Jane lowered her voice. "But Francesca, do you really think he's with a man?"

"I'm sure of it. I saw Quentin and Jett on the golf course last week, and that wasn't the first time. And then last night they were pretty cozy at Carousels. You never see two men alone there, unless . . ."

"They're a couple," Jane finished. "Okay?"

Quentin and Jett went to Carousels.

She wanted to tell her heart to really stop beating. To take her out. To take her away from this misery. She turned, moving as fast as she could before the two women discovered her listening.

Go back.

"No," she whispered to herself. "I can't."

Go back, her inside voice urged.

"What will I say?"

Go back.

It wasn't her will that turned her around. She trembled with each step. When she walked inside, their chatting ceased.

Francesca and Jane froze, their heads bent close together, their mouths still open.

It was Francesca who had the most nerve. "Sheridan." She paused, and her eyes wandered to Sheridan's hands.

What? Do you think I'm going to beat the crap out of you?

"How are you?" Francesca asked.

Help me, Lord. "I'm fine." Sheridan smiled. "And how are both of you?"

The women nodded as Sheridan stood in front of the mirror and finger-combed her hair.

"You look great," Francesca said, finally standing up straight. "Doesn't she, Jane?"

Jane only nodded.

While Sheridan powdered her face, Francesca added, "And I love that suit. Is it Chanel?"

Sheridan nodded nonchalantly and freshened her lip gloss.

Francesca said, "Oh, that's nice, isn't it, Jane?"

Jane only nodded.

The two women stayed in place, staring as if their legs were bolted to the floor.

Sheridan looked at them in the mirror. *Idiots. You should have run.*

Sheridan closed her purse. "Well." She smiled and faced the ladies. "You two biddies have a blessed day."

Her smile was genuine as she walked back into the sanctuary and took her seat a moment before Praise and Worship began.

Chapter Twenty-three

"Etta-Marie, is Pastor in?"

The pastor's assistant looked up from her computer. "Yes, Sheridan, but she's not taking any meetings today."

Sheridan sighed. "I just wanted to tell her something quickly." She'd spent several sleepless nights, hearing Quentin's words in her mind. But during the day she heard nothing from him. Although he'd called every night to speak to Tori, he hadn't asked to speak to her. She didn't know what worried her most — his fury or his silence.

"Okay, let me see if she has a moment," Etta-Marie said.

But the moment Etta-Marie stood, Pastor Ford opened her door. "Come on in, Sheridan."

Sheridan shook her head. The doors to the pastor's office were thick; she did counseling and never wanted to be overheard. And there were no cameras or intercoms. Yet Pastor Ford knew she was there.

"I wanted to get back to you about Quentin," Sheridan said as she walked into the office. "He doesn't want to come in for counseling."

Pastor Ford motioned for her to take a seat. "I figured that. He didn't return any of my calls." She shook her head. "Do you know if he's getting any spiritual guidance?"

"I don't know."

"It may be just as well. In today's times, there are so many ministers out there preaching and supporting this gay lifestyle straight from the pulpit. Many of them are even practicing . . ." She stopped and waved her hand. "Never mind all of that. I just want to make sure that Quentin is in a Word-teaching church."

Sheridan shrugged. "I haven't talked to him about church."

Pastor Ford nodded. "Okay, well all I can do for Quentin is pray. But Sheridan, I want to set up regular counseling with you." She opened her calendar. "You need to be ministered to throughout this." Pastor Ford leaned forward on her desk. "But first, tell me, how are you doing?"

Sheridan shrugged. "Fine, I guess. I realize that it is really over with Quentin, but now we have another problem." She paused. "Quentin wants the kids to stay with him for a weekend."

"At his place? With Jett?"

She folded her arms and nodded. "Christopher won't go, but Tori wants to." Sheridan jumped from the chair as if the leather were suddenly hot. "This is so hard because everyone has a different opinion about what I should do."

"What do you mean?"

"Well, my brother," Sheridan began, "says homosexuality is a spirit and that I can't expose my children to that. But then my mother says I have to remember Quentin is still their father."

"Your mother is right."

With her eyebrows raised, Sheridan turned to face the pastor. "I thought you'd side more with my brother."

"Well, first," Pastor Ford said, as she stood and joined Sheridan by the window, "don't get it twisted."

Sheridan almost chuckled. Pastor Ford knew the word of God, but she also knew the words of the streets. "Be very clear, Sheridan, because God makes it plain. Homosexuality, or rather the act of homosexuality, is a sin. Period. No matter what is going on in the world, no matter how many people call me judgmental or homophobic, I can't be politically correct. I have to be Jesus correct. I cannot help anyone if I don't tell the truth."

The pastor's words made Sheridan sadder. Deep inside she wanted to believe that the truth was a lie. That Quentin had been born that way. That the life Quentin had chosen was as acceptable to God as her life.

"Now, that said," Pastor Ford continued, "it is a sin like any other sin."

"That's what I say, Pastor," Sheridan said. "How can I judge Quentin when I have to ask God for forgiveness every day?"

"That's the point, Sheridan." The pastor motioned for her to sit down. "You ask God to forgive you for your sins. Right now, Quentin isn't doing that. There is a difference between struggling with homosexuality and wanting to leave it, and living in that lifestyle and being unapologetic and accepting of it. There is a difference when you don't call a sin a sin."

"Should I yank his children away from him? Never allow him to see Christopher or Tori again?"

"Oh, no. I don't believe that. What your mother said is true. He is their father. But you have to be concerned about how you handle their relationship with him."

Sheridan slumped over and held her

head in her hands. "So what am I supposed to do? Everyone has a different opinion."

"Why are you turning to man and not God? You need to ask the One who knows."

Beatrice had told her that.

"Normally," Pastor Ford continued, "I would give you scriptures to study, but I'm going to do something different.

"I want you to spend some time with God. Read the Word, talk to Him. Let Him lead you."

"But Pastor, I need to know what to do about Quentin and the children right now because I'm afraid of what he might do. I'm afraid we may end up in court."

"That's why you need to go to the Lord."

"But, suppose I don't hear anything?"

Pastor Ford squinted as if she were trying to see Sheridan better. "Don't let circumstances shake your faith. You know what God can do."

"My faith is strong. It's just . . ." She stopped.

"You have doubts," the pastor finished.

Sheridan nodded.

"Sheridan, never doubt in the dark what God has told you in the light. You know the truth." She took Sheridan's hands into hers. "Pray, Sheridan. For yourself. For your children. For guidance and wisdom. And pray for Quentin. God will speak to his heart too."

Tears burned behind her lids as she thought about praying for Quentin. Almost two months had passed since he changed her world. And instead of life getting better, it had become more complicated. All because of Quentin. How was she supposed to pray for him?

Sheridan hugged her pastor. "I'll try. I'll try to pray for Quentin." She fled from the office before Pastor Ford could challenge her to do more.

"Bye, Sheridan," Etta-Marie said, as Sheridan dashed by.

Sheridan barely waved, her mind still fixed on thoughts of praying for Quentin when she was sure she was about to enter a battle with him.

"Excuse me." A man's voice stopped her. She stumbled as she bumped into him.

"I'm sorry," Sheridan said without looking at his face. All she saw was his brown shirt and pants.

"Are you okay?" the man asked.

"I'm fine," she said, already rushing past him. She never looked up. Never looked back. Never saw the way the man's forehead creased or the way he stared until she was out the door.

Sheridan watched the neighborhood darken as light after light faded from each house, leaving the View Park homes blanketed in the midnight blackness.

She turned from the window and glanced at the Bible on her bed. More than seven hours had passed since she'd hurried into the house and rested in her bedroom with her Bible. Her children had ordered pizza as she'd spent hours reading her favorite scriptures and asking God to lead her to others. And then more hours passed as she meditated on what she'd read.

This afternoon she'd walked into her home in a knot of confusion. But now clarity filled her. It had come almost with the first scripture she'd read: *"If any of you lack wisdom, let him ask of God, that giveth to all men liberally, and upbraideth not; and it shall be given to him."* She had prayed for God to give her wisdom — to do right by Him, to do right by Tori and Christopher, to do right by Quentin.

Then she'd spent hours searching, reading, and rereading. More hours praying, meditating, and praying some more. And the answer had come to her. But she'd stayed in her place, in the peace she'd found with God's answer. She was sure. She was going to do the right thing for her children and for Quentin.

Sheridan turned off the light and dropped to her knees. "Father, thank you" was all she said. Still she stayed, silently giving thanks that peace had taken the place of confusion, shame, and grief.

Sheridan slipped her bathrobe from her shoulders and climbed into the bed. As she shifted her pillows, she saw her ring.

She stared at it for a moment.

"He's dead," she whispered in the darkness. Physically, the man she'd known lived, but the man she'd loved had passed away. She twisted the ring, turning it every way, trying to see the shine that was always there. But in the dark it would not glitter.

She opened the nightstand drawer and placed the ring on top of the tissue box. There was no need to keep it under her pillow anymore. No need to keep it that close to her heart.

She lay down, closed her eyes, and slept. It wasn't until morning that she realized the stalker who'd invaded her nighttime dreams for weeks had been arrested. The stalker had not come during this night.

Chapter Twenty-four

Sheridan closed her eyes and remembered the conversation.

"Quentin, it's me."

"What do you want, Sheridan?"

It was the first time she heard the edge of hate in his voice. In their worst times, he'd never spoken that way.

"I want to talk to you."

"About what?"

"Chris and Tori."

"I don't have anything to say unless you're calling me to tell me when I can pick them up."

She had taken a breath. "It's about that."

She had expected his tone to soften. It had not. "I have appointments until three. Should I just meet you at home?"

You speak as if you still live here. "No, let's go out." She knew he was praying that she didn't suggest Carousels. But she wouldn't. That wasn't their place anymore. "Denny's."

"I'm not going there," he had said, as if he couldn't believe she'd suggested that. "Let's go to City Lights. I'll be there at four."

There was no good-bye. Just the dial tone.

Now she opened her eyes, looked in the rearview mirror, took deep breaths, and went inside the restaurant.

She squinted as she looked around the dark space of City Lights, finally spotting Quentin motioning to her. As she approached his table, she wondered if he could see the way she trembled. Inside and out.

"Hi."

He nodded but did not get up, like he did all the years she'd known him. She wilted into her seat and tried to keep her smile. But when he stared at her as if he had never loved her, her smile faded away.

Before the waiter approached their table, Quentin waved him away. She looked at the glass of water in front of him. "Are you eating?"

"I'm not hungry." He paused, then added, "I haven't had an appetite for a few days. Anyway," he said, "let's get this over with."

She nodded. "First, I want to tell you, Quentin, that I'm sorry for the way I've handled this."

He looked as if he didn't care about the words she spoke, as if he just wanted to get to the point.

"Are you going to let me see my children or . . ." His unfinished sentence made his point.

"Quentin, why are you so angry?"

He leaned forward, and the heat in his eyes made her lean away. "Why do you think? You're trying to keep me from my children, and I won't have it."

She wanted to remind him that only one of his children wanted to see him, but that would only increase their divide. "I don't want to keep the children from you, Quentin."

Although his jaw remained stiff, his eyes softened, lightened; she could see the brown speckles once again.

She continued, "I want you to see Tori and Christopher anytime. You're their father, and no matter what has happened between us, you're not divorcing them. You're divorcing me."

Now, his eyes said, *I'm sorry.*

"But . . ."

All his hardness returned.

"Tori cannot spend the night with you . . . and Jett."

He leaned back in his chair, pushing against it as if he needed to get away from her. "How can you tell me that?"

Because I'm her mother. "Because I'm

responsible for her."

"And I'm not?"

"Not the way you used to be."

"So you're still going to use our children to punish me."

"It's not about that. I want you to have a relationship with them. I just won't allow Tori to spend the night in the house with you and Jett."

"What do you think I'm going to do to her?" he asked, as if her words offended him.

"Nothing, but I think by her being there, we'll both be saying we agree with the lifestyle you've chosen. We'll be telling her it's okay. And to me, it's not."

His was a bitter-laced chuckle. "You're actually sitting there judging me."

"No, I'm not. You've made a decision I'm not happy with and I'm working hard to live with it. But I'm still responsible for teaching my children what I think is right and wrong."

"No matter what you call it, it's judgment."

"Is it judgment just because I don't agree with you?"

He paused. "Call it whatever you want, but you're saying it's wrong for me to be living with a man."

It is. "I wouldn't feel any differently if you were living with a woman," she said, although she wondered if her words were true. "I don't want Tori in situations that will confuse her."

"She's not confused. She's accepted this. She understands."

"Don't fool yourself. Tori doesn't understand a thing. But she doesn't have to, because no matter what, she loves you."

He shook his head. "I'm not going to allow you to tell me when I can see my children."

With her eyes she pleaded for understanding. But with a strong voice, she said, "I'm not trying to hurt you, but I will fight to protect Tori and Christopher."

He pushed back in his chair and raised his eyebrows, surprised by her declaration. "Fight? This doesn't even sound like you, Sheridan. Who have you been listening to? Kamora? Your brother?"

It amazed her how he picked those two. "I talked to them, but it wasn't until I listened to God that I made this decision."

He sat silent, staring, waiting for her to come to her right mind.

"Quentin, I mean it when I say you can see the children anytime. Just not in the house with you overnight while you're there with your . . . Jett."

Quentin stood. "Remember one thing, Sheridan. You don't hold all the cards. Our divorce is not final and if I wanted to play with you the way you're playing with me, I could make things . . . difficult." He dropped a ten-dollar bill on the table. "I'd think about that if I were you."

She didn't turn to watch him walk away from her. She just sat waiting until she was sure he was out of the restaurant and away from the parking lot. She just sat waiting, and knowing that this awful dream had ended. Her life had just twisted into a nightmare.

Chapter Twenty-five

There was no surprise on Beatrice's face when she opened the door.

"Hi, Mom."

Beatrice hugged her daughter, then followed Sheridan into the living room.

Sheridan sank into the couch, relishing the comfort of the familiar. She wanted to take a moment to remember her life here — from the time she was nine until she left for college, and all the wonderful days in between.

"Aren't you wondering why I'm here?" she finally asked her mother.

"Do you need a reason to visit?"

Sheridan shook her head. "But I don't just drop by."

"Maybe you should more often."

Sheridan closed her eyes. "Mom, life is hard."

Beatrice chuckled. "If you're just learning that, then you've had a wonderful life. Some people learn that lesson before they're able to brush their teeth."

"Hey, I didn't know you were here," Cameron said, as he entered the room and hugged his daughter.

"Hi, Daddy. How're you feeling?"

"I'm great. Now what about you?" He sat on the ottoman facing her.

She shook her head. "I was about to tell Mom. I just left Quentin; I told him I'm not going to let Tori spend the night with him and . . . anyway, it wasn't good. I'm afraid he may take me to court."

"Did you pray about it before you talked to him?" Cameron asked.

Sheridan nodded. "For hours."

"And this is the answer you got from God."

"I'm sure of it, Daddy," she said with a strength she hadn't felt all afternoon.

Cameron slapped his knees. "Then you did the right thing. If it's from God, it's right. And He'll take you all the way through this."

"Daddy, I never asked you, and I know Mom's opinion, but what do you think?"

"I think you've done the right thing by going to God."

"I mean about Quentin. About his being . . . about what has happened."

Cameron remained silent.

Sheridan said, "Quentin says he was born this way."

Still, silence was Cameron's response.

"Please, Daddy. I'm not asking you what to do. I just want to know what you think."

Finally, he spoke. "Quentin's right. He was born that way." His words surprised her, but then he continued. "He was born that way — just like the rest of us. Born into sin." Cameron moved to the edge of his seat. "What I mean, Sheridan, is that Quentin wasn't born a homosexual. But he was born into sin, and homosexuality is the sin that he struggles with. But most people struggle with some sort of sexual sin — homosexuality, fornication, adultery, pornography. The list goes on. Our challenge as Christians is to fight through that sin, whatever it is. And call the devil a liar."

"But Quentin says it's not sexual for him. He says that his attraction to . . . men is not about who he sleeps with."

Cameron stood and waved his hand. "That's bull."

She sat back at his words.

He continued, as he marched in front of Sheridan and Beatrice, "It's just Quentin's way of justifying the sin. Just like people who say fornication is okay because times have changed. I could come up with a thousand excuses for every sin out there."

Beatrice looked at Cameron. He took a deep breath and then sat on the ottoman in front of Sheridan again. He took her hands into his. "I'm sorry, honey. I didn't mean to go off like that."

"No," she said softly. "I'm glad you did. I wanted to know what you thought."

"I think Quentin needs our prayers. And I think he knows the Lord. With all of that, God will take care of the rest."

"Do you really think so?"

Beatrice patted her daughter's hand. "Your father's right. Look at him and what he's been through. You know God's taken care of him. Doesn't he look good?" Beatrice beamed as she looked at Cameron, and then she added, "Doesn't he look good for an old man? You know that ain't nothin' but God."

The tension in the room popped like an overinflated balloon. Sheridan laughed with her parents. There was nothing like faith, the faith that her parents had shown her rather than told her about as she grew up.

But as their cheer continued, Sheridan felt sadness inside. Not just from her father's words, but from her parents' lives. Next year her parents would be celebrating their fortieth wedding anniversary. Forty years of love and life, not without sorrows and troubles. But forty years of making it through.

Forty years. That was something she would never have with Quentin. And she felt cheated. There was so much Quentin had taken away from her. But no matter what he did now, she would make sure that he would never take her children away.

Chapter Twenty-six

Sheridan glanced at the clock and gripped the telephone. It was almost midnight. Christopher was supposed to be home by eleven thirty. She kept her eyes on the grandfather clock until it struck midnight exactly.

She clicked on the telephone and dialed Christopher's cell again. "Hey, this is Christopher. Holla back."

She waited for the beep and then said, "Christopher, this is your mother. Call me."

Sheridan hung up. She didn't want to give room to worry, but she couldn't stop the thoughts. He was out with his new friends, whom she still hadn't met. She should have insisted that they come inside when they picked up Christopher. She should have insisted on getting their telephone numbers.

But she didn't think any of that was necessary. Christopher had a cell phone. And he knew the rule: to keep his phone on when he was out. Even at the movies, his cell was to be on vibrate.

Something had to be terribly wrong.

She tried to push her uneasiness down under, but it rose in her, creeping until it captured every thought in her mind. Every scenario that could take away her son went through her mind.

She dialed Christopher's number over and over as she paced. By the time the clock told her Christopher was an hour late, her tears had come.

It was time to call Quentin. They hadn't spoken since their showdown, although he'd called Tori. But even though their last words were ones of war, that didn't matter now.

She called Quentin's cell. "This is Dr. Hart. I'm unavailable . . ." She hung up and almost screamed.

She dialed again. Same result.

She paged him and waited. But after five minutes he hadn't returned her call, and she had to work to make sure hysteria didn't overtake her.

It was more than an hour past curfew, but it might as well have been five hours. Christopher had never done this. Never had been late. Never had not called.

Sheridan tried Christopher's cell again. Voice mail. She tried Quentin's cell again. Voice mail. And still no response from his beeper.

Sheridan went into her office and opened the drawer — the drawer with the card. The card with the number. The number she'd taken from the caller ID. Sheridan had vowed never to use the number. Never to call it and be forced to talk to the one who had replaced her.

Fear made her heart quicken as she dialed, fear for her son and fear for what she might hear when the telephone was answered.

"Hello." It wasn't the voice of her husband.

Sheridan hung up. A second before she lifted the handset to call the police, the phone rang and she grabbed it without looking.

"Sheridan, did you just call here?"

Caller ID changed the world. "Yes. Christopher's not home."

"Where is he?"

"He went out with friends," she said, fighting to keep her voice low so she wouldn't awaken Tori. "To the movies."

"With Nicole?"

"No. He's been hanging out with a new group. He went to the movies with Brendan and Gary and some of their friends."

"Who are Brendan and Gary?"

Just another sign that you're not here. "Guys he's been hanging out with since . . ."

"Sheridan, this is what happens when we're not working together."

"The last thing I need is a lecture, Quentin. I need to find Christopher. He's not answering his cell."

As she spoke, headlights flooded the living room through the drapes as a car eased around the cul-de-sac.

"Wait. This may be Chris now." Sheridan opened the door as Christopher jumped from the Navigator. He shouted his good-byes to his friends.

"Where have you been?" she asked, her face and voice tight with her anger.

"We took Déjà home. She lives in Pomona and on the way back there was an accident on the sixty."

"You're supposed to be home by eleven thirty."

"Mom, she's my girl. I can't let anyone else drop her off."

Your girl?

"Sheridan!"

She'd forgotten Quentin. "He went to Pomona?" he asked when she put the phone to her ear.

"I guess you heard."

"Put him on the phone," he demanded.

Gladly. She held the handset toward Christopher. "It's your father." He opened his mouth, but before he could protest, Sheridan said, "And remember you just walked into this house an hour late, without a call. So understand the situation."

He pressed his lips together and took the phone.

Sheridan crossed her arms and watched as Christopher listened, saying nothing. Minutes passed, and when he handed the phone back to Sheridan, he still hadn't uttered a word.

"Sheridan, I want to talk to Chris," Quentin said, as Christopher sprinted up the stairs. "We can't let this go on. I don't know what's gotten into him."

You're kidding, right? "When do you want to come by?"

Quentin continued, "I told Chris I'd be there in the morning. Is that okay?"

She took a breath. There was no way she could handle Christopher alone. And if Quentin didn't come back into his life now, one day they all might face regret.

"Tomorrow's fine. My mother is picking Tori up about ten. So come earlier if you want to see her."

He hesitated. "Thank you, Sheridan," accepting her attempt at peace.

She hung up, went upstairs, and glanced at Christopher's door before she opened her own. Part of her wanted to bust into his bedroom and beat him down for filling her with such anxiety. But tonight was not the time. Right now all she wanted to do was climb into bed. All she wanted to do was find some peace. But she had a feeling that peace was a long ways away.

Chapter Twenty-seven

Pancakes just seemed to be in order.

Sheridan couldn't remember the last time she'd awakened on a Saturday and had the urge to prepare a full breakfast. But by nine she'd awakened Christopher and Tori with the aroma of blueberries and sausages.

As Sheridan placed the pancakes on the table, she heard it. The sound she'd listened for over the years — Quentin's car, pulling into the driveway. Her husband coming home.

When he put his key in the door, Tori's eyes widened. "Daddy's here?" It was a mixture of pleasant surprise and caution.

"Yes, to see you." She paused. "And Christopher."

With her concern gone, Tori raced to the door.

Sheridan eyed her son. "Your father told you he was coming over, right?"

"Yeah," he groaned.

"Christopher, lose the attitude. After last night you're facing serious punishment. Keep that in mind."

Quentin came to the kitchen's doorway with Tori by his side. "Good morning."

Sheridan smiled; Christopher moaned.

In their past, at this moment he would kiss her. In the present he returned her smile and pulled out the chair next to Tori. "Mind if I join you?"

"Not at all." Sheridan sat and joined her family, as she'd done for years.

It was a one-sided conversation. One side of the table — Tori and Quentin — chatted about school and the dance recital and how she was beating all of her friends at chess. The other side of the table — Christopher and Sheridan — picked at the pancakes and sausages and scrambled eggs.

Quentin asked, "What's been going on with you, Chris?" Sheridan eyed him. "I mean Christopher," he said.

Christopher shrugged and fork-stabbed his eggs.

"How are your classes?"

"Fine."

"How's your golf game coming?"

It was the first time Christopher looked directly at his father. "I don't play any-more. I'm into basketball now."

Quentin sat back, shocked by the news. "I thought you loved golf."

You don't get any of this. Sheridan explained, "He plays basketball a lot . . . with his new friends."

"Oh."

Sheridan said, "Tori, go get your bag. Your grandmother will be here in a few minutes."

"Do I have to go?" Tori whined.

"This was your idea, sweetie. You asked her to take you shopping for the recital."

"But I didn't know Daddy was going to be here." She beamed at Quentin as if he were a national hero.

"Don't worry, honey," he said. "We'll get together tomorrow after church." He looked at Sheridan as he said, "I'll take you to lunch."

"Great." Tori ran to her room.

Christopher stood, dumped his plate into the sink, and then moved toward the door.

"Christopher, we want to talk to you," Sheridan said before he could disappear.

He turned, looking only at his mother. "Can I at least get dressed?" he demanded.

You're not going to get a reduced sentence that way. "Be back here in five minutes."

Sheridan waited until he was out of earshot. "Last night I prayed that God would bring him home. This morning I'm wondering if I should ask God to take him away."

Quentin nodded. "Teenagers don't make it easy."

Sheridan piled the empty plates on her arm and then in the sink. As she returned to clear the table, Quentin asked, "Do you want any help?"

She shook her head. "I'll take care of this later. I want to handle Chris now."

He moved toward the living room, but before he took two steps, he turned back. "I don't want to fight with you . . . about Tori," he whispered.

"I don't want to fight either, but I have to do what I believe is best."

His glance was intense, as if he were trying to see inside her. "It's hard to believe you don't think I'm good for our children."

"I know how good you are with both of them. That's why I'm always calling you about them." She sighed. "I wish you could understand my point."

"Funny, I wish the same thing."

The doorbell chimed, giving them a time-out. Sheridan rushed toward the door. "That's probably my mother." She paused. "Do you want to go upstairs?"

He frowned. "You don't think your

mother wants to see me?"

"No, but I thought you . . . never mind." She opened the door.

"Hey, honey," Beatrice said, as she stepped inside. "How are . . ." Her words stopped. "Well." She looked from Quentin to her daughter, then back to her son-in-law. "Quentin." There was love on her face and in her tone when she said his name.

"It's good to see you, Mom." His steps toward her were cautious, until Beatrice lifted her arms and wrapped him in an embrace. After a moment Beatrice leaned back, and her stare made Quentin turn his head away. With gentle fingers she touched his chin and encouraged him to face her. They stood, eye to eye. "If you ever want to talk, Cameron and I are here. We're praying for you."

The three stood like the family they used to be, and Sheridan wondered if Quentin harbored any regrets.

"Hey, Grammy." Tori bolted down the stairs.

"Hey, sweetheart." Beatrice kissed Tori's cheek. "Where's Chris?"

"He's getting dressed," Sheridan said.

Tori added, "We can't call him Chris anymore. He's Christopher now." Tori twisted her lips as if she still found her brother's demand ridiculous.

"I'm his grandmother and I can call him Chris if I want to." Beatrice chuckled. She turned to Sheridan. "What's that about?"

Sheridan shook her head as she straightened the collar on Tori's jacket. "You don't want to know." She kissed Tori. "You guys have a good time."

"Bye, Daddy," Tori said as she grabbed his neck. "Will I be able to come to your house next weekend?"

Without looking up, Quentin said, "Maybe."

"Yeah," Tori cheered.

Sheridan wanted to slap Tori for asking and beat down Quentin for answering.

When Sheridan closed the door, Quentin said, "It was good to see Mom."

"You shouldn't have said that to Tori. I told you that's not going to happen."

Quentin folded his arms and leaned against the banister. "Don't be so sure."

The certainty that covered each word made her shudder, just a bit. Before she could question him, Christopher strolled down the stairs.

Quentin stared at Sheridan a moment longer, just enough to make her shudder some more, before he turned toward the living room. Christopher followed, and with a deep breath, Sheridan did the same.

"I wanted to talk to you, son, because I don't understand what's going on," Quentin said, once they all sat. "The tattoo, and missing curfew, and even this morning your telling me you're not on the golf team. I don't understand. What's going on?"

Their son shocked them both with his laughter. "That's a stupid question."

"Christopher!" Sheridan yelled.

"Mom, I can't believe you and Dad are asking me what's wrong. You know what's wrong."

She had to agree with that statement.

"Well, maybe I'm not as aware as your mother . . ."

"I wonder why," Christopher said.

Quentin ignored his son's tone. "Explain it to me."

Christopher leaned back as if he were the one in control. "I dropped the golf team because everyone there knows you." He paused. "Everyone knows *about* you." Christopher glared at his father. "I hate that."

Sheridan sat on the arm of Christopher's chair.

Quentin said, "Chris, I'm so sorry —"

"Call me Christopher," he said, his stare

continuing. "Chris could be a girl's name, and I'm nowhere near that. I'm nothing like you."

A long stream of air pushed through Quentin's lips as if Christopher's words pricked his lungs. "I'm sorry, son —"

Christopher didn't let his father finish. "I hate school because my friends know. I can't hang out with Nicole or Darryl or any of my other friends. Because they know, Dad. Everyone knows you're gay, and I can't stand it. I know Nicole is talking to her friends about it."

"That doesn't sound like Nicole."

"And Darryl and the guys won't have anything to do with me," he continued, as if Quentin had never spoken.

It was Sheridan's turn to reassure him. "Christopher, Darryl's been your friend for a long time. He's not like that."

Christopher jumped from the chair. "You guys don't know what it's like. I had to make new friends. I had to get around guys who didn't go to my school, who didn't know anything about me."

"Christopher." Quentin said his name slowly, as if he was trying to remember to call his son by his full name. "None of this has anything to do with the way you're behaving."

"I just want the new guys to like me. I don't want them to think I'm some fag—" He stopped before he finished the word. With tears in his tone, Christopher said, "You ruined my life, Dad."

Quentin stood. "Christopher, that's not what I wanted to do. I love you too much for that."

"Well, if you love me," Christopher paused to control the quivering in his voice, "stay away, because I don't want any of my other friends to know about you."

Christopher rushed from the room.

Sheridan said, "Christopher, come back here."

"Let him go."

When she faced him, Quentin broke her heart all over again. But this time it wasn't with his words, but with his stance. He was a beaten man.

"I never thought Chris would react like this."

Sheridan squinted, trying to understand. "Quentin, are you really surprised?"

He nodded as if he were taken aback by her question. "Chris has always been such a good kid. I didn't think this would change that." He dropped to the couch.

"So what did you think would happen when you left your children?" Her tone screamed that she found his naiveté hard to believe.

"I just didn't think . . . it would be like this. I would have never . . ."

She sat next to him, let quiet minutes rest between them, and then said, "What happened? What happened to us?"

He looked at her. "Nothing. It all happened to me."

"But didn't you know that anything happening to you was happening to me?"

"It's a lot clearer looking backward. But I just wasn't happy," he said, shaking his head.

"I couldn't make you happy."

"I told you before, I was happy with you. I wasn't happy with me. I truly believed it would be better if I told you who I really was. I still think it was better . . . at least I did until all of this started happening with Chris . . . and with Tori." He looked at her, and the confidence he'd worn when he walked through the door this morning had faded away. "Maybe I should have just . . ."

She waited for him to finish, but he didn't. "You're doubting this now?" she asked.

"How could I not? I didn't want my family to fall apart."

She didn't want to ask, but she had to know. "What about the other side?"

He frowned.

"Are you sorry about" — she took a breath — "being with . . . Jett?" She couldn't believe she'd asked that question, and his momentary silence told her he couldn't believe it either.

He looked straight at her. "I'm only sorry because it's affected you." He paused. "Do you believe me when I say I still love you?"

She shook her head. "I have a hard time believing that you ever loved me."

"That makes me sad."

"How can you love someone for seventeen years and then one day just leave them?"

"I can't give you any scientific explanation. I can only tell you what's in my heart."

She let his words settle between them for a few seconds before she asked, "Are you afraid?"

He nodded. "I'm afraid I've lost Chris." He paused. "And I'm afraid that soon I might lose Tori."

"I don't think that's going to happen."

Doubt was in his eyes.

She paused for a moment. "What I was asking, though, was are you afraid . . . about God?"

He frowned.

"Are you afraid that you'll never be forgiven for this?"

He exhaled. "There's nothing I need to be forgiven for."

His words made her shake. His words made her remember that she had to pray for him.

He said, "For years I saw myself as a sinner because of this and I was tortured by that. But I'm free now. I've accepted that this is the way God made me."

"But what if you're wrong, Quentin? What if it's exactly the way the Bible says it is?"

He shook his head. "I can't believe I'll be punished for the heart I was born with. If I had a choice, I wouldn't be this way. This is not my will."

This is your will. She wished she had the words to save him. She wanted to tell him to read the Bible. And then read it again. Read it as many times as it took.

"I wish I could help you," Sheridan said. "I wish there was something I could have done. I wish there was something I could do now."

He looked down at her hand, resting between them, and he covered hers with his. "If I couldn't change my heart by praying to God every day for more than half my life, there's certainly nothing you could have done. You're where I used to be. Wanting, hoping, praying. My prayer now is that God will forgive me for hurting you."

Sheridan wanted to tell him there was much more he needed to be forgiven for. But she said nothing.

"I talked to my lawyer about custody."

Slowly she moved her hand away from his.

"But," Quentin continued, "I don't want to fight that way. I want us to work this out."

She stayed silent.

"For now, Sheridan, I'll see Tori the way you say, but . . ."

He left his thought unfinished, and she was glad he did. She didn't want to know his thinking, what his next steps would be; she just hoped he'd never want to finish whatever it was he was about to say.

"I'm willing to give you some time," he said.

"Thank you." She smiled, and tried to add warmth to her expression. She was relieved there wouldn't be a fight — for now. They had too many battles they had to face together.

"I need to go up and talk to Christopher. Let him know that he's on punishment until he's fifty."

They chuckled together, for a moment. "So, who are these new friends of Christopher's?"

"Some guys who live in the neighborhood. According to him, they're enrolled at L.A. Community College. But no matter how much I insist, I haven't met them yet. There's always some excuse." She paused. "And then there's this girl . . ."

Quentin raised his eyebrows. "So he's really not seeing Nicole?"

"Apparently not. And I'm not crazy about this new girl." She raised her hand. "Before you say anything, I'm not one of those mothers who believes no girl will ever be good enough for her son."

"Why don't you like her?"

"She's older."

"How much?"

"She's eighteen. Graduated from high school in June."

Quentin whistled. "So what does she want with a sixteen-year-old?"

Sheridan jumped from the couch at that question. "I don't know, but I have to do something."

"Telling him he can't see her won't work."

"I know." She paused as if she had a sudden idea. "I think I'll invite her to dinner. See what she's all about."

"That's a good idea."

"Maybe I can scare her away, and maybe you should be here too." A beat passed before they both shook their heads.

"I had to make new friends . . . get around guys who didn't know anything about me."

"I'll come next time," Quentin said.

She nodded.

He said, "Do you think I should try to talk to Chris again?"

"No, he knows where we stand, but I'm going to punish him. What do you think about two weeks with no driving privileges, no going out?"

Quentin nodded. "He's never been punished for that long, so he'll know we mean business." He stood. "I don't think we'll have any more challenges with Chris. He said what he had to say, and now that he knows we're watching, he'll be more careful."

Sheridan nodded, although she didn't agree. She had a feeling there were plenty of problems ahead. But she kept those thoughts to herself as she walked him to the door. "Thank you for coming, Quentin."

"There's nothing to thank me for. This is where I . . ." He paused. "I wouldn't be anywhere else." He picked up his jacket and reached for the doorknob. But a beat later he turned back to Sheridan and pulled her into his arms. Surprise kept her from stepping back. Inside his arms she felt love from the man she had once loved. Felt gentleness in the embrace from the man who wanted to be her friend.

Quentin let her go and then walked through the door without looking back.

She didn't bother to knock on his door.

Sheridan stepped inside Christopher's room and stared at her son, who lay across his bed with his eyes closed.

"Your father just left."

Still he didn't open his eyes. She knew he wasn't asleep, so she continued. "We decided you'll be on punishment for two weeks — no driving privileges, no weekend dates, home during the week, right after school."

His eyes popped open, and he leapt from the bed. "Mom, I said I was sorry, but I had to take Déjà home."

"It doesn't matter. You have a curfew. You didn't call. You didn't answer your cell."

"Because I knew you'd be mad."

"You were right about that."

"But next weekend is Déjà's birthday, and I'm supposed to take her out."

"You should have thought about that before you began breaking the rules."

"This isn't fair."

"You're right, because if your father and I were being fair and took everything into consideration, your punishment would have been much longer."

"Mom —"

She held up her hand. "This is a light sentence, and if you want to keep it that way, shut up now."

He bounced back on the bed, crossed his arms, and closed his eyes.

Slowly Sheridan walked to his bed and sat on the edge. "Christopher, I know you're hurt by your father."

He stayed in place.

"When your father first left, you told me you were going to be the man of the house. Well, I don't need you to do that because you're not a man yet. But you are a mature young man whom I'm very proud of. And I expect you to behave that way." She paused; when he still didn't move, she added, "I won't tolerate any more of this acting out, Christopher. No more tattoos, no more breaking curfews, no more being late to church, nothing."

She tapped his shoulder and he opened his eyes. "Sit up." She waited as he moved as if he were ill, sliding his legs over the side of the bed. "Christopher, you're a wonderful young man; that hasn't changed. And the greatest tragedy would be if you did change."

She was surprised when he said, "I'm sorry about everything, Mom."

"I know you are. I just need you to help me by being the young man I know."

"I promise, nothing more is going to happen."

She hugged him, but still she felt as if she'd lost part of him, a part she had to get back. She said a quick prayer, asking God to keep her son from the trials ahead. But even her prayer didn't end the stirring inside her soul.

Chapter Twenty-eight

He may have been on punishment, but Christopher had been excited all week.

"If Christopher can have friends over, and he's on punishment, why can't Joy and Lara come to dinner too?" Tori whined as she placed three plates on the table. It was her fiftieth request to have her friends join them, but all appeals had been denied. This was a dinner her children thought was for Christopher. But it was really for Sheridan.

They'd completed the first week of Christopher's punishment, but there hadn't been the normal parental grief that came with having one of the children sentenced to weeks in his room. Christopher had been beyond pleasant from the moment last Sunday when Sheridan suggested he invite his new girlfriend to dinner.

"I thought I was on punishment," he'd said, as if Sheridan needed reminding.

"You are, so don't take this as a sign of anything. I just want to meet her. Do you think she'll come to dinner?"

"Will she?" Christopher grinned. "She's been dying to meet you."

"Why haven't you introduced us before?"

"I didn't think you'd like her. But now I know that you will."

No, I won't, she'd thought at the time. But she'd only smiled.

"Can she come on Saturday?" he asked. "It's her birthday."

Sheridan paused. Saturday was her anniversary. The beginning of what would have been the eighteenth year of her marriage. She didn't want to spend that day with Christopher's new friend. "Let's do Friday."

"Okay." Anything was fine with Christopher.

Now Sheridan had spent the entire morning planning with Kamora, who tried to finagle her own invitation to this dinner.

"Girl, I just want to see what she's like. With a name like Déjà, you know she's ghetto," Kamora had said when she dropped Sheridan back home after they'd shopped.

Sheridan laughed; Kamora had expressed what she was too polite to say aloud.

"Let me come," Kamora had continued

begging. "He's my godson, and I need some entertainment after the week I've had. You know I broke up with Clark." After none of her protests worked, Kamora said, "Well, call me the moment the thugette leaves."

Sheridan had to make that solemn promise before Kamora drove away.

"Okay, Mom." Tori's whining invaded her thoughts. "Then can Lara and Joy sleep over next weekend?"

"We'll see."

Christopher barreled down the stairs. "She's here. She's here, Mom."

"Oh, brother," Tori said, rolling her eyes. "Why does she have to come to our house anyway?"

My thoughts exactly. "Tori, be nice to your brother's friend."

"He's never nice to mine. Ask Lara and Joy. He always calls them names and . . ."

Sheridan never heard Tori's complete complaint. She waited in the hallway as Christopher opened the door. Her eyes widened as the girl pushed up on her toes and kissed Christopher as if his mother were not standing there.

Sheridan cleared her throat.

"Oh. Mom." Sheridan hadn't ever seen a grin so wide on her son's face. Christopher entwined his fingers with the girl's. "Mom, this is Déjà."

"Nice to meet you, Ms. Hart."

Sheridan wondered how she could talk with a wad of gum in her mouth so large that it stretched her cheek. "You too, Déjà." For the first time she noticed her son's shirt — a white T-shirt with a huge red heart in the center. It was identical to the shirt Déjà wore, only while Christopher's was two sizes too big, Déjà's was at least two sizes too small.

"Let's go inside," Sheridan said.

Following Christopher and Déjà, Sheridan stared at their hands, clasped together as if they'd been bonded by industrial-strength glue. And she wondered if they'd purchased the glue at the same place where they bought the paint to cover Déjà's ample hips and thighs with what looked to be painted-on jeans.

They sat on the couch, and Sheridan parked herself across from them. Tori was already sitting Indian-style on the floor.

"Hi, I'm Tori."

"Nice to meet you, Tori. I'm Déjà."

"Hi, Deejay."

"No, it's *Day . . . zha,*" she said, pronouncing her name slowly.

Tori frowned.

"That's okay, people mispronounce my name all the time." She turned to Sheridan. "Thank you for inviting me to dinner, Ms. Hart."

At least she's polite, Sheridan thought, a moment before Déjà blew a bubble so large, Sheridan was sure the gum would pop over her entire face. But Déjà sucked in the air and returned the gum to her mouth as if she were a bubble-blowing professional, never smearing the violet-colored gloss that shined her lips.

Sheridan said, "Christopher never told me, where did you two meet?"

"Well," Déjà began, as she hooked her arm through Christopher's, "Chris and I met when I was at the park watching my cousin Brendan play basketball." She smiled into his eyes.

"His name is Christopher," Tori interjected.

Déjà grinned. "I know his real name, but I love calling him Chris. It's okay with you, isn't it, baby?" Déjà purred.

Who are you calling baby?

"And look." Déjà held up her hand showing fuchsia-colored inch-long nails with a letter painted in gold glitter on each finger. *C-H-R-I-S.* "I have my baby's name on my nails. Just so everyone knows he's mine."

Tori laughed as if she had never seen anything so ridiculous.

Surely this is a joke. But when Sheridan glanced at Christopher, he was gazing at Déjà, showing no signs of humor.

She cringed as Déjà squeezed even closer to Christopher, and Sheridan knew at any moment the girl would be on his lap. Or worse, he'd be sitting on hers.

"What school do you go to?" Tori asked, taking her place in the inquisition.

"I graduated," Déjà said proudly.

"Aren't you going to college?" Tori continued, as if she were the mother.

Déjà waved her other hand in the air, and Sheridan noticed all ten fingers claimed her son. "No, I'm going to beauty school in the summer."

Tori scrunched her face. "Beauty school? What's that?"

"None of your business," Christopher said. He looked at Sheridan. "Mom, make her stop."

"Tori, that's enough." Sheridan's words had never been truer. She didn't need to hear another thing.

But it wasn't until they sat at the table that she was convinced she'd have to break this duo up. Déjà chatted about her life goals: having babies, getting married, and if her husband made enough money, maybe one day buying a house.

Only Déjà spoke. Tori sulked because she knew dinner would have been much more uplifting if her friends had been invited. And Christopher couldn't speak. His eyes were glazed; he was hypnotized.

"Your son is wonderful," Déjà gushed, as Sheridan picked at her pasta.

Déjà spoke with the confidence of a woman who knew she had her man. And throughout dinner, the way she touched Christopher's hand, his arm, his cheek, let Sheridan know that Déjà was familiar with Christopher in ways that weren't obvious.

Oh, my baby. Sheridan shuddered. *Are they having sex?*

"Ms. Hart, you should see my baby play basketball."

He's my baby.

"He told me he used to play golf, and he wanted to teach me, but I don't wanna run around in the sun chasing a little ball." Déjà laughed.

So why are you running around in the sun chasing a sixteen-year-old?

"Plus, I told Chris he'd develop his body more by playing basketball." She rubbed his arm. "He's already developed more muscles."

Oh, my God.

"Ms. Hart, haven't you noticed the changes in his body?"

"No!" Sheridan asked, "Déjà, what time are you leaving?"

Christopher's eyes widened, horrified.

"I mean," Sheridan began again, "Christopher told me your cousin was picking you up. I just want to make sure we have enough time for dessert."

"Oh, we do," Déjà said. "My father doesn't care what time I get home."

"What about your mom?" Tori asked, and Sheridan almost smiled. One day her little girl was going to make every overprotective mother in America proud.

"My mother is dead."

Those words, spoken softly, covered the room with a blanket of sadness.

Oh, no. Well, that explains it. "I'm sorry, Déjà," Sheridan said. Her thoughts about the girl had been harsh. Déjà was doing the best she could without a female figure to guide her.

"It's not too sad anymore," Déjà said. "My mother died when I was four, and I have six older sisters. They helped my father raise me."

Sheridan wondered what her sisters were like if it took six of them to come up with Déjà.

It was still another painful ninety minutes filled with chocolate-chip cheesecake and endless, meaningless chatter. By the time Déjà called her cousin, Sheridan was ready to drive the girl home herself.

"Thank you for a wonderful evening, Ms. Hart," Déjà said, as Brendan's Navigator waited in front of the house. He'd been honking for almost five minutes, and Sheridan wanted to run outside and ask him if Déjà's sisters had raised him too.

"I hope we get to do this again," Déjà said.

Sheridan marveled at the girl. At times she spoke so maturely, so politely.

Sheridan walked Christopher and Déjà to the door and stood there as if they needed a chaperone. When Christopher glared, Sheridan turned to the kitchen. It didn't matter anyway. Not much could happen at their front door, and Christopher would be on punishment for another week. In that time she could come up with something to keep them apart. And if she couldn't, she knew Kamora had a trick or two. No matter what it took, Christopher and Déjà were not going to be.

Chapter Twenty-nine

It was 1993 and their first marriage retreat.

"We're going to Vail," Quentin had said when the marriage retreat had been announced at the new church she and Quentin had just joined.

For weeks she had counted down the days to their trip. It would be their first vacation. She knew they would have a wonderful time, especially since the weekend happened to fall on their anniversary.

Sheridan was beyond happy with her life as Quentin's wife. Her world was filled with the best of everything — a designer-decorated home, closets packed with expensive clothes, and every toy imaginable for their children. Quentin tried to pack her days with leisure, insisting they have a nanny and a housekeeper. But Sheridan wouldn't allow that.

"The reason I'm a stay-at-home mom is because I don't want anyone else raising our children." Quentin had acquiesced but insisted upon the three-times-a-week housekeeper who kept their home looking as if two children didn't live there.

But although her life overflowed with material possessions, they were secondary to Quentin's expressions of love. From cards to flowers to the words he spoke, not a day passed when she didn't know how much she was adored. Even in the midst of one of their rare arguments, he would declare his devotion.

"We can agree to disagree," Quentin would say. "But never doubt how much I love you."

It was his passion that she loved most. He worked hard but loved harder. So there was no doubt their first marriage retreat would be one of their most romantic times.

And she'd been correct. He'd held her hand in their workshops, pulled her chair close as they ate meals. And when they were alone in their suite, he made love to her as if his survival depended on their union.

On the last night of the retreat, Quentin had stood and recited a poem for her that thanked her for not only making him fall in love, but grow in love.

There was no doubt in her mind. Quentin Hart loved her and always would.

The alarm clock chirped, dragging her from the memories. Sheridan slapped the off button and then lay back in bed. Today was her anniversary. Eighteen years of marriage. The beginning of her first year as a single woman.

She waited for the feelings to come. The hopelessness. The despair. The tears.

But nothing. All she felt was peace.

She wondered if she had actually reached that place where there was no backward, only forward.

Sheridan rose, but before she could make it into the shower, the telephone rang. She smiled as she checked the caller ID.

"Hey, girl, what's up?" Kamora shouted.

"Nothing much. What are you doing?"

Kamora sighed. "Absolutely nothing. Just wondering what I'm going to be doing tonight. Looks like I might be spending my Saturday night alone watching *Columbo*."

"What's up with that? I can't imagine you without a hot date."

"Well, I told you I broke up with Clark, right?"

That lasted all of two weeks. What was there to break up? "Yeah, you told me."

"I'm beginning to wonder if maybe I just need a hiatus. Some me time, you know. But that's not why I called. Tell me — was she a ghetto chick or what?"

Sheridan leaned back on the bed. "I

cannot begin to tell you." She replayed the evening for Kamora, having to stop and repeat the part about Déjà's fingernails. Sheridan was sure Kamora was going to pass out from laughter.

"Well, girl, one thing I can say — she's a smart cookie. Home-chick wants a good husband who can give her a house and babies. Chris is perfect. She knows how to pick 'em."

"Well, she's not pickin' nothin' over here," Sheridan exclaimed. "I may need you to help me come up with a plan to break my son away from ghetto chick."

"Sheridan!" Kamora feigned surprise. "Don't tell me you're one of those bourgeois mothers who doesn't think any ghetto chick is good enough for her son."

They laughed.

Kamora said, "Just tell me what you want me to do." A beep interrupted their talk. "Girl," Kamora dragged out the word. "That's Spencer."

"Who's . . . never mind," Sheridan said, knowing she'd heard this story before. Only the names changed when Kamora was talking.

They hung up and Sheridan rushed into the shower. By the time she was out, the phone was ringing again.

"Hello, sweetheart," her mother and father sang when she answered.

"Is something wrong?"

"Now is that any way to greet your parents?" her father asked. "We were thinking about you and wondering if you wanted to come over for dinner tonight."

"That sounds good, but what's the occasion?"

"Well, it's Saturday and you know I'm a party animal," Cameron said. "But your mother won't let me go out and do my thing. So, I thought I'd ask you to bring the kids over instead."

"Sheridan, your father hasn't been out doing his thing since eighteen forty-two."

"Eighteen forty-two? What are you talking about? I ain't that old."

"Oh, I'm sorry. It was eighteen forty-three."

They all laughed.

"So, what about it?" Beatrice asked. "We'll see you and the kids tonight?"

"Okay," she agreed. "But let me bring the food. I'll pick up something."

"Fine with me," Beatrice said.

"I know it's fine with you," Cameron interjected. "You can't find the kitchen."

"Now you know the devil has gotten ahold of your tongue. Sheridan, ask your father who made the lasagna he ate last night."

"You know you didn't make any lasagna. That came from that restaurant on Pico Boulevard."

"Bye, you guys. I'll call you when we're on our way."

"Bye, sweetheart," they said in unison. Sheridan could still hear them laughing as they hung up. She stepped into the hallway and heard the sound of television coming from both bedrooms. It was a leisurely Saturday; there was no need to disturb the children.

As soon as she reached the bottom of the stairs, the telephone rang again.

"Hey, sis," her brother bellowed.

"Hey, what's up?"

"Not much. Just checkin' on you. How're you doing?"

"Great. Just spoke to Mom and Dad." She paused, knowing why her brother had called. Knowing why her mother and father and Kamora had called. No one wanted her to spend this first anniversary alone. "I'm going to Mom and Dad's for dinner tonight, so I'll be fine."

"That's great. How's Dad doing?"

"You know Dad. He's healed already. He's just waiting for the doctors to catch up with what God has already told him."

"In the name of Jesus. Well, sis, I gotta run." He paused. "Are you sure you're all right?"

"I'm better than that."

"That's my sister. Just let me know if you need anything."

When Sheridan hung up, she thought about what she'd said to her brother. *"I'm better than that."* It was true. Two months after Quentin had declared he was a different man, she was a different woman — stronger, wiser, and finding a way to be happy.

Christopher held Tori's arm as she staggered to the door. It was almost midnight, and Sheridan couldn't believe they'd stayed at her parents' this late. They'd feasted on specialties from P. F. Chang's, then played what seemed to be every board game in America, and then cheered when Cameron pulled her aside and declared that his treatments were over and in a few weeks he'd know if he was cancer free.

"Thanks for helping your sister," Sheridan said.

Sheridan locked the door, and just as she lifted her hand to switch off the lights, she saw them — the bright red roses. There had to be at least three dozen; their fragrance filled the air.

Who . . .

She picked up the oversized card and read the inside: "You were my first love. Thank you for the best years of my life. Q."

She dropped the card onto the table. He could still pull her heartstrings. But she didn't understand it. They were no longer husband and wife. No longer celebrating their union. Why would he send her roses?

What do you want from me, Quentin?

Sheridan was too tired to figure it out, but there were two things she knew for sure. One, she would have to set up some rules for Quentin's use of his key, and two, the roses would smell wonderful in her bedroom. She lifted the oversized vase and marched up the stairs.

Chapter Thirty

"Pastor, I really appreciate this, but I don't want to see you on your days off. Isn't there another time?"

This was their third meeting.

"Sheridan," Pastor Ford said, "it's fine. And I don't see these as real counseling sessions. It just gives us a chance to talk. So, how're you doing?"

Sheridan smiled. "Two months ago, if you had told me I would still be alive today, I wouldn't have believed it. I really thought my life was over."

"Not over, just altered. A new normal." Pastor Ford beamed. "You're a trooper. It's clear God is carrying you through."

"I still have lots of moments."

"Did you think you wouldn't?"

"No, but I'm looking forward to the day when Quentin Hart is totally behind me."

"That will never happen . . . not completely."

"I know. Because of the children. But I want our life as man and wife behind us. I think we're getting to the point where we could be friends."

"That would be good for you and the children."

"Definitely for Tori. But Christopher . . ." Sheridan sighed. "He concerns me. He won't speak to Quentin."

"He'll come around. There'll come a time when Chris will need his father, and Quentin will be right there for him. Are you having any challenges with Tori or Chris in school?"

Sheridan shook her head. "Both of them are maintaining their grades. Chris quit the golf team and . . ." She paused just before she told Pastor Ford about Déjà.

Christopher had been off punishment for more than a week, and from what Sheridan could see, he spent as much time with Déjà as he could. But her plan remained, and the first piece was to arrange some events he and Nicole could do together. Once Christopher started seeing Nicole again, Déjà would become a bad memory. Sheridan continued, "Except for Chris and Quentin, the children are really doing fine, Pastor."

Pastor Ford smiled. "I am proud of you, Sheridan. You're handling this with your head up. And with all the class that I knew you had."

It was a small bit of guilt that rained on

her when she remembered how she had called Francesca and Jane biddies. Pastor Ford wouldn't think that was very classy.

The pastor prayed before she hugged Sheridan with admonitions that she call if she needed anything.

"See you later, Etta-Marie," Sheridan said, as she rushed through the office. At the door she was almost knocked off her feet when she bumped into a gentleman entering.

"Excuse me," she said, trying to steady herself.

The UPS man reached out and helped her regain her balance. "Are you okay?"

"Yes," Sheridan said, and finally looked up. The man held two brown packages in his hand. But even with their collision, he stood steady. "We've got to stop meeting like this."

Sheridan frowned.

He continued, "You almost knocked me over a couple of weeks ago." There was a chuckle in his voice.

"I don't think it was me."

"Oh, yes. I wouldn't forget you. I think you were upset . . . about something."

And then Sheridan remembered. Her first meeting with Pastor Ford. "Oh, I'm sorry."

"No problem." He held out his hand. "I'm Brock. Brock Goodman."

"I'm Sheridan." Still he held her hand, held her gaze. "Well," she said, pulling away. It took her a couple of seconds to find something to say. "Have a blessed day."

She could feel his stare as she walked away. And even when she was outside, the way he looked at her stayed in her mind.

At her car she dropped her keys, then fumbled, finally unlocking her car. At that moment, the UPS truck pulled up beside her.

"Excuse me, Sheridan?"

Oh no. She turned around and smiled. "Yes?"

"I forgot to tell you something." He stared again, letting too many moments pass. "You look great in that suit."

If Kamora had been standing there, Sheridan would have kissed her. She was grateful to her best friend for two reasons: this was another one of those spree outfits, and she wouldn't have it on at all today if she weren't meeting Kamora for dinner at Crustacean.

"Thank you," she said. "And you look rather nice yourself — in that uniform."

He chuckled. "You're one of those

women who love men in uniform?"

"Not until now." Another reason to thank Kamora. It was obvious some of her friend's best lines had stayed with her. Sheridan could almost see the heat rise under Brock's milk chocolate skin.

"Listen, Sheridan, I was on my way to lunch. Would you like to join me?"

She stepped back a bit. "No, I'm sorry. I'm married."

She noticed the way his eyes roamed to her left hand and he stared at her ringless fingers.

"I'm almost divorced." She didn't know why she felt the need to explain.

"Then you're not married." He grinned. "And anyway, I'm not looking for a wife. I'm not even asking you out. Just thought you had to eat lunch sometime today and so do I. So we might as well do it together."

She couldn't help but smile. Still, she declined.

"Okay." He revved the truck's engine. "Let me know if you ever change your mind."

She watched the truck roll down the street and wondered how in the world she could let him know. Besides his name, and that he worked for UPS, she knew nothing else.

"Good thing," she said as she got into her car. "With the way I've been feeling, what I could do with him over lunch would be illegal." She giggled at the thought and looked in the rearview mirror.

That was fun.

She fluffed out her hair with her fingers and started her car. For the first time since Quentin left, she remembered that she was a woman.

Chapter Thirty-one

Jane Jones sauntered into the church bathroom, but the moment she saw Sheridan, she turned so fast, she bumped into the wall.

Sheridan bit her tongue to keep from laughing.

That's what you get, Sheridan thought as Jane rushed away. Then another quick thought followed: *Forgive me, Lord.*

She'd just left church and admonished herself for laughing at Jane. But it felt delicious. The entire morning had been good — the best Sunday since Quentin had left. Sheridan was sure most people had heard something by now. Almost three months had passed and she was sure the rumor mill was churning. Although it still bothered her, she realized she couldn't control it. So for weeks now she'd sat in the services, ignoring the real stares and the imagined whispers, and was simply grateful that God was using time to slowly heal her heart.

Sheridan wrapped her purse strap over her shoulder and rushed out of the bathroom. "Excuse me," she said the moment she stepped into the hallway and collided with someone.

"No problem, Sheridan. I was hoping to bump into you."

It took her a moment to recognize the voice, then the man. "Brock, right?" she said, surprised that she remembered his name. Weeks had passed since he'd stopped her on the street. "I didn't recognize you —"

"Without my uniform," he said, his lips moving into a one-sided smile.

"We've got to stop meeting like this." She laughed.

He put one hand above her and leaned against the wall. "I kinda like bumping into you."

"Really?" Her tone left no doubt she was flirting too. "Why's that?" *Sheridan, what is wrong with you?* "By the way, what are you doing here? I didn't know you attended Hope Chapel."

"You don't know anything about me. I think we should change that."

Sheridan smiled and then noticed Francesca gawking from a few feet away. She tightened the strap of her purse. "Well, Brock, it was good seeing you again."

He looked over his shoulder, following her gaze. When he looked back at

Sheridan, he said, "Why don't we grab a cup of coffee . . . or something."

Sheridan's glance moved back to Francesca, who had not taken her eyes away from them. Right now she needed her children. But both had deserted her; Tori was with Sheridan's parents and Christopher had run off as soon as services ended.

"No, I don't think so," she finally answered Brock.

"What are you afraid of, Ms. Sheridan?" he asked, lowering his voice. His question felt seductive.

"Not you," she said softly, and wondered again what she was doing.

"Then let's meet at Starbucks. The one in Ladera. Do you know it?"

"Sure. I'll meet you there." *Am I crazy?*

"Do I have to follow you to make sure you get there?"

"Nope. I know the way."

He nodded. "Just remember, if you don't show up, I know where you go to church."

She laughed and sauntered toward Francesca.

"Sheridan, good to see you." Those were the first words Francesca had spoken to her since the biddy incident.

"Good to see you too," Sheridan said,

not stopping, even though Francesca tried to block her path.

"Ah, wait a minute. That gentleman you were talking to. He looks familiar . . ."

Sheridan walked away without responding.

During the five-minute ride to Starbucks, she continued to question her mental state. But another part of her felt as if it was being awakened from a long sleep. She was doing something she'd never done before. In the Starbucks parking lot she checked her makeup, fluffed her hair. "I'm just going to have a quick cup of coffee," she told herself.

She slid from her SUV and noticed the men who made it their job to watch women enter the coffee shop. As she walked past the gawkers, she felt their eyes and she was pleased.

Sheridan walked in and looked around. No sign of Brock. She was surprised. She'd driven slowly and then stayed in the car for several minutes.

What if he doesn't show up?

"This was stupid," she whispered.

"Were you talking to me?"

Her smile was immediate when she looked up. "No, I was talking to myself."

He laughed. "I think the two of us will

make much better conversation."

She loved his confidence — the way he asked what she wanted, then paid for her Frappuccino and carried her drink as he led the way to a table he chose.

"So, Mr. Goodman, what's your story?" she asked, as she sat and pretended to be Kamora.

He shrugged. "I was born and raised in D.C., but my grandmother moved here, and a few years ago I followed her to make sure she was okay."

"You came across the country to be with your grandmother?"

He sipped his coffee and shrugged. "Family is important to me."

"Do you have one?" She twirled her cup in her hand.

"One what?"

"A family?"

"Yeah, my grandmother and my parents, who still live in D.C. I have a younger brother who visits every summer." He paused. "But that's not what you were asking. You wanna know if I have a wife and kids."

"Do you?"

"No. Why didn't you just ask me?"

"Obviously, I did. I got an answer, didn't I?"

He nodded. "Yeah, you're good. So what's your story?"

She shrugged the same way he did. "I don't have a wife." She paused when he laughed. "But I have two children, neither old enough to vote."

"Too bad. I've been working with the NAACP to register voters for this election. We're going to need all the votes we can get to win this one."

Sheridan put her drink down. "So you're interested in politics?"

"Very much so. Every black person in this country should be. So much is at stake."

As he continued to chat about what he thought about the president and the California election that recalled the governor, Sheridan sat amazed. This was not the conversation she expected from the man in the brown uniform with the shoulder-length locks and a body that looked like he spent as many hours working out as he did working. But she was engrossed in his words, sharing her opinion and debating whether one vote really counted.

"The two thousand election showed just how important each vote is. Barely five hundred votes put Bush in office."

She nodded, but said nothing. She

hadn't known that. He said, "I like the fact that Pastor Ford mentioned the elections in her sermon today. I think churches need to take it up a notch. Become more useful to the community."

"Pastor Ford believes in that. She's made sure the church is more than a building."

"I like her."

"She'll break it down for you and she'll get down with you, if it'll teach you how to stand on the word of God." Sheridan took another sip. "So, was this your first time at Hope Chapel?"

He nodded. "I was hoping to bump into you." She laughed. "I'm serious," he said.

"Where do you attend church?"

"I don't have a church home. I've visited a lot of the superchurches, but I can't get into them. Too big."

"They're only too big if you don't get involved."

"That's never been my problem. I taught Bible study to teens when I was in D.C."

She didn't know why that surprised her.

As he chatted about the time he spent with the teenagers, Sheridan watched his light brown eyes glow and his face beam. He kept smiling, that crooked smile that had captured her the first time.

How old are you? she asked inside as she

sipped and nodded in agreement with his words. And then she wondered why she'd asked herself that. Obviously, he was a bit younger than she was, but it didn't matter. The last thing she wanted in her life was a man — young or old.

"What do you think about what I just said?"

"What?" She focused, bringing her mind back to the conversation.

"You weren't listening to me."

"Yes, I was. I heard every word you said about the teenagers. And I think what you do is terrific."

"So you like what I said?"

She nodded.

He leaned forward, closing the gap between them. "So you agree with me? You know you are a beautiful woman?"

She opened her mouth, but no words came out. She didn't have one of Kamora's ready quips. She lifted her hand to the edges of her hair. "Thank you."

He grinned, and Sheridan was sure now: his smile was a trap, designed to capture her and make her do things she'd never dreamed of. It worked, because she said, "I think you are one fine man."

He sat back in his chair. "Is that a physical assessment or are you talking about my socially redeeming characteristics?"

She laughed. "Both," she said boldly.

"Then I thank you."

"Let me ask you something."

He leaned forward. "Anything," he whispered in that voice.

"Why aren't you married?"

"I haven't found the woman to share my life with . . . yet," he said.

"Are you gay?"

The words slapped away his smile and pushed him back in his chair. "Why would you ask me that?"

If only you knew. She shrugged. "I've just been reading a lot . . ."

"Oh." He nodded. "You've been reading those E. Lynn Harris books." He shook his head. "I hate that stuff. It makes it bad for the rest of us heterosexual guys."

"So are you gay?" She had no intention of letting the question go.

He leaned forward again. "No." He said the word as if it had five syllables.

"And you're not married."

"No."

She smiled but stayed silent even though everything about her said she didn't believe him.

"Have I passed the test?"

"I thought we were just getting to know one another."

He took a sip of his coffee. "Under getting to know each other, I want to explain."

"You don't have to."

He held up his hand as if he were taking an oath. "I want to. It's hard meeting women in a city that is filled with ladies who care more about what kind of car you drive than whether you even have a job."

The way he spoke almost made Sheridan feel bad she'd asked.

"That's one reason I like older women." He returned to his flirting mode.

She chuckled. "You think I'm older."

"I do. But it doesn't matter. You're just someone I'd like to get to know."

"Why?"

He frowned. "That's a strange question. Why wouldn't I want to know you better?"

She lifted her self-esteem back up and asked, "So, how old do you think I am?"

He held up his hands and laughed. "You're not going to get me. I'm not going to guess; I'm not going to ask. I told you, it doesn't matter to me."

"Okay, so how old are you?" she asked, taking the last sip of her coffee.

"I'm thirty," he said, as if he were proud.

Sheridan almost spit out her drink. "Actually, I'm almost thirty. I'll be thirty in May."

Her eyes widened. "You're twenty-nine?"

"That's what comes before thirty."

Sheridan laughed and stood up. "It is definitely time to go."

"My score just went down, huh?"

She laughed again. "You're a nice man, Brock, but . . ."

He shrugged, pulled out his wallet, and handed her a card. "Call me anyway."

"Thanks, but we won't be getting together again." She dropped the card inside her purse.

"I think we will."

She wiggled her fingers in a wave, then almost ran to her car. She couldn't stop laughing. *Twenty-nine. When he was in kindergarten, I was a teenager.*

Her laugh became almost hysterical. And she didn't stop laughing until she got home.

Chapter Thirty-two

The din was almost melodic as Sheridan stepped down the stage stairs to join her parents and Kamora chatting by their front-row seats.

"Is Tori ready?" Cameron beamed as if his granddaughter was about to perform before the queen of England.

"I think so. The best part for her is wearing makeup. I put pink gloss on her lips and you would've thought I told her she didn't have to go to school for a year."

They laughed.

"I tried to watch her practice last week," Beatrice said. "But she wouldn't let me."

"Tori's been that way with me for months. In January she laid down the law. No one would see her dance until today."

"Well, I understand," Kamora interjected. "She's about to be Cinderella."

"Here comes Chris." Cameron waved to get his grandson's attention.

Christopher shuffled down the aisle as if his feet were shackled. When he walked up to her, Sheridan kissed him.

"Mom," he whined, and backed away.

"Sorry, I forgot." She wiped her lipstick from his cheek. "Did you get the balloons set up at home?"

He nodded, then scrunched his face as if he were in pain. "Why did I have to come? I don't wanna see no little kids dancing around."

Sheridan put her hands on her hips. "Too bad, because you're going to stay. Tori goes to all your tournaments."

"Yeah, but at least they're good. This is —"

Sheridan held up her hand, stopping his protest. "Could you not be a teenager today?"

Christopher stuffed his hands into his pockets, tucked his chin into his neck, and turned away.

"Where are you going?"

He looked at Sheridan as if he wished she'd stop minding his business. "I'm going to sit in the back. Is that at least okay?"

This boy needs a spanking and a nap.

"Don't you want to sit up here with your godmother?" Kamora asked.

His glare told her not to ask any more stupid questions.

"Go on," Sheridan said, waving him away. "We want to have a good time. Just make sure you stay in the auditorium."

Sheridan sighed and turned to the three adults, who, with pity-filled eyes, told her they felt sorry that she was the mother of that young man. "Don't say anything," she said.

"He's just a teenager," Cameron said.

"He'll come around," Beatrice said.

"Quentin needs to realize what he's done to that sweet young man," Kamora said.

Cameron, Beatrice, and Sheridan stared at Kamora with expressions that asked why she had to go there.

Kamora's eyes widened. "What? I'm just sayin'."

Beatrice made a sound Sheridan could only decipher as annoyance, before she asked, "Is Quentin coming?"

Sheridan shrugged. "Tori told him. But she hasn't mentioned him and I didn't want to ask."

"I'd be surprised if he didn't make it," Cameron said. "Let's sit down."

Sheridan's glance wandered around the horseshoe-shaped auditorium. She smiled when Carlton Arrington waved.

"Who's that?" Kamora whispered, and wiggled in her seat.

"The father of one of Tori's classmates."

"He's cute, in a Danny Glover rugged

kinda way. Is he married?"

"Divorced," Sheridan said, praying Kamora wouldn't ask for an introduction. Although Sheridan didn't know Carlton well, she knew enough to protect him from her flighty friend.

"Divorced, huh? So are you."

Sheridan twisted in her seat. "So?"

"You're divorced, he's divorced. What more do you need in common?"

Sheridan laughed. "A little bit more."

"Look at him," Kamora said, leaning in closer. "He can't take his eyes off you."

Sheridan tried to face forward but kept shifting to glance at Carlton.

"Look, he's getting up," Kamora said, sounding giddy. "He's coming over here."

Five seconds later Carlton said, "Hello, Sheridan," with an inflection that left no doubt he'd been raised in the most prominent neighborhoods in Boston and had probably spent summers in Martha's Vineyard.

Sheridan took his outstretched hand. "Hi, Carlton. Have you met my parents?"

"Yes, at last year's recital."

Beatrice and Cameron smiled and waved.

"And this is my friend, Kamora Johnson."

He nodded and Kamora scanned Carlton in his silver-buttoned navy blazer. “Sheridan tells me you’re divorced.”

It was a reflex that made Sheridan stomp on Kamora’s foot.

“Ouch!”

“Oh, I’m sorry,” Sheridan said, before she turned back to Carlton. “Well, it’s good to see you.”

“I was trying to help,” Kamora whispered, as she rubbed her wounded ankle.

Carlton said, “Sheridan, I heard . . . well, anyway, I’d love to give you a call sometime.”

Sheridan smiled; Kamora said, “That would be good . . . ouch!”

Sheridan kept her smile trained on Carlton. “I’ll call you.”

“Looking forward to it.” He took two steps and said over his shoulder, “By the way, you look terrific.”

He was barely out of earshot before Kamora said, “Why are you trying to spike me to death with your Manolos? I was trying to help you get your groove on.”

“First of all,” Sheridan hissed, “I don’t need any help, and second, my parents are sitting right next to you.”

Kamora glanced over her shoulder. “Your parents are hardly paying attention to us. Look at them holding hands. They're planning how they're going to get their groove on as soon as they leave this joint."

"Do you want me to stomp on your foot again?"

"No."

They laughed.

"Hi, Sheridan." As Quentin interrupted their conversation, Sheridan smiled. She turned around. Quentin stood there. And next to him stood Jett.

Sheridan rose as if her seat were on fire. She could barely get her mouth open to return his greeting. While Quentin stepped over to greet her parents, Sheridan glared at Jett.

"What are you doing here?" she hissed.

"I was invited." He paused. "I'm not trying to start anything, Sheridan," he said, keeping his voice low. "I wanted to see Tori. Quentin said this was a big day for her."

"You shouldn't be here." She turned her fury to Quentin. "I cannot believe you did this without telling me," she whispered.

He kept his smile, although he fooled no one. "I didn't know I had to get your approval."

"How could you do this?" She felt the

tears, and with a breath she shoved them back inside.

Cameron stood and urged Sheridan to take her seat. "We'll see you later, Quentin," he said, dismissing his son-in-law.

She followed her father because that was all she could do. She battled her tears and prayed for the auditorium lights to dim so she could release her anguish in private.

Beatrice leaned across Kamora. "Are you all right?"

Sheridan shook her head. "But there's nothing I can do about it," she sniffed. "He's already embarrassed all of us."

Beatrice handed Sheridan a tissue. "He didn't embarrass us, sweetheart. He's just trying to live his life."

You're supposed to be on my side.

"Well, I agree with Sheridan," Kamora said, with her arms crossed and her lips poked out. "Quentin should be here, but he should have had the good sense to leave Jett in the car. Preferably in a closed garage. With the engine still running."

Mercifully the lights dimmed, and a moment later Christopher was by her side, taking the aisle seat. The look of disdain he'd worn earlier was gone; in its place was concern.

"You okay, Mom?"

She nodded, afraid she'd be sorry later for any words she'd speak now.

Ms. Lott, the studio owner and an accomplished dancer, came onto the stage and gave thanks for everyone attending. Sheridan tried not to turn around. But curiosity won over good sense, and she twisted in her seat. It was difficult to see, with her view blocked by the darkness and the rows of people behind her.

"He's on the other side," Christopher whispered. "Where I was sitting."

Sheridan turned around and pretended her eyes were following the performance. But she couldn't see through the tears that blurred her vision. She sat through the series of dances, clapping when she heard others clap, cheering when she heard others cheer. It wasn't her own strength that made her stand at the end. Kamora gently cupped her elbow and helped her to join the ovation.

When the lights came on, Sheridan rushed to the bathroom. It wasn't until she stood at the mirror that she realized Kamora had followed her.

"I cannot believe he did that," Kamora muttered.

Sheridan dabbed at the black tracks her mascara had left.

"I mean, to show up like that," Kamora puffed.

Sheridan pulled a brush from her makeup pouch and dusted her face with powder.

"And to bring his lover," Kamora exclaimed.

Sheridan banged the brush on the counter. "Are you trying to make me feel bad?" she asked her friend's reflection in the mirror.

Kamora stepped backward. "Of course not."

"Then let's not talk about this," she said with exaggerated calm.

Kamora returned her gaze. "I was trying to help," she said, before she turned and left Sheridan alone.

Sheridan stayed at the mirror and smiled as women filled the restroom. She graciously accepted the compliments offered for Tori's performance.

But as she smiled, inside she raged. And inside she cried. And inside the stalker returned, bringing his images — of Quentin and Jett, walking down the aisle together, sitting together, watching Tori together. The stalker returned, this time as a thief, stealing the peace she'd worked so hard over the last weeks to find.

It was a long, slow ride home.

Sheridan had tried, but she couldn't find enough cheer to go out to dinner.

"Mom, Daddy, you guys take Tori out," Sheridan had pleaded when Tori bounced off the stage and rushed to her family, ready to revel in their adoration. "I'm going home."

"I'm going with you, Mom," Christopher insisted.

Beatrice tried to encourage her, but Sheridan had been steadfast in her grief.

"Are you sick, Mom?" Tori had asked.

"I'm not feeling well," Sheridan said, eyeing Quentin and Jett as they walked toward them.

"Daddy," Tori had exclaimed, and jumped into his arms. "I didn't know you were here."

"I wouldn't have missed this. You were terrific, sweetheart."

"Do you want to come to dinner with us?" Tori asked.

"Well," Quentin paused, glancing at Sheridan.

"Mommy's not going," Tori said. "She's not feeling well."

Quentin looked at Sheridan and his eyes apologized. "Are you okay?"

"I think you make her sick." Christopher scowled. Then he turned his visual rage to Jett.

Christopher's words shocked them all, but only Kamora looked like she was ready to give the second standing ovation of the night.

Sheridan took Christopher's hand. "Mom, Dad, we're gonna get out of here." She kissed Tori. "You were fabulous, sweetheart. Have a good time, okay?"

Tori grinned, then frowned at Christopher. But a moment later her hand was back inside her father's, grasping him as if she couldn't let go.

Sheridan kissed her parents, hugged Kamora, all the while holding Christopher — afraid of what he might do if she set him free.

"I'll call you," Kamora whispered. "And I'm sorry about . . . you know."

Sheridan nodded, then rushed from the auditorium, keeping her eyes away from Quentin and Jett. Wondering how he could be so thoughtless.

Those questions stayed with her as she and Christopher got into her car.

He allowed her to be quiet as they drove,

allowed her to stay inside her feelings. She was beyond the shock now. Only sadness remained as she realized this was another turning point.

For months she'd prayed that Jett would be little more than a name, that her children would never have to deal with him. But now Jett had invaded her whole life — her children, her parents, her friends, her acquaintances. Her humiliation was public.

She left the car in the driveway and followed Christopher into the house. The balloons he'd hung on the banister for Tori bounced with the breeze. When he started to untie the string, Sheridan stopped him.

"Leave them."

"I'm going to take them to her room," he said, as if he wanted to dispose of any reminder of the day.

"No, I want her to see them when she comes home."

He nodded. "Are you okay?"

Why is everyone asking me that?

"Yes." She plastered on a smile so fake, she knew not even Christopher would believe it.

"Let me know if you need anything," he said as he moved up the stairs.

In the living room Sheridan flopped onto the couch and closed her eyes. *What was*

Quentin thinking? she wondered again. But then, on the other side, she marveled at her own naiveté — how could she not have expected this day? This day when their lives had to converge because of the children they shared.

"Mom." Christopher bolted down the stairs, invading her thoughts. "Can I go over to Darryl's after the teen all-night praise jam at church Friday?"

Sheridan opened her eyes. He hadn't mentioned Darryl in months. And if he wanted to be with Darryl and not Brendan and Gary, then something good had come from this day.

"I forgot that was Friday. What's going on at Darryl's?"

"His mom invited some of the guys over for breakfast and to just hang out."

Thank you, Lord, Sheridan thought. She'd have to thank Darryl's mother too. And she'd thank the Lord again. There was no mention of Brendan or Gary . . . or Déjà.

"Déjà is going with me Friday."

I was beginning to think something good was coming out of this day. "How is she going to do that if you're going to Darryl's?"

"Brendan will take her home, or she'll

stay at his house. She's been staying over there a lot."

Just what I needed to hear, Sheridan thought, as she remembered that Brendan lived just a few blocks away.

She leaned back and closed her eyes as Christopher returned to his bedroom.

She hadn't come up with a plan to keep Christopher away from Déjà, so she made a mental note to talk to Quentin. The thought of him made her groan.

"Mom," Christopher yelled again, not allowing her time to brood. "Can I order a pizza?"

She opened her purse, taking loose bills from the pocket, and a card fell onto her lap. She stood, staring at the card. "I'm going upstairs," she said as she handed Christopher a twenty-dollar bill.

As she moved, she looked at the card again — Brock Goodman. She remembered their time together. Remembered how he kept her engaged and entertained. Remembered how good he made her feel. Remembered he was twenty-nine years old.

I should call and thank him for his time, she thought before she dialed the number. Her heart thumped faster when she heard his voice.

"Brock, this is Sheridan. Sheridan Hart. From church. We had coffee on Sunday —"

He laughed. "I know who you are. I've been waiting for you to call."

She struggled to keep her smile away, but she didn't win. "You have?"

"Yeah, in fact, I was sitting here saying, 'I wonder when Sheridan is going to call.' "

She laughed, kicked off her mules, and curled up on the bed. "I told you I wasn't going to call."

"And I told you, you would."

"I'm only calling to thank you for Sunday."

"For the coffee?"

Sheridan could hear the amusement in his tone. "Yes."

"So," he began, "now that that's done, what else do you have to say?"

"Nothing, I'm finished," she kidded.

He laughed. "Well, I have something to say. Have dinner with me."

She sat up. "I . . . don't think . . ."

"Ah, come on. You didn't think you would ever call me. Now you know you can do things you never thought possible. So have dinner with me."

"I don't know."

"There you go again," he said.

She frowned. "What do you mean?"

"Thinking that I'm asking you to marry me. I just want us to go on one date."

"Just one?"

"Aha. You do want to do this."

Before she could stop her mind, the stalker returned, with his backpack of images. She thought about her life. She thought about Quentin's life.

"Brock, I haven't dated in years, and even then, I didn't date much. I guess —"

Before she could finish, he said, "I can help there. I've dated a whole lot, enough for both of us."

She laughed. "That's supposed to make me feel better?"

"No, dinner will make you feel better."

Her telephone beeped, interrupting them. "Brock, hold on a sec?"

The moment she clicked over, he said, "Sheridan, do you have a moment to talk?"

Quentin stole the smile she'd been wearing since she'd heard Brock's voice. "There's nothing for us to talk about."

"I didn't mean to upset you. I just thought . . . the other day when we talked . . . I thought we were in a place where you accepted my life. And months have passed now. It was time to bring Jett into my world the way he's brought me into his."

She wondered what that meant. Had

Quentin met Jett's family? Had he been accepted as Jett's partner? "I think there was a better way to do it."

"Maybe. But all of this is new to me. Everything I do, I'm doing for the first time. I just want you to know I wasn't trying to hurt you."

"I'm on the other line," she said, not acknowledging his words. When he stayed quiet, she added, "I really am on the phone."

"Okay, but please call me back."

"If it's not too late."

She said good-bye and then clicked back to Brock.

Brock said, "I was beginning to think you'd forgotten about me."

"That would never happen."

"It was time to bring Jett into my world." She said, "I would love to have dinner with you."

"Wow," he exclaimed. "I was prepared to give you the top ten reasons why you should go out with me."

"I'd like to hear that."

"I'll save that for dinner. So let's do this tomorrow. I don't want you changing your mind."

She laughed on the outside. "I won't, but the weekend is better for me."

"Okay, but let's do it Friday. Let's not waste any days."

Sweet words, just like the ones Quentin used to say.

She gave him her number and address and then hung up after she made multiple promises not to cancel.

On the bed, she hugged her pillow. She didn't need to have a psychology degree to know what was going on. Barely three months had passed; her divorce wasn't even final. She'd sworn that she would never get near another man who wasn't her father, brother, or son.

Yet on Friday, she was going out with Brock Goodman.

This is not about Quentin.

She closed her eyes and imagined what Quentin would feel, think, say if he knew about Brock.

This is not about Quentin.

She pushed aside her reservations. This weekend would be perfect. Christopher would be at church, and she'd been promising Tori a sleepover with her friend Joy. She'd call Joy's mother and find out if Friday would work.

She closed her eyes and the stalker invaded her space, dragged her back to the recital. And Quentin. With Jett. She squeezed her eyes and tried to expunge the image. A moment later, she opened her eyes. Friday would be a good day. Maybe Brock Goodman could help her erase her stalker permanently.

Chapter Thirty-three

This is just a dinner.

Sheridan shook the raw silk pants suit off the hanger. She slipped the tank top over her head, careful not to disturb the hairstyle Crystal had given her, then stepped into the cabaret-style pants. She posed before the mirror.

This is just a dinner, nothing special.

Her shoes waited at the foot of her bed and she eased into the open-back pumps. She returned to the mirror and, as quickly as she'd been doing for years, completed her makeup, using her fingertips to smooth on lip gloss. When she stepped back and took the full view, she smiled her approval.

This is just a dinner, nothing special, just a distraction.

She picked up her purse as the grandfather clock struck eight. Downstairs she peeked through the curtains, not wanting to be seen if Brock was walking up to the door.

Five minutes later she was pacing.

It's just five minutes. And then the other

side said, *Suppose he's changed his mind?*

When the telephone rang, she jumped and ran to the kitchen.

"What are you up to?" Kamora asked.

I've got to get caller ID for this phone. "Nothing."

"Do you want to hang out with your best friend?"

"What are you doing home?" Sheridan asked, not remembering a time when Kamora called her on a Friday night.

"I was supposed to be with Sheldon tonight, but he canceled. So I was thinking about curling up with my *Columbo* tapes, and then I thought about you."

Great. I come after Sheldon — whoever he is — and Columbo.

Kamora said, "Do you want to go to the movies or something?"

"Nah." Sheridan studied the moving hands of the clock. "I'm going to cool out tonight."

"What're you doing?"

"Nothing much. Christopher and Tori are out."

"Great, I'll come over."

"No," Sheridan said a bit too quickly. "I really don't want to do anything." Then she added, "Just wanna rest." It didn't even sound good to her.

"Okay," Kamora said slowly.

"It's been a hard week," Sheridan continued. "With the recital, and Quentin, and Jett."

"Oh, sweetie. I didn't think about that."

Headlights beamed through the living room curtains and Sheridan sighed, relieved.

Kamora continued, "Are you okay?"

You have no idea. "Yeah, I'm fine. Listen, I've got to go."

"Okay, but call me if you want to talk."

When Sheridan opened the door, her first thought was that as fine as he looked in his uniform, Brock looked even better in his tan suit. And then she wondered why she'd given him her address. But she didn't know the dating rules; and now she didn't care. Not the way Brock Goodman looked standing in her foyer.

Brock glanced around the entryway. "You have a beautiful home, Sheridan. I got lost coming into this place. This is not on my route."

"I'm surprised; the church is not far and you deliver there, right?" she asked, as he helped her slip into her jacket.

"Yeah, but I don't come across Manchester."

He waited as she locked the front door, and then helped her into his Camry. Before he pulled out of the driveway, he pushed in a CD, and Lionel Richie's voice filled the car. "Zoom, zoom. I'd like to fly away."

"This is my all-time favorite song," Sheridan said.

"You're kidding. Mine too."

She looked at him out of the corner of her eye. "Were you even born when this song came out?" She was kidding but then did the calculation. *This boy was born in 1974.*

"Yeah . . . I think," he said, as he maneuvered through the streets. "But I love old-school music."

"Who you calling old?" She laughed.

"I meant the music, not you."

They were quiet for a moment, letting Lionel finish his serenade.

"I didn't ask where you wanted to go," Brock said.

"You decide."

He smiled. "I like that. I was thinking of checking out a new place — well, new for me. Everyone talks about it, and I wanted to take someone special."

That's sweet.

"Have you ever been to Carousels?"

She was glad her groan stayed inside. "I've been there."

"Did you like it?"

She shrugged, trying to hide her deep breaths.

"Do you want to go someplace else?"

She thought about Quentin and Jett. In Carousels. "Carousels is fine."

"Great." He grinned. "So, who do you like besides Lionel?" He held up his hand. "Wait, let me guess. Luther."

"Check."

"And Marvin."

"Double check."

He laughed. "They're my favorites too. Now see, aren't you glad you agreed to have dinner? We were made for each other."

She joined his laughter. "So, you only like these old-school guys?"

"No, I listen to all kinds of music. Especially hip-hop and rap."

"Really? After Marvin and Luther, how can you listen to that?"

"I listen to the words."

She scrunched her face. "It's the words that make me keep that music out of my house."

"I listen beyond the cursing. Get rid of the words you hate, and these kids are telling quite a story. Of their world, their trials, their tribulations. Of what they see every day, of what they hope for in life. It's no different than other musicians. Take Marvin. He sang about the social issues that were troubling him. The things he wanted to change."

"I know you're not comparing them to Marvin."

"Oh, no, but I believe their objective — their desire to be heard — is the same as it was for Marvin. They're using their talent to speak out."

She nodded, although she wasn't sure she agreed.

"These kids are the same as everyone else," he continued. "We all want someone to listen, and they sing to be heard. Through music, they know someone is listening."

As Brock eased into Carousels' parking lot, Sheridan scanned the spaces for Quentin's Mercedes or Jett's Jaguar. Seeing neither, she took Brock's hand when she stepped from the car. Inside, Joseph greeted her.

"Mrs. Hart, good to see you." The maître d's smile vanished when he noticed Brock behind her.

Sheridan rescued Joseph from his surprise. "This is my friend, Brock Goodman," she said.

The men shook hands, and Joseph's professionalism returned. He led them to their table and chatted as if he'd always seen the two of them together.

Once alone, Brock said, "So you've been here often."

"I wouldn't say often."

"Enough for Joseph to know your name."

She shrugged and leaned back, and as a waiter filled their water glasses, she glanced around.

"Looking for someone?" Brock took a sip of his water.

A rush of heat blanketed her face. She shook her head, took her own sip.

Brock placed his elbows on the table. "It's no problem. I know you have a history." He paused. "I have one too."

She raised her eyebrows. "Tell me about it."

"Already did. You know about my grandmother, what I think about the president, what kind of music I like. You even know where I work. But I don't know anything about you except you have children who can't help me reach my new registered voters quota."

She chuckled. "There's not much more than that to tell," she said, and thought how pitiful that fact was. Her life had been about being Quentin's wife, being Christopher and Tori's mother. She still had Hart to Heart, but she could count on one hand the hours she'd spent working on the business since she lost the man who had inspired their enterprise. She had to do something about her life.

Brock said, "I look at you and know there's more." He leaned forward, and Sheridan loved the way the flickering candlelight made his eyes dance. "I look at you and want to know everything."

"Are you ready to order?" the white-clad waiter asked.

Sheridan wanted to kiss the young man for the reprieve. The waiter stepped away while she and Brock scanned the menus. Even when Brock put his card down, Sheridan kept the list of culinary choices in front of her. It didn't matter that she'd already decided before she walked through the door what she was going to have. But the menu gave her a stay; not a word needed to be spoken while she supposedly agonized over her choices.

"There's so much here," she said, feeling Brock's stare. *I bet he's wondering right about now if I can even read.*

"Take your time."

"Are you ready?" the waiter said as he returned with his pad in hand.

They gave their orders, and once alone, Brock asked for her life story again.

Sheridan took a deep breath and gave the short answer. "I've lived in California my entire life, went to college here, married young, had children, started a business, divorced . . ."

"Is that something you can talk about?"

No. "There's not much to tell. Just didn't work out."

"I'm sorry."

She nodded. "It's a little like our favorite song. I've had many days when all I wanted to do was fly away."

"Well, I hope tonight you'll allow me to help you do that."

Every muscle in her body relaxed when he didn't push. "You've already done it," she said, as their drinks arrived.

Over a chocolate martini and a Samuel Adams, Sheridan bragged about Tori's recital.

Over her pine nut halibut and his prime tenderloin of beef, Brock talked about Charles Gibson, the young man he was mentoring who lived with a great-grandmother too old to care what her fifteen-year-old grandson was doing.

Over tiramisu cheesecake, they shared dessert and thoughts about what was most important in life.

"I want my children to be happy, well-adjusted adults," Sheridan said.

"You have the most important job in the world."

"That's why I always wanted to be a stay-at-home mom."

"I'm impressed you did that. I believe the future lies within us. Not only in the children we parent but in the children we impact just by being — by being in their communities, by being in the political process, by being involved in any manner. I'm a big fan of each one teach one. I just hope I can reach and teach two, three, four . . ." He stopped, but Sheridan understood his point.

She had no response. She didn't want to say what she felt. Brock Goodman was a special man.

When the waiter returned to fill their water glasses for the fourth time, Brock held up his hand and handed the young man the check with cash. Then he stood and took Sheridan's hand. She peeked at her watch as she slipped into her jacket, and couldn't believe it was almost midnight. They'd talked for over three hours, yet it didn't feel like any time had passed at all.

At the valet Brock held the door as she slid into his Camry, then he jumped into the driver's seat.

"I hope you had a good time," he said, as he eased the car from the parking lot.

She nodded and wished there was more. "I enjoyed talking to you."

Brock slipped another CD into the player, and Marvin Gaye sang on the ride home. As they edged off the freeway and stopped at the red light, a man hobbled toward their car. Sheridan shuddered as the man begged with his eyes. At this time of night she would never open her window if she were alone. A second before she opened her mouth and her purse, she felt the car pull forward — the moment to help, gone.

"I need to make a quick run, would you mind?" Brock said.

She frowned, wondering what he could possibly need to do at midnight. But before she could ask, he turned into a McDonald's and, at the drive-thru window, placed an order large enough to feed both of them.

"Don't tell me you're still hungry."

He laughed as he exchanged money for food, then sped back to the corner. He pulled to the edge of the curb and stopped the car, and before she could ask a question, Brock opened his glove compartment, grabbed a small book, and jumped out of the car. He dashed across the divider, dodging two cars speeding down La Cienega.

With wide eyes Sheridan watched Brock hand the bags of food and the book to the homeless man they'd passed minutes before and then chat with him as if they were friends. Minutes went by and he pulled a card from his suit and handed it to the man before he trotted back to his car.

Wordlessly he jumped into his seat, shifted the car into gear, and took off. Sheridan twisted slightly so she could see him better.

"What?" he asked, when her stare stayed with him.

"That food was for him," she said, stating the obvious.

He nodded. "Wanted to make sure he had something to eat."

"And something to read?"

Slowing the car, he reached over her, opened the glove compartment, and handed her a book like the one he had pulled out before.

In the dark she could see the gold letters — *Holy Bible, Pocket Edition.* She looked at Brock as if she hadn't just spent hours with him.

Again he said, "What?"

She smiled. How could she tell him all that she thought when she looked at him? "Nothing. I just think . . . that was very nice."

He leaned across the console. Before she could imagine what was happening, his hand touched hers. The moment was tender . . . and electric. His long fingers wrapped around her hand and squeezed gently. Then just as fast as his touch was there, it was gone.

She kept her eyes away from his, looking through the windshield, remembering his touch and the shivers that had surged inside her.

It's a good thing he's just dropping me off, she thought, as he turned into her driveway.

Brock turned off the car, and Sheridan was surprised when she turned to him and he opened his door, leaving her. She'd been hoping he would touch her again. Give her a good-night kiss. Something to help her remember this night.

He's way too much of a gentleman.

He helped her from the car, then walked her to the front door. For years she'd been able to open the door with her eyes closed, but tonight she fumbled with the key. Finally the lock clicked, and she turned back to Brock. In the dark his eyes were like matches, burning right through her.

"I had a great time," she was able to say.

"I tried to tell you. Dinner with me is always a good time. So, I won't have to work so hard to get a date next time, right?"

Next time? She smiled. "I'll give you a call." She moved to turn, but he stepped closer, blocking her.

"I was hoping you'd give me something more."

The horror on her face made him laugh. "A good-night kiss, Sheridan. That's all." Then his cheer went away, and his fiery gaze made her smolder some more.

Sheridan's eyes darted around the surrounding homes, settling on Mrs. James's across the street. She imagined the old woman peeking from behind those heavy curtains, watching her kissing a stranger at midnight.

"Why don't you come inside?" she said.

It was his turn to show surprise and

Sheridan's turn to laugh. "I don't want my neighbors . . ."

He nodded and followed Sheridan. The light from the outside door illuminated the room, washing it in a golden glow.

She leaned against the banister. "You know, Brock, I don't know the rules, but I'm sure no one kisses on the first date."

He chuckled. "You're right. You don't know the rules. People do a lot more than kiss."

She shook her head. "Not this girl," she said playfully.

"Glad to hear that." She frowned, and he said, "Glad to know I was right about you. With what women are willing to do these days, it's nice to meet someone who holds on to their principles." He paused. "So good night, Sheridan."

When he moved toward the door, she wanted to scream that she'd only been kidding. She wanted to at least feel his lips on hers. But before the words rushed from her, he turned around.

"You know, technically," he began, rubbing his chin as if he were in deep thought, "this isn't really our first date. We've been out twice — really three times."

She laughed and crossed her arms. "You have to explain that to me."

"Well," he said, taking a step toward her, "the first time was when we met at church." He held up his hand, stopping her protest. "In many circles, those five minutes count as a date. Now the second time," he took another step, closing the space between them, "was when we were at Starbucks. Any time you spend a couple of hours with someone, it's definitely a date." He paused as he took another step. "And the third time," he held up his hands as if he were resting his case, "was this wonderful evening." The next step he took put him so close she could smell the lingering aroma of the cheesecake they'd shared. "So you see, Ms. Hart," he said in that voice that had the potential to bring her to her knees, "I've been waiting for a kiss for a long time."

She would have laughed if her heart weren't beating so fast. With the confidence he'd worn since the moment they'd met, he lowered his lips to hers. His kiss was tender, soft, wonderful, just as she'd imagined. When his arms wrapped around her, her purse slipped through her fingers, and she fell into the gentleness of his embrace.

And then the stalker returned.

The images of Quentin and Jett. Holding

hands. Touching. Kissing. Caressing.

She moaned, trying to push the images away. She moaned and he pulled her closer.

He leaned into her, and she could feel every inch of his desire. He wanted her. Quentin wanted Jett.

For a moment his tongue left hers, and he kissed her face, her neck, her shoulder, making her quiver.

"Sheridan," he whispered in that voice.

She was ready to bow down. The heat inside her rose, taking her to a place where she had to have more.

Still connected, she backed him toward the staircase until he hit the first step. He pulled back slightly, and his eyes asked the question. Her lips answered when she pressed her mouth to his, and they climbed the stairs, legs, arms, lips entwined.

She wasn't sure how they made it to her bedroom, but she was more amazed they were still wearing clothes.

He slipped her jacket from her shoulders and massaged her bare arms until goosebumps were on every part of her. He took off her top, and then his tongue teased her.

She wanted to scream, demand that he take her, take her quickly, or she would die. But she couldn't pull her lips away to tell him.

She was sure hours had passed before she was standing covered only by her La Perla bra and panties. He pulled back for a moment, and she hoped it was a smile of appreciation that crossed his face.

He laid her on the bed, but when she reached for the buttons on his shirt, he gently pushed her hand away and stood.

"I just want to look at you," he said.

He shrugged the jacket from his shoulders and unbuttoned his shirt. His eyes never left her as he stripped, slowly, seductively, making her a promise.

His eyes seared her. "You are so beautiful."

Still he stood above her, until his naked, muscle-packed body glistened in the dark.

Still he stood above her, and she felt as beautiful as he said she was.

Still he stood above her. His eyes whispering that he wanted her. Her eyes screaming that she needed him.

It was torture. It was agony. It was ecstasy.

When he finally lowered his weight onto her, she kissed him, grateful to feel him once more.

His lips, his hands, his eyes did things to

her she'd almost forgotten. He rolled over, pulling her on top. She removed her bra, and drank in the lust, love — it didn't matter what it was — that was in his eyes.

She was a woman.

Wanted by a man.

She kissed him, then frowned when he reached for his jacket. It took a moment for her to recognize the plastic packet.

What am I doing here?

But that questioning thought was gone when he joined with her and she moaned as if it were her first time.

"Are you okay?" he whispered.

She nodded, because she had forgotten how to speak English. But the memory of love rushed throughout her body. And she forgot who she was. The only thing she knew was she wanted this man.

He made love to her as if he loved her. Slowly, at times. Gently, at times. Urgently, always. He caressed her with words, telling her he wanted every part of her.

And she drank in all that he said.

Their love continued for hours, until there was no more within them. At the end she collapsed into his arms. And he held her. And planted small kisses on top of her head. And he held her some more. Then he slept.

She didn't close her eyes. She didn't want to sleep. She just wanted to rest and remember.

Her legs covered his. His arms covered hers.

Sheridan opened her eyes to the glow of the new day's sun peeking through the curtains. She had no idea what time it was, even though she'd fought to stay awake, wanting to be aware of each passing hour.

She twisted, trying to glance at the clock, but Brock's embrace tightened. She wondered if he was awake. But his eyes were closed, his breathing sleep-steady. Even in his unconsciousness, he wanted her near.

"You wake up early," he said, shattering that thought.

Still she smiled. "It's not early." She sat up and pulled a corner of the sheet over her. The clock told her she'd been right. It was just after ten.

"It's early to me." He turned on his side, rested on his elbow, and tugged the sheet from her, leaving her exposed.

She combed through her hair and turned away from his stare. With his fingers, he brought her back, making her look at him. "I had a wonderful time last night," he said, as if he knew those were the words she needed to hear.

She leaned back and he sat up. He kissed her, gently. But then passion grew and she begged him to take her again.

"Mom!"

Sheridan's eyes opened wide. "Oh. My. God." She tore from Brock's embrace and jumped from the bed. "That's my son."

"Okay." Brock held up his hands. "Go talk to him. I'll get dressed and then get out of here without him seeing me."

Sheridan grabbed her robe. She was shaking when Brock jumped from the bed and held her for a moment. "It's going to be okay."

"Mom!"

His voice was closer. Sheridan stepped into the hallway, closing her bedroom door behind her. "Christopher, what are you doing home?"

He grinned. "Is that any way to speak to your number one son? I thought you'd be glad to see me." He handed her purse to her. "This was on the floor downstairs."

She grabbed her bag and waved her hand in the air. "It must have fallen . . ."

He moved toward his bedroom. "I just came to change my clothes and get my golf clubs. Darryl's mom's going to take us to the course."

Darryl. Golf. She would have been delighted if she weren't terrified.

Christopher stepped into his bedroom, and Sheridan leaned against the wall. But before she could inhale a breath of relief, Christopher leaned back into the hallway.

"Whose car's in the driveway?"

Oh, my God. "Ah, it belongs to a friend. Who had to leave his . . . their car here overnight . . . because . . . he . . . they needed to leave it." She hoped it didn't sound as stupid to him as it did to her.

Christopher frowned, shrugged, and then stepped back into his room, and Sheridan tiptoed back into hers. She had a quick moment of relief when Brock stood before her, dressed.

"I'm ready," he whispered.

"Let me make sure he's still in his bedroom." Sheridan reached for the doorknob, but Brock pulled her to him. He kissed her, and even though her son was just feet away, she reveled in the embrace for a moment.

When she stepped back, he said, "I'll call you."

Sheridan peeked outside and then nodded to Brock. They stepped into the hallway.

"Mom!" Christopher came from his bedroom before they had taken three steps. "Mom?"

She decided this would be the perfect moment for Jesus to return. But then she wondered why she would turn to Him now. Although she had called His name a million times last night, she hadn't been thinking about Jesus at all.

Sheridan took a breath, turned around, and said, "Christopher," as if she were delighted to see him.

He moved toward her, his eyes all the time on Brock.

"Christopher, this is Brock Goodman." She wanted to say more but couldn't think of any new words.

Brock held out his hand. Moments passed, but Brock held his smile and his hand in the air. Finally, without a word, Christopher shook his hand, turned, and walked back toward his bedroom.

"Christopher, did you need anything?" Sheridan asked.

"Naw, never mind." This time, he closed his bedroom door, and Sheridan closed her eyes.

"I'm sorry," Brock said.

At the bottom of the stairs, he said, "I'm sorry about Christopher, but I'm not sorry about last night."

She allowed herself a moment to remember.

He touched her chin. "I'll call you," he said before he stepped out the door.

Her eyes followed him, and she stood until the Camry backed out of the driveway.

When she turned around, Christopher was at the top of the stairs with his golf bag draped over his shoulder.

Sheridan tightened her robe.

"I'm going back to Darryl's," he said, as he bounced toward her. He stopped at the door. "Is it okay if I spend the night over there?"

She swallowed the lump in her throat and nodded. She had to say something. "How was last night?" she asked.

"Fine." He looked at her. "How was last night for you?"

She wanted to slap him; wanted to slap herself even more. Didn't know what to say. "Christopher, I'm sorry about what happened. What you saw. I shouldn't have . . ."

He held up his hands. "It's cool, Mom. I understand. Everyone has their needs. See ya later." He closed the door, leaving her standing alone.

"Everyone has their needs"?

Sheridan didn't even want to imagine. With each step she took up the stairs, the dreadful moments played in her mind. Brock tiptoeing out of the room. Christopher charging out of his. The second their eyes met. Sheridan wished she could pray the last fifteen minutes from existence.

But when she entered the bedroom, the memories of the night rushed over her like a waterfall, washing away the guilt, dousing her with pleasure. She lay on the tousled sheets and bed cover, allowing her mind to revisit the hours. There were parts where she smiled, moments when she shuddered. Even as guilt crept back to her, she wished she could go back twelve hours and live inside each minute again.

She sighed as she rubbed the sheets where he'd slept. *I can't do that again.* It was beyond her wanting to do right by her children. This was about wanting to do right by God.

She closed her eyes and prayed. Asked God for forgiveness. Asked Him for strength. Asked Him for guidance, because there was no doubt she wanted to see Brock Goodman. And she wasn't sure what her walk with God would look like when they got together again.

Chapter Thirty-four

"Pastor, I have to cancel tomorrow," Sheridan mouthed as Pastor Ford stepped from the altar after the service. The pastor motioned for her to come closer, and Sheridan took a deep breath before she moved.

"You can't make it tomorrow?" the pastor asked.

Sheridan shook her head because she didn't want to lie out loud. Didn't seem like a good idea — to be telling a lie, on Sunday, in God's house, to her pastor, in front of the altar. Especially after what she'd done this weekend.

"Okay." The pastor took Sheridan's hand. "How are you doing?"

"Great. Well. Fine."

Pastor Ford squinted and Sheridan held her breath, praying that her pastor wouldn't have a vision. When Pastor Ford said, "I'll see you in Bible study on Tuesday," Sheridan nodded. She had no intention of seeing Pastor Ford alone for at least a week. By then, maybe God would have so many other things on Pastor Ford's mind that she wouldn't be able to look at her and immediately know Sheridan Hart was the church's biggest fornicator.

As Pastor Ford walked to her office, Sheridan sauntered toward the back of the sanctuary. Her eyes continued to do what they'd been doing all morning — searching for Brock.

She'd squirmed through the entire service, barely able to keep her eyes on the scriptures, barely able to keep her mind on the pastor. Instead, her body twisted as her eyes roamed through the church.

She'd been sure he'd be in church after she hadn't heard from him. Yesterday she'd expected him to go home, rest a while, then call to check on her and Christopher — and to remind her that he'd had a wonderful time.

But when her phone didn't ring, Sheridan had slept, knowing she'd see Brock in church today. But he wasn't there, and as Sheridan scanned the second-service worshippers, there was still no sign of the man she'd given herself to.

"Hi, Mom."

Her thoughts had taken her so far away that Sheridan hadn't seen Christopher approach her.

"Hey." She hugged him. "I didn't know

which service you were coming to."

"We came to the first one."

"Okay. So, do you want to ride home with me?"

He nodded.

As they walked toward the parking lot, Sheridan couldn't keep her eyes away from the thinning crowd.

"Are you looking for someone?" he asked, as if he already knew the answer.

She shook her head. In the car she asked, "Do you need to pick anything up from Darryl's?"

"Naw, I'll do it later. Darryl's going to his father's house today."

Sheridan eased into traffic and hoped to find words to say. *Should I wait until we get home?* "Do you want to pick up something to eat?"

Christopher nodded. "Can we stop at McDonald's?"

If she didn't need a bribe, she would have made another choice for him. But if he wanted twelve Double Quarter Pounders with cheese and as many supersized fries, she was willing to buy it all if it would help her now.

The next words Christopher spoke were to the drive-thru attendant as Sheridan searched for what needed to be said. While he yelled his order, Sheridan prayed, then waited until they turned back onto Century Boulevard.

"I want to talk to you."

Christopher popped a french fry in his mouth.

She said, "I'm really sorry —"

"I told you, Mom, it's okay."

"No, it's not."

"Maybe it's not, but I can't tell you that."

"Yes, you can. You know right from wrong."

"Yeah, but everyone makes mistakes. Even you, Mom." He paused. "I'm not mad about it or anything. I understand. It was because of Dad."

"This has nothing to do with your father."

He shrugged. "Okay. But it doesn't have anything to do with me either."

"Why do you keep . . ." She stopped. Christopher didn't want to have this discussion. Not about his mother — with a man who was not his father — having sex. And how could she blame him? She was almost forty and still wanted to believe her parents had had sex only twice, for the pure purpose of procreating. She'd never talked to her mother or father about sex.

Maybe I need to break this cycle, she thought. And then the other side of her said, *Maybe this isn't the time.*

"Oh, no, what's Dad doing here?" Christopher groaned, tugging her from her thoughts.

She turned into their driveway. "I don't know. I guess we'll find out."

She climbed from the SUV, but when Christopher got out, he said, "I'm going to Darryl's."

"I thought Darryl wasn't home."

"Then I'll go to the park or see if Brendan's home. Déjà may still be over there."

Sheridan watched her son trot down the street, away from his home, far from his father.

Inside the house, Quentin's jacket was tossed over the settee and he was on the couch, leaning back, his eyes closed, as Barbra Streisand sang his favorite song, "Evergreen," to him. Sheridan paused at the entryway, staring at Quentin posed in the way she had found him so many times before.

"Quentin."

He opened his eyes. "I didn't hear you come in."

She lowered the stereo's volume. "You

can't come in here anytime you want."

He shrugged. "I knew you were at church. I didn't think it would be a problem."

"Well, it is a problem, because this is my home now. I don't have a key to your house. And even if I did, I wouldn't just barge in there."

"Okay, but it's not like . . ." He stopped.

"Not like what? Not like I may have someone here?"

A slight grin slipped over his face. "Well, I *was* going to say that," he teased.

"Well, if you said that, you'd be wrong."

His smile left. "What do you mean?" He looked at her as if he was trying to discover the meaning behind her words.

She crossed her arms. "Did you want anything?"

He stood. "You called me about the mail. And I wanted to see if everything was all right with you and the kids."

"Why would something be wrong?"

"I didn't think anything was wrong, Sheridan. I was just checking."

"We're all fine." *Except for the fact that I haven't heard from Brock.* "Although Christopher was upset when we drove up and saw your car. He took off." As soon as the look of hurt swept over him, she regretted her words.

"Well," he slapped his hands against his legs. "I'll get going."

She sighed as she watched him walk away. Yes, she felt awful not hearing from Brock, but no, she didn't have to bring Quentin down with her.

Quentin picked up the pile of envelopes and slipped into his jacket. "Tell Tori I'll call her tonight."

Sheridan said, "She'll be back from Joy's around seven."

"Okay." He glanced at her. "I'm sorry about the key. Do you want it back?"

She shook her head. "Not yet. You may need it one time for the children or something. I just want you to call before you come over."

He nodded. And then, he left.

Sheridan felt no joy as Quentin swaggered to his car. And she felt even worse when she went upstairs and waited for Brock to call.

Chapter Thirty-five

Sheridan closed the door just as the school van pulled away. She glanced at the clock and counted again. It had been almost seventy hours since she'd seen or heard from Brock and he had consumed most of her mind for most of those hours. *If he doesn't want to call, that's fine,* she told herself.

But minutes later she was studying the clock, counting again, wondering if it was really approaching seventy-one hours since she'd last seen him.

"I need to do something," she said for at least the thousandth time. She searched, seeking tasks to keep her thoughts away from a man she'd spent no more than ten waking hours with. But it was those other hours — the ones they'd spent in bed — that consumed her.

She put this morning's plates into the dishwasher, then stood, staring out the window, until the machine stopped forty-five minutes later. Then she fluffed every pillow on the couch and chairs in the living room, changed the linen in all the bedrooms, and vacuumed the two levels of the house even though her housekeeper had done the same yesterday.

When there was nothing else to clean, she wandered into the office, praying to find peace in the midst of Hart to Heart. But in minutes, she raised herself from her executive chair and left the office without having moved one paper.

She leapt into a pair of jeans, brushed her fingers through her hair, grabbed her leather jacket, and rushed to the car. She turned on the ignition even though she had no place to go. But she had to get away — from the ticking clock that teased her with the passing of time, and the telephone that taunted her with its refusal to ring.

"Maybe this is what he does," she spoke aloud as she maneuvered through the streets. "Maybe he preys on desperate women." She never imagined herself to be like one of those women in those Lifetime movies. But here she was, wandering through the city like a nomad, with her mind fixed on one thing. She had turned into one of those girl-you-need-to-get-yourself-together Lifetime heroines.

"Gas is too expensive for this," she exclaimed as she made a right onto Lincoln Boulevard.

Ten minutes later, she parked her Explorer in the no-parking zone and clicked on her cell. Once she was put through, she said, "Do you have some time for your best friend?"

"Yeah, girl, what's up?"

"Need to talk."

"Wanna meet for dinner?"

"Look out your window."

"What?"

"Look out your window," Sheridan repeated.

She could hear Kamora's pumps clicking on the hardwood floor of her office, and then Sheridan looked up through her sun roof.

"This must be an emergency," Kamora said as she waved. "Come on up."

Sheridan pulled her car into the underground garage and took the elevator to Kamora's office. Once Kamora closed the door behind her, she asked, "What's up?"

Sheridan sank onto the couch. "Thanks for seeing me. I know you're busy."

"This is what we do." She sat next to Sheridan. "Is Quentin giving you a hard time?"

Sheridan almost laughed at her words. It wasn't Quentin who had given her a hard time. She shook her head. "This isn't about Quentin. But before I tell you, you have to promise you'll never repeat this."

Kamora looked at her as if she was crazy. "Who am I going to tell?"

"I don't even want you to say anything to any of your guy friends."

Kamora chuckled. "Girl, when I get with a man, I'm not talking or thinking about you."

"And you have to promise . . ."

"Enough with the promises. Just tell me."

Sheridan took a breath. "I had a date Friday night."

Kamora frowned. "The night I was going to come over to your house?"

Sheridan nodded.

"So, my girl is getting out again. Well, good for you. So, who did you go out with?" And then Kamora snapped her fingers. "Oh, that guy from the recital who sounded like a black Kennedy."

"No, not Carlton. This is a man I met at the church. Brock Goodman."

"A church guy. Well, at least he won't have his hands all over you."

Sheridan wanted to explain that he wasn't actually a church guy, but she was buckled over with laughter.

"What's so funny?" Kamora asked.

"He had more than his hands all over

me. He had his hands, and his mouth, and his . . ." She stopped.

Kamora's eyes widened. "Girl, don't tell me you did the nasty," she whispered as if they were in tenth grade exchanging secrets.

Sheridan nodded.

Kamora leapt from the couch and clapped as if she'd just won on *The Price Is Right*. "You are kidding me."

"I wish I was kidding. I cannot believe I did that."

Kamora rejoined her on the couch. "Why not? You're human. And I've been trying to tell you, this is a hard walk." She paused and waved her hands. "I know what you're going to say about God not being pleased . . ."

"He's not."

"And all of that," Kamora continued, ignoring Sheridan. "But it's just the way things are these days. You've got to know the whole man — know in the biblical sense." She bounced back on the couch and kicked her feet in the air. "I want details, girl."

Sheridan sighed. "Well, let's just say I know why God set it up like this. Why He says if you're not married, no sex, period."

Kamora closed her eyes and groaned.

"Because He knows it will end up like this," Sheridan continued. "He knows you will give yourself to a man and then never hear from him again."

Kamora opened one eye and peeked at Sheridan. "What you talkin' 'bout, Willis?"

"He hasn't called me," Sheridan wailed. "He left Saturday morning, right after Christopher found us."

"Christopher?" Kamora's scream lifted her from the couch.

Sheridan grabbed her hand and pulled her back. "I'll tell you about that later, but Brock said he would call, and I haven't heard from him."

"Was this the first time you guys went out?"

She nodded. "First time. We went out. We had sex. Wrong move on every level."

Kamora paced in front of the couch. "Well, I agree. I don't believe in first-date contact."

"You make it sound like football."

"Girl, with me, sometimes it is." She waved her hands. "But don't distract me. I've got to figure this out. So he said he'd call and then he didn't. And so you called him and —"

"I didn't call him," Sheridan said, as if she was offended. "I don't call men."

Kamora laughed. "You sleep with men *on* the first date, but you won't call them *after* the first date."

It sounded ridiculous to Sheridan too.

Kamora continued, "Girl, welcome to the new millennium. This is how we do it." She held her phone out for Sheridan. "Call him."

"I'll call him on my cell," Sheridan said, although she had no intention of doing that.

Kamora shook her head. "No, he'll recognize your number, and if he's playing possum, he won't answer. But this way you can trick his butt and catch him."

"I don't want him that way."

"I know, but the point is to find out what's going on with this bozo."

She wanted to tell Kamora that Brock was no bozo, but somehow Kamora's words made sense. She did want to know what was going on. With reluctance she took the phone and dialed the number she had already committed to memory.

She held her breath as it rang. And then after the fourth ring: "Hey, this is the good man. When you hear the beep, do your thing." *Beep.*

Sheridan did her thing and hung up. "Voice mail."

"Try again," Kamora encouraged. "You never know."

Sheridan followed her friend's advice, only to get the same message. Sheridan sighed, waiting for further instructions.

"So that didn't work," Kamora said. "Do you know where he lives?"

"No," Sheridan yelled, as if she couldn't believe the question. She could imagine what Kamora had in mind. "And even if I did, wouldn't be going over there."

Kamora looked as if she was disappointed. "Oh, well. We'll figure out something." She grabbed her jacket.

"Where are you going?" Sheridan asked.

"With you. First we're going to do a little shopping, clear our minds enough to come up with a plan. Then we'll go to dinner and discuss strategy."

"I can't. I have two children who'll be home from school in a couple of hours."

"Girl, please. Chris can take care of himself and Tori for a few hours. Call him, tell him to order pizza and you'll see him later."

Sheridan was grateful for the invitation. It would keep her away. Away from the clock. Away from the phone. "Okay, but I feel like a terrible mother. I'm always feeding my kids pizza."

"Honey, if Chris found you and what's-his-name doing the do, pizza is not what makes you a terrible mother." Kamora laughed.

Sheridan sucked her teeth. "Thanks for making me feel worse."

Kamora hooked her arm through Sheridan's, guided her toward the elevators, and asked, "So tell me now, what exactly did Chris see?"

Sheridan parked her car in the driveway. At least Kamora had kept her entertained. Shopping, dinner, then a movie. And she'd thought about Brock no more than one hundred times.

Through the sunroof, she glanced up to the darkened heavens, knowing this was just another lesson.

"How many more of these lessons about men are there?"

She was sure she'd never trust any man besides her father, brother, and son again.

As Sheridan moved toward her front door, she was surprised that the entire downstairs was dark. She stepped into her home, flicked on the light, and shrieked.

Her scream made Christopher and Déjà jump from the couch. But not before Déjà lowered her T-shirt over her naked chest.

Sheridan inhaled as much oxygen as she could.

"Christopher," she yelled. "What is going on?"

"Nothing."

That word and the fact that he didn't even look afraid fueled her fury. She marched into the living room. "What is going on? Where's Tori?"

"She's up in her room, Mom. I was just waiting for you."

"This is how you wait?"

He shrugged. "Déjà's stranded. She missed the last bus and Brendan is in Mississippi."

Sheridan wanted to ask why Brendan hadn't taken Déjà with him.

Christopher continued, "So I was going to drive her home. Can I borrow your car?"

She wanted to slap Christopher upside his head. "How are you going to do that? You can't drive after dark."

"I thought you'd let me do it this one time."

She had no idea how she kept the rest of her screams inside. What happened to her intelligent son? The one she had thought about minutes before — the one she believed she could always trust?

Sheridan turned her glare to Déjà. The girl smiled and then blew her signature bubblegum bubble. Sheridan wanted to smash the gum in her face.

"You don't have any way to get home?" Sheridan asked.

Déjà shook her head.

What about walking?

Déjà smiled. "I can stay here. My dad won't mind."

You have lost your mind. "I'll take you home," Sheridan growled.

Christopher said, "I'll ride with you."

She needed to get away from this boy before she beat him down. "Who's going to stay with Tori?" she asked in a tone that told him she thought he was stupid.

"She can come with us?" It was supposed to be a statement.

Sheridan didn't even bother to answer. "Get your things, Déjà," she demanded, looking at the girl because she couldn't stand looking at her son.

Déjà grabbed her bag. "This is all I have." As she held her purse up, Sheridan noticed that her nails still claimed Christopher; this time the long, curved nails were sapphire blue.

Sheridan marched toward the front door. "Christopher, check on your sister.

And make sure your homework is done. I'll speak with you when I get back."

She rushed to her car, but when she got inside, Déjà was not behind her. Christopher and Déjà were in the doorway, standing under the light, kissing as if they'd never see each other again.

Sheridan blasted the horn, startling them both. She shook with anger as she leaned on the horn again, not caring if she awakened Mrs. James. Not caring if she awakened everyone in the entire county of Los Angeles.

Déjà jumped into the front seat and waved until Christopher was out of sight.

"Where do you live, Déjà?"

"In Pomona. On Lemon Street, right off the freeway."

Pomona. Sheridan had forgotten. She glanced at the clock. By the time she drove this child home and then came back, it would be after midnight.

For more than fifteen minutes they exchanged no words. Déjà chewed her gum as if it were her job, and Sheridan drove, her anger simmering.

Finally Déjà said, "You don't like me much, do you?"

What was your first clue? "It doesn't matter if I do or don't, does it?"

"It matters to me," Déjà said softly, "because I love Chris."

Oh, brother.

"I really do," Déjà said, as if she knew Sheridan's thoughts. "And he loves me."

"Christopher is not old enough to be in love, Déjà."

"I think he is, Ms. Hart." She twisted in her seat and faced Sheridan. "You don't know him like I do."

Now Sheridan wanted to slap her too. "You've known Christopher for five minutes. I've known him since I carried him in my womb. Tell me again that I don't know him like you do."

Déjà sighed, popped another bubble, and said, "Why don't you like me?"

She couldn't say all of the words that would explain it, so instead she said, "Let me ask you this. You're eighteen. What do you want with a boy so young?"

"He's not that young, and he's really not a boy, Ms. Hart."

Sheridan gripped the wheel. "He *is* a boy, Déjà. He's a boy playing grown-up. And you should know better." As she said the words, her insides stirred. In some other place, at some other time, this conversation could be happening — but she wouldn't be in the driver's seat. Brock's mother could be glaring at her as if she were some misfit corrupting her baby boy. His mother could ask her what she wanted with a man so young.

But at least he's a man. Still, her thoughts didn't make her feel better. What was the difference between her and Déjà?

Déjà said, "I don't see anything wrong with me and Chris being together. We have fun and he's taught me a lot of things. He's not like all those other guys I've been with."

Oh, God. "I'm sure he's not like the boys you know," Sheridan said, and then tried to suck back her words. "Look, Déjà," she said, softening her tone. "In less than two years, Christopher will be going to college. He'll leave home, probably leave California." *If I have my way, he'll be going to school in China.* "Besides the fact that he's so young, that's another reason why it doesn't make sense for him to be in a relationship."

Déjà leaned back. "He told me you liked Nicole Blake. What's the difference between her and me?"

Only God's grace kept her from laughing and really hurting this girl. "It doesn't make any difference to me who the girl is. Christopher is too young, and I'm not going to allow this to go on."

Sheridan clicked on the radio, but when she heard Luther crooning about how love had been good to him, she flicked to another station. She settled on KKLA and the Christian broadcast *Focus on the Family*. This girl needed to hear something uplifting, inspirational — a message that would convince her to keep her behind away from Christopher Hart.

Forty-five minutes later Sheridan stopped her car in front of Déjà's home.

"Thank you, Ms. Hart," Déjà said, and hopped out of the car.

Sheridan glanced at the clock. It was just after eleven. Too late to go into anyone's home. But this was a desperate matter that called for a desperate measure. "I'd like to meet your father. Is it too late?"

Déjà frowned. "No, but I don't know if he's home yet. He usually hangs out when he gets off work."

Sheridan nodded. "Let's see if he's home."

They walked up the driveway of the stucco ranch-style home, past a gray truck with more rust than paint.

"What's your father's name?"

"Harold."

"No, I mean, what's your last name?"

"Blue. His name is Harold Blue."

Sheridan nodded but then almost tripped on the concrete path when she realized what that meant. *This child's name is Déjà Blue.* Before she had a chance to recover she stepped into the house.

It could have been the middle of the day, judging from the sounds of the Blue household. Although no one was in the front room, Sheridan's ears were accosted by a baby's cries and toddlers' squeals. Still, she was able to hear the sounds from a television that was slightly overpowered by a CD blasting, "Lean over to the front and touch your toes."

As her eyes wandered through the space, the first word that came to her mind was *brown.* Everything was the color of mud: the pleather couch, the stained recliner, the bookshelves, the carpet — even the curtains that hung at the window were a drab brown.

Déjà tossed her purse on the brown table and walked toward the hallway. "Daddy," she yelled.

"What are you screaming for, girl?" a voice bellowed back.

"Daddy, Chris's mom wants to meet you," Déjà shrieked. Then she turned to

Sheridan and spoke softly. "Have a seat, Ms. Hart."

Sheridan looked again at the couch, covered with empty KFC bags, soda cans, and toddler's toys. Her glance moved to the stains on the recliner and she wondered what they were. She shook her head and stepped back, moving closer to the door. "No, thank you. I won't be staying long."

"What did you say?" Déjà's father spoke as loud when he entered the room as he did when he yelled from the back. He stopped when he saw Sheridan and grinned as his eyes roamed over her body one inch at a time.

Sheridan pulled the belt of her trench coat tighter.

"Daddy, this is Ms. Hart, Chris's mother."

Harold Blue was a big man who stretched his clothes beyond their size. His white T-shirt hugged his chest and barely covered his stomach. He wore jeans that were hip huggers, not because of style, but because he couldn't get the pants to his waist over the rolls of skin that bulged from his side.

Sheridan kept her eyes on his eyes. "Hello, Mr. Blue."

"Yeah." His grin widened. "Nice to meet

you." He motioned for her to have a seat. "Do you want a beer?" he asked as he popped a cigarette into his mouth and sat on the couch.

And then she noticed it. His name shouldn't have been Blue; it should have been Brown. He was the same color as everything around him. "No, thank you," she said to his offer of beer. "Mr. Blue, I apologize for disturbing you so late."

"Ah, it's not late," he said. "It's not even midnight." Then he screamed, "Would you guys turn that noise down? We got company." But the chaos continued as if he hadn't spoken. He looked back at Sheridan and grinned again. "Sorry."

Sheridan didn't return his smile. "I drove Déjà home tonight because she missed the last bus."

His face stiffened when he turned to Déjà. "How'd you do that?"

Déjà flipped open the top of a soda can and shrugged.

He turned back to Sheridan. "Thank you. I know it was a long ride, because Déjà told me you guys live in one of those fancy homes near Ladera."

"Mr. Blue, when I came home, I found Déjà with my son." A baby's wail came from the back. She paused and looked at

Déjà. She leaned against the counter separating the living room from the kitchen. Sheridan was surprised; Déjà looked amused. "They were in . . . well, let's just say I was upset."

"Oh, yeah," Harold glanced at Déjà, who rolled her eyes.

"Yes. And I'm concerned because not only does Christopher have a curfew, but they were in the house with his sister. This kind of behavior is unacceptable to me, as I'm sure it is to you."

Harold shrugged. "What were they doing? A little kissing? A little making out?"

Sheridan took a breath. "That may have been the beginning."

Harold chuckled. "That's no big deal. Chris is your oldest, right?" Before she could answer, he said, "You haven't been through the hormonal teenage years. So let me tell you, that's normal. They're just kids being kids."

What kind of parent are you? "I don't allow that kind of behavior in my house, Mr. Blue."

"Oh, now I get it," he said. "You have a little one." He paused and looked at his daughter. "Déjà, from now on, you and Chris should hang out here. Don't be going over there, making out with that little girl in the house."

"Okay, Daddy."

He smiled at Sheridan as if he'd solved the problem.

Sheridan exclaimed, "Mr. Blue —"

"Please call me Harold."

Sheridan had to fight to keep her voice down. "The problem is not just my daughter being in the house. The problem is that . . ." She paused and swallowed, taking a moment to pray that what she was about to say wasn't true. "They were almost having sex."

Harold frowned as if he didn't understand her words. "What's the problem?" He turned to Déjà. "Chris isn't forcing you to do anything, is he?"

"No, Daddy."

He looked at Sheridan. "So, it looks like it's consensual."

She wanted to tell Harold Blue that there was no such thing as consensual sex between an eighteen-year-old and a sixteen-year-old minor, but she stayed silent. He took a puff on his cigarette, and then said to Déjà, "And if you do anything you'll use protection, right? With all those diseases out there."

"Yes, Daddy."

He might as well have driven a stake through her heart.

"Look, Ms. Hart," he continued, "I have seven daughters who I raised mostly by myself."

Obviously.

"Déjà is the youngest, and she's done well. She graduated from high school, and she's the first one to do that before she had a baby. But I ain't complaining about the others. They're good kids too. They all got little ones, but their babies' daddies are doing the thing and taking care of their children."

It was shock that kept her silent.

"Anyway," he continued, explaining real life to Sheridan, "Chris has a good head on his shoulders. And the best thing is" — he paused and winked — "he can't get pregnant."

"Mr. Blue . . ." And then Sheridan stopped. How could she explain what she wanted for her son? How could she tell him her son wasn't going to be anybody's baby's daddy? "Good night, Mr. Blue."

He stood. "Hey, don't worry, little lady," he said as he followed Sheridan. "I know these kids will be responsible."

Sheridan climbed into her car and wondered if Mr. Blue or his daughter could spell *responsible.* She started her SUV and then floored the accelerator. Still she didn't get away fast enough.

It wasn't until she was on the freeway that she realized how hard her heart was pounding.

"Don't worry, little lady." She heard Mr. Blue's raspy voice. "Don't worry," she said aloud. She couldn't do anything else. The man didn't care what was going on with Christopher and his daughter. It didn't matter to him. Christopher was probably the best thing ever to happen to that entire family — even if he was only sixteen.

Sheridan made up her mind. She didn't care if she had to lock Christopher inside his room like it was a high-security prison if it would keep him away from Déjà and the rest of the Blue crew.

Sheridan looked at the clock, and then took the SUV to eighty. She had to get home. She had a son she needed to talk to, a son she needed to save.

It was after midnight, but Sheridan didn't care. She marched into the house, up the stairs, and straight to Christopher's room. Without her perfunctory knock, she swung his door open, and turned on the overhead light.

He stirred before she called him and he sat up.

He squinted as his eyes adjusted to the light. "Mom, is Déjà all right?"

She wanted to shake this alien until he returned her son. "She's fine." He sighed as if he was relieved, and Sheridan wondered what he thought. Wondered if he imagined his mother taking Déjà for a long ride and then returning alone. She wished she'd thought of that.

As he turned to lie back down, Sheridan said, "We need to talk."

He yawned.

"Christopher, I cannot tell you how disappointed I am."

"I don't know why, Mom. I was just waiting for you. I didn't know you were going to be so late."

She paused, unable to understand his nonchalance. She'd caught him, in her house, on top of a girl who was almost naked. Months ago, he would have been trembling at the thought of what his parents would do. But tonight he looked like he didn't care.

And then she thought of Brock. In the hallway. With her and Christopher.

She pushed that memory to the back of her mind. "What was Déjà doing here anyway? You're not supposed to have company on a school night."

"She was helping me with my trigonometry homework."

If she weren't fuming, she would have laughed. She doubted if Déjà could add three numbers together.

He continued to plead his case. "And what could I do? She was stranded."

"It doesn't matter. Christopher, you are continually breaking the rules, and this is not acceptable."

"Why are you hassling me, Mom?" When he raised his voice, Sheridan raised her eyebrows. "You keep stressing me."

"Christopher, you have lost your mind. I'm stressing you?"

"Yeah. And I don't know why," he said more slowly, as if that would help his mother understand. "My grades are good; I don't get in trouble. I do everything you want me to do. And I'm nothing like that jerk you married."

It was a reflex, the way her hand pulled back. The way she used her body to increase the force. The way her palm hit him, leaving her hand stinging. Leaving an imprint of five fingers on his face.

"Don't you ever talk to me like that again," she said. Her teeth were so tightly clenched it almost hurt to speak. "And don't you ever say anything like that about your father."

His wide eyes filled with tears as he held his cheek. "Mom . . ."

"Don't say another word. Just listen." She pointed her finger in his face. "You are not to see Déjà. Not inside this house, not outside, not in Los Angeles, Inglewood, or Pomona. Not on the basketball court or on the golf course. If you see her walking down the street, you are to run the other way. You are not to see her anywhere on this earth, do you understand me?"

He nodded slowly.

"And if I find out that you have defied me — and you know I will find out — you will pay, Christopher. Don't test me. I'm serious. You . . . will . . . pay."

She stared at him, cementing her message, and then stomped from his room.

It wasn't until she was in her bedroom that her tears came. She laid her head on her pillow. First she'd lost Quentin. Then she'd had the news of her father's illness. Now she was sure she was on the verge of losing her son. And if she lost Christopher, there would be no one to blame but herself.

Chapter Thirty-six

"Well," Beatrice began in her calm, cautious way, "you did the right thing. Maybe Quentin needs to talk to Chris too."

Although they were speaking on the phone, Sheridan nodded, grateful for her mother. This conversation was so different from the one she'd had with Kamora. When she told her best friend about Déjà and the Blue crew, Kamora had hollered with laughter. Sheridan could imagine Kamora in her office, buckled over.

Kamora could barely speak the way she gasped for air. "Stop it, girl," she repeated, as if Sheridan's life were a sketch on Comedy Central.

But her mother didn't find the situation as humorous, and Beatrice was doing something she didn't often do: she was offering advice.

"I don't think it's serious, Sheridan," Beatrice continued. "This is the first time you've had any real problems with Chris, and we know the reason."

Sheridan closed her eyes. She wondered if silence was as bad as lying. She knew that her mother was talking about Quentin. But this time Sheridan couldn't blame her son's behavior on his father alone.

"Have you thought about counseling?"

Sheridan opened her eyes and tilted her head. "No, not really, but that may be a good idea, Mom." Maybe she didn't need to be seeing Pastor Ford alone. Maybe she needed to take Christopher and Tori with her.

Beatrice continued. "You and the children have been through so much. It may help to get guidance from a Christian counselor. Give you all a chance to talk through your feelings. And counseling could help Quentin too."

A car door slammed, and Sheridan peeked through her curtains. Her eyes widened. She jumped away from the window. "Mom, I have to go," she said.

"Okay, sweetheart."

Sheridan hung up. Her hands shook as she paced in the entryway. She looked down at her jeans and adjusted the collar of her shirt.

Get it together, Sheridan.

She had to show him. Show him that she was just fine. Show him that their time together had meant as little to her as it had meant to him.

The bell chimed, and she took a deep breath. When she opened the door, her face stretched with surprise, as if she hadn't just scoped him walking up to her front door. "Brock. Nice to see you." But her tone belied the flutters that made her feel faint. It had been five days, and he looked as good to her now as he had when he took her hand, kissed her lips, and led her to paradise.

His lips spread into his lopsided smile as he handed her a package. "Delivery for you."

Her inside flutters turned to churning. He wasn't even there to see her, just there to make a delivery. Her heart cried, but she kept her emotions inside.

She took her tone from casual to professional. "Thank you very much." Even her fake smile was gone. "Is there something I need to sign?"

His smile was gone too. "Listen, Sheridan, I'm sorry I haven't called, but . . ."

She held up her hand, stopping him. "No explanations necessary. I understand what last week was about."

He frowned.

She continued, "We were just kickin' it, right?" It didn't even sound right to her, the way she said it. But she wasn't going to stand there and be on the wrong side of joy. He was going to feel some of her pain.

"Is that what it was?"

"Yeah. It didn't mean anything." She reached for the package. "Is there something for me to sign?" she repeated.

He handed her the blue box. "Too bad," he said with narrowed eyes. "Because the time I spent with you . . . it meant a lot to me."

Now her insides rumbled.

"I came over to tell you that. And to apologize for not calling. But when I left you Saturday, my cell was blowing up. My grandmother had been hit by a car, and I stayed with her at Cedars the entire time. She just went home yesterday."

Sheridan gasped.

"I haven't even been to work, Sheridan." He paused. "I came here looking for a friend, but I guess I came to the wrong place."

"Brock. I didn't know."

"I know you didn't. But I don't want your sympathy. After all, I was just someone you were kickin' it with." He turned and trotted to his car.

Everything inside her dropped to the bottom. She closed the door when he sped away, leaving a trail of smoke from the exhaust pipe.

"It meant a lot to me."

"It meant a lot to me too, Brock." She wondered just how high she could lift her legs — to kick herself.

She glanced down at the box he'd given her, turning it every way, searching for the label. She frowned. There was no label. She sat on the couch and when she lifted the cover, she gasped.

She raised the porcelain flower basket from the box. Red, pink, and white roses sat on top of a ceramic basket. Sheridan lifted the roses, and soft music filled the room.

Tears came to her eyes as she let the music box complete the stanza of "Zoom." She replaced the top and noticed the card.

S, I had a wonderful time. I hope you had a chance to fly away . . . even if it was just for one night. B

She lifted the top again and let the chimes from her favorite song play out. And then she read the card again. Then played the music; then read the card. And all the time wondered how she could ever convince Brock Goodman to give her another chance.

* * *

Sheridan checked the locks on the door and then turned off the lights. She paused outside her bedroom. The lights were still on in Tori's and Christopher's bedrooms.

She was still concerned about Déjà, but she knew there was nothing more she could do. Without prompting, Christopher had promised her yesterday and again today that he wouldn't see Déjà anymore. She'd have to go with that. For now.

Sheridan stepped into her bedroom and saw the music box lying in the center of her bed. She picked up the porcelain piece and removed the top, as she'd done every hour since Brock gave it to her that afternoon.

And again, she read the card.

She took a deep breath and picked up the phone.

Maybe he won't answer, she thought when his line began to ring. By the fourth ring, she was sorry she'd had that thought; she did want to speak to him. On the fifth ring she imagined him sitting, looking at the caller ID. With the sixth ring, she made a promise to hang up if it rang one more time. On the eighth ring, he answered.

"Brock, this is Sheridan."

"Yes?"

"How are you?" she asked, knowing that was the dumbest question, since she'd just seen him hours before.

"Fine."

"Were you busy?"

"No."

She sighed. "You're not going to make this easy, are you?"

"Should I?"

"Yes. Because I called to tell you I shouldn't have said those things."

"What things?"

"I shouldn't have said that our time together didn't mean anything to me."

He stayed silent.

"Brock, please. I'm sorry."

She sighed when she heard his chuckle. "That's what I was waiting to hear."

She pouted. "You knew I didn't mean what I said?"

"Not right away. At first I was stunned. But when I drove away, I began to think about what you said. No way were you just kicking it. So I figured I had to decipher your coded message. Figure out what you were really upset about. Because with women, the problem is never what they say it is."

"Is that so?"

"Yeah, and after thinking about it for

two minutes, I figured you were upset because I hadn't called you. So, was I close?"

She sank under the covers at his psychoanalysis. "You should think about changing careers," she said lightly. Then she added, "I'm so sorry about your grandmother. How's she doing?"

"She's blessed, and she's told every doctor and nurse in that place. Only her ankle was broken, so she's able to get around a bit with a walker. She's a diabetic with high blood pressure. That's why they kept her in the hospital so long."

"I wish you'd called me. I would have been there for you."

"You were with me. In my mind."

She fingered the porcelain box resting on the nightstand. "I love the music box. Thank you."

"I saw a catalogue in the flower shop, and when I found out I could customize the music, I had to get it. It was delivered today, and I couldn't wait to get it to you . . . and to see you."

She paused. "I have . . ." She stopped.

"Tell me what you were going to say."

"I have a hard time believing your words."

"Are you calling me a liar?"

She could tell he was amused, but she

wasn't, as thoughts of Quentin passed through her. "No, I just wonder how you could say all of that when we've only known each other a few weeks."

"I was thinking the same thing. But one of the best lines I've ever heard is, 'A heart does what it wants to do,' so I've given up trying to figure out why I can't get you out of my head. I'm not analyzing it, just going to go with it."

"Is that what you want to do? Just go with this?"

"Yeah. As long as you don't say any more crazy things."

She almost smiled, then said, "Brock, what does a man like you want with me?"

"That's what I was wondering."

Her eyebrows almost fused together at his words.

He continued, "I wondered what a woman like you wants with a man like me."

"You say the right things."

"I'm not just saying that. I'm feeling that."

"I never thought I'd be seeing someone . . . after my husband. But then I bumped into you."

They chuckled together.

"I just want to warn you: I'm new at this

and I might make a few mistakes."

"You think?" he teased.

"Can you be patient with me?"

"Oh, yeah," he said with cheer in his voice, " 'cause I've made a few mistakes, too." With more seriousness he said, "Sheridan, this is not rocket science. Let's just go with this. We've already gotten the hard part out of the way."

She knew they'd get to this. Where she had to tell him and at the same time convince herself this was what she wanted to do. "There is something you should know." She took a breath. "What happened the other night — it can't happen again."

"Oh." He paused. "Was there a big problem with your son?"

She thought of all the trouble that had found them in the last week. "Yes, but it's not only that. I know this is may sound ridiculous, but I want to live my life right by God."

"Are you talking about . . . being celibate?" He said the word as if it belonged in another language.

"Yes," she said.

His whistle was low and long. "That's a big challenge when you're getting to know someone."

She thought of all the times Kamora had

said that. And how she'd tried to convince Kamora that celibacy was God's way. Then she thought about how it felt to be with Brock. His hands. His tongue. His body.

"I know it's a challenge," she said through her thoughts. "But it's what I want." She spoke those words as much for herself as for him. "And I have to be responsible for what Chris and Tori see. But" — she paused for a moment, preparing for her next words — "I understand if that's not the kind of relationship you want." She spoke the words quickly.

"There you go again, trying to get rid of me. Did I say that I didn't want that?"

"No, but —"

"But nothing. Look, Sheridan, I'm not saying I'm excited about this. For me, intimacy is an important part of bonding. But I'm curious enough, and intrigued enough, and impressed enough to want to see where this can go. So I'm willing to play . . . by your rules." He paused. "For now."

Her smile started on the inside. "I think you're a very nice man."

"Does this mean I won't have to beg you to have dinner with me anymore?"

She laughed. "You won't have to beg me and I may even prepare a dinner or two for you."

"That's what I'm talking about."

She laughed, and they stayed connected for almost two more hours. It was well after eleven when she finally hung up, agreeing to meet him on Saturday.

Sheridan lay down and tried to understand all that was going on inside her. She felt like a teenager on the brink of her first relationship, discovering a new life — a life that made her smile. But fear accompanied her joy. A fear that she'd never live up to the advice she'd so easily given to Kamora all these years.

This is a hard walk.

She fingered the music box, thought about Brock, and she knew for the first time in her life that her friend's words were the absolute truth.

Chapter Thirty-seven

Sheridan slowly closed the door, then clapped her hands. She looked at the clock. It was three thirty sharp, and she had done it, gotten everyone out of the house. Tori, this morning, for a Girl Scout outing. Then Christopher, just now, on his way to Darryl's house with his golf clubs. It seemed she'd put sufficient fear inside him. It had only been a few days, but Déjà appeared to be a memory.

Now she could wait for Brock in peace and not worry about his bumping into either of her children. And even if Tori or Christopher came back unexpectedly, there would be no surprises. Brock wouldn't make it past her living room.

Sheridan looked in the mirror, smoothed her knit skirt and turtleneck top, then dashed up the stairs for her pumps. As she started back down, the doorbell chimed. It was only three forty. He'd said fourish, but obviously he was as anxious to see her as she was to see him. She took a last look in the mirror and then swung the door open wide. And her eyes widened as well.

"Quentin."

He stepped inside as if she were waiting for him.

"What are you doing here?"

He frowned and shrugged his jacket from his shoulders. "You wanted to talk about Chris."

He tossed his jacket over the settee and then sauntered into the living room. Her eyes moved from his jacket, to him, back to his jacket. And she thought, *I've really got to get rid of this chair.*

With quick steps she followed him. "I can't talk about Chris right now."

He turned, and as if he were just seeing her, he said, "You look great. Got plans?"

"Yes."

"A Delta meeting?"

She shook her head.

"Something at church?"

She crossed her arms and shook her head.

He stayed quiet, as if he expected an explanation. When she offered none, he shrugged. "So what's up with Chris?" he asked, as he sat down.

"I just said, not right now. I'm on my way out."

"Well, we can talk while I walk you out."

You are just too nosy, Quentin. "No, I

have a few other things to do before I leave, but I'm in a rush."

He slapped his hands against his legs. "Okay."

Sheridan had never seen him move so slowly. She glanced at the clock again, and when she looked at him, Quentin grinned.

"So," he began, as he took his time shrugging into his jacket, "where are you going?"

"That's not something we need to discuss."

He smiled slightly. "Let me know when you'll have time to talk."

She nodded. "I will, but I think Chris is fine now. He and Darryl went to play golf."

"So he's settling down?"

"Seems to be. We all are," she said, looking straight at him.

"That's a good thing. What about his new girlfriend?"

"A girl of the past." She opened the door. "But we'll talk about this later."

He grinned. "I can take a hint."

"Took you long enough to take it."

"I just wanna know what's going on."

"We have separate lives, Quentin."

He lost his grin. "Sometimes that makes me sad."

She didn't say what she wanted to —

that she was moving away from the sad. "I'll call you, maybe tomorrow."

Quentin got into his car and then sat for a minute before he slowly rolled out of the driveway. She didn't breathe until he was out of sight. She was tempted to peek around the corner and see if he was waiting, but she chuckled at that thought. She didn't care if Quentin saw her with Brock. She just didn't want Brock to be surprised.

She dashed up the stairs again, grabbed her purse, and as she came down the steps, the bell chimed.

She swung the door open, and this time she moaned.

"Hey, girl," Kamora said, and stepped inside without an invitation. "Was that Quentin's car I just passed?"

"Probably."

"What was he doing here?" Kamora plopped down on the settee, and Sheridan knew for sure she was getting rid of that seat.

"He wanted to talk about Christopher. But I don't have time right now."

"I hear that. Girl, I am so tired of this. I was home alone last night, and then tonight I was supposed to be going out with Roger. But he just canceled. I don't know what's going on in my life right now." She sighed.

"Kamora, I would love to talk, but I can't."

Like Quentin, it took a minute for Kamora to notice. "You look good, girl. Going out?"

"I have something to do."

"Answer my question." Kamora stood and circled Sheridan, looking her up and down. "Looks to me like you have more than something to do. Looks to me like you got some*one* to do."

"Kamora . . ."

She grinned and stopped in front of Sheridan. "So, who's the guy?"

Sheridan knew she didn't stand a chance of getting Kamora far away unless she gave up the news. "I'm going out with Brock."

Kamora frowned. "Brock?" Then her eyes widened. "Brock. Brock!"

Sheridan sighed.

"You mean Brock. The take-you-to-bed, then-don't-call-you-for-a-week, hiding-his-sorry-behind-until-he-gets-good-and-ready Brock?"

"It wasn't like that."

Kamora dismissed Sheridan's words with a wave. "You're just saying that because you're so —" Her words were interrupted by the door chime once again.

Sheridan pointed her finger at Kamora. "Be nice. I'll explain later."

Kamora rolled her eyes as Sheridan opened the door.

"Hey . . ." Brock greeted her but stopped when she put her hand on his chest.

She smiled and motioned toward Kamora. "Come on in, Brock."

He stepped inside. "Hello." His greeting was cautious.

The grunt Kamora gave him couldn't pass as any kind of welcome.

"Kamora," Sheridan said her name slowly. "This is Brock Goodman. Brock, this is my ex–best friend, Kamora."

He extended his hand; Kamora took her time taking it.

"Nice to meet you," he said.

"Um-hmm." This time it was Brock whom Kamora circled like a vulture. "So you're the man who has my friend —"

"Kamora!" Sheridan shouted, as she pushed her toward the door. "I'll speak to you tomorrow."

"Call me tonight." Kamora paused and looked at Brock, and just before she opened her mouth, Sheridan closed the door in her face.

When she turned around, Brock was

leaning on the banister, watching her. "So I'm that man who has you . . . what?"

She shook her head. "I have no idea what she was going to say, but I know that I'm glad to see you."

He pushed her back against the door and kissed her. She soaked in as much of him as she could.

When he pulled back, he said, "So now go get dressed so we can get out of here."

She frowned. "I am . . ." And then she noticed his jeans and navy shirt. Her eyes wandered to her own outfit. "Where are we going? You didn't say."

He shrugged. "I'm not sure yet. But wherever, we're going to have fun. Don't have to worry about first impressions anymore. So go change, woman," he teased.

She grinned. "Okay." Before she could climb the first step, he pulled her back into his arms and kissed her again. "Hurry back."

She didn't need the stairs. She was sure she could have just jumped up to the second floor, because Brock Goodman had her floating.

Once again Brock didn't ask where she wanted to go or what she wanted to do. For some reason, she liked that, until

Brock took the Magic Mountain Parkway exit off the 5 freeway.

"You're kidding, right?" Sheridan chuckled.

He grinned. "Don't you wanna take a roller-coaster ride?"

I've already been on one with you. She laughed but then stopped when he turned the car into the colossal parking lot. "You're not kidding."

He shook his head, bouncing as if he were moving to a beat only he could hear. And she remembered again: he was still in his twenties. This was his idea of a good time.

Sheridan remembered the last time she'd visited the theme park. Christopher had been eight or nine, and the day had been full of headaches: running after children, standing in long lines, and trying to bear a heat that baked her brain. She'd sworn off ever returning and from then on left this children's task to Quentin. "I'm too old for this," she'd told Quentin then.

She remembered those words she'd said almost a decade before as she looked up at Brock. And then she forgot them when he gave her his smile.

He grasped her hand and they passed through the ticket gate. Even though it was

Saturday, the lines were March light and flowed with ease.

"Okay, what do you want to do first?" he asked, opening the park map.

Sheridan shrugged. "You've done all the planning. I'll just go with whatever."

"You sure you can hang with me?" He laughed with his eyes.

She accepted the challenge, snatched the map, and pointed to one of the attractions. "Let's go here."

"You sure you want to do Scream?"

She frowned, not sure she liked the name of that ride. But how bad could it be? "Yeah, let's go." She stopped when he stared at her. "What's wrong? You sure you can hang with me?"

He snickered and grabbed her hand, and they weaved through the streets of the park, finding their way to Scream. As they stood in line, Sheridan strained to get a view of the ride, but it was hidden behind the building and bushes. But neither hid the screams of terror coming from those already on the roller coaster.

It's just a ride.

"Have you been to Magic Mountain before?" he asked, as they moved closer to the front.

"Yeah, with the kids, but not too much.

Amusement parks aren't my thing."

"I love them. It's the only place I know where I can scream without anyone staring at me as if I were crazy."

I've got to be crazy, she thought, as the squeals became louder.

The line moved too fast, and Sheridan held her breath as she stepped to her place in the ride. She frowned as the assistant helped her. "Where do you put your feet?" she asked, as she was strapped in.

Brock laughed. "You leave them dangling. We're going to fly through the air," he said, as the attendant walked away.

I'm too old for this.

Then she heard the final click and the jerk of the beginning of the ride. She looked at the attendant with fear-filled eyes before the ride slowly moved forward. She wanted to yell to the operator to let her out, that she had made a mistake, that grown women didn't do things like this. But as Scream increased its speed, Sheridan closed her eyes and did the only thing she could; she screamed. And then she prayed for God to keep her safe. And after the first one-hundred-fifty-foot drop, she screamed to God to let her live.

She was trembling when the three minutes of terror ended and Brock helped her from her seat. "Wasn't that great?" he yelled, as if adrenaline was still thickening his veins.

All Sheridan wanted to do was bend down, kiss the ground, and promise God she would never do anything that stupid again.

She held on to his arms because her legs had not yet figured out they were on solid ground.

"Wow, I hadn't been on that one," he exclaimed. "That was great. Which ride's next?"

The ride home. "I don't know."

He looked at her. "You okay?"

"I will be as soon as I tuck my heart back into my chest."

He laughed. "Okay. Maybe we'll stay away from the rides for a bit. Wanna get something to eat?"

She nodded, even though she wasn't sure if she'd be able to hold anything down. But at least it would keep her away from flying through the air as if she were some kind of trapeze artist.

Once they settled at a table at the Chicken Plantation, Sheridan relaxed and devoured her fried chicken and fries as if it were her last meal.

Brock's eyes showed amusement, and

she expected him to say, "See, you can't hang with me." But he said nothing, and when they finished, he took her hand and they strolled through the park. He stopped to order a funnel cake (with extra sugar), which they shared, and then he ordered popcorn (with extra butter), which they shared as they watched the exotic bird show in the Baisley Theatre.

The sun had set when Brock, with his arm around her, led her from the park. She leaned against the car's headrest and closed her eyes. Only music filled the car on the hour-long ride back into the city. Two blocks from her home, Brock pulled over.

"What's wrong?"

He said nothing before he kissed her. "Thank you for another great time," he said, when he leaned back. He put the car back in drive and slowed it in front of her house.

"Maybe I'll see you in church tomorrow?" she asked.

"Is that your way of saying you want to see me again?"

By any means necessary. "No, it's my way of asking if you're going to church."

He chuckled. "You can say it, Sheridan. It's okay. I know you have a great time when you're with me."

He waited for her to answer, but when she only smiled, he jumped from the car and walked around to her side. Leaning against her open window, he said, "I want to kiss you again. But your children . . ."

She looked at the house. Just about every light was on, and she wondered if Tori and Christopher were crouched behind one of the windows, watching. It was only nine, much too early for them to be asleep on a Saturday night.

He walked her to the door. "I'll see you in church," he said, before his lips grazed her cheek.

Watching him drive away, she remembered the last time, when he hadn't left her standing at the door.

Sheridan stepped inside and heard squeals. In the living room, Christopher, Darryl, and Tori sat Indian-style on the floor with PlayStation 2 in the middle.

"Hey, guys."

"Hi, Mom."

"Hello, Ms. Hart."

Not one child glanced up, but Sheridan didn't mind.

As she climbed the stairs, Sheridan raised her eyes skyward. "Thank you, Lord," she whispered.

She was in her bedroom for less than a minute before her phone rang. She grabbed the receiver.

"Hey, girl."

"Hey," Sheridan said, her smile turning down just a bit.

"I was taking a chance that you'd be home this early."

Sheridan flopped onto the bed. "Yeah, Brock knew I had to get home to be with the kids."

"I can't believe you're going out with this guy. He didn't even call you back."

Sheridan wanted to remind Kamora how many times she'd complained about men doing that to her. Instead she told Kamora Brock's story. By the time Sheridan finished, Kamora was almost in tears.

"Oh, that wonderful guy. Staying with his grandmother until he was sure she was okay."

"He's pretty terrific."

"And he's easy on the eyes," Kamora said, her sadness gone. "He has muscles everywhere."

Sheridan laughed. "I can vouch for that."

"I know you can. But let me ask you, girlfriend. Just how old is this guy?"

Sheridan moaned inside. "Why?"

"Well, I can tell boyfriend is a bit young."

"Does he look a lot younger than me?"

"No, not at all. Girl, you know how good we look. But don't change the subject. 'Fess up."

"He's almost thirty."

"How close to thirty is he?"

"Closer to thirty than to twenty-eight."

"Oh, that's not so bad. I thought you were going to tell me he was hovering around twenty-five."

"Girl, do you think I would do that?"

"Before last week, I didn't know you would 'do' any of this." Kamora laughed. "But it's all good. So what have you two kids decided?"

"We agreed to be friends and take it slow."

"Now, you know that's not what I'm asking. Come on. What about doing the do?"

"That's personal, Kamora. You're all up in my business."

"As if you haven't been in mine for all these years. Just answer the question."

Sheridan sighed. "We're going to give this friendship thing a go — without sex."

Kamora screamed. "That's impossible."

"I know," Sheridan groaned. "It's going to be so hard."

"Welcome to my world."

Sheridan's phone beeped, and when she looked at the number on caller ID, she rushed her friend off the phone.

"Would you look at this?" Kamora said, pretending to be offended. "The tables have turned." She laughed. "Anyway, I'll call you when I get out of church."

When Sheridan clicked to the incoming call, Brock said, "I wanted to make sure you arrived home safely."

"You walked me to my door."

"I know, but anything could have happened before you stepped into the house. I'm glad you're safe."

She couldn't help smiling. "I'm safe. And the children are safe. And life is wonderful."

"Does that have anything to do with me?"

She stayed silent.

He chuckled. "One of these days, you're going to admit it, Ms. Hart. You're going to admit you have a wonderful time in my company. But for now, I'll just wish you a good night. And before you go to sleep, think about a brotha."

He hung up before she could say goodbye. She closed her eyes and pressed her hands to her chest, wanting to stay in this moment for as long as she could.

After a while she opened her bedroom door and yelled downstairs, "Tori, time for bed."

"Oh, Mom," Tori whined her usual response.

"And Darryl, make sure you don't miss your curfew."

"I won't, Ms. Hart," Darryl shouted up.

Sheridan put her arm around Tori's shoulders as she moped to the top of the stairs.

"Mom, why can't I stay down there with Chris? We were having a good time."

"I'm a mean mother, huh?" Sheridan said, as Tori dragged herself into her bedroom.

When Sheridan closed her bedroom door, she laughed out loud. She had Brock, and Christopher was hanging out with his old friends. Could life be any better?

She grabbed her Bible from the nightstand. She needed to spend a little time with God. Because it was obvious He had been spending quite a bit of time on her.

She couldn't wait to get to church. There was so much she wanted to give thanks for. First, she couldn't have been happier when Christopher yelled up the stairs to tell her he was walking Nicole to church.

How easy had that been? All this time she'd been trying to mastermind some undercover plot to rid her life of Déjà. But all she'd had to do was demand that Christopher not see her anymore. If she'd known it was going to be that easy, she would have done that as soon as she saw her son's name sprawled across the girl's fingertips.

But now, as she waited to give praise and thanks to God, her thoughts turned to Brock. She was surprised that he had not arrived. Through praise and worship, the offering, the sermon, and finally the benediction, Sheridan felt as if her neck were on a swivel, as she twisted in her seat in search of the man who had promised to join her this morning.

When Sheridan hugged the woman sitting next to her at the end of the service, she couldn't even fake a smile. She stopped at the back of the church to wait for Tori, sure that Christopher would walk home with Nicole.

As Tori walked over to her, Sheridan took a step and bumped into the person in front of her. "Excuse me . . . Brock!"

He smiled. “Good morning.”

“Were you here? I didn’t see you.”

“I was here before the service began. I sat in the back.” He paused and looked at Tori. “This must be your daughter.”

“Yes.” She introduced the two and then watched Brock ask Tori all the questions a nine-year-old was expected to answer. She breathed with relief when Tori chatted, comfortable with the man in the navy suit.

He turned back to Sheridan. “You look good.”

His words made her notice the watching eyes. “Let’s go outside.”

In silence they walked to her car. As she opened the door, he said, “It was good to see you.”

She faced him, her smile gone. “Oh . . .” She had expected to spend some time with him. After all, hadn’t they agreed to give this thing a try?

He has a life beyond you, Sheridan. She shaped her lips into a smile.

“I’ve got some things to take care of today,” he said.

Some things or someone?

He said, “I’ll give you a call tomorrow.”

She nodded to hide the truth of her emotions. And then she waved and drove away, without glancing back. She didn’t want to look again at the object of her disappointment.

She pulled into her driveway. The moment Tori jumped out of the car, Sheridan's cell phone rang.

"Hello, Quentin."

"Good morning. I was hoping you were out of church."

"What's up?"

"Wanted to finish what we started yesterday — talking about Chris." He paused. "That is, if you have time today."

"I have plenty of time," she snapped, as she stepped from the car. "My children are important to me."

"I was just kidding," Quentin said. "What's up with you?"

Brock left. "Nothing, but I don't think we need to talk to Christopher." She laid her purse and Bible on the settee and kicked the front door closed. "Things are better with him." *A lot better than they are for me.*

"What happened?"

Sheridan told him about Christopher's weekend with Darryl and then this morning with Nicole. "He hasn't mentioned Déjà at all."

"You mentioned that yesterday, but that seems kind of suspect to me. All of a sudden she's gone?"

"I threatened his life. And once Christopher started hanging out with Darryl and Nicole again, he must've realized I was right."

"Okay," Quentin said, as if he wasn't sure. "But let's keep an eye on him."

"I do that every day, Quentin. Every day when I'm here by myself with our children."

His sigh made her want to apologize. To explain that her words had nothing to do with him. "Anyway, do you want to talk to Tori?"

Sheridan called her daughter from the kitchen and handed her the cell. When Tori clicked off the phone, she said, "Mom, when am I going to spend the night at Dad's house?"

"When there's enough ice in hell to ice skate," Sheridan said, and stomped up the stairs. Her regret was instant. Now Tori was added to her apology list. But she would make amends later. And she would change her clothes later. Right now she just wanted to lie down and find a way to rid her head of the pounding that had suddenly overtaken her.

Sheridan wasn't sure what day it was.

It was dark, and she wondered if she had slept through to the next day. But the black outside her window wasn't the deep dark of night. She glanced at the clock. It was a little after six.

She sat up just as her telephone rang.

"Hello," the voice said.

It made her mad — the way she smiled at the mere sound of his voice.

Brock said, "What were you doing?"

Thinking of you. "Nothing."

"I wish we could have spent some time together today, but I was with my grandmother. She's doing better, and even though my mother is here, I'm the one who makes her smile."

You do that for me too. Sheridan didn't know what made her feel worse — the fact that she'd sworn he was with another woman, or the fact that she was relieved he wasn't.

"I'm sorry I didn't ask you this morning: how is your grandmother?"

"Good; it's taking her longer to recover than she expected, but she's a feisty sixty-eight-year-old."

Your grandmother is sixty-eight? My father is sixty-seven.

"But I'm grateful to God," he said. "He's healing her."

How old is your mother? I could be closer to his mother's age than his.

"Sheridan?"

"I'm sorry, did you say something?"

"Yeah, but you sound like you're distracted. I'll call you tomorrow."

She wanted to tell him to stay on the line because she loved the way he made her feel. But she kept those thoughts inside — away from him. "Please tell your grandmother I wish her the best."

When she hung up, there was still fear behind her smile. She feared all the emotions that Brock stirred in her every time she talked to him, every time she saw him. But no matter what she thought, her heart was beating on its own. She would just have to pray that her heart didn't take her to a place where she really didn't want to be.

Chapter Thirty-eight

The weeks passed like a whirlwind, and almost every other day she spent some time with Brock. At the movies, at the beach, even bowling. Their hours together taught her more about him. More about herself. More about them.

At home, life was almost as sweet. Tori didn't ask again if she could spend the night with Quentin. Quentin didn't ask if Tori could. And Christopher was spending his time with Darryl and Nicole, and Hannah, Darryl's new girlfriend.

The only challenge was Hart to Heart. Even now, as she sat at her desk, she couldn't get herself to care. Quentin had been gone for over four months, and in that time she hadn't spent four hours on their business. The fax machine was filled with requests: for order changes, for delivery confirmations, and for the new catalogue.

She flipped through the papers but studied none of the words. When the telephone rang, she welcomed the reprieve.

"Mom, how are you?"

"Just fine, sweetheart. And before you ask, your dad is doing great too. That's why I'm calling. You know Tori's birthday is next weekend."

Sheridan laughed. "How could I forget? Tori won't let me. She's been dropping hints on what we can do and what she wants." She laughed. "Reminds me of when I was turning ten."

"Well, your father and I want to give her a little party."

"You don't have to do that. I can have something, and you and Dad can come here."

"No, we really want to do something. Yesterday was your dad's third appointment since his treatments ended and it's official. He's cancer free."

Her tone was so casual, Sheridan paused, but only for a moment. She jumped from her chair. "Mom, that's terrific. Why didn't you call me?"

"I'm calling you now. Your dad and I wanted some time last night to rejoice ourselves and now we want to share it with the family. And our granddaughter's tenth birthday is the perfect time."

"God does answer prayers," Sheridan said.

"I could have told you that." Beatrice

laughed. "So, we want to have a party this Saturday."

"Absolutely. Tori will be excited."

"Great. Invite some of her friends. And tell Chris too. By the way, how's he doing?"

"My perfect son has come back to me. He hasn't mentioned that girl; she hasn't called. Life is wonderful."

"Good. Did Quentin talk to him?"

"Didn't have to. I think Christopher decided that I could be a very dangerous mother when angry."

"That works. You know I had you and your brother believing I was crazy."

They both laughed.

"Mom, you're the best."

"I was born that way, sweetheart. See you Saturday."

Sheridan was still laughing when she hung up. She looked around the office. Life was going too well to have to handle any of this right now. She'd work on Hart to Heart later. Much later.

Sheridan eased her car next to Brock's Camry. She'd been disappointed when after a counseling session with Pastor Ford, she'd heard Brock's message on her cell, canceling their lunch date. But she was more than delighted when hours later he called and invited her to Starbucks.

She sauntered into the shop and spotted him, still in his UPS uniform. He held up two cups and she laughed.

"You didn't wait for me," she said, as she slid into the chair across from him.

He kissed her cheek. "I know what you like."

"Oh, you do," she continued the flirtation. The sexual tension between them remained, although they'd been able to stay out of the bedroom. It was with a lot of prayer that they'd settled into a comfortable relationship, although it was not without its temptations.

He grinned and kissed her again, this time on the lips.

"Sheridan?"

His lips were still on hers when she opened her eyes.

"Francesca," Sheridan said, as Brock backed away. "How are you?"

"Fine," she shrieked to Sheridan, but her eyes were on Brock.

Sheridan took a sip of her coffee, not bothered by the long moments of silence that passed between them. Finally Brock introduced himself.

Francesca held his hand longer than she

had to. "Haven't we met?"

"I don't think so."

"I think we have. I'd never forget you." Sheridan was sure Francesca's grimace was meant to be seductive, but instead she looked like she had to go to the bathroom.

Sheridan said, "It was nice seeing you, Francesca," dismissing her.

Francesca stood in her place until Brock turned to Sheridan and said, "How was your day?"

Sheridan laughed as Francesca trudged away.

He asked, "What's her story?"

"That's the problem. She didn't get much of a story from us. She's the town gossip."

"I hope I didn't make things worse by kissing you in public."

Sheridan sighed. "Yeah, that's going to be tough, you know. You don't know who might see us when we do that."

"I'm sorry," he said. "I didn't think about that. That's my problem sometimes; I go with what I'm feeling rather than . . ." Before he could finish, Sheridan leaned across the table and kissed him, letting her lips linger with his for an extra moment.

When she pushed back into her seat, she said, "I have the same problem."

He laughed. "That's a good thing. Anyway, do you have some time tonight?"

"What do you have in mind?"

"Got a lot on my mind, but we're not doing that, remember?"

She smiled. "Sorry, I forgot."

"I want you to do something with me. It'll only take an hour or so. You can ride with me, and I'll bring you back here to get your car."

"Sure." She took the last sip of her drink and waved to Francesca. When Francesca rolled her eyes, Sheridan laughed.

She was still chuckling when Brock steered onto the 110 freeway. Ten minutes later, when he slowed his car, she asked, "Where are we going?"

He turned off the ignition in front of a 1930s-style Spanish home. "To my grandmother's house."

Do I look like Little Red Riding Hood? Her eyes widened. "Your grandmother's house? Does she live here?"

"Yeah, people usually live in their houses, sweetheart."

"Brock, I'm not ready to meet your grandmother."

"Why not?"

"Because . . ." She paused. How could she explain all of the reasons? *Because I'm wearing jeans. Because I haven't covered my gray in a few weeks. Because I'm almost forty and you haven't even yet turned thirty.* "Because," she continued aloud, "I'm sure she's not ready to have visitors."

"She loves company."

"I'm sure she does, if they're her friends."

"You're *my* friend." He paused. "What's the problem? My grandmother is important to me, and I want her to meet you. She knows there's someone special in my life, and it's about time."

"It's not like we've been seeing each other for years."

"Doesn't matter. I want her to meet you now."

"What's the hurry? You make it sound like we're about to get married."

"There you go again, woman," he kidded. "I'm not looking for a wife."

But as he got out of the car, she didn't laugh like she always had when he'd said that before.

Sheridan stayed silent as Brock took her hand. She didn't want to be holding on to him when they walked into his grandmother's house, but if she let go, she was sure she'd meet the ground.

She squeezed her hands together when he released her to open the door. “Big Momma,” he yelled.

Sheridan stood on the porch, wishing she could meet his grandmother from where she was — outside, in the open. In case she had to make a run for it.

Brock pulled her into the house and then closed the door, trapping her. She looked around the living room, which was somber with heavy, dark furniture. She sat on the edge of the plastic-covered sofa and waited.

“Big Momma?”

A moment later Sheridan heard a shuffling sound. And then a woman who was the antithesis of her name inched into the room, propelled by a chrome walker.

Big Momma was quite petite. The five-foot-three beauty could probably still hang out at a club or two, with her silver-black pixie haircut and green eyes that brightened her face. And Sheridan was sure the sixty-eight-year-old woman could still slip into a pair of size six jeans. All that aged Big Momma was the thin cotton, flowered housecoat of the type that Sheridan was sure only grandmothers wore. And the tattered slippers that looked as if they had seen more earthly days than her grandson.

Brock hugged his grandmother and helped her into a chair. Sheridan studied the way he handled her — with gentleness. Tenderness. And love. Kamora had told her she measured a man by the way he treated his mother. She wondered what her friend would say about Brock and his grandmother.

"How're you, Big Momma?"

"Boy, if you don't stop asking me . . . I told you I was fine when you called. I'm wonderful in the Lord. Now tell me," she said, and poked his arm, "where're your manners?" Big Momma looked at Sheridan and folded her hands in her lap. Her smile made Sheridan's anxiety thaw — just a bit.

Brock grinned. "This is my friend, Sheridan Hart."

She stepped forward when the woman reached for her. It was another of the few signs of Big Momma's age, the weathered skin, the soft touch.

"It's nice to meet you, Ms. . . ."

"Everyone calls me Big Momma." His grandmother chuckled. "At least everyone who is friend or family." She tilted her head. "And the way my boy here talks about you, you're a friend."

"Thank you, ma'am." Sheridan smiled.

Her apprehension continued to melt as the woman warmed her with her eyes.

"And the way my boy here talks about you," Big Momma continued, "I suspect you'll soon join the ranks of family."

"Big Momma!" Brock exclaimed.

"Why you yelling like that, boy?"

" 'Cause not only are you talking about me like I'm not here, but you're talking about things that are none of your business."

Big Momma twisted her lips. "At my age, everything is my business." Then she grinned at Sheridan. "If we waited for these men, none of us would ever be married." She rocked back in her chair. "So I'm just moving along the inevitable."

Brock shook his head and then sat on the couch next to Sheridan.

"So, Sheridan," Big Momma continued, "my boy here tells me you have two children."

Her uneasiness returned, and an image came to her mind — Déjà and Christopher sitting in front of her, prepared for their interrogation. Sheridan scooted a few inches away from Brock.

I am too old for this. "Yes, ma'am, I have two children."

"And how old is your oldest?"

Here it comes. "Sixteen."

"Boy or girl?"

"A boy. Christopher."

Big Momma leaned back and nodded. She continued staring, as if she were studying more than Sheridan's words. When the old woman's eyes narrowed, Sheridan could imagine Big Momma's thoughts. *"What do you want with my boy?"*

What goes around . . .

"You got your hands full," Big Momma said. "A sixteen-year-old boy. He's probably smelling himself, giving you all kinds of trouble."

"No, ma'am. He's a good kid."

"I'm sure he is in front of you, but you know kids these days. They'll tell you one thing, then do another. Tell you they're going to school, but never make it to class. Be doing all kinds of things you don't know about."

Big Momma's words made Sheridan pause. She swallowed the fear that came with the memories of what they'd been through with Christopher. Big Momma shook her head. "Did my boy here tell you he has a younger brother?" She didn't wait for Sheridan to affirm. "Brock has done wonders with his brother, and now he works with other young men. Even brought a few 'round here for me to meet." She peered at Sheridan another moment. "I know you're good for him. Making him smile all the time and taking his behind to church. But he can be good for you too. My boy here can help you raise your boy."

"Big Momma," Brock called, in a tone that was a plea for silence. "You shouldn't be talking about this."

"Why not? You won't."

"Big Momma," Sheridan interrupted both of them. "Christopher is a normal teenager and his father is very active in his life."

"Is his father living with you?"

None of your business. "No, ma'am, but —"

"Then it ain't good enough." Big Momma shook her head. "That's part of the problem. These boys on the streets with no direction from their fathers. Many don't even know who their fathers are."

Brock stood. "Okay, time for us to go." He took Sheridan's hand.

"Why you leavin' so soon?" Big Momma asked.

"Because if you keep talking, Sheridan may never go out with me again."

Big Momma waved her hand. "I doubt

that. Look at the two of you." She smirked. "All that chemistry. *Umph, umph, umph.* Well, at least I know my boy here will be in good hands."

You don't even know me, Sheridan thought, but said nothing.

"And you may think I don't know nothin' 'bout you," Big Momma said, letting Sheridan know she knew her thoughts. "But I know all I need to know. You love the Lord, right?"

"Yes, ma'am."

"And you love my grandson, right?"

Brock held up his hands. "Okay, Big Momma, that's enough."

"She don't have to answer. I know." Big Momma leaned back in her chair and rocked as if God had told her something. "Just look at you two. *Hmph, hmph, hmph.*"

Brock kissed his grandmother's cheek. "Do you want me to help you back to bed?"

"No, I was just resting before you came. But now I'm gonna stay up and watch a little TV." She picked up the remote.

"Well, don't stay up too late. I'll call you."

Big Momma nodded. "Nice to meet you, young lady. And maybe you can do me a favor."

"Yes, ma'am."

"Can you get my boy here to cut his hair?"

"Big Momma!" Brock protested.

She continued, "Walkin' 'round here with all that hair like a girl."

Brock shook his head and Sheridan laughed. She took the woman's hand again. "It was nice meeting you, Big Momma," she said before Brock pulled her from the house.

Sheridan slid into the car and bounced back in her seat. "Thanks for introducing me to your grandmother."

Brock rolled his eyes and turned his head. But even from the side, she could see his smile.

"Now that you've met my grandmother, there's only one thing left," he said somberly.

Sheridan's forehead wrinkled.

He eased the car onto the freeway. "I want you to spend my birthday with me."

"I'd love to," she exclaimed. "So you're finally going to be thirty."

He nodded and his locks swayed. "Yup." He took her hand and squeezed it.

"Let me plan something for you."

"A party?" There was a frown in his voice.

"No, something with just the two of us."

He glanced at her, grinned, winked, and then turned his eyes back to the road.

She slapped his leg. "Not that. But I want to do something."

"Okay. What?"

"I don't know yet. I'll surprise you."

"It doesn't matter what we do. All I want is to spend the entire day with you."

They settled into a comfortable silence that lasted until he stopped in the Starbucks parking lot. She jumped from the car, sauntered to his window, and leaned in.

"I'm looking forward to your birthday," she whispered, and let her lips graze his.

"I can't wait. Now get in your car, and call me when you get home, woman."

She watched him in her rearview mirror as she backed out. Then she pulled up next to him. She motioned for him to roll down his window. "I forgot to ask. When's your birthday?"

"Saturday."

A car behind him honked and Brock waved. "Call me," he said, before he pulled away from her.

Sheridan sat. This Saturday. May fifteenth. Tori's birthday. She put her car into drive and tried to gather her thoughts.

Tori's birthday. And her party. With her family. There was no way she could spend the day with him.

She couldn't invite him to the party. Her children would be there. And her parents.

She'd call him and explain.

What if he wants to go?

"He'll never want to go to a children's party. That's no way to spend his birthday."

"All I want is to spend the entire day with you." She remembered his words.

She pulled back into the parking space she'd just left and dialed Kamora's number.

"Hey, girl," Kamora said.

"Starbucks, in ten minutes."

"Girl, I'm already in my pj's."

Sheridan raised her eyebrows. "Boy, your life has changed."

"Don't I know it? Can't we just talk over the phone?"

Sheridan remembered all the times when Kamora had called, pleading for some face-to-face time. Well, it was her turn.

"Please come," Sheridan said. "I need you."

Kamora said, "Okay, but don't be mad when I show up looking like I'm going to a slumber party and embarrass you. I ain't takin' off my nightgown."

Fifteen minutes later Kamora strolled into the coffee shop. She was right; she'd been dressed for bed. And as promised, she hadn't taken off what she'd been wearing. She wore her silk, low-cut, mid-thigh nightie over a pair of jeans with a short denim jacket. It may have been her sleepwear, but she looked like she was going to a party.

Kamora rolled her eyes when she spotted Sheridan at the table, but Sheridan didn't mind. She knew Kamora was eager to hear whatever she had to say. Not much could get Sheridan pleading for some time at Starbucks.

Kamora ordered her drink, made eye contact with no one, even though she knew many eyes were on her, and then strutted to the table with her drink in hand.

"Okay, so what problem do you need me to help you solve?" Her tone was blasé, but her eyes were wide, as if she couldn't wait to hear. "It's about Mr. Muscles, right?"

Sheridan nodded. "His birthday is Saturday and I promised to spend the entire day with him."

"And you want to know how you're going to spend all that time together and not jump his bones, right?"

"No. The problem is Saturday is Tori's birthday."

"Oh, that's right. Your mom called. I'll be there."

"That's my point. You'll be there. My parents will be there. My children will be there." She paused as if Kamora would understand.

Kamora shrugged. "So Brock will go to the party with you and then you guys can do something afterward."

Sheridan shook her head. "You're not listening. How can I ask Brock to come with me?"

She frowned. "It's like that? He doesn't want to spend any time with your people?"

"No, he does. He wants to spend time with Christopher and Tori. And today he took me to meet his grandmother."

"Whoa, when a man introduces you to his folks, it's serious." Kamora took a large gulp of coffee. "Okay, so, I must be tired, because I'm not getting this."

Sheridan threw her hands into the air. "I can't have Brock meeting my family. No one knows about him except for you."

"And Christopher." Kamora grinned.

Sheridan sighed. "Well, Tori met him too, but nobody knows that we . . . slept together."

"Except Christopher." Her grin spread. "Look, I don't get the problem. It's about time your family met Brock. You're always together; he's introducing you to his family. What are you ashamed of?" Kamora paused. "Oh, 'cause he's a baby."

That's one thing. "No."

"So explain it to me so I can go home," Kamora whined.

Sheridan knew why Kamora didn't understand; she didn't get it herself. She knew what was in her heart; she just couldn't put words to it.

"Well, here's my opinion," Kamora said, standing. "If you're ashamed of Brock, then stop seeing him." She patted Sheridan's shoulder. "Look, I got a big date today. With my king-sized bed and seven-hundred-thread-count sheets. Call me if you wanna talk some more. But I'm out."

Sheridan watched her friend walk into the night, leaving her alone with the confused thoughts that continued to whirl through her mind.

For some reason she didn't want to call from home.

"Hey, baby," Brock said, as soon as he answered the phone. "I've been waiting for you to call."

"I'm sorry. I met Kamora for coffee."

"At Starbucks? You need to buy stock in the place." He laughed, but there was nothing within her to join him.

"I have something to tell you." She took a breath. "I forgot that Saturday is Tori's birthday."

"Really, we share the same day? How great is that?"

"We planned a party for her . . . on Saturday."

"Oh. Well, that's okay, sweetheart." She breathed. "I don't mind going to Tori's party. I can't wait to spend some time with her and Christopher."

His words took her relief away. "I don't want you to spend your birthday at a children's party," she said, as casually as she could through a thumping heart.

"I don't mind."

"There'll just be kids there."

"Sounds like fun."

"And you'll be bored."

He paused. "Sheridan, are you listening to me?"

She said nothing.

"Okay," he spoke slowly. "You don't want me at Tori's party."

"I just think it would be better . . ." She didn't have an excuse real enough to finish the sentence.

"No problem."

This time they were both silent. Finally he said, "I'll speak to you later." He clicked off the phone before she could say good-bye. Before she could say she was sorry. Before she could figure out what was wrong with his going to Tori's party.

His words no longer meant anything.

Sheridan flipped through pages of Quentin's love notes, searching for inspiring pieces that could fill a catalogue, but every line felt empty, meaningless, as if the man who wrote them had no depth.

Was it always like this?

It made her pause. What a person did to another was a great indication of who they were. Sheridan stared at her phone for only a moment before she dialed. It rang and rang, and just before she shifted the handset to hang up, he answered.

She could hear the sleep in his voice.

"Brock, it's me."

"Is something wrong?"

"No. I'm fine."

She heard his sigh of relief. And then with his next words, she heard his anger. "Okay, so it's three in the morning. What's up?"

His tone was low on the rage meter, but she knew he was still furious. And his fury had nothing to do with the time.

"I want you to come with me to Tori's party."

He sighed. "Why do you want me to come now?"

"Because I've had a chance to think about it. I can't even sleep."

"I don't want to be an afterthought in your life, Sheridan."

"That's not what this is about, Brock. It's just scary. When I arrive at that party with you, things are going to change."

He may have been asleep when she called, but he was alert now. "Why do you think I'm going to change?"

"Not you, not me. But the 'us' will change. Because everyone will know we're a couple."

"That bothers you?"

"Not when it's just me and you." She sighed. "I don't want the pressure of the questions that will come. My parents will start asking about you, and my brother will want to know more about you, and my children will expect to see you."

"And that's scary?" His concern was back.

"It's the unknown. It's the fact that if we

decide this is not what we want to do, I have to lose someone in public again."

His silence told her he was wondering again about her and Quentin.

"And," she continued, "it's been so wonderful, just the two of us."

His deep sigh made her wish she hadn't made this call. Wish she'd kept it all to herself, stayed with her first thoughts and not invited him to the party. She closed her eyes, suddenly very sleepy.

"I understand."

Her eyes popped open.

"But Sheridan," he continued, "look at it this way. Life is a risk. When we met, you were convinced you would never go out with a dreadlock-wearing, UPS-delivering twenty-nine-year-old."

"Your job never bothered me." She knew she'd made him smile. She said, "You were convinced we couldn't have a relationship without sex."

"Well, I'm still working on that. But I don't want you to be scared. I'm not. We can't see the future, but also" — he paused for just a moment — "don't hold your past against me."

Is that what I'm doing?

He continued, "If I'm willing to go for it, will you do the same?"

I don't know. "Yes."

"Great."

"Will you come with me to Tori's party?"

"Oh, yeah. I had planned on it. I was just waiting for you to realize it."

She laughed. "You were taking a chance. I only had a few days to change my mind."

"No problem. I knew my baby was brilliant."

My baby. It was a warm smile that came before her yawn. "And I know you're sleepy," she said.

"Yeah. What were you thinking, calling me at three in the morning, woman?"

"I was thinking about you."

"Now that's what I like to hear. But even though I could bask in the sound of your voice for the rest of the night, I've got to get some sleep. Will you continue to think about me?"

"Yes."

For the second time that night, they hung up without saying good night. But this time, they didn't have to say it. They both knew that it had already been a very good night.

Chapter Thirty-nine

Sheridan didn't know why her nerves remained. Yesterday, when she had announced she was bringing a friend to the party, her family had responded casually.

Christopher had shrugged.

Tori had asked, "Does Mr. Brock know it's my birthday?"

Her parents had spoken in unison, "That's nice."

And Kamora had cheered as if Brock were her own date.

Sheridan had felt like she was making much ado about nothing. And so she had slept last night, but this morning everything inside her fluttered.

"It's the last house on the right," Sheridan directed, as Brock slowed the car. In an instant she was taken back to 1984, when she'd brought her first boyfriend, Kevin, to meet her parents. She'd been terrified, knowing her parents were going to interrogate Kevin about his intentions. Now, more than twenty years later, she felt the same way.

"Are you ready?" she asked, when Brock

turned off the ignition.

Brock twisted to face her. "I'm beyond ready." He squeezed her hand. "Don't worry. I'll use a fork when I eat, and I'll wait until I get home to scratch any itch."

She laughed but then quickly became serious. "I hope you know that I love who you are."

"Okay, so I won't use a fork." He grinned and then slid from the car, grabbing Tori's gift. Sheridan was already standing outside the car when he came around to her side. "Anxious, huh?"

"No," she said, as she tried to breathe her nerves away. She looked at him and wondered why she worried. He was gorgeous in his black jeans and black shirt. This time his locks were tied back. How could her family not love him?

She led him to the front door and took one final breath before she stepped inside.

"Hey," she yelled over the squeals of Tori's friends and the TV in the living room.

It was Tori who rushed to her first, with six of her friends in tow.

"Hey, Mom." She hugged her mother. "Hi, Mr. Brock."

"Hey, happy birthday." He handed her the gift. She squealed her thanks and then turned away, with her friends following behind.

Sheridan had expected a rush — curious adults dashing to meet her and her guest at the door. But besides Tori and her entourage, no one came. She could hear the clatter of pots and pans in the kitchen. She peeked into the living room and decided she'd conquer its occupants first.

Her father stood the moment she walked into the room. "Hey, sweetheart. I was just explaining the intricacies of basketball to my other daughter here. You would think after all these years she would've learned something."

"Ah, come on, Mr. Collins. You're not being fair. I've only been your sports student for twenty-five years." Kamora grinned and waved. "Hey, Brock."

"Hey." Then Brock held out his hand to Cameron. "Mr. Collins."

"Nice to meet you."

As her father and Brock exchanged greetings, Christopher and Nicole walked over. Sheridan hugged Christopher and then Nicole, hiding her surprise at seeing the two together.

She said, "Christopher and Nicole, this is —"

"I met him before," Christopher said, as

he took Brock's hand.

She wanted to cover her face, hide her eyes from her son, but when Christopher introduced Nicole, to Brock, as his girlfriend, that news made her forget her embarrassment.

"Did I hear Sheridan?" Beatrice asked, as she brought a tray of cheese and crackers into the living room.

"Hi, Mom."

But Beatrice had no words for her daughter, turning instead to the man by her side. "Brock. Welcome to our home."

"So, Brock, are you a Laker fan?" Cameron asked, pulling him away from Sheridan's side.

Sheridan couldn't hear his response as he moved with her father to the other side of the room.

Beatrice said, "Honey, can I speak to you?" She motioned with her chin toward the kitchen.

Sheridan glanced at Brock, who with his expression waved her away.

Inside the kitchen Beatrice said, "Just want you to know, Quentin's coming."

Sheridan groaned. "How'd that happen?"

Beatrice shrugged and pulled a tray of ribs from the oven. "He called this morning. Asked if it was okay. I couldn't tell him no." She paused. "Didn't you think he'd want to come?"

"I thought he'd be happy having her to-morrow." She inhaled. "Oh, well. We're all adults. And I've got to get used to seeing him with Jett." She paused. "But I don't know how Christopher will react."

Beatrice waved her hand. "Chris will be fine. He's not going to do anything in front of me or Cameron."

Sheridan shook her head in doubt. "I don't know. For four months Chris hasn't said four words to Quentin. Even Quentin and I have found a way to get along. Well, sort of. I'm learning to accept and live with what's happened."

"And that young man out there is making it a bit easier."

Sheridan couldn't tell if it was a statement or a question, so she said nothing.

Beatrice said, "Don't worry about Chris." She opened the refrigerator and handed Sheridan a Mountain Dew. "He seems fine now. I was happy he brought Nicole with him."

"Yeah, he's been hanging out with her and his other old friends," Sheridan said. But still the worry stayed inside her. She didn't know what Christopher would do when Quentin arrived with Jett.

"If you want, I'll have Cameron tell Chris that there'll be none of that teenage nonsense in this house. We let that kind of stuff go when we got rid of you and your brother."

"No. Let's just see how it plays out." She paused. "But maybe you can send up an extra prayer right about now."

"I will." Beatrice chuckled. "But there's nothing to worry about. I know my grandson."

And I know him better, she thought before she turned to the living room. The doorbell rang, but before she could get to the door, Kamora opened it. Over her shoulder Sheridan saw Quentin.

It was a long, silent moment as Kamora stared at Quentin, and Sheridan wondered why she hadn't thought about Kamora. Her friend wasn't much better than her son.

"Come on in, Quentin," Sheridan said, because it was obvious Kamora had no intention of making the invitation.

He stepped to the side, since Kamora hadn't made a space for him to pass, but before he could say anything, Tori rushed to him.

"Daddy!" It was like Tori had radar.

She'd been in the den with her friends, but the moment Quentin stepped into the house, she found him. "Thank you for coming to my party."

"I wouldn't miss this, sweetie."

Kamora rolled her eyes and walked into the living room.

"Daddy, we're playing chess. There's three of us on one team, and three on the other, but you can play with us too. Come on."

"Just a minute, sweetheart. I want to talk to your mom first."

Once alone, he said, "I hope you don't mind my being here."

"Not at all," she said. "I just want to warn you, Christopher's here."

"I expected him to be."

"He's with Nicole" — she paused when he raised his eyebrows — "so maybe he won't act like a total fool."

Quentin chuckled. "Anything else I should know before I head inside?"

She looked over Quentin's shoulder to where Brock sat with her father on the couch. "Where's Jett?" she asked, not answering him.

He looked away from her. "I didn't think I should bring him. This is a day for our family." He paused. "I learned a lesson from the recital."

Oh, great.

Sheridan watched as Quentin walked into the front room. She stayed still as Cameron greeted his son-in-law and then introduced Brock. The girls' shrieks from the den and the Laker game in the living room drowned her father's words, but she exhaled when Brock shook Quentin's hand and a moment later Quentin walked away. Only then did she join her father and Brock.

"Are you okay?" she asked Brock.

"He's fine," Cameron answered for him. "This guy has a good head on his shoulders. First, he's a Laker fan, and he agrees we shouldn't let Shaq go. And then we've been talking about whether there really are lost books of the Bible."

"He must really like you," she said to Brock. "Those are his favorite subjects."

Sheridan turned when Christopher tapped her on her shoulder and motioned for her to step away.

"I didn't know Dad was coming," Christopher whispered.

"I didn't know either." She took a sip of her soda.

"Are you all right?" he asked.

She cocked her head. "Of course. I'm not hurt by your father anymore, Christopher. And I don't think you should be either."

"Yeah, well. I'm fine with him. As long as he leaves me alone." He smiled when Nicole joined them, and the talk turned to their SATs.

Kamora sauntered over to the group and pulled Sheridan away. "I didn't know Quentin was going to be here."

Sheridan chuckled. "That's exactly what Chris said."

"Are you okay?"

"That's exactly what Chris asked."

Kamora chuckled. "I was wondering . . . how does it feel to be in a room with your husband and your boo?"

"Do women call men that anymore?"

"What? Husbands?"

They laughed together. Kamora said, "I'm just sayin'," she whispered, "it's gotta feel kinda good, showing Quentin he's nothing more than a few years in your history."

He was a lot more than that, but Sheridan wasn't going to explain that to Kamora.

"I'm glad Mr. Muscles has helped you get over Quentin."

"It's not because of Brock that I feel this way."

"Um-hmm." Kamora popped a cracker into her mouth. "But I know Mr. Muscles has helped to move the healing process along," she said, before she sauntered back to Christopher and Nicole.

Sheridan leaned against the mantel and glanced through the pictorial history of her life. And then she looked at Brock. He felt her stare, looked up and smiled.

For the next hour Sheridan wandered through the rooms, joining Quentin and the girls, then Christopher, Nicole, and Kamora. She went into the kitchen to help her mother, who just shooed her away.

"It's just hamburgers, hot dogs, and ribs," Beatrice said. "I'm getting the beans ready now."

The day was easy, more effortless than she had ever imagined. Once Brock was released from her father, he flowed with the family like he belonged.

"Okay, everyone," Beatrice finally called. "Grab a plate. Let the birthday girl and her guests go first," she admonished the adults.

Sheridan packed her plate with food and then said to Brock, "Let's eat outside." She led him through the sliding door to the table under the gazebo.

"Your family's great," Brock said. "Especially your dad. And I'm glad Christopher . . . well, I'm glad he doesn't hold a grudge."

The sliding door opened and Quentin stepped outside. "Mind if I join you guys?"

He moved too quickly for Sheridan to respond, and a second later he was sitting next to her.

With a rib in his hand, Quentin asked Brock, "How long have you known Kamora?"

Both Sheridan and Brock frowned at the oddity of the question. And then it hit them at the same time.

"Quentin, Brock is here . . . with me."

It took several seconds for her words to reach the understanding part of his brain. His eyes looked like he was watching a game of Ping-Pong, the way his glance moved back and forth between the two of them.

"You're . . . together." His tone was full of humor.

"Yes," she said.

"You're not here with Kamora?" he said to Brock.

With one of his lopsided grins, he said, "No. I'm here with your . . . with Sheridan."

Quentin's smile faded. "Oh."

The minutes that followed were filled

with only the sound of forks scraping against the softness of the paper plates.

"Daddy!" Tori slid the doors open. "Can you come and —"

"Sure." Quentin jumped up before she finished her request.

The moment Quentin stepped into the house, Brock said, "At least we got that over with."

"It felt beyond strange. But you know what? It felt good."

"Because it gave you a chance to get back at Quentin?"

"No, exactly the opposite." She reached across the table and touched his hand. "Because it felt good to say I was with you."

He squeezed her hand. "So you're not ashamed of me anymore?"

"I was never ashamed of you," she exclaimed.

"Yes, you were. But you're not anymore. Because at least from today forward, you can tell people that we share the same decade."

She balled up a napkin and threw it at him. They laughed. Brock stood and pulled her to her feet. "Happy birthday," she whispered. He kissed her and Sheridan didn't care if anyone was looking.

★ ★ ★

"Are you sure you're okay with this?" Sheridan asked, as Brock stopped the car in her driveway. "I wanted to do something special for you today."

He took her hand. "I had a great day."

Sheridan wanted to believe him, but this was not what she'd planned. After dinner she'd hoped to rush away, the way Kamora had done a moment after she tossed her empty plate into the trash. But still they stayed, even after Quentin left, offering to drive Tori's friends home. By eight o'clock Christopher and Nicole had hurried off to a party at their school.

But when she'd tried to leave, Brock insisted that they stay.

"It'll be fun to watch *Finding Nemo*," he'd said.

Now he leaned over and kissed her. "If you feel so bad about my day, why don't you make me feel good about my night?"

"How?"

"Well, Tori's with your parents. And Christopher's not home either. I could always come in for a good-night kiss."

"Remember what happened the last time you came in for just a kiss?"

"I remember. That's why I want to do it again."

This time, when he kissed her, she remembered too. *It's a hard walk.* And she wanted him. *It's a hard walk.* She wanted to do it again — just once. And then she could pray for forgiveness.

She pulled away. She knew she'd gone over the edge if she was thinking about the sin and the redemption at the same time. "I'd better get inside."

"I think you'd better too." His voice was husky.

"Thanks for spending your birthday with my family." She kissed the tips of her fingers and then placed them on his lips.

She rushed away, glad he didn't decide to walk her to the door, knowing that she would never turn him away if he was by her side. She stepped into the house, stood at the window, and watched Brock sit in his car. She wondered if he was waiting for her to change her mind. She wondered what she would do if he came to her door.

Minutes passed before he started the car and backed out of the driveway.

"This is a hard walk."

The phone interrupted her thoughts and she smiled. He missed her already.

"Hey." Lust mixed with joy in her tone.

"Hey yourself, sis."

She changed her tone. "What's up?"

"Nothing. I just talked to Mom, Dad, and Tori, and I heard all about your new man."

She sighed. This was the part she'd feared.

"So tell me about this Brock."

"There's nothing to tell," she said, sitting at the table.

"Don't you think it's a little too soon for you to be going out?"

"No, if your husband leaves you for a man, there's no grieving period. You gotta get right back out there." She chuckled.

He was silent for a second. "Good point," he said, taking her words seriously. "So, do I need to get down there and check this one out?"

"The only thing you need to do is stay out of my business."

"Yeah, yeah. Anyway, Mom told me Quentin showed up too. Ain't that some s— well, praise the Lord anyway."

Sheridan was glad for that detour.

He said, "Can't believe he showed his face."

"He's my children's father."

"Maybe I need to move down there. I can do better for those kids than he can."

"Keep your butt in San Francisco, little brother. I can take care of my children.

And I know no matter what, Quentin loves them too."

"He has a fine way of showing it."

"So is this why you called? To berate me?"

"I called because I care."

"You called because you're nosy."

"I'm just looking after my family."

"I've had a long day. I'm going to bed."

"You always do that. When you don't want to hear what I have to say, you rush off."

"Good night." He was still talking when she clicked off the phone. She sighed when the phone rang again.

"What do you want?" she said, her annoyance apparent.

"I want you."

Her tone changed again. "I want you too. I just have to do this right."

"Is wanting a sin?"

"Some people might say it is, but I don't."

"Good. Because I want you, badly." He sang the last word and she laughed.

"Are you home yet?"

"Almost, but I was thinking about turning around and bringing you home with me. No children will walk in on us here."

She smiled at the thought. “Good thing I live fifteen minutes away.”

“I can be there in ten.”

“Good night, Brock.”

“Good night.” Before she hung up, she heard him call her name again.

“Yes?”

He was silent. “Never mind. Just have a good night.”

When she clicked off the phone, she whispered, “I’ve had a very good night, already.”

Chapter Forty

"Honey, we had a wonderful time with you and the kids Saturday," Beatrice said. "And it was nice meeting Brock."

Sheridan held her breath, bracing for the questions. She didn't want to answer any inquiries about Brock and she exhaled when all Cameron added was, "He's a nice guy."

"We had a good time too," Sheridan said. "But the best part of everything is that you're cancer free, Daddy."

"Well, I always knew I'd be healed, but I want to go beyond my healing, and that's why we called."

Beatrice said, "Sheridan, your father has come up with a wonderful idea."

"Let me tell her, woman," Cameron teased.

"You're taking too long."

Sheridan laughed. "Come on, guys. Tell me. You sound so excited, but I'll never know what it is if you keep going at each other."

They laughed with her, but then Cameron turned serious. "Sheridan, you know the deadliest part of prostate cancer is not the cancer. What kills is not catching it in time. And that's because men aren't aware and don't get examined. Early detection is almost guaranteed curable. I want men to know this."

"So," Beatrice jumped in, "your father wants to do workshops. Isn't that terrific? We've already talked to our pastor about it and I'm sure Pastor Ford would be open to having this at Hope Chapel too."

"That's a great idea, Daddy. I'll speak to Pastor Ford, but in the meantime let me know when you'll be speaking at your church and I'll be there."

"That's why I called." Cameron paused. "I want you to do the workshops with me."

Sheridan frowned. "How will I do that?"

Beatrice said, "These workshops are about survival. And your father and I believe you would be terrific."

"Yes," Cameron continued. "I'm calling these My Life as a Survivor Seminars. There'll be quite a few of us presenting. Mrs. Maloney has agreed to speak about surviving breast cancer and Mr. Johnson is going to speak about surviving his wife's suicide."

Sheridan could feel the fear building. Surely her parents weren't asking her to speak about her husband being gay.

Cameron said, "And you can speak about divorce, sweetheart."

Oh, no.

He continued, "Now, I know you may not want to talk about Quentin specifically, and that's okay. But you have quite a testimony. And testimonies are not for you alone. They're meant to be shared. I can't do these workshops without you, Sheridan. You're a survivor."

"We've been talking about this all week," Beatrice said. "Don't you think that's a great idea?"

For moments only silence was Sheridan's answer. Finally, she said, "I don't think I can do that."

This time, the Collinses responded with silence.

"I'm sorry, Daddy."

"That's okay," Cameron said with disappointment inside his words. "Let me know if you change your mind."

"I will," she said, although she knew she would never do that. Never stand up in front of anyone. Never give her testimony. Never tell anybody that she'd survived her husband's preference for a man.

Chapter Forty-one

Sheridan was livid.

"I don't know where he is, Ms. Hart," Nicole said in her soft manner. "He never came to services this morning."

Sheridan stood in the middle of the hallway, across from the Youth Center, where the teens held their Sunday services. She squinted, recalling this morning's conversation with Christopher.

"Mom, I'm going to walk to church," he'd said when she came downstairs.

He'd been walking to church with Nicole for the past few weeks.

"Maybe he wasn't feeling well and went back home," Nicole suggested.

That had to be it. "Thanks, Nicole."

Sheridan marched to her car. *That's what happened. He was walking to church and didn't feel well.* But not even that made sense. She'd watched him walk out the door; he'd been fine.

She jumped into her car and as she drove her anger grew. Just when she believed life was moving fine. Everything had been going well with Christopher — her model son had returned. No more missed curfews, no new tattoos, no other disorderly conduct. The only challenge had been that he still wouldn't speak to his father. But Sheridan had even accepted that for now, believing one day soon father and son would reconcile.

"Obviously, I was wrong," she thought as she rounded the curve of the cul-de-sac. A rusted pickup truck sat in her driveway. She frowned.

She pulled up next to the car, half expecting to see Jett Jennings, ready to ambush her once again, although she couldn't imagine the star golf pro in a truck like this. She looked toward her house. There was no sign anyone was inside, but still her stomach lurched.

The moment she entered her home, she knew why her insides were churning. She moved in slow motion — closing the door, stepping into the living room. Taking in the sight of her son. And Déjà.

Sheridan put her purse on the chair. "Hello, Déjà."

The girl smiled, but she didn't possess the ignorant arrogance she'd worn the last time she was in their home. She sat on one end of the couch, with Christopher at the other. "Hello, Ms. Hart."

Although she kept her eyes on Déjà, Sheridan asked, "Christopher, what's going on?"

His silence made her look at him, and she noticed the way he shook. And she did the same.

"Mom," he said with his eyes lowered. "We have something to tell you." Only then did he look at her. "Do you want to sit down?"

"No." She had to stand; her legs didn't have the power to move. "What is it?" When he remained silent, Sheridan said, "Christopher?"

Déjà reached across the massive space and took Christopher's hand. But he jerked away and then clasped his hands under his chin as if he were praying.

"Christopher?" Sheridan called him again.

"I'm pregnant," Déjà said.

Christopher's head snapped back. "I was supposed to tell her."

"You were taking too long." The movement of her head emphasized each word. Déjà's arrogance was back.

Sheridan watched the drama unfold. Only this wasn't television.

"What did you say?" She faced Christopher as if Déjà hadn't spoken.

"I'm pregnant," Déjà repeated, "and Christopher is my baby's daddy."

No, she didn't just say that. She shook her head, not allowing Déjà's words to touch her. As long as the words stayed away from her head, as long as they stayed away from her heart, this wouldn't be true.

It couldn't be true anyway. Couldn't be happening. Not to her son. Not in her perfect family.

Then she remembered: they weren't the perfect Harts anymore.

Finally her legs moved, and she fell into the chair facing them. It was the same space she'd sat in when she'd met Déjà two months before.

This baby can't be Christopher's.

"Déjà, you haven't known Christopher long enough to be pregnant by him."

Déjà frowned as if she wanted to ask Sheridan if she'd ever taken biology. "It only takes one time, Ms. Hart," Déjà said, breaking it down. "And I was with Chris plenty more than once. But if you don't believe me, we can take a test. 'Cause since I met him, I haven't been with anyone except for Chris." Her hands moved with her words, and Sheridan noticed that this time Déjà's fingernails didn't claim her son. Sheridan allowed her glance to move to

Déjà's stomach. And she wanted to cry. The girl didn't need glitter on her nails to stake her claim anymore.

"So what are you going to do?" Sheridan asked, looking between the two of them.

Christopher frowned. "Mom, I thought you would tell me —"

"I'm going to have the baby," Déjà interjected, as if Sheridan should have known this. "We should get married."

Christopher's eyes widened, and in spite of it all, Sheridan laughed. "How can you get married, Déjà? Christopher's sixteen. He can't marry anyone."

"He can if he has your permission. My father checked it out." Déjà blew a bubble and then let the gum pop, sealing her words.

Christopher shook even more.

"You told your father?"

She nodded. "He don't have no problem with this."

Why would he?

"He says I'm grown. So I want to get married."

Christopher looked as if he would begin convulsing at any moment. Sheridan wanted to rush to him, rest his head on her shoulder, and convince him everything would be all right. But first someone had to do that for her.

Sheridan closed her eyes, hoping to still the shock that was making her shiver.

"Do we have your permission to get married?"

Sheridan opened her eyes. *Was this your plan all along?* she wondered as she looked at Déjà.

"Mom!" Christopher's tears were just seconds away.

"Déjà, I need to think about this, talk it over with Christopher and his father."

"Mom!" he exclaimed, as if he couldn't believe she was giving him away.

Sheridan ignored him. She wanted him to stew in the shock that he'd just given to her.

Déjà smiled, on the verge of winning a prize. "That's fine. I'll go now, so you can talk." She stood and glanced at Christopher, but he kept his eyes away from her. With a sigh she walked past Sheridan and out the front door.

Sheridan sat, staring at her son. Christopher sat, staring at the floor. Neither said a word until the rattle of the old truck's engine faded.

"Mom," Christopher finally spoke. "Please."

"Please what, Christopher?"

"Please don't make me get married." He trembled with his words.

Like I would really do that. "Why shouldn't I? You're going to be a father. Don't you think you should marry your child's mother?" It sounded even more absurd when she said the words aloud.

"Mom, I can't."

"Why not?"

"Because I'm too young."

"But you're not. You're going to be a father."

"And because I don't love her."

"But you had sex with her."

"Yes, but people have sex all the time and they're not in love." She wondered where he'd learned that piece of fact. And then she remembered. Brock. Then Christopher. In the hallway.

Sheridan stood. "I haven't decided anything yet. I have to talk to your father."

He stood. "Mom, please." She half expected him to drop to his knees.

She turned and then said over her shoulder, as calmly as if he'd just told her what college he'd selected, "Don't leave this house, Christopher." She stomped up the steps and slammed her bedroom door. She needed to call Quentin, but first she had to get her heart back to its normal pace. Her sixteen-year-old son was going to be a father. How could this have happened?

Sheridan was catatonic.

She didn't know how long she sat, staring, thinking about all that had gone wrong. All the reasons why her family continued to crumble like a tower of cards.

Finally she gathered the strength to pick up the phone and punched in Quentin's cell.

"This is Dr. Quentin Hart. I'm unavailable . . ."

She hung up and paged him, but when after five minutes he hadn't called back, she scrolled through the caller ID, found his number, and called his home.

Her heart pounded with each ring.

"Hello." It wasn't the man who was once her husband.

"Jett, I need to speak to Quentin."

"Is everything all right, Sheridan?"

No, she almost screamed. *Nothing is right because of you.* "I need to speak to Quentin," she repeated.

She heard his sigh, but she didn't care.

"Hello."

"Quentin . . ." She had planned on telling him all of it, but the thought of what she had to say made her lips tremble.

"Sheridan? What's wrong?"

It took moments to swallow the lump that blocked her words. "We need you here."

"I was on my way to pick up Tori from your parents."

She had forgotten about her daughter, who had spent the night with Beatrice and Cameron. "Quentin, I'll call my parents, but I need . . . you. Here."

Only a beat passed. "I'll be there in twenty minutes."

She hung up the phone and let the tears she'd been holding flow. She cried for the lost dreams — the ones she knew Christopher had, the ones she had for him. She even cried for Quentin and what this news would do to him. She cried for her parents and Tori and Nicole. She cried for all who would be affected.

Finally she stood and stepped into her closet. She dropped the skirt and matching top and left the designer outfit on the floor. Then she reached for her black sweat suit. She was dressed in seconds. When she opened her bedroom door, Christopher was coming up the stairs.

She looked at him, but the young man in front of her was not the son she knew. He was a son who would be a father in just months.

"Your father will be here in a little while."

"Why do I have to talk to him? He's not a part of my life anymore."

Sheridan wondered, if sex had made him so bold, then why hadn't it made him smart? She said nothing; just walked past him, leaving him standing in the hallway. Downstairs, she called her parents, and was relieved when the answering machine came on.

"Hey," she said into the machine. "Quentin's going to be a bit late picking up Tori, but let her know he'll be there, okay? Speak to you guys later."

She only had to wait a few more minutes before she heard the key in the front door. Quentin stepped inside, tossed his jacket over the settee, and then came into the living room.

"Hi," he said, eyeing her.

Her response was tears. They gushed from her, as they had the day he left.

"Sheridan, what's wrong?" He held her.

"Dad?"

Quentin's arms released her, and Christopher moved toward them, slowly. Then his tears came.

Quentin held his son as if he were a newborn, and Sheridan cried some more.

Finally Quentin stepped away. "What is going on?" He looked from Sheridan to Christopher and back to his almost ex-wife again.

"Dad, Déjà is pregnant and I'm the father."

Quentin's eyes widened, and he returned his glance to Sheridan. She nodded and sank into the chair. Quentin and Christopher sat on the couch together.

"Tell me everything."

Sheridan listened as Christopher told how Déjà had called this morning. He ended by telling his father that Déjà wanted to get married.

"Mom wants me to get married too."

Quentin looked at Sheridan as if she had lost her mind, but she held up her hand. "I didn't say that."

"You didn't?" Christopher's voice was soft; he sounded the way she remembered him. Before he'd met Déjà.

Christopher's shoulders relaxed with relief. "But I still don't know what to do."

"What do you think you should do?" Quentin asked.

Sheridan could see Christopher was surprised by the question. He expected her and Quentin to make the decisions for him. "I don't know," Christopher said. Sheridan and Quentin stayed quiet, and Christopher continued, "I don't want to get married." He paused. "And I'm not supposed to believe in abortion." He paused again, as if waiting to see if his parents agreed. When they still said nothing, he said, "But I can't be a father, because I don't even have a job. And I want to finish school." He paused. "And Dad, I really want to go to college."

The doorbell chimed, and the three sat still for a moment, wondering who was interrupting their catastrophe. It wasn't until their visitor knocked that Sheridan rose to answer the door.

"Ms. Hart, is Chris here?"

Sheridan stepped aside, allowing Déjà to enter. She walked into the living room like she was supposed to be there.

"Mr. Hart, I'm Déjà."

Quentin stood and took her outstretched hand. Then, she took his place on the couch next to Christopher.

"I was on my way home when Chris called and told me you were coming over, Mr. Hart, and I wanted to be with him."

Sheridan moved to Quentin and they

stood, shoulder to shoulder, looking at their son.

Déjà continued, "I wanted you to know that my father says it's fine if I get married."

Quentin crossed his arms. "That's not an option. Christopher is a minor." He held up his hand, stopping her protest. "I know we can give him our permission, but both of you are too young."

His words made Sheridan freeze. Those were the words Cameron had spoken all those years ago when she and Quentin insisted on being married. Would Christopher do what she and Quentin had done? Could Déjà convince him that being married was for the best, just as Quentin had convinced her?

Sheridan exhaled when she looked at her son, his eyes full of terror. Not even she would be able to convince him that being with Déjà was for the best.

Quentin said, "But Déjà, although we won't give our permission for Christopher to get married, we will be there for you."

Déjà smiled. Christopher didn't.

"I guess I understand," Déjà said. "It'll be better for Chris to graduate. I can wait. It'll only be a year."

The three Harts exchanged glances.

"Let's just get through this part first," Quentin said.

"Okay." Déjà shifted her glance to Sheridan. "Ms. Hart, I know you're not happy about this. But like I told you, I love Chris." She paused and rested her hand on her stomach. "And I love my baby too."

Sheridan swallowed and nodded.

Déjà continued, "I have my first appointment at the clinic and maybe . . . you can go with me? So I won't have to go by myself."

A clinic?

The three Harts looked at each other again.

Sheridan's expression made Quentin say, "Ah, Déjà, did you know I'm a doctor? I deliver babies."

Déjà frowned. "Yeah, but aren't you expensive?"

"We take insurance."

"I don't have any."

Sheridan said, "Déjà, we'll handle your expenses. Don't worry about that."

Déjà smiled. "Okay."

"I'll refer you to one of the doctors in the medical center. I'll make the appointment tomorrow, and Ms. Hart will call you."

"Okay." Déjà stood. "I'm late getting my

dad's truck back to him. And I'm a little tired anyway." She took one step and then looked down at Christopher. He didn't move.

Quentin said, "Christopher, walk Déjà to the door."

"Thank you, Mr. and Ms. Hart."

Sheridan waited until Déjà and Christopher were out of the room before she turned to Quentin. "I want a paternity test."

"No doubt." Quentin sat on the couch.

"And I'm thinking about calling the police. Christopher is a minor."

Quentin shook his head. "Sheridan, that's not going to change anything. It will be a misdemeanor, at best. And Déjà will still be pregnant. If Christopher is the father, do you want our grandchild's mother to have a police record . . . or worse?"

Before she could answer, Christopher returned.

"Thanks, Dad." When Quentin frowned, he continued, "For not being mad."

"Oh, I'm upset, Christopher," Quentin said, his voice tight. "And I'm disappointed. But we have to do what we have to do." He paused. "Did you and Déjà talk about a paternity test?"

He nodded. "Yeah, I told her I wanted

one, but she said there was no need."

Where was I when this world changed? Sheridan wondered. Her sixteen-year-old son was demanding a paternity test.

"We're still going to have a test done, Chris," Quentin said.

Christopher nodded and smiled slightly for the first time since Sheridan had come home. "Do you really think I'm not the father?"

"The only way I could say that is if you tell me you didn't have sexual intercourse with Déjà."

Christopher said nothing.

"Then the purpose of the test is to make sure you're the father."

Christopher nodded, but his smile was gone. He turned, but stopped and faced his parents. "Mom, Dad, I'm really sorry." He paused as if he had more to say, but then he trotted up the stairs.

They were silent while they watched him, and then Sheridan fell onto the couch next to Quentin.

"Wow" was all he said.

"Christopher is just a baby himself."

Quentin shook his head. "It's unbelievable that this would happen . . . to us."

"A lot of things have happened that I never thought would happen . . . to us."

He looked away. "Do you think this happened because . . ."

She wished she could blame it all on him, but she had let Christopher down too. "There were a lot of things. Who knows? Even if . . ." She paused and sighed. "This may have still happened."

Quentin shook his head. "I don't think he would have met Déjà if I were still home."

Sheridan shrugged. "All I know is that I have a baby who may be having a baby. His whole life is going to change."

Quentin nodded. "I'll take care of this tomorrow. But I'd better get going and pick up Tori. I don't want to disappoint her." He sighed. "I'm not in the mood to go out right now."

Sheridan stood with him and sadness walked them to the door.

"I don't plan on saying anything to Tori."

"Of course not." Sheridan hadn't even thought of that. "I don't think we should say anything to anyone until we know for sure."

He moved in slow motion, slipping the sleeves of his jacket over his shoulders. Then he reached for her and held her, trying to bring them both peace inside the embrace.

When he pulled away, he said, "We'll get through this. Just like we've gotten through everything else."

She nodded, then watched until he'd driven away.

"Mom?"

Christopher walked down the stairs and sat on the bottom step. "I'm really scared." His voice was so soft she barely heard his words. But his expression, face tight, shoulders lifted, told Sheridan all she needed to know.

She sat next to him, and her anger fell away. All she wanted to do was hold her son. "Your father and I are here for you no matter what."

He nodded.

"And you always have God. He'll never let you down." *Like your father and I did.*

"God is probably mad at me."

"I'm sure He's disappointed, but all you have to do is pray, tell God what's in your heart, and He'll forgive you."

"I never thought something like this would happen to me."

Neither did I.

"Mom, how am I going to go to church now?"

She frowned. "You'll go to church just like you always did."

"But what about the people? What are they going to say?"

Sheridan remembered her same concerns. She remembered Francesca and Jane. She remembered the other comments she'd never heard but was sure were made. "It doesn't matter what people say, Christopher. As long as you do what's right, people's opinions don't matter."

"But I know they're going to be asking a lot of questions and talking about it." He paused and his voice became softer. "I don't know how I'm going to tell Nicole."

"Why didn't you think about any of this before?"

He shrugged. "I don't know. I just wanted to feel better, and Déjà made me feel better. She said I was the first man she ever loved."

Sheridan kept her response inside.

"I had never had a girl tell me that before."

You're only sixteen.

"But I guess I should have thought more about it."

You think? "Yes, you should have."

With tears in his eyes, he said, "Mom, I'm sorry."

She put her arms around him and they stayed together, marinating in the same thought: what was life going to be like now?

Finally Christopher pulled away. "Mom, there is one more thing."

She looked at him and the shaking returned. What else could there be? She braced herself, waiting for the next words that would rock her world.

"You don't have to call me Christopher anymore. I'm fine with being just Chris."

Sheridan stroked his face and wished she could take him back. Back to before he knew Déjà. To the days when he was innocent. To when he was just Chris.

"You've always been just Chris to me," she whispered, as she held him again.

Sheridan glanced at the caller ID. She took a breath before she answered.

"Hey, baby," he said, after she said hello. "I missed you today."

"I missed you too."

"What's wrong?" he asked, and she could hear his worry.

"Nothing. Just a long day."

"You sound like it. Want me to come over? No, wait, it would be better if you came over here. I could make you forget whatever happened today."

She sank onto her bed and closed her eyes.

Brock said, "So what do you say? Want some comfort?"

"I can't talk right now."

The concern was back in his voice. "What's wrong?"

"Nothing. Everything. I'll call you tomorrow." She hung up, not able to talk to him. Not able to listen to his voice. Not wanting to be reminded of that day. Of her and him. Then Christopher in the hallway.

"Is this my fault?"

Sheridan lay in the bed, still in her sweat suit. Her eyelids were heavy from exhaustion, but she fought to stay awake. She didn't want to sleep, didn't want to dream. Didn't want her subconscious to confirm what she already knew — that even though God had forgiven her for what she'd done with Brock, what happened with Christopher proved that even forgiven sins had consequences.

Chapter Forty-two

"Hi, Mom."

Sheridan turned around. "Chris, you're going to be late . . ." She stopped as she took in her son. He was dressed in khaki pants and a navy golf shirt, his bomber jacket in hand and leather backpack over his shoulder. Even his loafers were back. The Chris of old. Softly she said, "You're running late. Do you want some cereal?"

"I'm not hungry."

"You have to eat."

"I'll grab something at school."

The blare of the van's horn announced its arrival, and Christopher hugged her like he used to. He said, "Have a good day, Mom."

After he disappeared, she was still standing, wondering what this school day was going to be like for him. How was he supposed to concentrate on English lit and chemistry and trigonometry when all he could think about was that he was going to be a father?

The telephone rescued her from more despair.

"Sheridan, I've made the appointment," Quentin said. "Can you bring Déjà this afternoon?"

"I don't know. I didn't know you were going to do it this soon."

"Oh, yeah."

Sheridan wondered if he had even slept. She was sure he was in the office before anyone else, just waiting until he could arrange the appointment. She almost smiled. Last night her son had returned. And now here was the man who was once her husband. The man who took charge and controlled their home.

"Chris just left for school."

"Not a problem. I'll pick him up this afternoon and bring him for his tests. But I want to get Déjà in here this morning."

"Okay. I'll call her."

"One thing, do you know how far along she is?"

Sheridan tried to remember if Déjà had said. "I don't know. I guess a couple of months. She can't be too far along."

Quentin released a long breath of air. "She has to be at least ten weeks for a CVS. But just get her down here; we'll figure it out."

"I'll call you when we're on our way." It took only seconds for her to hang up and call the Blue household. At first the phone rang ten times, with no answer. Still, she hung up and dialed again. This time the phone was answered on the first ring.

"May I speak to Déjà, please?"

"Hold on," a female voice said.

Sheridan heard the scream that beckoned Déjà to the phone and then the same sounds that had met her the night she took Déjà home — the squeals of toddlers, the roar of the television, the blasting of a CD.

"Hello."

"Déjà, this is Ms. Hart." Sheridan paused and wondered what Déjà would call her if it did turn out that she was the mother of her first grandchild. She shuddered. "My husband . . . Dr. Hart scheduled an appointment for this morning. Can you make it?"

"I don't know. My father was supposed to be home, but he traded times with one of his friends. He'll be home tomorrow, and I can use the truck then. Can we do it tomorrow?"

"I'll come and get you right now." Today Sheridan had no concern about the distance. She'd drive five times those miles to get this done.

"But I'm so far away."

"It's fine. What time can you be ready?"

"Ms. Hart, can you hold on a sec?"

Sheridan paced as she listened to the muffled conversation before Déjà said, "My sister can take me. Where's the clinic?"

"Have your sister drop you off here. We'll ride together."

"Okay." The cheer in Déjà's voice told Sheridan she thought that this was a peace offering. But it was far from that. Sheridan was not taking any chances with misread directions; she would get Déjà to the hospital herself.

Déjà promised to be there within two hours. Sheridan took a shower, dressed, grabbed her purse, then the phone, and went downstairs. She sat on the settee by the door, with her purse by her side and the phone in her lap. And she waited. And thought about the future that sprawled in front of them.

The telephone rang and made her jump. But when she looked at the caller ID and saw that it was Kamora, she didn't answer. Then, minutes later, when she saw Brock's number, she let the phone ring again. Even when her parents' number showed up, Sheridan let voice mail greet them. There was no one she wanted to hear from right now. Except for Déjà. And all she wanted to know from her was that she was on her way.

Inside Quentin's office, Sheridan paced.

Hours had passed since Quentin had called this morning. It had taken Déjà and her sister more than three hours to get to Los Angeles, but Sheridan had been ready. When Déjà and her sister rounded the cul-de-sac, Sheridan was sitting in front of the house, in her car, with the engine running.

Now it was almost one and the waiting was beyond painful. She just wanted to know — wanted to know if her son was going to be a father.

"It normally takes two weeks to get the paternity results, but we'll rush it," Quentin had told her and Déjà when they arrived. "We'll still have to wait a day or two though."

Sheridan grimaced as she remembered Déjà's response. She sat calmly, as if she had expected the request for the paternity test. As if the joke was on them if they wanted to waste time and money.

The door opened and Sheridan stopped moving. She watched Quentin take slow steps to his desk.

"Well, she is pregnant," he said.

"I never doubted that. She's too smart to tell that lie."

"But we have a problem. She's only eight weeks."

Sheridan frowned.

He continued, "We have to wait at least two, possibly three weeks to do the paternity test."

Sheridan groaned.

He said, "It's not that long."

"It's a lifetime to me."

"Sheridan, you need to prepare yourself, because Déjà is insisting that Chris is the father."

"How many girls say that?"

"There's something about the way she says it. Maybe she does love Chris."

Is every man this gullible? "And that would mean what?"

Quentin stared at her for a long moment, then shook his head.

Sheridan sank into the chair across from Quentin. "How am I supposed to wait three weeks?" She closed her eyes and tried to imagine the time. The minutes, the days, the weeks of nothing but waiting. And worrying. And wondering. Sheridan leaned back in her chair. There was no way. She would never make it.

Chapter Forty-three

Sheridan was getting on everyone's nerves.

For the past week she had avoided most calls. But when she knew she couldn't get away with that anymore, she had curt conversations, wrapping everyone who loved her into a ball of confusion.

When she told Beatrice that she couldn't talk on the phone, her mother had said, "Just know that we're here if you need us." Beatrice spoke in that motherly tone that showed she knew something. "We're praying," was all she would say.

Brock had said, "Whenever you're ready for me, I'll be here for you."

And then Kamora said, "Girl, why you getting all brand new? Are you going through the change or somethin'?"

Not even Kamora's berating could free Sheridan from her angst. She hadn't slept more than three hours on any night, and she hadn't eaten three meals in five days. But she had prayed without ceasing. Prayed that God would be merciful. Prayed that inside that mercy, Christopher would not be the father of Déjà's baby.

Now she turned over in bed, took a breath, and decided it was time to get up. Get up from her bed and get up from the despair she'd wallowed in. There was nothing more she could do. Except leave it in God's hands. And believe that His will was the same as hers.

Sheridan sighed as she thought about Déjà, who had already shifted into Chris's-baby's-mother gear. She was easing her way into the Hart family fold, reporting to Christopher daily, chatting with Tori, always asking to speak to Sheridan. And she took every opportunity to convince Sheridan of the inevitable.

"I know how the paternity test is going to turn out, Ms. Hart, but I don't mind that you and Dr. Hart wanted the test," she'd said, as Sheridan drove her home on Monday.

On Tuesday Déjà asked, "Ms. Hart, which would you prefer, a grandson or a granddaughter?"

On Wednesday Déjà queried Sheridan for names.

On Thursday she said to Sheridan, "I was thinking about doing some shopping for my baby. Do you want to come with me?"

Yesterday, when Déjà had asked if they

were going to prepare a room for her and the baby so that she could stay there sometimes, it was only the grace of God and the sense she'd been raised with that prevented her from using every curse word she knew.

Sheridan shook her head as she looked in the bathroom mirror. She had to get past the emotions. Get to a place where she could accept Christopher as a father and Déjà as her son's baby's mother. And herself as a thirty-eight-year-old grandmother.

"Mom!"

Tori's scream froze Sheridan, but only for a moment. She bolted from her bedroom and raced down the stairs. Then she froze again at the sight before her. "What happened?" she asked, as she found her legs and knelt at the bottom of the stairs.

Déjà was sprawled across the marble floor, by the door, her eyes closed.

"I don't know," Tori cried. "When I opened the door, Déjà was there and said she was supposed to meet Chris. And then she said she wasn't feeling well. And then she fell."

Gently Sheridan lifted Déjà's head and rested it in her lap. "Where's Chris?"

"At Darryl's house. Mom, what's wrong with her?"

"I don't know, sweetheart." Sheridan spoke with calm, although her heart was pounding its way through her chest. "Get me the phone."

As Tori dashed into the kitchen, Sheridan lifted Déjà's head slightly and called her name. "Can you hear me?"

When Tori returned, Sheridan said, "I'm going to call nine-one-one. Get my cell and call Chris at Darryl's."

Tori took the steps two at a time, as Sheridan dialed. By the time she had given the information and begged the operator to hurry, Tori was back at her side.

"Chris and Darryl are on their way, Mom."

A moan stopped both of them. Déjà's eyelids fluttered and another groan slipped through her lips. She twisted in Sheridan's arms.

"Déjà, can you hear me?"

Her eyes opened slowly, and Sheridan could tell she had trouble focusing. "Ms. Hart." She licked her lips.

"Déjà, don't move. You're going to be all right. I called the paramedics."

"What . . . what happened?"

Her question came as Chris bolted into the house, slamming the door against the wall. "Mom!"

"Chris?" Déjà moved to sit up. "Oh." Her moan was louder this time, and she clutched her stomach. "Ms. Hart."

"Don't move," Sheridan pleaded. And then she saw the dark stain seeping through Déjà's jeans. She was grateful that no one else seemed to notice.

"Chris," Sheridan said, moving into command mode, "stay with Déjà. Tori, call your father. Track him down. Darryl, come upstairs with me." Sheridan stood. "Chris, don't let her move."

It was Sheridan's turn to race up the stairs. In the bathroom she soaked two towels. "Put these on Déjà's forehead," Sheridan told Darryl. "I'll be right down."

As Sheridan jumped into a sweat suit, Tori tore into her bedroom. "Dad wants to talk to you. He's at the golf course."

Sheridan grabbed the phone at the same time that she heard the front door open. "Quentin, the paramedics are here. I'm going with Déjà."

"What happened?"

"I don't know," she said, surprised by the tears she felt coming. "She fainted, I think." Then Sheridan lowered her voice. "I think it's bad. She's bleeding."

A groan was his response. "Okay, they're probably going to take her to Daniel

Freeman. I'll be right there."

Sheridan grabbed her purse.

"Mom! The doctors are here," Chris screamed.

She hurried to the door, but before she stepped into the hallway, she stopped. "Please, Lord, please. Keep Déjà and this baby safe." She repeated her prayer once more before she dashed down the stairs.

Chapter Forty-four

"We cleaned up the bloodstains in the hallway," Beatrice said. "And we're about to take Tori home with us. Poor thing. She's still upset."

Sheridan massaged the bridge of her nose. "Thanks, Mom. I'll call as soon as we know something."

"We'll be praying."

Sheridan clicked off her cell. She knew she wasn't supposed to use her phone inside the hospital, but there were no pay phones in sight.

She sighed and sank deeper into the hard leather of the waiting room couch. An hour had passed since Déjà had been admitted, and Sheridan had never felt so helpless. Even though Quentin was with Déjà, Sheridan wanted to be there too — to give her comfort, to tell her that everything would be all right.

"Chris," Sheridan said, "why don't you sit down?"

He shook his head. "I can't. I'm scared, Mom."

She nodded, understanding his feelings.

For days she'd wished this girl and her baby would fade into oblivion. But not like this.

Please, God. This is not what I meant. This is not what I wanted.

"Chris!"

Sheridan looked up as a woman with three children in tow rushed toward them. And then she saw Harold Blue.

"Hey, Bogus," Christopher said.

Bogus.

Christopher turned to Sheridan. "Mom, this is Déjà's sister, Bogus. And her dad."

"Hello, Mr. Blue," she said. "Hello . . . Bogus."

"What happened?" Bogus asked.

Sheridan let Christopher tell all that was known, which was not much beyond Déjà's being admitted. As her son spoke, Sheridan eyed the twenty-something-year-old woman in front of her. A toddler hung from her hip, and two other children, not much older, stood at her side. She would have been able to pick Bogus as Déjà's sister without being told — from the jeans that seemed to be dyed on, to the T-shirt that was stretched across her chest. Sheridan read the words painted on Bogus's chest — "I Did Rashaad Three Times." She wondered what that meant, and then her eyes passed over the three children. She almost laughed out loud.

"Your husband hasn't come out yet, Ms. Hart?" Harold Blue asked, as he sat next to her.

"No, but believe me, Mr. Blue, Déjà is in very good care. I can promise you."

He nodded and clasped his hands. "She's my baby. I just want her to be all right." Then he whispered, "I don't like hospitals much. This was the last place I saw my wife alive . . ."

Before Sheridan could reassure him, the doors to the emergency room swung open and Quentin, dressed in a white lab coat, walked out. As he stood at the entrance to the waiting room, every eye turned to him. But only Sheridan knew what his eyes were saying.

The trembling began in her toes and climbed through her until it reached her lips. "Oh, no," she cried softly.

Quentin walked over to Christopher and hugged him. "I'm sorry."

Harold Blue looked at Sheridan. "What happened? My baby . . ." He fell into his seat, and Sheridan took his hand.

She swallowed before she asked, "Quentin . . ." Her voice trembled. "How's Déjà?"

"She's fine, although she is taking this pretty hard."

Sheridan almost collapsed with relief.

"My baby . . . she's okay?" Harold Blue sounded as if he was confused.

"Yes. Yes, she's fine."

Harold Blue rested his face in his hands. "Thank you, Lord," he spoke loudly.

Sheridan closed her eyes. She couldn't have said it better herself.

The black of night was all Sheridan could see as she waited.

"Here you go," Kamora said, as she returned to the waiting room with two Styrofoam cups.

They sipped in silence until Kamora said, "You doing okay?"

Sheridan nodded. "Just numb. Exhausted emotionally. For the past week, I've had every emotion known to man."

"I can't believe you kept this from me."

"I didn't want to tell anyone until we knew for sure that . . . the baby was Christopher's." Sheridan had to pause. This morning she would have paid any ransom to be told Christopher was not this baby's father. But now she felt a loss so overwhelming, it knocked all feelings from her.

"I'm really sorry, Sheridan," Kamora said, taking her friend's hand.

Sheridan nodded.

"There's a bright side." Before Kamora could continue, Sheridan held up her hand. She could imagine the joke her friend was going to share. Something about the Blue crew. Something about Bogus's shirt. Something that yesterday would have made her laugh but today would make her cry.

"I don't see too many bright sides, Kamora. I don't know what this is going to do to Christopher."

"My godson is smart. He'll be relieved."

Sheridan took another sip of her coffee and doubted that Christopher felt relief. He was like her. All week he'd probably begged for this kind of pardon. Today he probably wished he could take back all those thoughts.

The emergency room doors swung open, and Quentin escorted Harold Blue out. Sheridan watched the two fathers shake hands and pat each other's back. And then Harold walked away, his shoulders just a bit lower than when he had come in this afternoon.

"How is she?" Sheridan asked, as Quentin came over to them.

"She's fine. It's more emotional than physical."

"Why did she miscarry?" Kamora asked.

He shook his head. "That's a question we haven't been able to answer. The only thing we know about miscarriages is that the baby wasn't developing normally. Unfortunately, miscarriage is common — almost fifty-fifty — in the first twenty weeks."

"But she's so young," Kamora said.

"That's the good news," Quentin said. "She'll be able to have more children."

At that moment Christopher stepped into the waiting room, and Sheridan was sure they were all thinking the same thing: Déjà could have more children, just not with Christopher Hart.

"Mom, Déjà wants to see you."

There was a part of Sheridan that had been waiting to see Déjà, to be there for her and comfort her the way she was sure Déjà's mother would have. But there was the other side — filled with guilt. The side that Sheridan wasn't proud of.

"I'll be here when you get back," Kamora said, as Sheridan stood.

Christopher took his mother's hand and escorted her to Déjà's room. Outside he stopped.

"You're not coming in?"

He shook his head. "She wants to talk to you."

But I don't want to be in there alone.

Sheridan took a deep breath and then entered. Déjà leaned back against the half-raised bed. If Sheridan didn't know what she'd just gone through, she wouldn't have believed it. Déjà just looked like she'd been up for a few too many hours. Nothing like someone who had to mourn the death of what would have been her first child.

That thought brought tears to Sheridan's eyes. She moved to the side of the bed and touched the railing. "How are you?"

Déjà nodded. "I'm fine." She paused. "I'm sad."

Sheridan touched her hand. "I know. I'm sorry."

Déjà cocked her head a bit. "Are you really?"

Sheridan swallowed the lump in her throat. "I am."

"I didn't think you'd be sorry. I didn't think you wanted me to have this baby."

She didn't want to lie, so she said nothing.

Déjà continued, "I know you don't like me, Ms. Hart."

"It's not that, Déjà."

"I know what it is." She looked down at her hands. "You don't think I'm good enough for Chris."

Sheridan pressed her lips together.

Déjà said, "When I first met Chris, I thought he was too good for me too. But my dad told me that no one was too good for me and that I had something to offer every boy." Her eyes lifted to Sheridan. "And what I offered Chris was love. I loved him, Ms. Hart. I still do."

It was the first time Sheridan believed her. "I know, Déjà." She paused, wondering if this was really the time to say what she thought. But then she continued, knowing neither one of them wanted her to hold back. "Déjà, you have so many years in front of you to discover what you want to do and who you want to be."

"Ms. Hart, it's not like that in my world. Where I'm from, I knew when I was a little girl what I wanted to be. I've known for a long time that I wanna be a mother and a wife."

Sheridan took her hand. "I think you'll be a wonderful wife and mother someday. But before then, there's so much you can do."

"But what's wrong with the plan I have?

Why can't what I want be enough? Why do you think it's not good enough?"

Her questions surprised and startled Sheridan, and she wondered, what was wrong with what Déjà desired? It wasn't any different than what she'd done — married young, become a wife and mother above all else.

Sheridan took Déjà's hands into hers. "I'm not saying you shouldn't be what you want. I just want you to know you have options. Does that make sense?"

She nodded. "I never thought about choices before. Didn't really think I had any."

Sheridan tried to smile. "Would you mind if I prayed with you?"

Déjà looked like she wanted to protest, but she nodded.

Sheridan closed her eyes. "Heavenly Father, we come to you, thanking you for being God. We worship you because you are God. We praise you and thank you for all the wonderful things you've done for us." Sheridan felt Déjà pull away, just a bit, but she held her hands tighter. "We thank you, Father, for protecting us, and guiding us. We thank you for caring for us. And we thank you for everything you've done for Déjà." She had to pause for a moment as she felt Déjà stiffen. "And though we don't understand everything that happens, we know that you are sovereign, you are in control, and everything will move for your glory. So Father, we ask for your peace tonight. We may not understand, but I know that you will hold us, and we will both know that you are with us. Thank you, Father, for this day. And thank you, Father, for all that you do every day. In Jesus' name, Amen."

When Sheridan looked up, Déjà's eyes were already open.

"You have a lot of faith, Ms. Hart, don't you?"

"I don't know what I would do if I didn't have God."

"No one's ever prayed for me before."

That made Sheridan sad.

Déjà said, "Thank you for coming to talk to me."

Sheridan squeezed Déjà's hand. "Just know you're going to be all right. God will take care of you."

Sheridan moved toward the door, but before she put her hand on the doorknob, Déjà said, "Ms. Hart, you said God will take care of me."

Sheridan nodded.

"I don't know a lot about God. Maybe I

can go to church with you one day."

Sheridan smiled. "I'd like that. If you're feeling up to it, what about Sunday?"

Déjà nodded.

"I'll give you a call, okay?"

Déjà smiled, and Sheridan stepped from the room. Outside she hugged Christopher. As she watched him push open the door to go back inside with Déjà, Sheridan had never been more proud of her son. They didn't know whether the baby had been Christopher's, but today he'd stepped up to the plate of responsibility.

Sheridan worked her way back through the hospital maze with beds and carts blocking the walkways, while the words she'd shared with Déjà whirled in her head. When she stepped through the emergency room doors, Brock stood on the other side.

He held his arms open, welcoming her, and she rushed to him.

"What are you doing here?" she asked.

"I called this morning, and Tori told me you had just left for the hospital. I've been calling you all afternoon."

"I'm so glad to see you."

"Kamora and Quentin filled me in a bit," Brock said, as he led her to the couch. "Are you okay?"

She shook her head. "It's been a long week."

He held her hand as they sat.

Quentin stood. "Christopher will only be able to stay another hour or so."

Sheridan asked, "When will Déjà be released?"

"Tomorrow. It's really not necessary for her to stay tonight. I just don't want her taking that long ride home."

Kamora stood. "Okay, I'm out." She hugged Sheridan and then turned to Quentin. She faced him for a long moment before she hugged him too. "I'll call you tomorrow," she said to Sheridan, before she waved good night to Brock and sauntered into the night.

Quentin said, "Give me a minute. I'll let Christopher know I'm going to take you home and that I'll come back for him."

Sheridan frowned. "That's not necessary. Brock will take me home."

It surprised her, the way Quentin's lips pressed together as if he needed to keep words inside. Brock took her hand into his.

Quentin nodded slightly. "Well, then, I'll pick up Tori. Come back. Get Christopher." He stopped. "Then I'll be home."

You'll be home? "Okay."

Sheridan could feel his eyes on them as

they walked to the parking lot. But when Brock pushed her against his car and released some of her stress with his lips, all consciousness of Quentin evaporated. And all her thoughts of Déjà and Christopher faded into the cool night's air.

They had been sitting in front of the house for at least an hour. The quiet felt good. And Brock's hands over hers felt even better.

"I want you to get some rest," Brock said. "It's been some week for you."

Sheridan leaned back. "This week is just a piece of the puzzle. A puzzle that began at the beginning of this year."

Brock twisted in his seat. "I hope I'm a good piece of your puzzle."

She smiled.

He said, "I guess it's been difficult getting used to Quentin being gone."

Her smile went away. "Yes, but it's getting easier."

She could feel the question coming — the one she was sure he'd almost asked a million times before. "How long have you and Quentin been divorced?"

Time to tell. "Not very long. Actually, not at all." She spoke faster when his eyes widened. "Our divorce will be final soon."

He paused. "So, I've been sleeping with a married woman?"

"We only did that once."

"Good thing. Adultery . . . not my thing."

She was quiet for a moment. "Are you upset?"

He shrugged. "Should I be?"

"No, because in my mind, I've been divorced since January fifth — the day Quentin left. It's just hard for me to talk about it with you."

He was thoughtful for minutes. "Was it very difficult? You both seem to be in that place where mature people who divorce find themselves, mostly because they want to do what's best for their children."

"Are you a divorce expert?"

"No, but I see a lot of divorce — especially with some of the boys I work with. And rarely does it look as civilized as it does with you and Quentin."

She thought about all the times when her thoughts had been far from civilized. "Separation is hard."

"I always wondered why you never talked about Quentin."

"I thought that was one of the rules — never talk about your ex with your new . . ."

He grinned. "You don't know what to call me, do you?" Before she could answer, he leaned across the seat and kissed her. For a moment she wondered if Mrs. James was watching. But then with his tongue he took away thoughts that weren't centered on him. When he pulled away, he asked, "So are you going to tell me about Quentin?"

"Quentin who?"

They laughed, but then she turned serious. "Why do you want to know about him?"

"I don't want to know about him, I want to know about you." He shrugged. "It's just that sometimes, Sheridan, I feel there is an emotional wall around you. You let me get close but only so close."

"I don't feel that at all."

"Like right now. You know how to direct the conversation. You almost had us going off on another subject."

"I guess I haven't accepted my separation from Quentin in my head yet."

"Have you accepted it in your heart?"

She shrugged. "I don't know. What comes first — the heart or the head?"

"You tell me."

She was quiet and looked away. "Quentin's out of my heart. I've worked hard to close that door. But maybe he's not out of my head."

Brock nodded slowly, digesting her words. "So, if he's out of your heart, is there room for someone else?"

More time passed. "I didn't think I had any room." She stopped, still not looking at him. "But you've opened that door a bit for me."

"Is that a good thing?"

"I think so."

With his fingertips, he turned her head so she faced him and kissed her gently. He pulled back and said, "If there's room in your heart, I'd like to submit an application for residence."

She shook her head. "I just don't know if I'm capable of loving again," she said softly. "How can I love when I still may have a broken heart? How would . . ."

He covered her lips with his fingers. "A while ago, you promised to just go for it with me. Stop asking the questions. Just go."

Her stare was intense. "Is that what you're doing?"

He kissed her, gently, tenderly. Then, urgently. When he leaned back, he'd taken all of her breath away. "What do you think?"

She didn't answer. She didn't have to. The door to her heart cracked open just a bit more. And she knew then that maybe, just maybe, she could make a little space and perhaps let Brock Goodman inside.

The couch enveloped her like a soft leather glove.

Sheridan eased further into the crevices, dipping deeper into the comfort. And then she did what she'd wanted to do all day. She closed her eyes.

She couldn't count the hours since she'd last rested. For the past days her slumber had been filled with images of Christopher, Déjà, and a baby. She'd awakened every morning tangled in tousled sheets as if she'd been battling an enemy.

But now she wondered what would fill her dreams tonight. Today all of her wishes for her son had been granted, but not the way she wanted. Never did she expect to feel such overwhelming loss. She wished now that she had never prayed those prayers.

"I know you're sovereign, Lord," she whispered. "I know everything is for your purpose and glory. But please forgive me for my thoughts. Please understand my heart."

She sat, relishing the peace that came with that prayer, and minutes later, her calm ushered in a vision of Brock. And her entire body smiled.

"You look happy."

Slowly she opened her eyes and took in Quentin. He leaned against the wall, arms crossed, standing as if he were home.

"Happy is not exactly the word I'd have used."

He joined her on the couch, leaned back, and rested his legs on the table. "Been a long day," he said.

"Longer than long."

He smiled.

"How's Tori?" she asked.

"She's okay. I stayed with her until she fell asleep. I think this was traumatic for her."

Sheridan nodded. "I thought about letting her stay with Mom and Dad tonight. But when I called, she said she wanted to come home."

"Told me the same thing." He paused. "I think when things like this happen, people want to be around those they're closest to. Makes them feel safest."

It was the way he spoke that made her twist to face him. "You miss this."

She wasn't sure herself whether she was asking a question or making a statement. She wasn't sure at all what she thought he missed. But he nodded — understanding and agreeing.

In the silence Quentin's eyes slowly took in the room as if he was digesting memories, saving the nourishment for sometime later. His eyes rested on the family pictures on the mantel.

"I miss all of this," he finally said. He sounded as if he were drowning in sadness.

"Is it because of what happened . . . with Déjà?"

"No. Well, maybe. I don't know. Even though it was killing me that Chris could be a father, in other ways, it felt good. I felt like I was home again. I was needed by my children." He turned to her and placed his hand over hers. "And it felt good that you needed me too."

I've always needed you, Quentin.

His hand stayed, but he turned his glance away. "I was surprised to see Brock at the hospital."

She said nothing.

A moment passed, then, "This may be none of my business, but how serious are you about this guy?"

"You're right. It's none of your business."

He turned back to look at her and then smiled when she smiled.

"It just seems . . . he's around quite a bit."

"You've only seen him a few times."

"But I can do the math. If I see him once a week, I know you're seeing him more than that. So what's the deal?"

His tone was light, as if he were just asking a friend a simple question. But in his eyes Sheridan saw seriousness. She tilted her head. "You know, over the past few months there've been times when I actually thought . . . some of the questions you've asked me . . . you almost sound jealous."

He shrugged. "I'm not jealous. Just a little sad that you've moved on with your life."

"Why? You've gone on with yours."

He nodded, opened his mouth, and then closed it.

"Quentin, are you happy?" she asked.

His glance roamed to the mantel again, where the history of their love remained, even though he'd left almost half a year ago. "I thought I was. I wanted to be. But . . ."

This time she reached for his hand. They settled in the comfort of the familiar, until he said, "I'm leaving Jett."

His words froze every part of her. Finally she was able to ask, "What happened?"

"I've been asking myself that." He stared

at the wall. "I haven't been happy."

"That's what you said about being . . . with me."

He nodded. "If I were a psychiatrist, I'd diagnose myself as being totally confused."

"So then I won't say it," Sheridan said, wanting to lighten the mood. But then, she asked, "Quentin, is all of this based upon today? It's been an emotional day. I don't think you should make any decisions . . ." She stopped herself. Couldn't believe she was actually talking to Quentin about this. Couldn't believe that she wasn't jumping up and down, shouting, "Hallelujah."

She said, "So what's going on?"

"I wish I could explain it. But being with Jett didn't solve any of what was going on inside of me."

She exhaled a long breath.

"Now, I'm not saying I'm not gay. What I'm saying is that I never felt right with Jett. I don't know if that's a function of Jett not being the one for me or whether none of that life is right for me. I don't know. What I do know is that God's not finished with me. This isn't my final stop."

For months she'd been praying — first for Quentin to come home, and then just for God to speak to his heart.

I know he loves the Lord. If Quentin will

just pause and listen, he'll hear God's voice.

Sheridan recalled Pastor Ford's words. Was Quentin listening to God's voice?

"What are you going to do?"

He grinned without happiness. "Don't worry. I'm not going to ask if I can move back home." He chuckled just a bit when she exhaled. "I think you and Chris and Tori have all found your way through this. I'm just going to take some time for myself." He shook his head. "I'll probably move out next weekend."

"You have a place already?"

"Been looking at a few spots, but I'll grab a hotel room for now."

She nodded.

He said, "It's amazing. I'm over forty and I'm searching for an apartment and myself at the same time."

She squeezed his hand. "Do me a favor and really spend some time with God."

"I will, just like I always have. Through all of this, I've maintained my relationship with God. He's been with me." He paused. "I want you to know that I continued to ask God to take this desire away from me. And I still feel it, Sheridan. It's real. It's who I am."

She took a deep breath. "Maybe that's

the challenge. Maybe you keep asking God to take the desire away when all He wants is for you to give it up."

He was silent for long minutes. "You still think it's wrong for me to be gay."

She held up her hands. "I'm not judging you. I just keep you in my prayers. I'm just asking you to look at this through God's eyes." She took his hand. "You should consider talking to Pastor Ford."

He shook his head. "I know her position on this."

"Her number one position is as your spiritual leader. She's only concerned with your spiritual health. This isn't a personal opinion or judgment for her. You know how she is."

"I'll think about it."

"I know that Tori and probably now even Christopher would love to have you back at church with them."

"I'll think about it," he repeated. He looked at her, and for the first time she saw the new lines in his face. It looked like sadness had etched itself deep inside his skin and made itself at home. "I will always love you, Sheridan."

She nodded. "I know that, now."

"We still have quite a life in front of us

— together." He paused. "We were almost grandparents."

"Isn't that scary?"

He nodded. "But one day we will be. You'll be a terrific grandmother."

"And you'll make a wonderful grandfather."

"I hope so. In the meantime" — he dropped her hands and stood — "I've got to figure out my life so that I can be here totally for my children. And their children. And their children."

She held up her hand. "Please, I can't think about any of that."

He gently pulled her from the couch. When he put his arm around her shoulders, she inhaled. With each step they took toward the door, Sheridan was aware of Quentin's touch, the way his arm folded naturally over her shoulders as if it belonged there. When they stopped moving, she could feel her heart beating, and then she realized it was his heartbeat she felt.

He looked down at her, and her heart hammered more. It was a familiar stance, but one she'd missed for months. He stood so close she could see the speckles in his eyes and smell the fragrance of his breath. And tonight, on his face, she saw the same love that had been there so many years before.

Minutes stopped moving and Quentin leaned, his lips aimed for hers. As the edges of his lips touched her, she turned her head, so that his mouth landed on her cheek. He kissed her and let his lips linger against her skin. Softly. Easily. Sadly.

When he leaned back, there were tears in his eyes but none in hers.

"I'll call you tomorrow."

She nodded.

"Good night."

He opened the door and stepped outside. She watched until his Mercedes joined with the night. And then she closed the door.

Sheridan couldn't sleep.

Her mind was a tousled mass of thoughts — Christopher, Déjà, Brock, Quentin. It was enough to keep her eyes stretched open as if it were three in the afternoon. But it was three in the morning and she gave up trying to win the battle to rest.

Sheridan tightened her robe and then wandered downstairs. Inside the office, she looked around the room. Six months ago, only pain stayed with her as she studied

Quentin's words. Now, she felt nothing. Next time she saw Quentin, she'd have to tell him — she would be closing their business.

She sat at her desk and frowned when she saw the FedEx envelope. She wondered where it had come from, and then remembered that her parents had come to pick up Tori when she rushed with Déjà to the hospital. Maybe it had been delivered then.

She glanced at the return address, and her heart pounded. Slowly, she ripped open the envelope. Her eyes stayed on the large letters. And she waited for the tears to come.

"Final Divorce Decree."

No tears, but sadness filled her nonetheless. It was over. Officially now. All that was left for her and Quentin was a lifetime of sharing their children. And a love for him that she knew was there — but it was tucked away into a corner of her mind.

She stared at the paper for a moment longer and then filed it inside her drawer under "Important Papers." But even though the notice that legally recognized Quentin's deception was in the file cabinet, the thoughts stayed with her.

Six months ago, he'd told her about Jett.

She remembered that day and all of the horrific times in between. And then, she recalled the good days. When she knew that she and Christopher and Tori were going to make it. She had quite a testimony.

She paused. That's what her father had said.

You have quite a testimony. And testimonies are not for you alone. They're meant to be shared.

Sheridan pulled out a pad. *Maybe I'll just make some notes,* she thought. But the pen wouldn't move, even though her mind was racing, even though she had ideas — remembering the way Quentin had come to her. Remembering her fear of AIDS. Remembering the emotional devastation that rocked Christopher and Tori.

Quentin may not have had down-low behavior, but he had a down-low attitude, keeping the secret from her for far too long, hiding who he was, sending their world into chaos.

Down low.

And then her pen moved across the paper. She wrote the first words, studied them and smiled: *My Life as a Survivor: How I Learned to Live Up High.*

Author's Note

Whew! This was the most difficult novel I've written to date. Not only because of the subject matter, but because I have friends who are gay whom I love dearly. I decided to write *Grown Folks Business* (in 2002) for two reasons. One, I know the Word of God and the truth of God's Word. I know what He says about the act of homosexuality. I wanted to write a book about that. However, the other reason for this novel is that I often hear the judgment of Christians regarding homosexuality and how Scripture is often misquoted in this regard. I've heard people say that homosexuality is a sin on a different level — that it is an abomination and the only sin that is an abomination. That's not true. So, I wanted to write a book that addressed those issues as well.

While I understand God's direction on how we should judge one another as Christians, I also once heard wonderful words from a friend who was about to get married. He said, "You can love someone into submission." I believe as Christians, we can love someone so much that we can lead them to know the truth. I prefer the love approach. And that's what I wanted to show in this book.

Also, please note that this story is told from just one point of view. This novel is not about Quentin Hart and why he is gay or why he chose a particular time to leave his family. *Grown Folks Business* is *just* about Sheridan Hart's journey. This novel is about what would happen if your husband came home and told you he was in love with a man. I had the pleasure of speaking with a wife who experienced this and also with men who have left their families. I thank all of you for your candor.

My hope is that this book will open up discussion in a positive way and that we all come to know the truth — which is the Word of God.

About the Author

Victoria Christopher Murray is the *Essence* bestselling author of the novels *Truth Be Told*, *Joy*, *Temptation*, and *Blessed Assurance*, a collection of inspirational short stories. Visit her at www.victoriachristophermurray.com. She lives with her family in Inglewood, California.

Touchstone Reading Group Guide

Grown Folks Business

1. Quentin tells Sheridan that he's in love with someone else, but that he hasn't been having an affair. Do you think that an extramarital affair includes sexual infidelity by definition? What do you think constitutes "cheating"?

2. Sheridan feels that she is suffering the worst kind of betrayal by her husband. Is it harder for her because Quentin loves another man and not another woman? Do you think Sheridan would have felt differently if Quentin confessed to sleeping with a man, but not having fallen in love? How would you feel if you were in Sheridan's shoes?

3. *Grown Folks Business* presents situations that cause us to reconsider what makes a man a man. Consider Quentin's sexual identity crisis,

Cameron's prostate cancer and Christopher's attitude toward his father. What do you think the defining characteristics of a real man are?

4. Similarly, *Grown Folks Business* asks questions about womanhood and femininity. Kamora, with her sexy clothes and active love life, resides at one end of the femininity spectrum. Sheridan, with her sweat suits and celibacy, believes she resides at the opposite end — and, in fact, blames Quentin's abandonment on her lack of femininity. What do you think it means to be a real woman?

5. Homosexuality is an increasingly sensitive issue in our communities. What are some of the different views on homosexuality presented by the various characters in *Grown Folks Business*? How do you feel about these opinions?

6. Kamora tells Sheridan, we're all "only human." What do you think is the difference between the hypocrites in this novel and the people who are "only human," but are trying to do right by

God? To which camp would you assign each of the following: Sheridan, Quentin, Sheridan's brother, Kamora, Beatrice and Cameron, Déjà, Francesca, Christopher, Brock, and Pastor Ford?

7. When we are first introduced to Brock, he doesn't seem a likely candidate for Sheridan's affections beyond the initial physical attraction. Why do you think Sheridan is able to open her heart to him? Have you ever dated someone much younger than yourself? How do you feel about women who date younger men?

8. There are many thinks about Déjà that Sheridan doesn't like. Do you think Déjà is right in saying that Sheridan doesn't think she is good enough for Christopher? What reasons do you think are significant enough for a parent to forbid her/his teenager from dating someone? Where do you draw the line between a difference in taste and knowing that a relationship is a bad idea?

9. When Sheridan and Quentin explain to

Déjà that Christopher is too young to marry her, Sheridan recalls being on the receiving end of a similar lecture from her own father. What is different about Sheridan and Quentin's young, rushed marriage and Déjà and Christopher's situation?

10. Do you think Quentin was ever truly in love with Sheridan, or do you think he married his best friend, someone he could make a life with, in order to cover up his repressed homosexuality? What is the difference? Do you feel any sympathy for Quentin?

The employees of Thorndike Press hope you have enjoyed this Large Print book. All our Thorndike and Wheeler Large Print titles are designed for easy reading, and all our books are made to last. Other Thorndike Press Large Print books are available at your library, through selected bookstores, or directly from us.

For information about titles, please call:

(800) 223-1244

or visit our Web site at:

www.gale.com/thorndike
www.gale.com/wheeler

To share your comments, please write:

Publisher
Thorndike Press
295 Kennedy Memorial Drive
Waterville, ME 04901